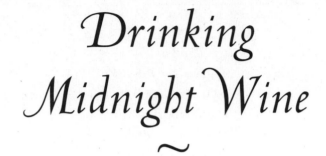

# Drinking Midnight Wine

# Drinking
# Midnight Wine

~

## SIMON R. GREEN

A ROC BOOK

ROC
Published by New American Library, a division of
Penguin Putnam Inc., 375 Hudson Street,
New York, New York 10014, U.S.A.
Penguin Books Ltd, 80 Strand, London WC2R 0RL, England
Penguin Books Australia Ltd, Ringwood,
Victoria, Australia
Penguin Books Canada Ltd, 10 Alcorn Avenue,
Toronto, Ontario, Canada M4V 3B2
Penguin Books (N.Z.) Ltd, 182–190 Wairau Road,
Auckland 10, New Zealand

Penguin Books Ltd, Registered Offices:
Harmondsworth, Middlesex, England

Published by Roc, an imprint of New American Library,
a division of Penguin Putnam Inc. Originally published in Great Britain by Victor Gollancz.

ISBN 0-7394-2690-7

Printed in the United States of America

PUBLISHER'S NOTE
This is a work of fiction. Names, characters, places, and incidents either are the products of the author's imagination or are used fictitiously, and any resemblance to actual persons, living or dead, business establishments, events, or locales is entirely coincidental.

Bradford-on-Avon is a real town, with a real history.
Most of the places described in this book really exist,
as does much of the history.
Anything else . . .

There is a world beyond the world.

There is a world beyond the world, a place of magics and mysteries, evils and enchantments, marvels and wonders. And you are never more than a breath away from all of it. Open the right door, walk down the wrong street, and you can find waiting for you every dream you ever had, including all the bad ones. Secrets and mysteries will open themselves to you, if something more or less than human doesn't find you first. Magic is real, and so are gods and monsteres.

There is a world beyond the world. But some things never change.

## One ~

# When Lives Collide

BRADFORD-ON-AVON is an old town, and not all of its ghosts sleep the sleep of the just. Nestled in the rolling hills and valleys of the county of Wiltshire, in the ancient heart of the southwest of England, many kinds of people have lived in Bradford-on-Avon down the centuries, and some of their past deeds live on to trouble the present. The Romans have been here, and the Celts and the Saxons and the Normans. And other, stranger folk, less willing to be recorded in official histories. In this small county town, far and far from the seat of those who like to think they run things, the fate of two worlds will be decided, by one ordinary man who dares to love a woman who is so much more than she seems.

She was there on the train again that evening, in her usual seat—the woman with the most perfect mouth in the world. Not too wide and not too small, not too thin and not full with the artificial plumpness of injected collagen or surgically implanted tissues from cows' buttocks. Just a wonderfully warm and inviting mouth, exactly the right shade of deep red that made the fuller lower lip look soft and tender and touchable. Toby Dexter wasn't usually preoccupied with mouths, as opposed to the more prominent curves of a woman's body, but there was something special about this one, and he liked to look at it and wonder what it might sound like, if he ever worked up the courage to introduce himself and start up a conversation.

Toby was traveling home from work on the 6:05 train, heading back to Bradford-on-Avon after a hard day's work in the famous Georgian city of Bath. It was a tribute to that city's relentless public relations machine that he always added the prefix *Georgian* whenever he thought of Bath, though the city was of course much older. The Romans built their famous baths there, that still stand today. They did other things there too, some of them quite appalling, in the name of the Serpent's Son; but you won't hear about those from the tourist board. Georgian society made visiting the baths the very height of fashion, and that was what people preferred to remember now. The past is what we make it, if we know what's good for us. Now, at the beginning of the twenty-first century, Bath is a busy, bustling, prosperous modern city, and Toby was always glad to see the back of it.

The early-evening train was crowded as always, all the seats occupied and all the aisles blocked, carrying tired commuters home to Freshford, Avoncliff, Bradford-on-Avon and Trowbridge. Packed shoulder to shoulder, perched on hard seats or leaning against the closed automatic doors, men and women forced into physical proximity concentrated on reading their books and magazines and evening papers, so they wouldn't have to talk to each other. The seats were fiendishly uncomfortable: there was no room to stretch your legs, and anyone who felt like swinging a cat would have clubbed half a dozen people to death before he'd even managed a decent windup. It was a hot and sweaty summer evening, and the interior of the long carriage was like a steam bath. Toby didn't think he'd mention it to Great Western Railways. They'd just call it a design feature, and charge him extra for the privilege.

Toby was pretending to read an unauthorized *X-Files* tie-in edition of dubious veracity and unconcealed paranoia, while secretly studying the woman with the perfect mouth who sat opposite him. He didn't have the energy to concentrate on the book anyway. He'd been on his feet all day, and the constant rocking back and forth of the carriage was almost enough to lull him to sleep, safe in the arms of the train, but he fought it off. Dozing on a train always left him with a stiff neck and a dry mouth, and there was always the danger he'd sleep past his stop. And you couldn't rely on any of this bunch to wake you up. Toby looked briefly around him at the neat men in their neat suits, with bulging briefcases and tightly knotted ties, no doubt listlessly considering another endless day of shuffling papers from one pile to another . . . and sometimes back again. Deadly dull people leading deadly dull lives . . . Toby envied all of them because at least they had some kind of purpose.

Toby worked at Gandalf's bookshop, right in the busy center of Bath. He was officially in charge of the Crime & Thrillers section, but really he was just a shop assistant with a few extra duties. It wasn't a bad place to work. The other assistants were pleasant company, and the shop itself was full of interesting nooks and crannies and intriguing out-of-print treasures. Gandalf's consisted of four sprawling floors, connected by old, twisting stairways and the occasional hidden passage. It was an old building, possibly even Georgian, with many unexpected drafts, and floors that creaked loudly as you walked on them, despite the thick carpeting. And everywhere you went, there was the comforting smell of books; of paper and glue and musky leather bindings, of history and dreams compressed into handy volumes.

Every wall was covered with shelves, packed tightly with books on every subject under the sun, and a few best not mentioned in polite company. There were standing displays and dump bins and revolving wire stands, filled with more knowledge, entertainment and general weird shit than any man could read in one lifetime. Gandalf's prided itself on catering for every taste and interest, from the latest paperback best-sellers to obscure philosophical discourses bound in goatskin. From science to mysticism, Gothic romances to celebrity biographies, from aromatherapy to creative knitting to erotic feng shui, you could be sure of finding something unexpected in every genre, on any subject.

Gandalf's had books on everything, including a few it shouldn't. The shop's owner was fearless, and would stock anything he thought people wanted. There'd been a certain amount of controversial publicity just recently, when the owner refused to stop stocking the new English translation of the infamous *Necronomicon,* even though it was officially banned. Toby didn't care; he'd already survived far greater scandals over selling copies of *Spycatcher* and *The Satanic Verses.* He'd flipped briefly through the *Necronomicon,* just out of curiosity, but found the dry prose style unreadable and the illustrations frankly baffling. People were still paying twenty quid a copy though, proof if proof were needed that you could sell absolutely anything if people thought they weren't supposed to be reading it. He'd been much more taken with *The Joy of Frogs,* a sex manual where all the illustrations featured cartoon frogs going at it in unusual and inventive ways. Some customer had ordered the book over the phone, but so far hadn't worked up enough courage to come in and pick it up. Just as well, really—the shop's staff had pretty much worn the book out between them. One had even made notes. The real money still came from the never-ending turnover of brand-name best-sellers: Stephen King, Terry Pratchett, J. K. Rowling and whoever the hell it was who wrote those marvelous children's fantasies about Bruin Bear and the Sea Goat.

The only thing Toby really disliked about his current occupation was having to get up so damned early in the morning. He lived alone, in a characterless semi-detached he'd inherited from an uncle, and most mornings his bed felt like a womb. He'd had to put his alarm clock on the other side of the room, so he'd be forced to get up out of bed to turn it off. So, up at seven a.m. to catch the train at eight, in order to get to work at nine. No doubt there were those who had to get up even earlier, but Toby preferred not to think about them because it interfered with his self-pity. Shit, shower, and shave, not necessarily in that order, grab the nearest clothes, and then downstairs to breakfast. A quick bowl of All-Bran (motto: eat our cereal and the world will fall out of your bottom), two large cups of black coffee, and then out of the house and down through the town to the railway station, with eyes still defiantly half closed. The body might be up and about, but the brain still wasn't ready to commit itself.

Though he'd never admit it, Toby quite liked walking through the town first thing in the morning. Down the seemingly endless Trowbridge Road, with its ranks of terraced houses with their bulging bay windows and gabled roofs on one side and old stone houses on the other, each one almost bursting with proud individuality. The street was mostly empty that early in the day, and there was hardly any traffic as yet. The town was still waking up, and only early risers like Toby Dexter got to see her with a cigarette in the corner of her mouth and no makeup on. Down the hill and turn sharp left, past the old almshouses, and there was the railway station, supposedly designed by Isambard Kingdom Brunel himself, on a day when he clearly had a lot of other things on his mind. So far it had successfully resisted all attempts at modernization, and the small monitor screens offering up-to-date train information had been carefully tucked away in corners so as not to detract from the building's ambience. The occasional recorded announcement sounded almost apologetic for disturbing the peace.

The station's general elegance and smug solidity was entirely lost on Toby, who tended to stand on the platform like one of George Romero's zombies, all dull-eyed and listless. Most mornings he had to be nudged awake to get on the train when it arrived, sometimes on time, and sometimes not. It all depended on how the train company felt about it. And if you didn't like it, you were, of course, free to take your custom to some other train company. Except that there wasn't another train company.

By the time the train lurched into Bath, the city was already wide awake and bustling with eager, impatient people hurrying to their jobs, positively radiating motivation and can-do. Toby tried not to look at them. He found them depressing beyond words. The streets were crowded, and the roads were packed bumper to bumper with snarling, cursing commuter traffic. At this time of the day, the air was so thick with pollution that even the pigeons were coughing, and the noise level was appalling. Head down, shoulders hunched, Toby trudged through the din, wearing his best get-out-of-my-way-or-I'll-kill-you look.

Toby didn't care for cities. They had far too much personality, like a bully forever punching you on the arm to get your attention. Toby had spent three years living in the East End of London, back when he was a student, an area that would have profited greatly from a heavily armed UN peacekeeping force. Lacking the funds necessary to reach the more civilized areas of London, Toby endured three very long years to get his B.A. (English Literature and Philosophy, Joint Honors) and then ran back to his hometown at the first opportunity. Cities crammed too many people together in too confined a space, and then the powers that be wondered why people fought each other all the time. Toby thought cities were like natural disasters; enjoyable only if viewed from a safe distance. Bath, for example, had interesting places to look at like a dog has fleas, but for the most part Toby couldn't be bothered to fight his way through the crowds to get to them.

Toby had worked in Bath for over a year, but had never once considered moving there to live.

By the time he got to Gandalf's, ready for the great unlocking at nine a.m., Toby was usually awake enough to know where he was, but not nearly together enough to interact with customers, so the other staff usually provided him with useful, mindless activities to occupy him until he was fully conscious. "Carry these boxes down into the cellar. Carry these boxes up from the cellar. Plug in this Hoover and follow it around for a while."

Toby quite liked working in the bookshop. Stacking shelves appealed to his sense of order, and he liked dealing with customers, even the ones who came in ten minutes before closing time looking for a book, but couldn't remember the title or the author's name, though they were almost sure they could describe the cover . . . But at the end of each and every day he was still just a shop assistant, another faceless drone in the great hive of the city, doing the same things over and over, achieving nothing, creating nothing. Every day was just like every other day, and always would be, world without end, amen, amen.

Toby had just turned thirty, and he resented it deeply. He didn't feel old, far from it; but his youth, supposedly the most promising part of his life, was now officially over. When he was younger, he'd always thought he'd have his life sorted out by the time he was thirty, that all the important decisions would be made by then. He'd have a chosen career, a wife and kids and a mortgage, just like everyone else. He'd have worked out who he was, and what he wanted out of life. But thirty came round as just another year, just another birthday, and brought no special wisdom with it. He'd had jobs, but none of them meant anything, and girlfriends, but none of them came to anything. He had ambition, but no focus; he had dreams, but no vocation. He drifted through his days, and years, and didn't realize how much time had passed until he looked back and wondered where it had all gone.

Most of his contemporaries were married, usually for all the wrong reasons: companionship, regular sex, baby on the way. Peer pressure, fears of growing old, alone. There were remarkably few great loves or passions that Toby could detect. Some had already divorced, and were on their second or even third marriages. Sometimes Toby felt like a late developer. But in his own quiet way he was stubbornly romantic, and was damned if he'd marry just for the sake of getting married. It helped that women weren't exactly beating down his door to get to him. And as for a career . . . Toby was still looking for a role to play that interested him; something to live *for*, to give his life purpose and meaning. He didn't know what he needed, only what he didn't want, and so he drifted through his life, sometimes employed and sometimes not, achieving nothing, going nowhere. Knowing that his life was slipping away like sand through his fingers, but somehow unable to do anything about it.

Toby looked at his own reflection in the carriage window, and saw only a pale face under dark hair, with no obvious virtues; just another face in the crowd, really. He wore a rumpled jacket over

T-shirt and jeans, the official uniform of the anonymous, and even his T-shirt had nothing to say.

He looked through the carriage window at the passing countryside, stretched lazily out under the dull amber glow of the lowering sun. Summer was mostly over now, and heading into autumn, and already the countryside was unhurriedly shutting up shop for winter. But still, it was home, and Toby found its familiar sights comforting. There were wide woods and green fields, and the River Avon curling its long slow way toward the town. There were swans on the river, white and perfect and utterly serene, moving gracefully, always in pairs because swans mated for life. They studiously ignored the crowds of chattering ducks, raucous and uncouth, darting back and forth on urgent errands of no importance to anyone except themselves—and perhaps not even to them. Ducks just liked to keep busy. Every now and again a rowing team would come sculling up the river, the long wooden oars swinging back and forth like slow-motion wings, and the swans and the ducks would move ungraciously aside to let them pass. The rowers never looked up. Heads down, arms and lungs heaving, all effort and concentration and perspiration, too preoccupied with healthy exercise and beating their own times to notice the calm beauty and heartsease of their surroundings.

There were animals in the fields. Cows and sheep and sometimes horses, and, if you looked closely, rabbits too. And the occasional fox, of course. Giving birth, living, dying, over and over and over, Nature's ancient order continuing on as it had for countless centuries. Seasons changed, the world turned, and everything old was made new again, in spring. And everywhere you looked, there were the trees. Not as many as there once were, of course. The ancient primal forests of England's dark green past were long gone. Felled down the years to make ships and towns and homes, or just to clear the land for crops and livestock. But still many trees survived, in woods and copses, or slender lines of windbreaks; tall dark shapes, glowering on the horizon, standing out starkly against the last light of day.

A single magpie, jet of black and pure of white, hopped across a field, and Toby tugged automatically at his forelock and muttered, "Evening, Mr. Magpie," an old charm, to ward off bad luck. Everyone knew the old rhyme: *One for sorrow, two for joy, three for a girl and four for a boy* . . . Toby usually got lost after that, but it didn't really matter. It was a rare day when you saw more than four magpies at once. Toby watched the countryside pass, and found what little peace of mind he ever knew in contemplating the land's never-ending cycle. The trees and the fields and the animals had all been there before him, and would still be there long after he was gone; and some day they'd lay him to rest under the good green grass, and he'd become a part of it all. And then maybe he'd understand what it had all been for.

The train paused briefly at the request stop for Avoncliff, a very short platform with stern DO NOT ALIGHT HERE signs at both ends, just in case you were too dim to notice that there was nothing there for you to step out onto. The usual few got off. There was never anyone waiting to get on, at this time of day. The train gathered up its strength and plunged on, heading for Bradford-on-Avon like a horse scenting its stables. Toby closed his paperback and stuffed it into his jacket pocket. Not long now; almost home. He felt tired and heavy and sweaty, and his feet ached inside his cheap shoes, already on their second set of heels. He looked out of the window, and there, on the very edge of town, was Blackacre. An old name and not a pleasant one, for a seventeenth-century farmhouse and surrounding lands, all set within an ancient circle of dark trees, cutting Blackacre off from the rest of the world—dead land, and dead trees.

A long time ago, something happened in that place, but few now remembered what or when or why. The old farmhouse stood empty and abandoned, in the center of a wide circle of dead ground, on which nothing grew and in which nothing could thrive. The deep thickets of spiky trees were all dead too, never knowing leaves or bloom, scorched long ago by some terrible heat. Animals would not go near the area, and it was said and believed by many that even the birds and insects went out of their way to avoid flying over Blackacre.

Local gossip had it that the house and the land had a new owner, the latest of many, probably full of big-city ideas on how to reclaim the land and make it prosper again, to succeed where so many others had failed. Toby smiled tiredly. Some things should be left alone as a bad job. Whatever poor fool had been conned into buying the place would soon discover the truth the hard way. Blackacre was a money pit, a bottomless well you threw money into. Dead was dead, and best left undisturbed.

Sometimes the local kids would venture into the dark woods on a dare, but no one ever went near the farmhouse. Local builders wouldn't have anything to do with the place either. Everyone knew the stories, the old stories handed down from father to son, not as entertainment but as a warning. Bad things happened to those who dared disturb Blackacre's sullen rest.

Which made it all the more surprising when Toby suddenly realized that there were lights in some of the windows of Blackacre Farm. He pressed his face close to the carriage window, and watched intently as a dull yellow glow moved steadily from one upper-floor window to the next. Some damned fool must actually be staying there, in a rotten old building without power or heat or water. Toby shivered for a moment, though he couldn't have said why. A dark figure appeared against a lit window. It stood very still, and Toby had a sudden horrid feeling that it was watching him, just as he was watching it. And then the light went out, and the figure was gone, and Blackacre Farm was dark and still again.

Toby's upper lip was wet with sweat, and he brushed at it with a finger before settling back into his uncomfortably hard seat. He would soon be at his stop, and he wanted one last look at the woman sitting opposite him. She was reading the *Times* with great concentration, the broadsheet newspaper spread wide to put a barrier between herself and the world. In all the time they'd traveled on the same train, Toby had never seen the woman speak to anyone. Most of the *Times*'s front page was given over to a story about unusual new conditions on the surface of the sun. Toby squinted a little so he could read the text of the story without having to lean forward.

Apparently of late a series of solar flares had been detected leaping out from the sun's surface; the largest and most powerful flares since records began. There seemed no end to these flares, which were already playing havoc with the world's weather and communications systems. Toby smiled. If the flares hadn't been screwing up everyone's television reception, such a story would never have made the front page. People only ever really cared about science when it bit them on the arse.

He looked away, and surreptitiously studied the woman's face, reflected in the carriage window beside her. She was frowning slightly as she read, her perfect mouth slightly pursed. Not for the time first, Toby thought she was the most beautiful woman he'd ever seen. She had a classic face, with a strong bone structure and high cheekbones, and a great mane of jet-black hair fell in waves well past her shoulders. Her eyes were dark too, under heavy eyebrows, and her nose was just prominent enough to give character to her face without being distracting. For all her serious expression, there was still a smile tucked in one corner of her perfect mouth, almost in spite of herself.

She wore a pale blue suit, expertly cut but just short of power dressing, with the kind of quiet elegance that just shrieks money. There was no jewelry, no wedding ring. Looking at her was like diving into a deep pool of cool, clear water. Hard to tell her age. She was young, but still very much a woman rather than a girl, and there was something about her eyes that suggested she'd seen a thing or two in her time. Her fingers were long and slender, crinkling the edges of her newspaper where she held it firmly. Toby wondered what it would feel like, to be held firmly by those hands.

She changed her outfits regularly, and never looked less than stunning. But no one ever hit on her. No one ever tried to chat her up, or impress her with their charm and style, the kind of stuff attractive women always had to put up with, even if they wore a large sign saying, GO AWAY; I HAVE AIDS, LEPROSY AND THE VENUSIAN DICK ROT, AND BESIDES I'M A LESBIAN. Men would always try it on. Except no one ever did, with her. Toby could understand that. He'd been secretly admiring her for months, and still hadn't worked up the courage to talk to her.

Sometimes he thought of her as the Ice Queen, from the old children's story. In the fairy tale, a boy looked at the distant and beautiful Ice Queen, and a sliver of her ice flew into his eye. And from that moment on, he had no choice but to love her with all his heart, come what may. Toby was pretty sure the story ended badly for both the boy and the Ice Queen, but he preferred not to think about that. What mattered was that he and she were fated to be together. He was sure of it—mostly. He turned away to look at his own reflection in the window next to him, and sighed inwardly. He was hardly worthy of a queen. Hardly worthy of anything, really.

He often wondered who she was, *really*. What she did for a living; where she went when she left the railway station at Bradford-on-Avon, and why he never saw her anywhere else in town. Whether there was someone else in her life . . . To stop himself thinking about things like that, Toby often indulged himself with harmless little fantasies. On leaving the station she'd be accosted by some mugger, and he would bravely see the villain off and comfort her afterwards. Or maybe she'd stumble and break the heel on her shoe, and she'd have to lean on him as he escorted her home. All the fantasies ended in the same way, of course, with the two of them having amazing sex on some huge, luxurious bed. Always her place, rather than his. His place was a dump.

The train finally pulled into Bradford-on-Avon station, the carriage jerking to a halt in a series of sudden jolts as the driver hit the brake pedal just that little bit too hard. Toby often thought that train drivers went to a special school, where they were taught how to stop a train in the most distressing way possible—there was no way you could be this annoying without practice. Finally the train stopped, and everyone surged to their feet. Toby waited until the woman with the perfect mouth had closed and neatly folded her paper and stuck it under her arm, and then he rose to his feet as she did. They stood side by side as they waited for the automatic doors to open, but she didn't even know he was there.

The doors opened, and a rush of passengers streamed out onto the narrow platform. Toby let the flow carry him along, as the crowd headed for the black iron gate that was the only way out of the station. (Being only a small station for a small town, the station building itself always closed at midday.) The air was suddenly cool and bracing as they filed out into the parking lot beyond, and Toby looked up to see the last of the summer sunshine swept away by dark, lowering clouds. At once the rain fell heavily, as though someone up above had just pulled out a plug, and the commuters ran for waiting cars and buses with shocked cries of surprise.

Toby tucked himself away under a convenient railway arch, and struggled with his stubbornly awkward umbrella. No waiting wife or family for him. The umbrella was a collapsible job, just right for his coat pocket; but every now and again it would refuse to open so he wouldn't take it for granted. He could have made a dash for one of the waiting local buses, but unfortunately he was supposed to be on a diet. Eat less and exercise more—he didn't know which one he detested most. Either way, his waistline was *still* expanding, so he had no choice but to walk home, regardless of the weather. If he started allowing himself to make excuses, he'd never get *any* exercise. He knew himself too well.

Cars were already jostling for position as they fought their way out of the car park, as though it mattered one jot whether they got home in twenty minutes rather than fifteen. The two local buses were revving their engines impatiently as the last few commuters climbed aboard, filling the wet air with heavy exhaust fumes. It was Friday, the beginning of the weekend, and everyone was eager to start celebrating finishing the working week. They'd all survived another run of nine-to-fives, and now they couldn't wait to forget it all in pubs and at parties, dinners and clubs, and with special treats they'd been promising themselves. Or perhaps they just wanted to get home, bury themselves in the bosom of their family and batten down the hatches for two precious days of small domestic things. Toby had no plans. He was tired of pubs, of the same conversations with the same people, and no one invited men like Toby to dinner parties. There were no clubs or parties on the horizon, and no one at home to care whether he was in or not. Toby often felt that life was passing him by, while he reached out with desperate fingers for someone to throw him a lifeline.

Soon enough all the cars and buses were gone, and a blessed peace fell over the parking lot as a small scatter of pedestrians trudged off homeward through the increasingly heavy downpour. There was an unseasonal chill now to the early-evening air, and overhead the sky was almost pitch-black. Toby fought his umbrella and the umbrella fought back, just to spite him. But Toby was dogged and determined and quite prepared to beat the umbrella against the nearest wall until it realized he was serious, and finally it gave in and sprang open with bad grace. Toby relaxed a little as the rain drummed loudly on the stretched black cloth over his head. The walk home was tedious enough without having to do it soaking wet. And it was only then that he noticed he wasn't alone.

The woman with the most perfect mouth in the world was standing not ten feet away from him, holding her folded paper above her head, and glaring about her as though the rain were a personal affront. Her light blue suit was no match for a downpour, for all its expensive elegance, and it was clear she'd be soaked through before she could even get out of the lot. Toby could hardly believe his luck. It was raining, she was stranded, and he . . . he had an umbrella! All he had to do was walk over to her, casually offer to share his umbrella, and they could just walk off together. It would be perfectly natural for them to get talking, and maybe agree to meet later, so she could . . . thank him properly. He might even finally find out her name. If he could just bring himself to cross the gaping abyss of the ten feet that separated them.

Toby stepped forward into the rain, and then watched in utter amazement as the woman glanced at the station house, not even seeing him, and snapped her fingers imperiously. The sound seemed to hang on the air, impossibly loud and distinct against the din of the driving rain, as she strode toward a door in the station-house wall that Toby was sure as hell hadn't been there the moment before. He'd been buying his ticket here for years, on and off, and there had only ever been the one door, and one way in. Only now there were two doors, side by side. The woman pushed at the second door and it swung open before her, revealing only darkness.

And all through the parking lot, and perhaps all through the world, everything stopped. The noise of the town and the rain was suddenly gone, as though someone had just thrown a switch. The silence was so complete that Toby could hear his breathing and his heartbeat. The rain was stopped, every drop suspended in midair, glistening and shining with a strange inner light. It seemed as though nothing was moving in the whole damned world but Toby and the woman before him. The air was full of anticipation, of imminence, of something vitally important balanced on the edge of becoming. There was a feeling deep in Toby's bones and in his water that, perhaps for the first time in his life, what he did next mattered.

The woman walked through the door that shouldn't be there, disappearing into the darkness beyond, and the door slowly began to close behind her. Toby ran forward, desperate not to lose his chance with her, and plunged through the narrowing doorway. The door closed behind him with a loud, definite sound, and in that moment, everything changed.

Forever.

Toby stepped through the door and found himself standing in the lot again, with the station building behind him. He stopped dead, and blinked a few times. The feeling that the world was holding its breath was gone, but something new and rather more frightening had taken its place. The parking lot looked just as it had done before, and the distant sounds of the town had returned, but it was no longer raining. It was bright and sunny, with a clear blue sky and not even a trace of dampness on the ground. Everything looked just as it normally did, but everything felt different. And the woman with the perfect mouth was standing right in front of him, studying him silently with an unreadable expression on her face.

"You really shouldn't have done that," she said finally, and her voice was everything he could have hoped for: deep, warm, music to the ears.

"Done what?" said Toby. "I mean . . . what just happened here? Where are we?"

"In the magical world. It's all around you, all the time, but most people choose not to see it, for the sake of a sane and simple life. But sometimes people from the everyday world find their way here by accident. Go where they shouldn't, follow someone they shouldn't . . . and then nothing can ever be the same again." She looked at him almost sadly. "You now have a foot in both worlds; in the real world of Veritie, and the magical world of Mysterie. And it's a dangerous thing, to be a mortal man in a world of magic."

"OK," said Toby. "Hold everything. Let's start with some basics. I'm Toby Dexter. Who are you?"

"I'm Gayle. I should have noticed you were here, but I was . . . distracted. The weather was supposed to be sunny all day. There wasn't even a chance of rain. And I am never wrong about these things. But today something changed, in your world and in mine, and it worries me that I can't see how or why such an impossible thing should happen. Why did you follow me, Toby Dexter?"

"I wanted to talk to you. Ask you if you'd like to go out, for dinner, or something . . ."

Gayle smiled and shook her head. "I'm afraid that's quite impossible."

"Oh," said Toby, disappointed but not incredibly surprised. "Well, I suppose I'll see you around."

"Yes," said Gayle. "I'm rather afraid you will."

She turned and walked off into the bright sunny evening, and didn't look back once. Toby stood there, with his dripping umbrella, and there was no sign of rain anywhere at all.

# Two ~

# The Reality Express

A GHOST TRAIN is coming to Bradford-on-Avon, thundering down the tracks, puffing smoke and steam. It is coming in the early hours of the morning, long before the dawn, in the hour of the wolf, the hour when most babies are born and most people die, when no train is scheduled to run.

A great black iron train, with hot steam raging in its boiler, avatar of a different age, it fills the night air with dirty smoke and flying cinder flecks, pulling old-fashioned carriages that bear names from companies long since vanished into the mists of history. The heavy black iron of the train's body is scored all over with runes and sigils and names of power. The great wheels are solid silver, striking singing sparks from the steel tracks. The smoke billowing from the tall black stack smells of brimstone, and the whistle is the cry of a damned soul. The train plunges headlong through the night, faster than any train has a right to go, ancient or modern. The carriages shake and sway, rattling along behind, the windows illuminated with the eerie blue glow of underwater grottoes. The Reality Express is coming into town, right on time.

Eager faces press against the shimmering glass of the carriage windows, desperate for a first glance of their destination, excited and fearful at the same time. Not all the faces are human. They have paid for their tickets with everything they had, or might have been, and it is far too late now to change their minds. They are refugees from the magical world of Mysterie, seeking asylum and safe harbor in the cold sanity of Veritie. The Reality Express is a one-way trip, and only the desperate and the truly needy need apply.

The great iron beast hammers down the tracks, as fast as misfortune and as implacable as destiny, sounding its awful whistle as the town of Bradford-on-Avon draws near. And standing quiet and calm in the shadows of the chimney stack on the station's waiting-room roof is Jimmy Thunder, God For Hire, with his great hammer in its holster on his hip. The only private eye in the magical realms raises his head and smiles as he hears the terrible cry of the dark old train, and looks up the tracks, curious as to what the night will bring. The product of gods and mortals, Jimmy Thunder has a foot in each world and a home in neither—a dangerous man to both.

And somewhere in the dark, waiting for the train's arrival, two figures stand, scarier than the Reality Express or a God For Hire could ever hope to be.

Jimmy Thunder stood on the sloping tiled roof of the station's waiting room, leaning casually against the disused chimney stack. There was a cold wind blowing, but he didn't feel it. He'd chosen the roof for his stakeout because in his experience, people rarely look up, even when they're expecting unwanted interest. And the shadows were so very deep and comforting tonight, almost as if they knew something. Jimmy pricked up his ears as he caught the exact moment the Reality Express dropped out of Mysterie and into Veritie, its awful cry of the damned Dopplering down into nothing more than the rush of escaping steam. The train would be here soon, disgorging its cargo of the lost and the wretched, and then he would see what he would see.

Jimmy Thunder was a great bull of a man, with long red hair and a jutting red beard. He had a chest like a barrel, muscled arms the size of most men's thighs, and shoulders so broad he often had to turn sideways to pass through doors. He had legs that could run for miles, and feet that never complained, despite all the standing around his job entailed. He wore black leathers adorned with brightly gleaming chains and studs, and looked every inch what every biker wants to be when he grows up. His eyes were as blue as the sea, and twice as deadly, though he had a charming smile, when he could be bothered. Descended, at many, many removes, from the Norse god Thor, Jimmy was fast and strong and disturbingly pow- erful—when he put his mind to it. Long-lived, though by no means immortal, he was a god by chance and a private eye by choice. His godliness was diluted by a hell of a lot of generations of mortals, but the power of storms, of thunderclap and lightning strike, was still his. Not many people worshiped him anymore, for which he was quietly grateful. He'd always found it rather embarrassing.

Also his was the ancient mystical hammer Mjolnir, a (mostly) unstoppable force that (sometimes) came back when he threw it. The hammer had once been Thor's, and in its day had changed the fate of men and nations. It was his only material inheritance. It stirred in its sleep in its holster, snoring quietly. Mjolnir was a good weapon, but it was getting old and forgetful. Forged from stone or crystal or metal at the dawn of Time, or perhaps from some starstuff that no longer existed in the material world, Mjolnir was not what it once was. It was created to be immortal, a weapon that would en- dure till Ragnarok or Judgment Day; but nothing lasts for ever. Ask Thor, if you can find his body.

Jimmy Thunder was the only private eye in Bradford-on-Avon, in reality or otherwise, and he had a reputation for getting things done, whatever the cost. During his long life he'd investigated many cases, both mundane and bizarre, and his unwavering pursuit of the truth had seen to it that a lot of not very nice people had good rea- sons for wanting him dead. Just as well he was a god, really. Even if he did have to chase after his hammer sometimes. He poured the last of the hot sweet tea out of his thermos and into the plastic cup, and sipped at it carefully. It was still pleasantly warming, but not nearly bracing enough for the early hours of a very cold morning, so he goosed it up a bit with a tiny lightning bolt from his index finger.

The wind had no damn business being so disturbingly cold this deep into summer, but then the weather had been strange of late— whimsical, almost willful. Jimmy was quietly hoping someone would hire him to look into that.

Not that he was complaining about the cold, or the early hour of the morning. Jimmy liked stakeouts, especially when there was a fair chance of a little hurly-burly in the offing. Smiting the ungodly was right up there on his list of favorite things. He lived to the hilt the role he had chosen, and the more he played it, the less like play it was. A god became a private eye, and an old myth became a new. Jimmy believed in progress. It's always the legends that cannot or will not change that wither and fade away. Faced with being just another minor deity in a long line of godlings, with no fixed role or future in the modern world, Jimmy had cheerfully embraced a different destiny. The first time he saw a private investigator at the cinema, solving impossible crimes and pursuing awful villains, while surrounded by dizzy dames and femmes fatales, he knew that that was what he wanted to be. It helped that his long life gave him plenty of time to learn from his mistakes, while his divine abilities kept him alive while he learned.

Jimmy liked to know things and had an insatiable hunger for the truth. Especially things other people didn't want him to know. He had no time for subterfuge, always preferring to meet things head-on. He had a fondness for the underdog, and a real weakness for damsels in distress, and if he had a fault, it was his constant determination to follow a case through to the bitter end, revealing every last truth or secret, come what may. He never could bring himself to accept that while his clients always said they wanted to know the truth, the whole truth and nothing but the truth, they didn't always mean it. Not when lies or evasions can be so much more comforting.

Jimmy always got to the bottom of a case, but he wasn't always thanked for his trouble.

Sometimes cases ended messily. As in the case of Count Dracula's mandolin, where no one got what they wanted, and everyone got hurt—even him. And sometimes Jimmy went into cases knowing from the start that it was all going to end in tears. The Lord of Thorns still hadn't forgiven Jimmy for proving his fiancée was a golem. But if he'd made enemies, he'd made friends, too. Even the Vatican owed him a favor.

(A few years back, Jimmy had been called in by the pope to investigate a curious case where all the statues in the Vatican had spontaneously started bleeding from vivid stigmata. They'd had to close everything down and run superhuman damage control to keep it out of the media. All the top-rank exorcists did their best, with gallons of holy water and top-class cross action, and got absolutely nowhere. So Jimmy got the call, on the grounds that while the Vatican certainly wasn't prepared to accept that he was a god, he could at least be relied on to bring a whole new perspective to the problem. Jimmy had expressed surprise that the Vatican had even heard of him. The Holy Father had smiled and said, "The Vatican has heard of everybody, Mr. Thunder."

(Jimmy had sorted it out, mostly by asking questions and knowing when he was being lied to. It turned out that the pope had forgotten someone's birthday. As a reward, Jimmy was allowed access to the Vatican's secret library for a whole afternoon and an evening, to browse where he pleased. The really dangerous books were kept under lock and key and were chained to the shelves, or in extreme cases immersed in holy water or kept in a vacuum inside a sealed vault, but he still managed to turn up some interesting stuff. Not necessarily useful, but interesting. The Gospel According to Judas Iscariot was a real eye-opener, though the Fourth Prophecy of Fatima turned out to be just what everyone thought it was.

(The one story Jimmy was really interested in remained stubbornly elusive. There were no records, and no one would talk to him about it. Which only convinced him all the more that there had to be something to it. It was common knowledge that Vatican scientists had been experimenting with computers and Artificial Intelligence for over fifty years, though they kept their achievements to themselves. No one would admit that there had been any success in creating an AI, but it was said that deep in the heart of the Vatican there was a room where no one went, where the door was always locked. And that if you could find your way to that abandoned room, and put your ear to that locked door, you would hear the sound of something crying. . . .

(There are many mysteries inside the Vatican, and only some of them have anything to do with Christianity.)

Jimmy drank the last of the very hot sweet tea, flicked the cup a few times to empty it and then screwed it back onto the thermos. He'd only half filled the thermos, anyway. Bad idea to drink too much on a stakeout, especially when you didn't know how long you'd have to hold your ground. He put the thermos down on the roof beside him and leaned back against the chimney stack, which shifted slightly under his great weight. Stretched out before him lay the sleeping town, still and quiet now, just an army of streetlights pushing back the darkness. There was the tower and spire of Trinity Church, and beyond it row upon row of terraced houses and cottages, ascending the steep hills that enclosed the town—ordinary people sleeping in their ordinary town, all's quiet, all's well. But that was just in Veritie.

In the magical world, every bit as clear to Jimmy Thunder's semi-divine eyes, the town was never quiet. Bradford-on-Avon was an old, old locality, littered with all the remnants of the past. The very old creature that lived Under the Hill stirred restlessly, as though it could feel the thunder god's gaze, and deeper still, things and shapes and presences out of times past slept and dreamed down among the bones of the town. On the last day, when the earth gives up its dead for judgment, many of those buried in Bradford-on-Avon's cemeteries will be surprised to find out who some of their neighbors have been.

Old buildings flickered in and out of sight, ghosts of the town that was. Pale figures sat glumly at the base of the old gallows in the Bull Pit, swapping hard-luck stories and old, old claims of innocence, while in the park next to Westbury House, old soldiers guarded the war memorial and made rude comments about the new pale green Millennium Statue in the gardens opposite. From the River Avon came undine songs of unbearable melancholy, sometimes drowned out by the terrible cry of the Howling Thing, still imprisoned in the chapel on the bridge. Powers and Dominations sat at feast in the ghostly remembrance of what had once been a seventeenth-century eating place, The Three Gables, sharing secrets in loud, carrying voices and deciding men's fates with a laugh and a shrug and a careless quip. King Mob still held sway in the town center, as men and women long dead rioted over the changing fortunes of the cloth trade. And all across the town there were flaring lights and voices in the earth, and unnatural creatures flying on the night winds.

Business as usual, in Bradford-on-Avon, in Mysterie.

Jimmy Thunder looked up at the full moon and nodded hello. He'd always been on good terms with the Moon, unlike some of his predecessors, though her skittish ways made her difficult to understand and dangerous to know. But you never knew when you might need a friend. The town was jumping tonight, and the Reality Express was fast bearing down on the station. Jimmy let his sight slip out of Mysterie and back into Veritie, as the big black train came roaring in, right on time.

The Waking Beauty had hired Jimmy Thunder to investigate the matter of the Reality Express, and Jimmy had nodded politely and said of course he would, no problem, because no one said no to the Waking Beauty if they knew what was good for them; not even a god. She hadn't offered to pay, and he'd known better than to ask. He was just building up credit that he might someday need to redeem. The Waking Beauty was older than the town, and the town was very old indeed. She hadn't volunteered why she was suddenly interested in the Reality Express, or what he was supposed to be looking for. A lot of people disapproved of it, for all kinds of reasons, but as yet no one had actually got around to doing anything about it. The trade in refugees between the two worlds wasn't exactly illegal, but it did tend to undermine the status quo. And a lot of people had a great deal invested in maintaining the status quo. No one had any idea who owned or operated the Reality Express, and those foolish enough to go looking for answers tended not to come back. So it was just there, a service for those who needed it.

Jimmy didn't even know who drove the damned train.

It irked him that he was working for nothing. Normally he charged all that the traffic could bear, on the grounds that, after all, even gods had to eat; and because he lived in horror of someday being required to get a proper job. His few remaining worshipers would have been only too happy to provide him with everything he might need or desire, but that was a dangerous road to start down. He didn't want to become dependent on his worshipers. It would have given them a measure of control over him, and Jimmy Thunder took pride in being his own man. Or god.

With a roar and a cry and a blast of escaping steam, the great black train finally slowed to a halt beside the opposite platform. Jimmy stood very still in the deepest of the shadows, but his eyes missed nothing. Steam billowed out onto the narrow platform like low fog, as doors began opening down the length of the carriages, their slamming back sounding loudly on the night like a long roll of applause. People stepped slowly down onto the platform, looking confusedly about them, unsettled to be suddenly only human. They clung together in little groups, all wide eyes and chattering mouths, finding what comfort they could in the familiar proximity of old friends or enemies.

The magical world is like an overlay on the real world, and though the real cannot see the magical, it can sometimes still be affected by it. But there has always been traffic between the two, mostly from Mysterie to Veritie, as beings of various kinds exchange the gaudier joys of magic for the more secure bedrock of reality. And there have always been those with a foot in both worlds, like Jimmy Thunder and the Waking Beauty. Many apparently ordinary people and things cast powerful shadows in Mysterie, and, of course, vice versa.

There are always those willing to leave magic behind so that they might live out normal, finite lives in Veritie. Some come to be free of their responsibilities, some to escape the obligations of their particular natures. But just lately there had been whispers that Something Bad was coming to Mysterie. Something awful and unstoppable, that would put an end to the old familiar dance of magic and reality. Jimmy had heard the rumors, and mostly discounted them. There were always rumors. But still people packed the carriages of the Reality Express and paid their fare with gold and gems, magical artifacts and personal power. They all had their reasons: vampires and werewolves who wanted to be freed from the demands of their curses, or undead who craved to know the sensual pleasures of the living, or just to know the simple joy of daylight. In Veritie, they could be mortal men and women, free from fate or duty or geas. The price was always more than they expected. Some of the newcomers were already shaking and shuddering on the platform, shocked at how much smaller they seemed here, how much more diminished and vulnerable the human condition really was.

Some of them had never even been cold before.

Two figures appeared suddenly out of nowhere to welcome the newcomers, and Jimmy leaned forward just a little for a better look. He was surprised, bordering on astonished, that they'd actually been able to arrive at the station without his noticing. And then he saw who the two were, and understood much. The man in charge of this small welcoming committee, speaking so calmly and graciously and comfortingly to the uncertain refugees, was Nicholas Hob, the Serpent's Son. Very old, very powerful, and irredeemably evil. Jimmy hadn't known Hob was back in town. To the best of his knowledge, no one had. It had been a hundred years and more since Nicholas Hob had gifted the town with his poisonous presence.

As always, he looked utterly perfect, in style and manners and everything that counted. He was handsome, elegant, apparently in his late twenties, in great shape and dashing with it. Blond, blue-eyed, and almost overpoweringly masculine, Hitler would have loved him on sight. (And probably had, if some of the rumors were true. There were a lot of rumors about Hob.) His suit was of the very latest cut, and quite clearly the most expensive money could buy.

Gold and silver gleamed all over his person, and he was charm personified as he welcomed one and all to their new lives in Veritie. He might have been a politician, a successful businessman or a film star, and had been all of those and more, in his time. But they were only the faces he hid behind, the masks he wore for other people. He was the Serpent's Son, cunning and vicious, potent and foul, who walked through lives and destroyed them, just for the hell of it. No one had ever been known to stand against him and live. He was his father's son, and he could shine like the sun when he chose.

(It was said that flowers and women withered when he smiled on them, and that he left a trail of blood and suffering wherever he walked. Jimmy Thunder was quite prepared to believe it.)

Hob's companion looked like a woman, but was actually Angel. In her own disturbing way, she was just as powerful and terrifying as Hob. Incredibly tall, impossibly pale and slender, she dressed in black tatters held together with safety pins and lengths of barbed wire. The pins pierced her flesh, and the wire broke it, but she didn't seem to care. She wore her jet-black hair cropped brutally close to her skull, and her face was coarsely good-looking, sensual rather than beautiful. Her skin was as pale as death, and her mouth and eyes were the same deep, vivid red. She smiled meaninglessly at the new arrivals, and her hands curled impatiently at her sides, as though impatient to be hurting or breaking things. At her belt hung a rosary made from human fingerbones, and a clutch of supernaturally white feathers that came from no material wings. The newcomers avoided her gaze, as though the very sight of her was painful to them. They all knew her name was more than just a name.

She really had been an angel once, descended now from the immaterial to the material world, and though she was much diminished from what she had once been, she was still a force almost beyond reckoning. No one knew what kind of angel she'd been, from Above or from Below, and whether she fell or was pushed, or what terrible, unforgivable thing she'd done, to be sentenced to the mortal miseries of flesh and blood and bone. No one asked; no one dared. She was Angel, and that was all anyone needed to know.

Jimmy hadn't known she'd allied herself with the Serpent's Son. And he hadn't known that either of them were involved in running the Reality Express. It couldn't help but make him wonder what else was going on, on his own doorstep, that he didn't know about.

Hob's calm voice and presence was finally having a soothing effect on the uneasy crowd of the newly human, as long as they didn't look at Angel, and he was soon bustling among them, smiling and shaking hands and checking names and numbers against a list on his laptop. He'd clearly done this before. At his murmured suggestion, Angel had moved away to lean against the station-house wall, and was idly digging out long curls of mortar from between the stones with a bored fingernail, clearly uninterested in the proceedings. Presumably she was just there to ride shotgun. Jimmy realized with a start that Hob and Angel were the reasons why he was there. The Waking Beauty had wanted their presence confirmed. The train and its passengers were largely irrelevant.

Jimmy studied Angel from the darkest and most concealing shadows he could find on the waiting-room roof. A line from an old song ran through his head, subtly altered: *Did you ever see a nightmare walking? I did* . . . Just standing there, with her pale arms now crossed over her small high breasts, she looked as dangerous and malignant as all hell. She hadn't been in town long, and everyone had been wondering which way she would jump. When God wanted a city leveled, or all the firstborn slaughtered in one night, he sent an angel. They were Heaven's stormtroopers. Angel's very presence in Bradford-on-Avon was enough to unsettle any sensible person, man or god.

(Only one other angel had been reduced from the immaterial to the material in present times, and that had been voluntary— supposedly. But the old city of Maggedon was no more, and the angel was still chained to his rock in the cold dark heart of the earth, with nails through his wings. A little humanity can be a dangerous thing.)

Jimmy Thunder let his hand fall to the great hammer at his side. It had been a long time since he had been genuinely frightened.

Perhaps he made a noise, or he'd moved too suddenly; either way,

Angel's head snapped round, and she looked up and glared right at him with her bloodred eyes, seeing him clearly through the concealing shadows of the chimney stack. She shouted a warning to Hob and ran forward, the crowd scattering before her. She jumped from the platform, across the tracks and up onto the waiting-room roof in one impossible bound, as though borne aloft on invisible wings. Roof slates cracked and exploded under her bare feet as she landed, her long legs barely flexing as they absorbed the impact. She held her hands like claws, and her wide smile could just as easily have been a snarl. Jimmy Thunder drew his hammer from its holster and moved reluctantly forward to face her.

Down below, on the far platform, the newly arrived refugees were panicking. Everyone was shouting and milling about, and trying to get back into the carriages, but the doors wouldn't open for them. There was pushing and shoving, and some fell to the ground and were trampled underfoot. Hob moved quickly among them, trying to calm them with his voice and his presence, but no one was listening. Newly human, no longer protected by their old natures or powers, the refugees were naked and vulnerable and they knew it. This was a perfect time for old enemies to strike, and pay off old scores and blood feuds. The crowd suddenly seized on the notion of escape, and headed en masse for the only exit, the black iron gate beside the station house. Hob was yelling now at the top of his voice, but no one gave a damn.

Up on the waiting-room roof there was neither time nor space for subtlety. Jimmy and Angel slammed together head-on, like two crashing trains. They exchanged blows that would have killed ordinary mortals, and took no hurt at all. Jimmy ducked one punch, and Angel's fist went on to shatter the chimney stack behind him. It all but exploded, showering bricks and rubble down the sloping roof and onto the platform below. The two fighters circled each other silently. They had nothing to say. More slates cracked and shattered under their feet as they threw themselves forward again. Jimmy made no attempt to block Angel's blow, taking it unflinchingly as he raised Mjolnir above his head and brought it down with all his strength. But Angel was still too fast for him. She leaped aside and the hammer came rushing down to strike the sloping roof, which broke open under the impact. The entire roof collapsed, plunging down into the waiting room below, and Jimmy and Angel went down with it, in a roar of disintegrating masonry.

Smoke and debris blew out the waiting room's windows, while the large oblong room filled with rubble and dust. Jimmy and Angel hit the floor hard, but were immediately back on their feet again, not even out of breath from their fall. They saw each other through the dust-choked air, and surged forward once again. Angel caught Jimmy in the chest with a powerful blow, and he was thrown backwards, knocking a hole through the wall behind him with his semi-divine body. It wasn't enough to damage him, but it still hurt like hell. And in the moment it took him to shrug off the hurt and rise out of the collapsed wall, Angel seized the advantage and went for his throat. Mjolnir leaped to Jimmy's defense, and lashed out to strike Angel a vicious blow on the right temple. Her head snapped right round under the impact, her neck bones squealing, but her neck held and her skull didn't break. Jimmy was frankly astonished, but that didn't stop him lashing out with his other hand, driving her back while she was still off balance. He charged forward, broken masonry falling off him like raindrops, wound up and threw Mjolnir at Angel with all his strength, sure that even a descended angel couldn't stand against the power and momentum of the legendary hammer that had split mountains in its time. Perhaps Angel wasn't sure either, and at the very last moment she ducked, and the hammer sailed harmlessly over her head to punch a hole through the wall behind her. Jimmy yelled for the hammer to return to him, but nothing happened. Bloody thing was getting senile. He lurched forward and Angel came to meet him, and for a long time they stood toe to toe, giving and receiving blows of terrible force that could normally shatter anything the mortal world had to offer. Neither of them would give an inch, and they fought on remorselessly as the last of the waiting room collapsed around them.

Hob was still trying to keep his panicking refugees under control, barking orders now in a cold, authoritative voice that as a rule would never be ignored, but no one was listening to him. They'd pressed themselves into a tightly packed crowd before the narrow exit gate, and were all but fighting each other in their need to get away. A few had made it out into the parking lot, and were running wildly in all directions. Hob lost his temper.

He took his ancient aspect upon him, glorious and terrible, and glowed, bright as the sun, brilliant and blinding. A wave of impossible heat blazed out from him, boiling along the platform, and engulfed all the refugees in one moment, even those running in the lot. Men and women burned alive and were gone, their bodies utterly consumed by an unbearable heat. They didn't even have time to scream before they were nothing more than a few ashes drifting on the night air.

Hob yelled to Angel, and she reluctantly turned away from the stunned thunder god, and vaulted back across the tracks to join her partner. They both disappeared into the parking lot, and a slow, sullen silence fell across what was left of the deserted railway station.

Jimmy Thunder kicked his way through the rubble of what had once been a waiting room, emerged out onto the platform and looked about him. The Reality Express was gone, returned to whatever place or state it called home. There was nothing left of the refugees but a few dark scorch marks on the station-house walls. For a moment it had been as though the sun itself had reached out and touched the earth, but it was Hob's power, and it touched only what he chose to touch. Jimmy looked back at the building he and Angel had destroyed during their fight, and swore briefly in Old Norse. Early hour of the morning or not, someone had to have heard the noise. He'd better leave before someone official turned up to investigate. Doubtless they'd come up with some real-world explanation—a gas explosion, probably. He stared up the empty tracks, still and silent now. He doubted there'd be any more runs on the Reality Express for the time being. No one would accept Hob's promises of a new and better life in Veritie anymore; not after he'd roasted his last lot of customers.

Jimmy wondered briefly how he was going to explain all this to the Waking Beauty. It really hadn't been one of his better showings. He sighed and started searching through the rubble of the destroyed waiting room for his lost hammer, calling to it as to a deaf and rather dim dog.

# Three

# Dead Man Walking

LEO MORN was having a quiet drink in the Dandy Lion when the dead man walked in. Leo put down his glass and glanced quickly about him, but no one else seemed to have noticed. This was Veritie, after all, and in the real world there was no magic, no enchantments, and definitely no walking dead men.

It was ten thirty on a Saturday, a quiet morning in a quiet country town. Bradford-on-Avon's narrow streets and lanes were full of shoppers and tourists and running children, making the most of a warm summer's day. Steady traffic rolled up and down the steep hill of Market Street, while harried motorists fought savagely over the limited parking space in adjoining Church Street. Just another Saturday morning, really, and Leo Morn was taking his ease at his favorite watering hole. The Dandy Lion was a very pleasant public house right in the center of town, in an old, old building that had been many things in its time, and known many names, but these days it was a warm and cozy resting place, with wood-paneled walls, raftered ceilings, good booze, and better food, where the lighting was kept just dim enough to be easy on the eyes. It was a good place to put your feet up, quench your thirst, and soothe the inner man.

Leo was sitting with the arty set, local writers, musicians, and artists who liked to get together of a morning, to exchange hard-luck stories about how harshly today's commercial world treated the suffering artist, steal each other's ideas, and indulge in as much mean-spirited gossip as possible. The company was always good, and the conversation could be sparkling and acerbic by turns. Coffee was usually the order of the day, in all its more dramatic forms, dispensed by a loud shuddering thing of steel and steam that squatted darkly at the end of the long wooden bar. Leo didn't actually care much for coffee, with or without whipped foam or chocolate sprinkles. He much preferred Dry Blackthorn, a locally produced cider that would bite your head right off if you weren't careful.

Leo considered his half-empty glass, but he couldn't blame the booze this time. He knew a walking dead man when he saw one. Not least because he'd been to this one's funeral only two weeks before. Reed Smith had been one of his few friends. A fortnight underground hadn't affected Reed much. He was still wearing the good suit he'd been buried in, and his slack face was pale under the last remnants of the undertaker's makeup. He held his head at an angle, where the motorcycle crash had broken his neck. His eyes were open, but barely focused, and his mouth was still held closed by the tiny stitches the undertaker had put in, so that there wouldn't be any unfortunate expressions on the dead man's face during the viewing. His hands hung limply at his sides, as though he'd forgotten they were there. Leo had a brief vision of those hands scrabbling at the underside of a closed coffin lid, and quickly pushed the thought aside. There was a lot to be said for cremation, especially in a town like this. Reed stood very still, just inside the swing doors of the pub, looking slowly about him as though trying to remember why he'd come in.

There was no disputing Reed was dead. One look was all it took. He didn't breathe, his chest didn't move, and he had no body language at all. Everything about him shouted his unnatural condition to all the world. In Mysterie, everyone would have known what he was the moment he walked in. But this was the real world, where such things just didn't happen; so no one noticed anything.

Leo always drank with the arty crowd on a Saturday morning. So had Reed. They were currently tucked away in their favorite corner, where the table was set right next to the big bay window looking out onto Market Street. It was semiprivate, a comfortable distance away from the damned jukebox and its fixation with minor seventies hits, and the window meant that when the conversation flagged, they could always look out at the world going by. People and traffic were always going up and down, back and forth, as they had for centuries past. Though the traffic these days moved a hell of a lot faster. Familiar faces were forever passing by the window, to be greeted with a wave and a smile, and perhaps a pointed comment it was just as well they couldn't hear. And there was always the primitive drama of Church Street, as motorists tried to squeeze cars into parking spaces manifestly too small for them. There was a lot of lurching back and forth, revving of engines, and jockeying for position. Conflicts here started with road rage and then escalated to open hysteria and blood lust, happily viewed by those around. The arty set were currently ignoring the dead man in favor of laying bets on whether the poor fool in the Rover Rio Grande was going to be able to back his car into the space he'd chosen without first cutting a few inches off both ends. He was on his twelfth attempt now, and a small crowd had gathered, sensing trouble. The arty set were fascinated.

"He'll never get that in there."

"Or if he does, he'll never get it out again."

"Not without a crowbar."

"Maybe we should just go down and offer to smear his bumpers with Vaseline."

"It always comes back to sex with you, doesn't it?"

"Not nearly as often as I'd like."

There was general laughter, and mouths and nose tips acquired layers of foam as everyone drank their frothy coffee. Leo liked to hear them in full flow. He'd been there the day they invented gut-barging, the English answer to sumo wrestling. He still couldn't believe it had actually caught on.

Leo Morn was a tall, slender, almost Gothic figure, all pale and interesting, who looked as if he should have been starring in a Tim

Burton film. He wore black cords and a black T-shirt under a black leather jacket, and was so thin a breath of fresh air might have blown him away. In his early twenties, with a misleadingly amiable face under a permanent bad hair day, Leo played bass guitar in a punk-folk band whose name kept changing so that promoters would book them more than once. He was currently resting between engagements. The band did a lot of resting. Leo mostly kept himself busy giving guitar lessons to teenagers who had more ambition than ability.

He was also prone to gambling with money he didn't have, making promises he had no intention of keeping, and having brief but torrid affairs with married women whose husbands understood them only too well. As a result, he had also become very proficient at pulling off a disappearing act at very short notice when it all inevitably came crashing down around his head. Leo had heard of responsibility, but wanted nothing to do with it. He did try to be a nice guy, when he remembered, but mostly he just didn't have the knack.

Meanwhile, the arty set's conversation had moved on, to discussing the overnight destruction of the railway station's waiting room. Theories were flying thick and fast. The current official explanation, of a possible gas leak, had been dismissed out of hand, on the unanswerable grounds of being both unlikely and boring. Much more exciting was the possibility of a terrorist bomb. A lot of Ministry of Defense people lived in Bradford-on-Avon, commuting in to the MOD centers at Bath and Bristol. As to which terrorists—take your pick these days.

Leo listened, but kept his mouth firmly shut. He knew the Reality Express had been running last night. He'd heard its unholy whistle sounding in the still of the night, and the roar of silver wheels hammering down the steel tracks into town. Leo was a half-breed: he had a magical father and a real mother, which meant he had a foot in both worlds and a home in neither. He lived in the real world by choice, but sometimes his father's legacy sang in his veins, and the secrets of Mysterie paraded themselves before him whether he wished it or not. He'd walked by the railway station on his way to the town center and paused awhile to watch the police studying the mess from a safe distance. There was so much magic hanging on the air that Leo could smell it, even in Veritie. Some heavy hitters had clearly gone at it hammer and tongs somewhen in the night, and not for the first time one of Mysterie's little wars had spilled over into reality. Leo had sniffed loudly and moved on. He didn't approve of the Reality Express. In his experience, Veritie and Mysterie worked best when they were kept strictly separate, an opinion for which his own existence was one of the best arguments. Love might conquer all, but it can be hell on the offspring.

He drank his cider, kept a watchful eye on the dead man, and listened with half an ear as Jason Grant, a local author, complained loudly to the rest of the arty set about his latest project.

"Crop circles! Bloody crop circles! I ask you, who cares about that rubbish anymore? Well, all right, somebody must, or the publishers wouldn't be paying me good money to write the bloody thing. It's a part-work; twenty-four monthly issues guaranteed to build up into an unsightly mess in your living room, until you're so far behind you give up and throw the lot out."

"So why are you doing it?" said Malcolm Cragg, an artist who specialized in portraits of people's pets, constructed from pressed flower petals.

"They found my weak spot," Grant said glumly. "They offered me money."

"The unfeeling bastards!"

"Right. So: it's put a bag over its head and do it for the money, one more time. Write interesting comments to accompany the hundreds of glossy color photos that are the real selling point. I mean, there just aren't that many ways to say *We don't know what it is either, or what might be causing it, but isn't it pretty? And/or impressive?* Heaven forfend we might even hint that we wouldn't be at all surprised if it turned out to be nothing more than half a dozen pissheads with planks on their feet, shuffling about in the corn in the early hours of the morning, going, *Hee hee, I'm a Martian.* God, *The X-Files* has a lot to answer for. . . ."

"Oh, I like that Gillian Anderson," said Cragg immediately. "You've got to admire a woman who can spout reams of scientific dialogue every week and still make it sound as though she's talking dirty."

"True," said Grant. "And it has to be said, if it wasn't for unauthorized *X-Files* tie-ins, I wouldn't be able to pay the rent some months. But crop circles have to be a new low, even for me. You can't just say, *Look at the pretty pictures*; you have to talk knowledgeably about UFO landings and wind vortices, and how there are always these strange molecular changes in the flattened corn. . . . I swear, much more of this and my brains are going to start dribbling out of my ears. . . ."

"It's your own fault," Cragg said unfeelingly. "They only hire you because you can make it sound convincing, no matter what crap you're writing about this week. Do you believe any of it?"

"Hell no! I might be an old hippie, but the only time I ever saw a UFO was when I scored some dodgy blotter paper in London, back in the seventies. There are no UFOs, no ghosts, and no secret conspiracies. And I should know because I've written about all of them, at one time or another." He smiled suddenly, and brightened up a little. "Hey; I had a great idea for a new *Crow* film the other day! Princess Diana comes back from the dead, with an Uzi in each hand, and hunts down French paparazzi! Easy enough to find a good look-alike and put her in *The Crow* makeup . . . You're looking at me strangely again."

The arty set started talking determinedly about the hippie commune that'd recently taken over the old Manor Farm on the edge of town. There were supposed to be a dozen of them, six men and six women, but so far they'd outraged local gossip by keeping themselves strictly to themselves. They'd come down from some dark corner of London, according to a girl who worked at the estate agents' who handled the sale, looking for peace and quiet and inner calm. Leo quietly wished them the best of luck in a town like Bradford-on-Avon, where the barriers between fact and fantasy had been rubbed a little thinner than most people were comfortable with.

What made the hippies so fascinating was that all details of the purchase of Manor Farm had been handled strictly by post. Not even a telephone call had been made. The commune had arrived en masse one morning, rumbling through the town in a converted double-decker London bus, and had settled into their new home without any help from anyone. And no one had seen neither hide nor hair of them since. The few things they needed were ordered by mail, and delivered by curious locals who found the money waiting for them on the doorstep. All the farmhouse's windows had been boarded over, and there was neither sight nor sound anywhere of the new occupants. There were rumors of drugs and orgies and dancing naked in the moonlight, but no one knew anything for sure.

"Hippies should have stayed in the sixties, where they belonged," said Grant, pushing his empty coffee cup forward, in the hope that some kind soul might offer to refill it for him. "Back with Love and Peace and Flower Power. It all seemed to make some kind of sense at the time. These days we're all too cynical to believe in Brotherhood and 'make love, not war.' Great music, though. There's never been any really good music since the Beatles split up."

"Oh, come on," Leo said automatically. "There's more kinds of popular music now than there's ever been. Something for everybody."

"Rubbish," said Grant. "It's all white kids getting off on pretending to be gangstas, and girl groups so young they're probably still doing homework. And most rap should have the letter *C* in front of it . . . Oh, God, listen to me. I sound so *old*. I hate kids' music and I can't stand the fashions. I have become my parents."

"Everybody does," said Cragg. "But the Manor Farm bunch do worry me. What have they got to hide? What are they afraid of our finding out? Nothing good will come of this, mark my words."

"You always say that," said Grant.

"And I'm usually right. Another coffee?"

Everyone immediately pushed their empty cups at him, and he went over to the bar to order more industrial-strength caffeine.

Grant scowled after him. "He may be a gloomy bastard, but he has a point. I just hope they don't turn out to be another of those bloody doomsday cults. End up drinking poisoned cider and burying themselves in the back garden. Before you know it, the whole town will be crawling with TV documentary crews, making programs called *Town of Terror,* or *The Hippies from Hell.* And I'll get called on to do another bloody part-work on them . . ."

Leo was looking at the dead man again. He'd been hoping against hope that his old friend Reed might have gone away by now, or at least had the good manners to be just an illusion, but no; it was looking more and more like Leo was going to have to Do Something. Reed had made his slow way over to the long wooden bar, and was staring uncertainly at the rows of spirits on the wall behind, as though sure they'd once meant something to him. People walked by him unconcernedly, and even pushed past him to give their orders, but so far no one had recognized him for who and what he was. On the rare occasions when the unnatural insisted on pushing its way into the real world, people mostly tended to ignore it for as long as possible. Leo sighed heavily and put down his glass. He wasn't thirsty anymore.

The dead shouldn't be *able* to walk in Veritie. It took a lot of magical power to raise the dead from their graves, and even more to keep control of them once they were up and about. And there was no magic in the real world: that was the point. Leo, however, being a hybrid derived from both worlds, could see more than most. In particular, he could see the magical field currently surrounding the dead man, containing him like a soap bubble, insulating what he was from the implacable laws of physics in the real world. Leo didn't even want to think about how much power such a field would take up. Reality was not easily defied, and even then not without terrible cost, for somebody. Leo knew most of the heavy-duty movers and shakers in the magical world, but unfortunately far too many of them knew him. And they certainly wouldn't take kindly to him pushing his nose in where it wasn't wanted.

Leo grinned suddenly. It was a wide, unpleasant, distinctly wolfish smile, and the people sitting around him shrank back in their seats a little, giving him more room, in case he decided to do something unpleasant. Leo tried to be a nice guy, but he wasn't at all averse to being a complete bastard when necessary. This wasn't just any dead man. This was his friend, Reed. Leo had many acquaintances, but few friends; even he knew that when someone drags your friend up out of his grave, you're supposed to do something about it. Leo felt like doing something very nasty. The more he considered the matter, the less he liked it. He didn't know a lot about zombies, apart from what he'd seen in bad Italian horror movies, but he knew they tended to come in two basic versions. One was just an empty shell, an untenanted body being operated at some remove by someone else. Which was disrespectful, if nothing else. Leo felt he could give someone a serious slapping for that. But there was an even worse alternative. Reed's soul could still be trapped inside his decaying body, a helpless victim under someone else's control. Endlessly suffering, denied his rightful rest, just because some heartless bastard had a use for him. Leo's mouth widened, his lips thinning as his smile became a snarl. Around him the arty set began getting to their feet and making noises like *Well, look at the time* and *I really must be going*. Leo didn't notice. His anger had escalated from hot to boiling to ice cold in just a few seconds. Someone was going to pay for what had been done to Reed. No one messed with a friend of Leo Morn and lived to boast of it.

Reed used to drink here, at the Dandy Lion. If he stood around long enough, people would be forced to notice him. And some might even recognize him, and that was when the screaming would start. Real people might like to titillate themselves with ghost stories and crop circles and the like, but when faced with the unreal thing, they couldn't cope at all. It destroyed their ideas about how the universe worked.

Leo decided it was time he talked with his Brother Under The Hill.

*"Brother,"* he said, in his mind. *"I have a problem. The shit is in the air, and it's right on course for the fan."*

*It's your own fault,* said the other voice in his mind. *I told you she was never sixteen. Tell me you used a condom at least.*

"Get your mind out of the gutter. I'm sitting in the Dandy Lion—"

*Now there's a surprise.*

"Looking at a dead man walking."

*All right, you've got my attention. Go to Red Alert and buckle yourself in. What the hell is a dead man doing in Veritie?*

"I was going to ask you that."

*What's it doing, right now?*

"For the moment, just standing around, looking confused."

*Oh, good. For one horrible moment I thought you'd wandered into a Lucio Fulci movie.*

"Zombie Flesh-Eaters *is a classic of the genre, and I won't hear a word said against it. Any ideas as to what I should do next?"*

Leo had no idea who or what his Brother actually was. He admitted to being extremely old and not entirely human, and lived, if that was the right word, buried deep under one of the hills surrounding the town. The last time he saw light, the Roman Empire was busy declining and falling. Leo inherited his Brother Under The Hill on his father's demise, and from that moment on he and the Brother could talk to each other, mind to mind, no matter how great the distance separating them. Whoever or whatever the Brother was, he'd been doing it for centuries. He liked to say he was raising Morns, and would keep at it till he got it right. The Brother saw, heard, and knew everything that happened in the town below him, in Veritie and Mysterie, although he only existed now in the magical world. The Morns were his only means of communicating with the two worlds. Leo was the first Morn who had chosen to live in the real world, which had been the cause of a certain amount of friction between them.

But Leo was determined to be nothing like his father.

*Keeping a dead man up and walking in the real world isn't something your average necromancer or dabbler in the dark arts could manage,* mused the Brother. *This has to be the work of one of the major players.*

*"I had managed to work that out for myself,"* said Leo, just a little testily. *"I've been running through the usual suspects, but . . . Jackie Schadenfreude is out of town at the moment, the Lord of Thorns is still sulking in his tent after getting his fingers burned in the Cup of Tears fiasco, and Jessica Sorrow the Unbeliever wouldn't bother herself with anything this trivial. Damn, that woman scares me."*

*I told you not to sleep with her.*

*"She didn't exactly give me a choice. Look; what do you think we should do about my dead friend?"*

*I love the "we" bit. Stuck as I am beneath this bloody hill, it's up to you to do something. And do it pretty damned quickly, before the mortals are forced to notice what's come visiting their fragile little world. The last thing we need is a panic in the town, and intrusive media people.*

*"Can't you see who's behind this? I thought you were supposed to be all-knowing."*

*Normally I am; but whoever did this is hidden from me. Which is worrying.*

*"Wonderful,"* said Leo. *"Don't you have any suggestions? If I try to drag Reed out of here, that's going to attract the very attention we're trying to avoid. And I really don't see him listening to reason—oh, shit . . ."*

*What? What?*

*"The Waking Beauty is glaring at me from her corner. If she's manifesting in the real world, the situation must be even worse than we thought. From the way she's looking at me, it's clear she expects me to do something pretty sharpish. Interfering old biddy. You are sure she can't hear us?"*

*Only you can hear me, Leo. Only you.*

*"Yeah, but this is the Waking Beauty we're talking about."*

*True. She's the only creature in this town who's older than I am.*

*"I wish you were just a voice in my head. Life would be so much simpler if I was just crazy. Hold everything: What was that?"*

A communication had come and gone so quickly Leo couldn't overhear or track it, but the dead man had heard and understood. He turned and walked unhurriedly out of the pub. People got out of his way without knowing why. Leo scrambled up from behind his table, realized for the first time that the arty set were all long gone, shrugged, and set off after the departing dead man. The mind voice hadn't lasted long, but it had still made one hell of an impression, scoring through Leo's mind like a length of barbed wire.

*Major* player.

Leo emerged blinking into the bright sunshine outside the Dandy Lion and hurried after the dead man, at what he hoped was a discreet distance. Reed strode firmly off down the hill, people parting on either side to let him pass without seeing him. Leo tried hard to keep thinking of his quarry as *the dead man,* an object rather than a person, but it wasn't easy. Reed had been one of his few real friends. He'd gone to Reed's funeral, tried to say the right things to the grieving relatives, had stood at the graveside and made his goodbyes; and now Reed was up and about again, a pawn in someone else's dirty game. Leo's hands clenched into fists at his sides. Someone was going to pay for this, and pay in blood. Leo's wolfish smile flashed again as he considered the awful mess he was going to make of whoever had been foolish enough to raise his anger. He didn't care how big or powerful or influential the bastard might turn out to be. He never did. He was Leo Morn, and no one messed with him and his. His mind filled with happy thoughts of broken bones and torn flesh and spurting blood, and people moved aside to let him pass, too.

The Brother Under The Hill maintained a neutral silence.

Leo followed the dead man through the center of the town and across the old bridge over the River Avon. Green reeds poked up through the dark waters, while crowds of ducks competed noisily for bread crumbs thrown by tourists. A pair of pure white swans watched disdainfully from a distance. The dead man passed the Chapel on the Bridge, a solid square of ancient stonework jutting out over the river. It had been there so long no one now remembered who built it, or why. Some said it had been a private chapel, others that it had been an overnight lockup for local drunks. There was one door, always locked, and small barred windows. Even in Veritie, it was a squat, brooding presence. As the dead man passed the Chapel, the Howling Thing stirred ominously.

Although it was a part of the magical world, forever separated from reality, the Howling Thing was still a powerful enough presence that its rage caused ripples in both worlds. People passing the Chapel often crossed themselves, even if they didn't know why. The Howling Thing reacted to the necromantic energies surrounding the dead man and hurled itself furiously at the locked door. It raged and beat against the four confining walls, old stone sealed and consecrated by ancient sorceries, and fought to be free. Its awful voice rose and fell, never-ending, promising revenge and retribution. It never stopped, never rested, but still its cage held it, as it had for centuries past and would do so for centuries yet to come.

There were those who said the Howling Thing founded Bradford-on-Avon, long, long ago. Others said it tried to destroy the town. And some claimed it was the town's spirit, and that if it ever escaped or was released, the town would come to an end. The truth was, no one knew anything for sure anymore. But absolutely no one was prepared to risk setting the Thing free, even if they knew how.

Leo padded on after the dead man, all through the town and out the other side. As buildings gave way more and more to open countryside, Leo began to get a really bad feeling about where they were going. And soon enough, all too soon, the open fields butted up against the silent, dead trees of Blackacre. Reed walked unhesitatingly into the dead thickets, but Leo paused for a moment, wondering if he really was that determined to avenge his friend. Nothing good ever came out of Blackacre.

Even Leo Morn had enough sense to be scared of Blackacre.

But in the end, he plunged on into the thicket of dark, lifeless trees, if only because he didn't want to. Leo had his pride. As he entered the woods he dropped suddenly out of the real and into Mysterie, with a sharp shock that for a moment took his breath away. He'd never known a place so strongly magical as to rip him out of one world and into the next, against his will. His senses became sharper, more focused, as using his father's legacy he adapted to the magical world, and with a slow sense of horror he realized that Blackacre no longer existed in the real world. Only its shell remained in Veritie, an empty vision of what had once been as real as earth and rock. Something, or more likely someone, had torn the guts out of Blackacre and pinned them firmly in Mysterie. Blackacre was a wholly magical place now, where dark, bad, magical things could be done.

Leo's pace slowed, almost despite himself. As his father's son, he was a powerful presence himself in Mysterie; but he'd never cared for that. Legacies and destinies were for other people. He preferred the simpler, subtler, more real pleasures of being just a man.

*"Are you still with me, Brother?"*

*Of course.* His Brother's voice was clear and sharp, with a much stronger sense of presence, now that they were both in Mysterie. *This is bad, Leo, really bad. Whoever gutted Blackacre to make it his own has to be one of the Powers and Dominations. In which case, we are both well out of our depth and sinking fast. It disturbs me that I sensed nothing of such a presence operating recently. Or that I knew nothing of Blackacre's destruction in the real world. I should have known. Proceed cautiously, Leo. These are deep, dark waters we find ourselves in.*

Leo didn't need telling. Just walking through the dead woods was enough to put all his hair on end. Blackacre felt like long fingernails scraping down his soul. The blackened trees bore no leaves or blossom, and never would again. Thick black boles and stark black branches were held utterly still, undisturbed by any trace of a breeze. Nothing moved in Blackacre, not even the air. Nothing but Leo Morn and a dead man. The ground was inches deep in ashes, and Leo's every footstep made loud crunching sounds, for all his stealth, announcing his presence. He let himself fall farther back, still keeping Reed in sight, as he glanced warily about him. There were no animals, no insects, no birds. This was a dead place, where perhaps even time stood still.

It was like walking on the moon. Life had come and gone, and nothing would ever thrive in Blackacre again. Once, there had been a great fire here, some awful heat that had scoured all life away and left only dead things behind. Which rather raised the question of where the dead man was going, and who or what was waiting to receive him. Like the rest of the town, Leo had heard rumors of a new owner of Blackacre Farm and its surrounding land, but he'd assumed that was only in Veritie. Reed seemed to be heading straight for the deserted farmhouse, and whatever occupied it now—something so powerful it could even hide itself from The Brother Under The Hill.

Leo was breathing hard now, cold beads of sweat standing out on his forehead, but he didn't slow his pace any further. He'd come this far. He wanted, needed, to *know*.

He could feel a pressure building on the still air as he neared the center of the dead woods and the farmhouse. The air seemed to push back against him, until it was like walking headlong into a harsh, relentless wind. He had to lean forward as he walked, digging his feet into the ash-covered ground. Each step became an effort, and he grunted and growled deep in his throat as he forced his way on. His eyes were narrowed and his teeth were showing. If someone was determined to keep him out, there had to be something worth knowing about at the end of it. He'd almost forgotten his earlier intention to avenge his friend Reed; this had become personal now. No one kept Leo Morn out when he wanted in.

He could feel necromantic energies growing all around him now, crackling on his skin and spitting sparks from his hair. He'd never encountered magical defenses this strong before. They would have stopped any normal man, and most magical creatures. But Leo was born of both worlds, and his dual nature seemed to confuse the defenses, so they couldn't get a firm grip on him. He trudged on, stronger and more stubborn than any mindless defense could ever be. And then suddenly the pressure broke, and he almost fell forward.

He stopped for a moment to get his breath back, glaring about him. There were dead trees everywhere he looked, for as far as he could see, as though the Blackacre woods were now much bigger on the inside than they appeared on the outside. As though Blackacre was growing, expanding, under the influence of its new owner. Leo sniffed at the still air, but there were no living scents. Just the dry and dusty air, the kind you find in a room that's been left locked up and abandoned for many years. The silence was so complete now he'd stopped moving that he could hear every sound he made, from his harsh breathing to the rustling of his clothes to his own heartbeat.

*Stand very still.*

"Why?" Leo said quickly. "What's happening?"

*I sense something. It's hard for me to see anything in Blackacre; it's like trying to see things out of the corner of your eye, but I think I'm getting the hang of it. You're not alone here, Leo. I can sense ten, maybe twelve, dead men in the woods with you. Can you see them?*

Leo looked quickly about him, into the artificial gloom of the thick woods, but couldn't see or hear or smell anything; except Reed, moving farther away from him, up ahead.

"All I can see are trees. Are you sure about this? What are these other dead men doing?"

*Of course I'm sure. I'm always sure. Make it twenty dead men. I'm finding more all the time. As far as I can tell, they're just . . . standing in the woods. Standing guard, presumably. Don't get too close to any of them. Proximity probably triggers an alarm. Proceed with extreme caution, Leo. Are you sure you can't see any of them? You're right on top of half a dozen.*

"Great," growled Leo. "Just bloody great. This gets better all the time. No I can't see any bloody dead guards. You'll just have to guide me. Steer me clear of the bastards. Brother, who the hell are we up against? This is more than just some rogue necromancer."

*Powers and Dominations,* said his Brother Under The Hill. *Would I be wasting my time if I suggested you make a strategic retreat, and not come back until you've acquired a few more powerful allies of your own?*

"Yes."

*I thought so.*

"Would you shut up a minute and let me concentrate? I may not be a Power or a Domination, but I can still be pretty damned sneaky when I put my mind to it."

Leo moved slowly forward, setting each foot down so carefully that the ashes burying the ground accepted his weight without a murmur. He swiveled his head slowly back and forth, not even blinking his eyes, and at last he caught sight of one of the dead men, standing as still as the dead trees. Leo froze in place and studied the dead man for a long time. It wasn't anyone he knew, and it seemed to be in a good state of preservation. The corpse's utter stillness was quietly unnerving, inhuman, like some machine waiting for instructions. People weren't supposed to look like that. Leo moved on, giving the dead man a wide berth.

Defensive spells formed on the air before him like static snowdrops, intricate and elegant, shimmering with unearthly colors; magical antipersonnel mines. Invisible to ordinary eyes, there were change spells and death spells, and a whole bunch of curses Leo didn't even recognize. He slipped cautiously between them, bending at awkward angles to avoid touching and activating them. He had no doubt that there were other, subtler defenses, too, so complex even he couldn't hope to sense them in time, but he trusted to his dual nature to protect him, and pressed on. He'd come too far to turn back now. Leo had few positive qualities, but stubbornness was definitely one of them.

At last the dark trees fell away to reveal a great open clearing, with the farmhouse standing at its center, like the bait in a trap. It was a long two-story building, in the old half-timbered style, its mottled exterior filthy and corrupted, the victim of nature's relentless working and long neglect. Leo crouched at the edge of the clearing, and just looking at the farmhouse made him feel sick. There was a disturbing wrongness to it, as though it was both more and less than just a house. The gaping black windows were like eyes, and the great front door a mouth with concealed teeth. It wasn't a sane place, where sane and normal people might live. The angles were all wrong, and the decaying features played tricks of perspective on him, as though parts were rushing toward and retreating from him, at the same time. It was a structure from another time and another place, where they did things differently. An alien place, perhaps neither real nor magical, but something . . . worse.

The slumping rotten heart of Blackacre stood all alone, with no obvious defenses. No dead men on guard, no attack spells floating on the air, nobody watching from the empty windows. It had to be a trap. Leo crouched where he was, considering his options, and then almost jumped out of his skin as Reed walked out of the woods some ten feet away and headed straight for the farmhouse. Leo seized his chance. He padded quietly across the open clearing, keeping close behind Reed, following in his footsteps. No one challenged him. Reed pushed open the front door and went in, while Leo dropped to the ground beside it, struggling to control his breathing and his heartbeat.

He pressed his back against the wall, and the moist surface gave disturbingly under the pressure. The dead woods were still and quiet. Leo swallowed hard. Now that he'd got this far, he wasn't absolutely sure what to do next. Just walking in the front door like Reed did not strike him as a good idea, and he didn't even know if there was a back door. A light suddenly appeared at one of the downstairs windows; a calm, golden light quite at odds with the rest of the farmhouse. Leo slid along the wall, as quiet as a mouse in carpet slippers, until he was right underneath the lit window. All he had to do now was rise up and peek in, but somehow that didn't appeal to him at all. For all his stubbornness and curiosity, that last step seemed so big as to be almost overwhelming. He didn't want to look in, for fear of what might look back at him.

There were monsters in Mysterie. Things much nastier than a little half-breed like Leo Morn.

And then he thought of Reed, his friend Reed, his dead friend Reed, walking helplessly into this house at the call of whoever or whatever had summoned him up out of his grave, and the chill in Leo's veins was driven out by a hot flush of anger. It wasn't courage, but it would do to get him moving. He sucked in a deep breath, held it, turned slowly, and carefully rose up to look in at the glowing window.

At first, the glass was so filthy he couldn't see a damn thing. But as his eyes adjusted to the glare of the light and the smeared fog on the window, his preternaturally keen gaze was able to make out two distinct figures sitting at their ease in what had once been a parlor. Nicholas Hob, the Serpent's Son, was having coffee with the woman Angel. Now that he saw them, Leo couldn't say he was totally surprised. Shocked, scared, and in urgent need of a toilet, but not actually surprised. If Hob had returned, then raising the dead was just the kind of unpleasantness you'd expect from the Serpent's Son. He was a Power *and* a Domination, and more besides. Nicholas Scratch. Hob. Old names for the Devil, the Enemy of Man. And Hob was all that.

Angel was more of an enigma. You couldn't really use terms like *good* and *bad* with her; they were just too limiting. Brutal and vicious certainly, and capable of anything . . . but applying morality to Angel was like ascribing motives to a force of nature. Angel was new to the material plane, and couldn't be expected to understand minor concepts like right and wrong. She was probably still working on life and death. Angel was dangerous precisely because she was so unpredictable. If she had fallen under Hob's influence . . .

*Now would be a really good time to leave.*

"*I told you to shut up!*" said Leo, in the mental equivalent of a shocked cry. "*That's Hob and Angel in there!*"

*They can't hear us. I've been probing their defenses for some time, and they haven't even noticed.*

"*Now he tells me.*"

*You run for the trees. I'll cover you.*

"*Hell with that. I didn't nearly wet myself getting this far to turn back without finding out what the hell is going on here. I didn't know Hob was back. Did you know Hob was back?*"

*No. I can't see him. Or Angel. Usually. They're just too . . . different. Veritie and Mysterie mean nothing to such as they.*

"*I really should have stayed in bed this morning, or maybe under it. Now shut up and let me concentrate on what's going on in there.*"

He pushed his face as close to the filthy window as he dared, straining his more than natural senses to their limit. Hob and Angel were sitting on opposite sides of an ornate and decorative coffee table, antique by the look of it, polished and gleaming and no doubt hideously expensive. The delicate china coffee set they were using was practically a work of art, but Hob treated it quite casually as he refilled Angel's cup. All around them, the parlor was filthy and squalid and utterly vile. It was more than a century since anyone had actually lived in the Blackacre farmhouse, and it showed. The bare walls were cracked and bulging and pockmarked with huge craters, running with slow viscous damp like pus from leaking sores. Thick clumps of bulbous white fungi filled the angles where the walls met floor and ceiling. Leo could almost taste the stench of corruption that filled the room, even through the closed window. The room was full of a golden light, but from no obvious source, as though the parlor itself glowed with the unclean light of underground phosphorescence. No one with human sensibilities could have lived in such a room, or even tolerated it for more than a few moments, but then, Hob and Angel only looked human. They drank their coffee and talked together, quite undisturbed by their surroundings, while outside Leo fought hard not to vomit.

He had come to a bad place, and just its proximity was enough to sicken him to his soul.

In the room, Angel looked at the steaming hot coffee in her cup, added four spoonfuls of sugar, and then stirred the boiling-hot liquid with the tip of her finger, with no obvious distress. Hob's aristocratic mouth moved briefly in a faint moue of distaste, but he had enough sense not to say anything. Leo pressed his ear against the windowpane, though his cheek crawled and jumped at the contact, and listened as they spoke.

"I understood you were banished from this town," said Angel. "Where have you been all these years?"

"Traveling the world, and walking up and down in it," Hob said easily. "Dabbling in politics and revolution, just for the hell of it. Mostly in parts of the world where politics and revolution are the same thing. People will rape, torture, and kill each other for the most amusing reasons, if you know the right buttons to push. I always feel most alive when everything else is dying all around me. And I was never banned. I chose to leave, to avoid . . . unpleasantness. I hadn't thought of dear old Bradford-on-Avon in a long time, but my father called me back, so here I am. One doesn't say no to the Serpent."

Angel leaned forward in her chair, suddenly interested. "Your father. Have you ever seen him? Do you know what he is?"

Hob frowned and looked away, developing a sudden interest in his coffee cup. "No. My father is as much a mystery to me as anyone else. I don't think there's anyone now living who knows for sure what the Serpent actually looks like. Except for dear Luna, of course. And she's still crazy. That's what looking in the eyes of ultimate evil will do to you, even if you are a Power or a Domination. Poor Luna. My father has never shown me his face, and I have never been tempted to ask to see it. But sometimes he talks to me. I hear his voice, in my mind."

"What does it sound like?" asked Angel, sipping coffee daintily with her little finger crooked.

"He sounds like a sword cutting through flesh. Like the sounds of children dying. Like everything we dream of in our worst nightmares. It is not a human voice, or even a living voice, in any way that you or I could comprehend. Though since you were once of the immaterial . . ."

Angel scowled and put her cup down sharply. "I am material now, and much less than I was. Any memories I might have had of things other than the material were taken from me. That was part of my punishment. Or perhaps my reward. It's so hard to be sure."

"Ah, well," said Hob. "Easy come, easy go. All you need to know is that I follow my father's wishes; and as long as we follow his plan, you and I will bring down both the worlds of reality and magic, and watch as my father tramples them beneath his ancient spite. The Serpent In The Sun will bring an end to Veritie and Mysterie, and you and I will have ringside seats as our reward, and afterwards we shall frolic in the ruins and glory in the damnation of our enemies."

"You say the sweetest things," said Angel. "Just as long as I'm not bored. I do so hate to be bored."

They both looked round as the door behind them opened and Reed walked in. Hob checked his Rolex and sniffed. "About time you got back. Off you go and join the others in the woods. Usual rules; if it moves and it isn't us, kill it. And don't go wandering off again, or I'll cut you off at the ankles."

The dead man turned and left the room, shutting the door quietly behind him. Leo let out his breath slowly. He'd been wondering if Reed would report being followed, but it seemed his dual nature was still protecting him.

"What was the little thunder god doing at the railway station this morning?" said Angel. When she spoke, she sometimes put emphasis on unusual words, as though she was still struggling to understand the subtler mechanisms of speech.

"Being a bloody nuisance, mostly," said Hob. "I suspect the Waking Beauty's hand in his presence. I can hide myself from most of the higher orders, but the Waking Beauty is something else. Even I'm not sure what. Luckily, she's never been of an active nature. Much prefers getting some other poor fool to do her dirty work. Don't you worry about Jimmy Thunder, Loser For Hire. The divinity's running very thin in his bloodline. If he shows his face again, I'll rip it right off."

"Tell me more about this Waking Beauty," said Angel. "Is she real, or magical?"

"Both. Neither. I don't think anyone knows. I have an uncomfortable suspicion that she's above such things. She's very old, and she never sleeps, and she knows things. Disturbing things. I met her once . . . and she wasn't frightened of me. Unusual, that."

"Thanks to the godling's interference, the Reality Express is no more," said Angel. "After your little outburst, it will be a long time before any refugees will trust their safety to you again. What will you do for the power you need, now that you can no longer bleed the refugees dry?"

"I do hope I didn't detect a teeny note of criticism there, dear Angel," said Hob, smiling with his mouth alone. "Never forget, I am the one who makes the decisions here, because I am my father's voice. I will do what it pleases me to do, and I will not be questioned. As I will, so mote it be, as dear little Aleister and I used to say in my somewhat younger days. The loss of the Reality Express is but a trifling thing. I can always raise more dead and send them out to murder the living. There's a lot of power to be gained from necromancy. And the dead do make such excellent servants; they're completely obedient and they never talk back. Bit short in the initiative department, but that's usually all to the good. I'll empty this town's cemeteries and send the dear departed lurching through the streets in broad daylight, if I have to. Killing a whole bunch of people always makes me feel better."

"Yes," said Angel, smiling for the first time. It was a disturbing sight. "To kill, to diminish the spark of light, to destroy the Creator's work. Such things are food and drink to me. But say the word, and I will set the town's streets awash with blood."

"Thanks for the offer," said Hob tactfully. "But my father's plans don't call for us to attract so much attention just yet."

"Perhaps you should have thought of that before you burned all those refugees," said Angel.

Hob looked at her, and there was something in his gaze that silenced her. "You forget," he said softly. "You forget who and what I am, little Angel. I am the only son of The Serpent In The Sun, and this whole world, real or magical, is mine by right. I could destroy you with a thought, and then raise you from the dead to serve me again. Get down on your knees."

"Please," said Angel. "Don't."

"Down. On your knees. Now."

Angel rose jerkily to her feet, leaving her cup on the table. She looked stonily at Hob, and then knelt before him.

"Now kiss my foot, little Angel," said Nicholas Hob.

And she did.

Hob looked down at Angel's bowed head and slowly emptied his coffee cup over it. The hot liquid ran down her face like dark brown tears, but Angel didn't move. Hob laughed softly. "Get up, Heaven's droppings."

Angel rose slowly to her feet and sat down in her chair again. She made no move to wipe away the coffee still dripping from her chin.

"Now, my dear," said Hob. "Is there anything else you feel you need to discuss with me?"

"The dead man," Angel said slowly. "The one who went walking into town. Could any of the others break free, like him?"

Hob frowned, and Angel could not meet his gaze. "I was distracted," Hob said finally. "When I lost my temper, at the station. My mind wandered for a moment, and my concentration lapsed. It took me a while to realize that one of my slaves had slipped his leash. But it won't happen again. I've taken steps to see to that. And as you should know, I never give up on anything that I have made mine."

Perhaps Leo started at that, or made a noise. Either way, Hob and Angel turned sharply in their chairs to look at the window, and for a moment Hob and Leo looked right into each other's eyes. It was only the barest moment, and then Leo was off and running, bolting across the open clearing as fast as his legs could carry him. He could hear Hob shouting something behind him, and then he was in among the dead trees and running hard. He could feel the magical defenses snapping on and off around him, trying to get a fix on him, confused by his hybrid nature. His Brother Under The Hill spoke urgently in his mind, giving him directions.

Dead men came lurching out from between the dead trees, looking for him with their cold unblinking eyes, but he was too fast for them, racing through Blackacre Wood with puffs of ashes flying up every time his feet hit the ground. One of the dead might have been Reed—he didn't stop to look. More figures appeared ahead of him, closing together to block his way. His Brother roared, filling the aether with mental static, and the corpses driven by Hob's will were suddenly blind and uncertain. Leo raced right through them, and they couldn't even touch him.

Leo grinned as he ran, moving quickly and confidently through the last of the dead trees. Hob couldn't find him now, and the stalking dead men were too far behind to give him any trouble. Just let him reach the open countryside beyond the woods, and cross back into Veritie, and he'd defy Hob or anyone else to bring him down. And then there was thunder on the air, high above him, and despite himself he looked back. Angel was coming for him, walking on the air.

Some twenty feet above the ground, higher than some of the trees, Angel strode across the sky, and the air shuddered like thunderclaps where her feet trod. She was coming faster than her stride could carry her, sweeping through the air like a hawk with fiery eyes. Leo ran at full pelt through the dead trees, dodging back and forth, heart and lungs straining, and Angel closed remorselessly in on him, like an owl hunting a mouse. Leo pushed himself to his limits, while his Brother yelled for him to make the change, and with anyone else he might have, but even in his changed state he doubted he would have lasted long against Angel. Veritie was his only hope.

He pushed himself even harder, crying out at the pain now as he forced his body past its human limits, and then suddenly he was out of the trees, out of Blackacre, and reality crashed down around him. Leo threw himself to the warm and living ground and lay there, panting for breath. His muscles were trembling with the strain he'd put on them. After a while, he turned slowly and looked back at the border of Blackacre, where Mysterie butted up against Veritie.

And there was Angel, standing quite normally on the ground, in Blackacre. They looked at each other for a long while, Angel's face completely expressionless, and then she turned and walked back into the dead woods, and Leo's heart started beating again. He lay on his back on the good warm grass, looking up at the blue sky and waited for his breathing to return to something like normal.

"*Brother,*" he said finally.

*Yes?*

"*We're going to have to talk to someone about this.*"

# Four~

# Some Things Are
# Meant to Be

TOBY DEXTER woke up comparatively early on Saturday morning, without knowing why. He rolled slowly over in bed and looked resentfully at the alarm clock on the bedside table. Mickey Mouse's hands pointed unfeelingly at nine o'clock. The alarm was still silent. Toby liked to lie in on a Saturday morning, preferably till ten or eleven or even later. One of the joys of Saturday morning was knowing he wasn't going to be driven from his nice warm bed by Mickey's shrill clamor at seven o'bloody clock. Toby lay back in his bed, vaguely contemplating the ceiling. Something had woken him up. Almost as though someone had called his name, in a voice that could not be ignored.

Saturday morning. He always looked forward to Saturdays, especially at the beginning of the week, when the days and the hours and the minutes at work seemed just to crawl past, stretching endlessly away before him, and Saturday night might as well have been another planet. But what did he actually do, when Saturday and the weekend finally came around? He'd sleep in. Get up only when he absolutely had to (usually forced out of bed by bladder pressure), and stagger downstairs in his dressing gown to watch kids' cartoons on television, usually while eating a big bowl of whatever sugary cereal he was currently addicted to. All the while grousing, sometimes aloud, that today's cartoons weren't a patch on the cartoons of his youth. *Scooby Doo* in particular had deteriorated dreadfully. He wouldn't even watch the ones that contained Scrappy Doo. (Once voted by the readers of a leading men's magazine as the cartoon character they'd most like to punch in the head repeatedly. Even more than Jar Jar Binks.) And where did the two good-looking kids always disappear to, while Shaggy and Thelma were busy being chased by men in monster masks? They'd probably found a bedroom and were rutting like crazed weasels.

Come midday he'd get dressed and wander down into town for a drink, to see what was happening and who was around. And it was always the same old faces, doing the same old things. Which was sometimes comforting, but more often not. Then back home, to open a packet and stick it in the oven, and that was dinner. Usually eaten straight from the plastic container because that saved on washing up. Then sit slumped in front of the television all afternoon, watching the sports. Any sports—he wasn't fussy. And in the evening, call around to see if anyone fancied a drink. And after drinking too much, in the company of people who only counted as friends because he saw them every weekend, stagger home and try to get to sleep with his bedroom revolving slowly around him.

Repeat on Sunday. Then back to work again. Not much of a life, really. Not much of a life at all.

Toby tried really hard to get back to sleep again so he wouldn't have to think anymore, but his body was having none of it. His body felt decidedly restless. Like it needed to be up and about, doing things . . . important things. Even though Toby had no idea what they might be. He turned onto his side, pulling the blankets up around his neck, trying to get comfortable so he could fool his body into dozing off, but the bed felt cold and hard and unwelcoming, as though it knew he shouldn't be there. In the end, Toby swore briefly but feelingly, threw back the covers, and lurched out of bed. It was clearly going to be one of those days.

He pulled off his pajamas and threw them roughly in the direction of the dirty laundry basket, and got dressed. It didn't feel like a dressing-gown-and-cartoons day. He stomped downstairs, yawning and scratching as the mood took him, collected the usual pile of junk mail from his doormat and headed for the kitchen, trying to decide whether he could be bothered to make himself a proper breakfast. One bowl of milky cereal and a compromise glass of orange juice with added vitamin C later, he rinsed the bowl and glass under the hot tap and put them on one side to dry. He sat down again at the kitchen table and considered the morning's mail. Which turned out to be strange and weird enough to snap him fully awake.

A folded glossy pamphlet offered six foolproof ways to avoid elf-shot, proven cause of most chills and fevers. The six ways included medicines and herbs he'd never heard of, prayers to someone called Mannan Mac Lir, and a series of healthy exercises that made Toby wince just to look at the illustrations. He turned the pamphlet over, to see if it was advertising a book or a film, but there was just the usual form to fill in, and an address in Findhorn, wherever that was. Toby blinked at the pamphlet a few times and then put it carefully to one side.

Next up was a sober, businesslike letter from one of the big established pharmaceutical companies, offering to supply him with the very latest in lust potions, suitable for all occasions. *Shouldn't that be love potions?* Toby thought vaguely. He checked the small print for mention of pheromones and the like, but the letter seemed entirely serious and straightforward. There was even a money-back guarantee. The sliding scale of prices was entirely reasonable, so Toby put that letter on one side, too, for further thought.

Next: Turn lead into gold! Crush coal into diamonds! Split the atom with a single blow! Gain mastery over the material world with the Junior Alchemist's Set! A philosopher's stone included with every kit! (Subject to availability.) We take Visa and MasterCard. Parent or guardian's signature required. Allow six moons for delivery. Toby blinked at that one for a while, and put it on one side.

Finally: You may already be a Superhero! Send for the origin of your choice. Design your own costume or choose from our wide range of cloaks, tights, and masks. Rubber and leather a specialty.

Return this form before the end of the month and choose two extra powers, one from Column A and one . . . Toby screwed that one into a ball and binned it with more than necessary force. Someone was setting him up. Had to be.

He turned on the radio. The news was almost universally depressing, as usual, and he felt on firmer ground again.

He puttered around the house for a while, wandering into rooms and out again, but he couldn't settle. The feeling of restlessness was getting worse. More and more he felt he should be somewhere else, doing something . . . important. That this Saturday, this morning, was important. Which was odd, because he'd never thought of himself or his life as mattering a damn to anyone, even him. He was just another faceless drone, a small cog in a small wheel that kept other wheels turning because . . . well, wheels had to turn, or where would we all be? The sudden bitterness in that thought surprised him; the feeling that he could have made something of his life, but somehow never had.

He sniffed. That was what hitting your thirties did for you. It made you bloody morbid.

He fought the restlessness for another half an hour, but in the end it forced him out of the house. He pulled on his new leather jacket and slammed the front door behind him just a little harder than was really necessary to make the lock catch. Truth be told, it was a bit warm for the jacket, but he liked the creaking sounds it made as he moved. He looked around him. It was a bright sunny day, but no one else seemed to be about. An impulse made him look up, and he was astonished to see an absolutely huge rainbow glimmering against the deep blue sky. The colors were almost painfully sharp and distinct, and the great arch seemed to fly up into the sky for ever. The earth-fixed end seemed so close he felt as though he could walk right up to it, and the whole thing was so damned beautiful his breath caught in his chest like it would never let go. In all his life, he'd never seen a rainbow like it. In the end, he tore his gaze away and walked off down the road, heading into town.

Something was calling him.

And as he walked through the town, everything was utterly familiar yet subtly different. The streets and the houses and the sights were all the same as they had ever been, but it was like seeing them afresh, as though he were recognizing them again after many years away. This was the same route he'd taken the night before, plodding home through the pouring rain, but now he felt like a stranger in his own town. There was a charge, a tension, on the air, something he could feel but could not put a name to. Home didn't feel like home anymore. It occurred to him that this was the kind of perfect summer day you usually only saw in films, all bright and sharp and Technicolor dazzle, with every detail spot on. The birds were all singing in tune, there was hardly any traffic on the road (unheard of for a Saturday morning), and the air . . . had a charge to it, a feeling of anticipation. Toby was surprised to find that there was actually a spring in his step as he headed for the town center.

And yet he couldn't shake off the feeling that something was wrong . . . out of place. Some of the houses he was passing didn't seem quite as he remembered them. There were too many windows, or too few. Front doors were the wrong color or even the wrong shape. Gabled roofs he would have sworn were solar-paneled the day before. Gardens were full of tall flowers, swaying in the gentle breeze, and trees were bright with blossom, when he was almost sure . . . He shrugged a few times and increased his pace. Amazing what one good night of rain could do.

He made his way down to the St. Margaret's Street parking lot, and that was where he got his first shock. Instead of the usual polite sign informing visitors to the town that cars could be left for a maximum of two hours during the day (GET YOUR TICKET FROM THE MACHINE, HAVE YOU PAID & DISPLAYED?), one wall was now covered with a large handwritten warning, painted in what looked very like fresh blood, saying, *Get it out of here by sundown or you'll never see it again! Repeat offenders will be defenestrated!*

Toby stopped at the top of the slope leading down into the car park and studied the new sign for some time, before looking around to see if anyone else had noticed it. Everyone else was bustling back and forth on their own business, paying the sign no attention at all. Toby stood considering for a moment, making sure that defenestration meant what he thought it did, and then frowned. His first thought was to dismiss it as graffiti, vandalism . . . and not very funny at that. But somehow, he didn't think so. There was something horribly official about the wording and the penmanship. Good thing he didn't own a car.

He started down the slope, threading his way through the tightly packed vehicles, and that was when he got his second shock. There were cars all around him, filling the lot from wall to wall, and every damn one of them looked as weird as hell. He passed what he was pretty sure was a Model T Ford; bright shining black and perfect, as though it had just rolled off the production line. A replica, obviously, but . . . as Toby slowed his pace and looked around him with growing confusion, it seemed to him that he was surrounded by makes of car from every period there ever was.

A great monster of a 1930s Bentley, in racing green and red, stood next to a powder-blue Hillman Minx Superior from the fifties. A blatantly purple DeLorean stood next to a silver-gray Aston Martin DB5 that looked like it had come straight from the set of a James Bond film. And then . . . It was long and sleek and gleaming, shining silver like a medieval church chalice, streamlined to within an inch of its life, and impressively low slung; but if it was a car, then where the hell were its wheels? Just looking at it, Toby knew it could go from zero to sixty while you were still turning the ignition key. The car of the future, just like in all the comics he'd read as a boy.

Toby walked slowly through the lot, his head swiveling back and forth, his arms tucked in close at his sides, so he wouldn't accidentally touch anything. He had a horrid suspicion that if he did, the car might pop like a soap bubble, and he didn't think he could cope with that. Toby was beginning to feel very strange. He kept trying to tell himself there must be a convention of rare and unusual cars in town, just for the day, that he'd managed to avoid hearing about . . . but he didn't think so. Somehow, during the night, while he'd slept, all the rules had been changed. He just knew it. Someone had yanked the rug out from under the world he knew, and he was beginning to have a strong suspicion as to just who that was.

He left the parking lot and crossed the new bridge. (*New* because it had only been constructed in 1962, as opposed to the main town bridge, which was at least thirteenth-century, and maybe older.) Halfway across, Toby heard something splashing loudly in the river down below and automatically looked over the dark railings, only to look quickly away, shocked by something he was sure he couldn't have seen correctly. It wasn't the bare flesh, or the bobbing breasts, or the wicked smile on the pointed face; it was the long green gleam of a fish's tail . . . He refused absolutely to even *think* the *m*-word, but he couldn't deny what he'd seen. He made himself look back over the railings again. Ducks. Swans. Swirling dark waters. Nothing else. Of course there was nothing else! Toby walked on, looking straight ahead. Behind him, someone was singing a song of great beauty in a warm, breathy contralto. He didn't look back, even when the bridge was safely far behind him.

He walked on into Church Street and it seemed to him that there were a lot of people around, even for a Saturday morning. What was more, quite a few of them seemed to be looking at him strangely. Which was odd, because this was, after all, his hometown, he a Bradfordian born and bred, and he was, if nothing else, a familiar face to most people. He checked himself unobtrusively, for spilled food or undone flies, but all seemed to be in order. He lifted his chin a little and stared back, and everyone looked away again.

It occurred to him that he was a bit short of money, so he stopped at the cash machine in the wall outside his bank. But even as he was fumbling in his coat pocket for his cash card and mentally rehearsing his PIN, the cash machine suddenly spoke to him.

"Oh, you needn't bother with that, dear. It's only money. How much do you want?"

Toby froze with his hand still in his pocket, and then looked quickly about him. There was no one else anywhere nearby. He looked reluctantly back at the glowing computer screen before him.

Instead of the usual green lettering, there were two yellow circles that might have been eyes, and a wide curve for a smile. As he watched, the smile widened, and one of the eyes winked at him. Toby cleared his throat.

"Uh . . . hello?"

"Hello there! Isn't it a simply super morning?"

"Am I speaking to a machine . . . or something?"

"Oh, something, dear, definitely something. You just tell me how much you need, and I will shower you with largesse."

"Is this some kind of joke?" said Toby, after a pause. "One of those hidden camera jobs? Because I never thought they were funny, even when I was just watching them."

"No joke, sweetie," said the cash machine briskly. "You can have as much as you can carry away, and do you know why? Because I like your face!"

"Maybe I didn't get up this morning," Toby said wistfully. "Maybe I'm still in bed, and dreaming all this. It would explain a lot."

"Oh no, this isn't The Dreaming. That's next door but one."

"And you . . . want to give me money?"

"Of course! Have as much as you want! I've got lots!"

And the cash machine sprayed banknotes into the air, tens and twenties shooting out in a great stream of multicolored paper, fluttering to the ground like so many leaves in autumn. Toby stood there gaping. He'd never seen so much money in one place in his life, and there seemed no end to it. He finally grabbed a few handfuls in self-defense, and then decided that this was just too damned weird, and quite likely to get him arrested as well. He stuffed the notes in his pocket without even looking at them and hurried off down the street, not looking back once. Behind him, banknotes slowly gathered in a pile on the pavement as the cash machine sang mournfully to itself.

Toby decided very firmly that he needed a drink. In fact, he quite probably needed several drinks, one after the other, and perhaps a swift slap to the side of the head while he was at it. He hadn't been so confused since that gorgeous blonde in the wine bar turned out to have a flat male chest under the padded bra. He headed straight for the Dandy Lion, in many ways his second home. He waited agitatedly at the pedestrian crossing, and nearly lost it again when a shocking-pink Rolls-Royce cruised past, and a strangely familiar aristocratic female face looked out of the window and smiled sweetly at him. Toby averted his eyes. Maybe if he just refused to accept all this weirdness, it would go away and bother someone else.

He dived across the road at the first chance he got and hurried into the pub. Once again, everything looked the same, but the place was full of people he didn't recognize, many of whom stopped talking to stare at him as he paused in the doorway. Toby squared his shoulders and headed determinedly for the bar. This was getting ridiculous. People slowly started talking again as he ordered his usual pint of bitter from the familiar face behind the bar. For once, wonder of wonders, the jukebox was actually playing something worth listening to. But as Toby listened, he felt the strangeness creeping over him again. It was quite definitely a Beatles song, but not one he'd ever heard before. And Toby was a Beatles fanatic. He had everything they'd ever done, including quite a few of the bootlegs. The hairs on the back of his neck stood up as he realized that this was no early Hamburg tape; this was Lennon and McCartney at the height of their songwriting powers. Singing a song he'd never heard before . . .

His pint arrived. He paid for it automatically and took a good hard drink. And then he stopped, considered, and took another, slower drink. It was good. *Damn,* it was good, the best bitter beer he'd ever tasted. And most especially one hell of a lot better than the stuff he usually drank. Must be a new brand. He was about to ask the barmaid when someone called his name in a sharp, commanding voice.

He looked around and there was Carys Galloway, sitting tucked away in her usual corner, underneath the stairs leading up to the restaurant floor. Toby smiled, relief washing over him. It was good to see that some things hadn't changed, on this most unusual of days. Carys spent more time in the Dandy Lion than he did. She was the foremost gossip of the whole town, a title not easily gained, and if anyone knew why today was acting as if it had got its medication mixed up, it would be Carys Galloway. She knew everything. Or at least, the few things she didn't know weren't usually worth the knowing.

Toby hurried over to join her at her usual table, and for the first time ever it occurred to him to wonder about Carys. It seemed as though she had always been around, sitting in her gloomy corner, always ready to lend an ear, to sort out a problem, or just to swap gossip about everyone and everything. There was no malice in Carys. She just liked to know things, and she liked to share what she knew with people she felt she could trust. Always cheerful, always smiling . . . That was it. Toby's pace slowed as he realized what it was that looked different about Carys this morning. For the first time in all the years Toby had known her, Carys wasn't smiling. In fact, Toby thought, as he sat gingerly down opposite her, Carys looked very different today.

It was the same familiar face, with its sharp chin and prominent cheekbones, and more than a hint of ethnic gypsy. Dark russet hair fell in thick ringlets to her shoulders and beyond, and her eyes were so dark and huge you felt you could fall into them and drown forever. Her long bony hands, the fingers heavily knuckled, were weighed down with rings of gold and silver set with unfamiliar gems. She had an unconventionally pretty face, that of a woman who could have been anything from her twenties to her forties. She always wore traditional Romany clothes, *gypsy chic,* complete with necklaces and bangles. Quite a romantic figure, usually.

But today she looked . . . harsher. Brighter. More *intense.* Almost overpoweringly *there,* as though she were the only thing, the only person that mattered in the whole place.

Toby tried to say something, but his mouth was suddenly dry. Up close, Carys actually looked forbidding; like one of the Fates, the Norns of Scandinavian lore, the wise women who measure out the threads of our lives and cut them off when they reach their end. But

as Toby settled himself opposite her, he realized suddenly that the
restlessness, the pressure, the need that had driven him from his bed
and from his house, was gone. Finally he felt that he was where he
was supposed to be. Toby put his pint glass down on the table top
with unnecessary force and looked hard at Carys Galloway.

Even though he was quaking inside, because some part of him
didn't want to hear what he knew she was going to tell him.

"All right, Carys; what's gone on? Why is everything in the town
so . . . different? The whole place is like Bradford-on-Crack. And
why is everybody looking at me? Am I paranoid, or did the whole
damned world change overnight while I was asleep?"

"No," said Carys, her voice only a little amused. "You aren't
being paranoid."

"Oh, shit," said Toby, slumping in his seat. "I could have coped
with being paranoid. OK; hit me with it, whatever it is."

"You have become part of the magical world," said Carys, her
dark eyes holding his. "You have left Veritie and now you are in
Mysterie, a place of marvels and wonders, banes and malignancies.
You are living in a much larger world now, Toby Dexter, by your
own choice, and you must widen your mind to accept it."

"Is everyone here magical?" said Toby. "Are you?"

"I'm more than magical. I'm older than the town. They call me
the Waking Beauty, because I never sleep. Ever."

"Ah. So . . . am I magical now?"

Carys looked at him hard. "No."

Toby nodded glumly. "I thought not."

"But you're not entirely real anymore, either." Carys frowned.
"You have a foot in both worlds. You could stay human, by return-
ing to Veritie, or you could stay here and become magical. You must
make your own choice. But beware; whatever choice you eventually
make will have consequences: for you, for everyone. For all the
worlds that be. You have become important, you poor bastard! You
met someone yesterday, someone of great significance. Because of
her, you are now aware of the magical world, and it is becoming
aware of you."

"It was her," said Toby. "Gayle. I should never have followed her through that door."

"But you did, and that changed everything. You must pursue Gayle, for your destiny and hers are now irrevocably linked. She won't like that any more than you, but destiny's often funny that way. Gayle lives close by. I will give you directions. What happens next is up to you."

"I don't believe in destiny," Toby said flatly.

"Tough. It believes in you."

"OK," said Toby. "I'll go and talk to her. What's her other name?"

"She is only what she is, whatever name she might be using. Hers is a most singular nature."

"Ah. Am I supposed to understand any of that?"

"Not yet."

"Well, what makes her so important?" said Toby, almost desperately. "And what on earth makes you think I might be important? I've never mattered much to anyone, not even myself."

"Self-pity suits you," said Carys. "But you'll have to put it aside. It's too small an emotion for what you are now."

"What am I?"

Carys leaned forward, fixing Toby with her dark, bottomless gaze. "You are a focal point, Toby Dexter. The patterns of fate surround you. Your role in things has been decided where everything that matters is decided, in the Courts of the Immaterial. And neither you nor anyone else has any say in the matter. The decisions you make in the next few days will be vital, for all of us . . . though I cannot see what or when or why. Which is in itself almost unprecedented. Whatever's coming must be momentous indeed, if it is hidden even from me."

"Is this . . . going to be dangerous? For me?"

"Very."

"And there's no way out of it?"

Carys leaned back in her chair, her face suddenly guarded. Her bangles made soft, eerie clanking sounds as she crossed her arms.

"You could try to walk away from your fate; insist on your humanity, at the cost of everything else. Few things are set in stone. But to
walk away from the role chosen for you would mean walking away
from Gayle. You could never see her, never speak to her again. Only
you can decide how much that matters."

Toby nodded slowly. "Give me the directions. I'll go and talk to
her. And then I'll decide . . . what I'll decide."

Carys smiled. Gayle turned out to be living almost literally just
around the corner from the Dandy Lion. Somehow Toby wasn't entirely surprised. He got to his feet, looked briefly at his pint glass,
and then left it standing on the table. At the thought of meeting
Gayle again, his stomach was suddenly full of butterflies. Dancing.
With clogs on.

"One last word of advice," said Carys. "You be careful around
Gayle. She's more than she appears. Hell; she's more than anyone appears."

"But you're not going to tell me what," said Toby. "I'm getting
really tired of mysteries, Carys. It was only by accident that I followed Gayle through that magic door of hers last evening."

"There are no accidents," said Carys Galloway, the Waking
Beauty. "Some things are just meant to be. Now get out of here, and
let the rest of us drink in peace."

Meanwhile, back in the real world, in Veritie, where she lived entirely by choice, Gayle was reluctantly getting out of her very comfortable bed. Thank the good Lord for snooze alarms. She could
sleep through or ignore one alarm, but half a dozen in a row would
have had Lazarus himself stomping out of his tomb to complain
about the noise. Gayle stood naked before her full-length bedroom
mirror and thought, not for the first time, that she looked pretty
good, all things considered. Bit of a tummy, and the breasts weren't
everything they once were, but you could say that about a lot of
things these days. The world turns, and we all get just that little bit
older. She pulled on a white silk wraparound, made a few half-
hearted stabs at doing something with her hair, and then decided it

was far too early for shit like that. She padded downstairs, stifling a yawn behind one elegant hand, and picked up the post and the morning papers from the welcome mat.

The post was the usual junk mail and a handful of bills. Didn't these people have anything better to do than pester her for the few paltry sums she owed them? Wasn't there a law against demanding money with menaces? She'd get round to them. Eventually. When she damned well felt like it. And as for the entirely unsolicited junk mail: *You may already have won a major prize?* How about: *You may already have felled irreplaceable rain forests,* just to make the paper this crap is printed on, dickhead? God help you if the South American Indians ever discover voodoo. Maybe she should send them a few useful instructional books on the subject. . . . They really liked the last one, on how to make explosives out of everyday kitchen products. She still got letters. Gayle sighed and dropped the lot into a nearby wastebasket.

She took a quick look at the main headlines in the morning papers. Gayle took the *Times,* the *Guardian,* and the *Independent,* covering the main political positions. She had no use for tabloids. She wanted information, not gossip. If she really wanted to know who was sleeping with whom, she'd ask Carys Galloway. The headlines were surprisingly quiet for once. Most of them were still wittering on about the continuing weird weather, that might or might not be the result of disturbances on the sun's surface. Gayle folded the *Independent* and tucked it under her arm, and laid the others on the side table for later. First things first. She went into the downstairs toilet, undid her wrap, and settled herself comfortably on the porcelain throne. (One good thing about not living with a man; you didn't have to keep checking whether he'd left the seat up.) She opened the newspaper to the political pages, supported the weight of the paper on her thighs, and sighed contentedly as she felt the first stirrings in her bowels. Ah . . . Quality Time.

Afterwards, she considered breakfast. Normally all her meals were lengthy affairs. Gayle liked to cook and she liked to eat, and breakfast was, after all, one of the most important meals of the day.

Everyone said that. Maybe sausage, bacon, and eggs—a cholesterol special. But the more she thought about it, the more she thought she'd better get dressed first. She wasn't expecting anyone, but she had a strong feeling company was coming.

So, back to the bedroom. Gayle chose a long, dark green dress with a white leather belt; comfortable, but still presentable. Flat shoes, no tights. It was Saturday, after all. Slap on some basic makeup (heavy makeup was for women with no faces of their own), and then attack her hair with a hairbrush until it sulkily assumed some shape and sense. She looked in the mirror. She looked good. In fact, for this early on a Saturday morning, she looked damned good. Relaxed, informal, chic. Heartbreaker, even. She laughed, blew a kiss at the mirror, and went downstairs again, humming an old Jacobean protest song. Whoever was coming to see her, they'd better be worth it. By her own choice, Gayle didn't get many visitors. If she needed to see someone, she paid them a visit, whether they wanted to see her or not. Humming quite loudly now, she floated around her kitchen putting together a hearty, organic, free-range breakfast. She laid the table for two, using the good crockery, and remembered to put the milk in the milk jug. She made a good strong pot of tea, and stirred it briskly with the end of a spoon. (Stir with a knife, stir in strife.) She stood back to take a look, and the doorbell rang, right on cue. Gayle went to answer the door. Whoever it was, they'd better have a really good reason for needing to see her.

Outside the front door, Toby was in serious danger of hyperventilating. His heart was hammering in his chest, his breathing was short and rapid, and the butterflies in his stomach were kicking the hell out of each other. He just hoped he wasn't sweating as well. Toby always found meeting new people socially rather difficult. Especially if they were women. Really attractive women he'd only worked up the courage to talk to yesterday. It didn't help that she was, apparently, a for-real magical creature of great significance to one and all, and that he and she were destined or fated or cursed to become involved with each other. Toby wasn't at all sure how he felt about that. His life might not be much, but he liked to believe he was in charge of it. He'd stopped along the way to buy half a dozen long-stemmed roses, for a frankly extortionate price, and hoped they'd serve as a peace offering, at least to show that his heart was in the right place.

How much longer before she was going to answer the bell? It had taken him ages to work up the courage to press the bloody thing, and now she was taking forever to answer it. He debated whether to ring the bell again, but decided against it. It might make him seem impatient, even aggressive. Not a good first impression. There was always the chance she wasn't in. Who said Carys had to be infallible? Toby was almost relieved at the thought that Gayle might be out. Then he wouldn't have to go through with . . . this. But all he had to do was remember all those times he'd sat opposite her on the train . . . and the thought of meeting her again brought a daft, happy smile to his lips and a spring to his heart.

The door opened suddenly, and there she was, even more beautiful than ever. The more casual look suited her. And her mouth was every bit the perfect thing he'd thought it was. Unfortunately, her mouth wasn't smiling at him. In fact, she was looking at him as though trying to figure out what he might be selling. Toby tried to say hi, but his breath was still trapped in his throat, so he thrust the roses at her, to speak for him. Gayle accepted the roses, carefully avoiding the thorns.

"Oh, how nice," she said. "You killed some flowers for me."

Her tone wasn't exactly what he'd been hoping for. In fact, for a moment Toby was sure she was going to throw the roses back in his face, but she just sighed and stepped back, indicating for him to come in with a jerk of her head. Toby stepped quickly forward into the narrow hall, just in case she might change her mind. Gayle pushed the front door shut and then headed back into the house, leaving Toby to follow her. He looked quickly about him as he hurried to keep up, trying to get some sense of Gayle's character from how she chose to live. The walls were decorated with pretty flowered wallpaper, the furnishings were basic but elegant and the carpeting had a cozy, worn-down look. An old-fashioned barometer hanging on the wall was stuck on CHANGEABLE. Toby tapped the glass with a knuckle, but the needle didn't even quiver. Gayle went into the kitchen, and Toby hurried after her.

The kitchen was bright and airy, morning sunlight streaming through the open window. The walls were painted in pale pastel colors, and there were lots of polished wood surfaces. The fittings were elegant, some old enough to be classified as antiques. There were large posters on the walls, mostly of dolphins, swimming and frolicking in the open sea, and one very large poster from Greenpeace, with the word *peace* crossed out, and *war* written in above it in a large feminine hand. There were thick colored candles, hanging wind chimes, and pots and pans and crockery all neatly arranged on shelves. Toby was impressed. His kitchen usually looked as though a grenade had gone off in it.

Gayle ran some water in her gleaming, spotless sink and put the roses into it. Then she sat down at the breakfast table and gestured briskly for Toby to sit opposite her. There was a lot of food laid out, as though she'd known he was coming. It was good food, and smelled delicious, but Toby was so nervous and on edge by now that he couldn't have eaten a forkful even if she'd put a gun to his head. It didn't help that he still couldn't think of anything to say that wouldn't sound trite or forced or just plain simpleminded, and Gayle was still looking at him expectantly, waiting for him to explain himself. For a long while they just sat and stared at each other.

She really was beautiful. Toby thought of telling her that, but decided she probably already knew. She wasn't beautiful like a fashion model or a film star, with that artificial, high-gloss look, all the little imperfections carefully removed by computer. Gayle looked . . . utterly female. Womanly, lovely, warm. As if he could curl up with her and be safe and happy forever. As if she were the other half of his life and could finally make him complete. Sexy, but in a calm, unhurried way. Confident, as though she no longer felt she had to prove anything. In fact, for first thing on a Saturday morning, she looked pretty damned amazing. All of which made Toby feel even more scruffy. His leather jacket creaked loudly as he shifted in his seat, and for one horrible moment he thought he'd farted. He quickly took the jacket off and draped it over the back of his chair.

"You came to me from the magical world," Gayle said suddenly. "When you passed through my door, you were translated back into reality. I felt it. How are you finding the magical world?"

"Confusing."

"Understandable. I have always preferred to live in the real world as much as possible. Also I usually prefer to keep my own company, in my time off. How did you find me?"

"Carys Galloway told me where you live." Toby felt a little easier now they were on neutral ground. "She said I was a focal point. That you and I were fated to be together." Once he'd started talking he couldn't stop, and he actually blushed as he heard himself say the bit about fate. It sounded appallingly arrogant. "Fated to meet, I mean. This morning. Here."

"If the Waking Beauty sent you here, then there must be a purpose to this meeting." Gayle frowned. "Damn it. I really didn't need more complications just now. And focal points are always trouble. For everyone."

Toby almost jumped out of his skin as something brushed against his leg. He looked down and found that a large tabby cat was rubbing itself against him with sensual thoroughness. He smiled and reached down to scratch its head, and it purred loudly, pushing up against his hand. Toby looked round the kitchen, and suddenly it seemed that the whole room was full of cats. There had to be at least a dozen of them, of varying types and colors, all of them looking rather . . . well, battered, really. Knocked about by life. Gayle smiled at them all.

"I collect strays. They turn up out of nowhere, the products of bad lives and worse luck, and I haven't the heart to turn them away. They come and they go, but there are always more to replace those who leave. I seem to attract strays." She looked at Toby, but he didn't get the point. She sighed quietly. "What do you want from me, Toby?"

*Love. Sex. Walking hand in hand for the rest of our days, under a perfect blue sky, with all the birds singing . . .*

That was what Toby wanted to say, but he couldn't, so he played for time by looking round the kitchen again. He couldn't believe how clean it was. His kitchen always looked . . . lived-in. He noticed abruptly that there was a lacy black bra lying crumpled beside the sink where his flowers were, and he looked quickly away, obscurely embarrassed. Gayle sighed again, and poured him a cup of tea. It smelled sharp and clean, with a hint of herbs he didn't recognize. He reached out to take the cup she handed him and there was a definite spark as their fingers touched. Toby saw Gayle's eyes widen just a little, and knew she'd felt it, too. Neither of them said anything. Gayle busied herself with her cup. Toby sipped cautiously at the steaming tea. It was delicious; probably didn't dare be anything else in a perfect kitchen like this. Toby studied the delicate china of the cup and saucer. It was decorated with an intricate design of owls made out of flowers.

"You seem vaguely familiar," Gayle said finally. "Did we ever meet before last night?"

"We take the same train home from Bath every evening," said Toby. "I've seen you lots of times."

Gayle shook her head. "Sorry. Doesn't ring any bells."

Toby felt disappointed and a little crushed, even though he'd always gone to great lengths to avoid being noticed as he watched her. He felt somehow that she should have known.

"So," he said, for want of anything else to say. "What do you do, in Bath? What's your job?"

"I work at a center for children with problems. It's privately funded. It's part refuge, part doctor's office, part school. We get all kinds. Kids that are deaf or blind, handicapped, traumatized . . . survivors of sexual abuse. Some have AIDS, some ADS."

"ADS?"

"Attention deficit syndrome, or whatever the hell they're calling it this week. Kids too bright for the system, who can't or won't fit in.

They play havoc with normal teaching systems and disrupt class-rooms, and the usual practice is to drug them up to the eyeballs. Turn them into obedient little zombies. Which is understandable, they can be right little bastards. But we try to channel their energies into more productive, more sociable patterns. It's slow, hard work, but it has its rewards. Do you like children?"

"Yes, but I couldn't eat a whole one." Gayle laughed at that, almost despite herself, and they shared a smile. Toby hurried on. "I like kids in the abstract, but I don't have much practical experience of them. I don't know if I'd have your kind of patience. Do you have . . . children of your own?"

Gayle smiled. "I like to think they're all my children. I care for them, help where I can, and do my best never to give up on them. What do you do for a living, Toby?"

"Ah," said Toby, thinking quickly. "I'm connected with publishing. On the retail side. Interesting work. Look; can we please talk about what's going on? All the weird shit I've seen today? What really happened last night? Why does the town I've lived in most of my life suddenly seem so different? And please don't use the word *magic* again. I don't believe in magic, or any of that stuff. I've read everything from *The Golden Bough* to *Chariots of the Gods,* and I've never been convinced by any of it. Have I crossed over into some kind of alternative dimension? That at least sounds scientific."

"Science arises out of the real world," said Gayle, almost sympathetically. "That isn't all there is. The universe is much bigger than that. You can't think in such limited terms anymore, Toby."

"Let's start with last night," Toby said doggedly. "There was a door, where there wasn't a door before. We walked through it. Everything changed. How?"

"We were in the real world last evening," Gayle said patiently. "You and I, on the train, on the platform. Then in the car park. It was raining. I was . . . impatient. So I opened a door, between the real world and the magical world. Between Veritie and Mysterie. I can do that. I have powers, responsibilities. I decided it wasn't raining in Mysterie, and so it wasn't."

"You made the door appear. I thought there was no magic in the real world?"

Gayle nodded approvingly. "You're starting to catch on. There are doors everywhere: natural fault lines, fractures, between the two worlds. People like me, and now you, with a foot in both worlds, can see these doors, these openings, and can pass through them. Sometimes people fall through by accident. There are many stories of people disappearing suddenly. Look them up if you want. Down the centuries people have blamed the disappearances on everything from fairy rings to UFOs. Anyway, the point is, you followed me through the door I opened, and into Mysterie. You are now part of, and aware of, the magical world, and it is becoming aware of you."

"What . . . were you, originally?" said Toby slowly. "Real, or magical?"

"I've always been both," said Gayle, smiling. "It's part of my nature. But I prefer to live in the real world; it keeps me grounded. Still; don't you go thinking that what you and I have done is in any way normal or ordinary. Usually the worlds are strictly separate, and people are discouraged from traveling back and forth. Science and magic are never supposed to meet, or interact." She frowned, choosing her words carefully. "Magic isn't illusion. Mysterie is the reality beyond the reality you know, the world from which your world unfolds. Veritie, the real world, is the subtler of the two realms."

"So which came first?" said Toby. "Veritie or Mysterie?"

"Which came first, you or your shadow?" said Gayle. "They're just two aspects of the same thing. Look, you're getting the Easy Readers version here. You're not ready to go wading too deep into philosophical waters. People have been deliberating the nature of these and other realms for countless centuries. There is no rule book, no instruction manual. We live in our own worlds, and we learn by doing. I'm just trying to explain enough to keep you out of trouble. Mysterie is a much more dangerous place than Veritie."

She stopped, and looked at him silently with her dark, all-seeing eyes. Toby never once considered looking away. Gayle sighed again.

"Toby, I couldn't help but notice the way you've been looking at me, and I have to tell you, it's not going to happen. You mustn't fall in love with me. Trust me on this. There are reasons why not. Good reasons."

Toby just grinned. "Too late: I'm yours. I fell in love with you the first time I saw you, and that was months ago. You might as well ask a salmon not to swim upstream, or a butterfly to change back into a caterpillar. It's a done thing."

"I'm just trying to prevent you from getting hurt. You don't know what you're getting into."

"I know all about being hurt," said Toby. "I've been hurt by experts, and I'm still here. Sorry; that sounded self-pitying, and I do try not to be. What I meant was, I'm not afraid of wading into deep, dark emotional waters."

"You don't understand, Toby." Gayle steepled her fingers under her chin and looked at him almost sadly. "Do you remember all those old folk tales and songs, about mortal men falling for magical women and coming to sad, horrible ends? Those songs were written about women like me as a warning, to save men from themselves. I'm much older than I look, Toby, and there is more to me than you could ever hope to understand. Mortal must not love immortal."

"And vice versa?"

"You're determined not to listen, aren't you? Let me say this as plainly as I can, Toby Dexter. You seem a nice enough sort, but I don't love you, I don't fancy you, and I never will. We can't even have enough in common to be friends. You should never have followed me through that door. But now you're here, let's talk about why the Waking Beauty saw fit to send you to me. I take that very seriously. Focal points can be dangerous to all concerned, if they're not properly directed. In fact, that's the only reason I haven't kicked you out already. You and your damned roses and your sweet, helpless smile. I have been here before, and it's never ended well. Will you please stop smiling at me! I don't need a big clumsy puppy dog getting under my feet and cluttering up my life!"

"So you're not going to throw me out?" said Toby, blithely ignoring everything he didn't want to hear.

Gayle had to smile. "You're a trier, aren't you? Forget that, and concentrate on what matters. The Waking Beauty did say you were a focal point? You couldn't have been mistaken?"

"No. It's one of the few things I am sure about."

"Damn. Focal points mean change. Often involving violent up-heavals in the way the worlds run. Whatever happens, you're not going to be popular, Toby."

"Well, who decided I was going to be a focal point?" demanded Toby, just a little plaintively. "No one asked *me*. I didn't get to vote on it. Isn't there anywhere we can go to ask for a recount, or something?"

"Not if you like living," said Gayle, thinking hard. "We're dealing with the immaterial here . . . the higher realities, the shimmering realms, the Courts of the Holy. You really don't want to go there. Especially not with your attitude. No; it's up to us to try to figure out why you're so important, or why you're going to be. Focal points can bring about change by their actions, or inaction, or simply by interacting with others. The reasons usually only become clear in retrospect, after everything's gone to hell in a handcart and we're all busy trying to pick up the pieces."

"But . . . I'm just me!" Toby protested. "I don't feel any different. I certainly don't feel at all powerful."

"That's the worst kind," said Gayle darkly. "The subtle ones. You'd better come with me, and meet some of the movers and shak-ers in this town. Maybe between us we can figure out what you're supposed to do, or be, so we can either defuse you, or at least point you in the right direction so you do the least possible damage. You're going to have to stick close to me for a while."

"Suits me," said Toby, trying not to grin too widely.

"Please don't smile like that. You don't have a single clue what's lying in wait for you. There are forces in Mysterie who would quite cheerfully rip your guts out if they knew you existed, just to keep you from upsetting their precious status quo. Come on; finish your tea. We're going visiting. Try to make a good impression. You're going to need friends and allies if you're to survive long enough to do whatever it is you're supposed to do."

"This is Saturday," Toby said firmly. "I am not putting on a suit and tie for anyone. Besides; good impressions aren't exactly what I do best. With me, what you see is pretty much what you get."

"Oh, hell," said Gayle. "In that case, we're in real trouble."

"Cheer up," said Toby. "I can pretend to be civilized, if I have to. What I can't take seriously is the idea that anything I might do could possibly change the world. Worlds. Now don't look at me like that; I am taking your warnings seriously. There are people out there who want to kill me. Got it."

"Not necessarily people," said Gayle.

"All right; that's scary. But it was my decision to follow you through the door, and I wouldn't take it back if I could. I wanted to meet you, and be with you, and here I am. That's all that matters. You really are rather special, you know."

"Trust me," said Gayle. "You have no idea how special." She stopped and looked at him thoughtfully, appraisingly. "Toby . . . there are alternatives. You're only in danger as long as you remain a focal point. And you can only be that here, in the magical world. I could make you forget everything. I could send you back through the door into reality, into Veritie, back to where you belong. You'd just wake up in your own bed, a little later than usual, and remember none of this. You could resume your old life, an ordinary man in an ordinary world. Safe from the burden of destiny, no longer a threat to the powers that be."

"Go back to my old life?" said Toby. "I'd rather die. And it would mean forgetting you, wouldn't it? I won't do that. You're the only special, beautiful thing that ever came into my life; and I'd rather die than give that up. I didn't choose to fall in love with you; I just looked at you one day on the train and that was it, done. I've never felt about anyone the way I feel about you. And just when I was beginning to think that love was something that happened to other people. Giving you up would be like giving up the only part of my life that matters. You can't *make* me forget, can you? You need my consent. And I don't give it."

"You do like the sound of your own voice, don't you?" said

Gayle. "I've never met a man that didn't. I could warn you till I'm blue in the face, and you still wouldn't hear a damn thing you didn't want to. Listen to me, Toby; please. You don't matter to me, except for the danger you represent. I don't love you. I never will. But no, you're right. I can't *make* you forget. It would be the safest, sanest thing to do, but there's no arguing with a man who thinks he's in love. Just remember, when everything's gone to shit and I've had to abandon you to die horribly for the sake of both worlds, I did offer."

"Why offer, if you don't care for me?"

"Because I am more than I seem. I have responsibilities. Even to complete idiots who won't be told what's best for them."

"It's more than that," said Toby remorselessly. "I can hear it in your voice."

"All right!" Gayle threw her hands up in the air. "I collect strays. It's a weakness of mine. But in the end you mean no more to me than some sad old tom with fleas and a chewed-up ear. You've got about as much sense. Why risk your life, your security, to be a focal point, when you're incapable of understanding what that means, and what it's worth, if anything? There's no guarantee that anything good will come of this, especially for you."

"You're cute when you're angry," said Toby. "Don't hit me! Look; don't think this is entirely about you. I've never been important before. Just once, I need to feel that I'm worth something, that what I do matters. That's worth dying for. Hell; that's worth living for."

"Let me ask you a serious question," said Gayle. "What value do you think one ordinary man can have in a magical world? What can one mortal man bring to the affairs of immortals?"

"Beats me," said Toby. "Maybe whoever chose me to be a focal point knows the answer. Or maybe we're supposed to work it out for ourselves."

Gayle sighed heavily and looked down into her empty teacup for a long time. Toby let her. It meant he could adore her beauty uninterrupted, while at the same time concentrate on ignoring the sinking feeling in his stomach. He felt more and more that he had just jumped in at the deep end in lead-lined boots, and that someone

had thrown a shark in after him. For all his brave words, he wasn't
at all sure he was doing the right thing. The thought that there were
people, and perhaps things not at all people, who would cheerfully
kill him just for existing, scared the crap out of him. Part of him
wanted to go straight home, hide under the bed, and not come out
until it was all safely over. But he'd meant what he said. Gayle mattered more to him than his own safety, and perhaps even his life.
Love could be a hard old bitch, sometimes.

   Love was supposed to come to you when you were a teenager,
when both of you were already half crazy anyway, driven out of your
heads by raging hormones and ready to do six irresponsible things
before breakfast. When you had your best years still ahead of you,
and lots of time to learn from your mistakes. It shouldn't barge its
way into your life when you're well into your thirties, and used to
the idea that you're always going to be alone. But this, all of it, was
what he'd dreamed of, prayed for, wanted so desperately for so many
years: his dreams come true. So; suck it in, square your shoulders,
take a deep breath, and get on with it. Because anything was better
than going back to his old, nothing, nowhere life.

   And if he had to fall hard for someone, he was just glad it was
someone as beautiful and special as Gayle. It would be nice if she
cared something for him, just a little bit. But then, you couldn't have
everything.

   "Tell me," Gayle said suddenly, fixing him with her gorgeous
eyes so that his heart jumped in his chest again. "Have you ever had
any kind of supernatural experience before? Seen anything strange,
encountered anything you couldn't explain in safe, rational terms?"

   "You mean before today?"

   "Of course before today."

   Toby thought hard. All kinds of people came into Gandalf's
bookshop, looking for all kinds of books, some of them so esoteric
they had to be ordered specially from foreign publishers. Some of
the stranger tomes even came with little locks and keys. Toby had always been willing to listen while these people talked, but he'd never
taken any of it particularly seriously. In all his life he'd never once

seen a ghost, or had a strange feeling in an old building. He'd never seen a UFO or a black helicopter, or one of those big feral cats that were supposed to roam the countryside. He'd never got a message on a Ouija board, never experienced déjà vu, and never once been abducted by little gray aliens keen to play amateur proctologist—even though there was practically an epidemic of those, according to what he read in the papers. No: for Toby the world had always been a simple, sane, and boringly normal place.

Until now.

Since it obviously meant so much to Gayle, he tried hard to think of something to say. There had been that time in Sally in the Wood, that long, winding road leading down a steep hill through the great swath of ancient forest on the Wiltshire and Somerset border. The area had long been said to be haunted by the ghost of an old gypsy woman called Sally. There was one particular sharp curve on the hill, where cars and lorries were always shooting out over the edge and into the long drop, despite all the warning signs, crash barriers, and its infamous reputation. *An accident black spot,* said some. *Sally,* said others, usually in a hushed voice, as though *Someone* might be listening.

And once, just once, coming back from a party in Bath in the early hours, in the back of someone's car, Toby could have sworn he saw . . . something, standing in the trees at the side of the road, in the woods, a tall dark shadow with eyes brighter than any eyes had a right to be. Toby was drunk, and by the time he had roused himself to say something, the car had swept past the corner and left it behind and the shape, or the shadow, or whatever it had been, was gone.

Toby related all this to Gayle, and looked at her hopefully, but she was already shaking her head. "It's hardly the *Blair Witch Project,* is it? Much more likely you saw a deer. There are still a few running wild around there, mostly because they've learned to stay out of the road when there are cars around." She sighed again and shook her head. Toby was getting really tired of that sigh. She looked him straight in the eye and her expression softened. "I know this is hard for you, Toby, thrown in the deep end without warning, but you can't get away with just treading water. There are bad things in the water with you. There are forces and influences in the magical world, and it's best to tread softly so as not to wake them. Especially in Bradford-on-Avon, a town with far too much past for its own good. I think we'd better start our grand tour right now, while the Waking Beauty is the only one that's noticed you. In fact, I think we'll start with her. Maybe she can talk some sense into you."

She frowned suddenly, and her gaze turned inward. "I'd been planning to make the rounds soon, anyway. There have been strange currents and dark undertows in the aether just recently. Maybe you're the disturbance everyone has been sensing . . . Damn! Everything's such a mess! Why did I give in to such a stupid impulse, to open a door between the worlds just to get out of the rain? What was I thinking of? And how the hell did I manage to avoid seeing you standing there? I'm always so careful. . . ."

Toby shrugged happily. "Carys said there are no accidents. That some things are meant to be."

Gayle looked at him. "Now that really is bullshit."

# Five~

## Secret Histories

THEY LEFT the house together, after Gayle had spent a certain amount of time looking for her good coat and her mobile phone, decided she didn't need either of them after all, checked her appearance in two different mirrors and finally bustled out without looking back to see whether Toby was following. She waited impatiently for him to step out of the front door, and then slammed it hard, making sure the lock had caught properly. "You can't be too careful these days," she muttered, and Toby nodded solemnly. Determined as he was to keep in her good graces, at that point he would have agreed to anything, up to and including his own evisceration, provided it wasn't too imminent. He was also observing her closely, without being too obvious about it. The door they'd just passed through was supposed to translate them out of Veritie and back into Mysterie, though Toby couldn't honestly say he'd felt anything, and he was curious to see if Gayle would look any different now, as Carys Galloway had in the shadowy corner of the Dandy Lion. But no; she still looked exactly the same: utterly magnificent. Gayle caught him looking at her, and smiled briefly.

"What were you expecting? That I'd suddenly sprout wings and a halo, or horns and a tail? This is me, Toby, whatever world I'm in.

I've put a lot of thought into my appearance, and it hasn't changed for centuries."

Toby raised an eyebrow. "Centuries?"

"Yes. Now do you begin to understand why there can never be anything between us?"

"I've always preferred the more mature woman," Toby said calmly. "Especially when she looks as good as you. Tell me about these doors of yours, that allow us to pass between the worlds. How does that work, exactly?"

"It works because I want it to," said Gayle. "If only people could be so reliable. Now follow me."

"To the ends of the earth and back again, and all points in between. Where are we going?"

"First, to the Dandy Lion." Gayle glared at Toby. "If only to find out why Carys Galloway thought it necessary to inflict you on me. She'd better have a really good reason, or I'll hit her with a rain of frogs again."

"She was very insistent that we needed to meet," Toby said diffidently. "I didn't have to bribe her, or anything. She gave me the distinct impression that she knows something about what's going on here."

"Oh, Carys always knows what's going on," said Gayle, setting off down the street at a fast pace, her long legs striding away as though half hoping she could leave Toby behind. He stuck close to her elbow, so she couldn't slip suddenly into a side alley and lose him. Gayle scowled, looking straight ahead. "The problem with Carys is getting straight answers out of her. She does so love to hint and tease, and play at being mysterious. I think she was an oracle once, and she's never got over it. Well, she'll talk straight to me or I'll bounce her off the nearest wall till her ears bleed. Don't dawdle, Toby. If you really are what you're supposed to be, we're going to have to cover a lot of ground this morning, and I don't want to miss my soaps this afternoon."

With Gayle striding away as if she was in a race, and Toby hurrying to keep up with her, it didn't take them long to reach the

Dandy Lion. Gayle barged straight through the swing doors and then stopped so abruptly it was all Toby could do to keep from bumping into her. He peered over her shoulder to see what the hold-up was, and was astonished to see that everyone in the now silent pub was staring openly at Gayle. As Toby watched, they all fell to one knee and bowed their heads to her. She could have been their love, their queen, their goddess. None of them looked afraid. Most looked radiantly happy, eyes filling with tears of joy. Some were actually wringing their hands. Gayle slowly shook her head and moved forward into the bar.

There was awe and wonder on every face as she approached them, open joy that she should be gracing them with her presence. A few were actually weeping, as though they'd never thought to see such a day. It occurred to Toby that he should feel jealous, but the emotions beating on the air in the crowded bar were just too big, too overwhelming to be any threat to the simple everyday feelings in his heart. Everyone here clearly loved her, but as they'd love a pope, or a saint. They worshiped what she was, rather than who, and Toby had to wonder if perhaps he would worship her, too, once he finally found out what Gayle really was.

It wasn't a comfortable thought.

Gayle advanced slowly, with Toby all but forgotten behind her, and people came forward to greet her in quiet, reverential tones. Some tried to kiss her hand, or the hem of her dress, but she wouldn't let them. She was polite but firm, and no one tried to argue with her. Some looked curiously at Toby, obviously wondering what the hell a scruff like him was doing with someone like her, but no one said anything. Which was just as well, as right then Toby was damned if he could have justified his presence. It felt a bit like he'd wandered into a urinal at the Vatican, and looked round to find the pope splashing his boots beside him. Whoever or whatever Gayle might be, Toby just knew he was well out of his depth.

But then, that was true with most women, where Toby was concerned, and especially with Gayle. It was a bit like finding out that your blind date was actually Madonna.

Finally Gayle shooed away the last of her admirers and drew up a chair opposite Carys Galloway, who was still sitting in her dark corner under the stairs. Toby pulled up another chair and sat down beside Gayle. She didn't look at him. Behind them, the buzz of conversation in the bar slowly started up again.

"This is why I prefer to stay real," said Gayle. "I love them, of course, I care for them all; but I do hate it when they get so *clingy*. Carys, talk to me. Why did you presume to send love's young dream here to see me? What's going on that I don't know about? And why am I so absolutely sure that I'm not going to like the answers you're about to give me?"

"We can't all bury our heads in the sand," said Carys, utterly unmoved by Gayle's presence or the roughness of her manner. "Some of us take our responsibilities seriously. I've never understood why you limit yourself to being human, when you could be so much more. When you could be *doing* so much more. It's perverse. If I had your power, your capacities . . ."

"You'd interfere far too much," Gayle said flatly. "It's a human world now, so let the humans run it. I have abdicated." She looked sharply at Toby, and he almost jumped in his seat. Her voice was calm and cool as she spoke to him, as though he was a stranger. "The trouble with the Waking Beauty is that she could have been so much more, but she never had the nerve. Could have been a repository for a whole people's history, but settled for being a gossip and an agony aunt. Even I don't know how old she really is. Certainly she's been around far longer than any human has a right to be. She lives here, in Bradford-on-Avon, because more ley lines cross in this place than in any other part of the British Isles. She subsists on the tiny amounts of energy she's able to draw from the lines of power, like a happy little parasite."

"Ley lines," Toby said tentatively. "I've heard of those. Invisible lines of force that crisscross Britain, following the ancient roads?"

"The roads follow the ley lines," said Carys. "The lines are older than man, older than any civilization. They were here before us, and they'll still be here when we are all gone. And the power they carry dwarfs anything your modern science could produce. It's because so many lines converge on this town that it's so special. Such power and possibilities attract magical beings of all ranks and station. Things are possible here that are only dreamed of in the great cities of the world. And that's why I stay here. Why travel, when all the wisdom and wonders of the world will come to me?"

"If these lines are invisible," Toby said cunningly, "how can you be sure they're really there at all?"

Gayle turned to him, her face suddenly cold and expressionless. "Do you want to see them?"

"No!" Carys said urgently. "You mustn't do this! He isn't ready! He's only human, damn you!"

"He wants to see them," said Gayle. "He needs to know what he's getting into. Take your first step into a larger world, Toby."

Her left hand slammed down on top of Toby's right, where it rested on the table, and before he even had a chance to enjoy the contact, a sudden force tore through him, swift and merciless. His back straightened with a snap, his head jerked up and his breath caught in his chest between inhale and exhale. A horrid relentless pressure built behind his eyes, as though trying to force them forward out of their sockets. Toby cried out in shock and hurt, but couldn't even hear his own voice. He tried to pull his hand away, but Gayle, implacable, held it in place. His whole body was rigid now, his muscles stretched so tight they screamed. He felt a sudden helpless horror, of something huge and unendurable bearing down on him. His teeth were chattering, his mouth stretched in a mirthless grin, and still the pressure built behind his eyes, until finally it swept forward, *through* his eyes, and Toby saw what had been hidden from him.

The lines of light were everywhere, great beams of shimmering blue-white, blasting through buildings and furniture and people, unseen and unnoticed, burning with so much naked energy they were almost impossible to look at directly. Never beginning, never-ending, crisscrossing in a lattice of unworldly energies, it was like looking at the building blocks of the world, the lines on God's architectural plans. Beautiful and terrifying and utterly alien, the light was so bright Toby could almost hear it, the lines so powerfully present he could almost feel them. It was light to make the stars seem dim, beautiful enough to make the rainbow nothing more than a gaudy smudge. And they burned him, inside and out, like a moth held in a flame.

*Ley lines.*

Gayle took her hand away, and the lines were gone. The everyday world crashed back in upon Toby, and he slumped in his chair, shuddering all over. He slowly turned his head and looked at Gayle. Sweat ran down his face and dripped from his chin.

"How could you do that to me?" he said, his voice rough with shock and pain. "You didn't have to do that to me."

"Yes, I did," said Gayle, meeting his gaze unflinchingly. "You only think you know what you're getting into; what just being around me can cost you."

"I won't leave," said Toby. "No matter how much you hurt me."

"Wonderful," said Gayle. "You know, if I'd wanted a stalker, I'd have advertised. Toby, I collect stray cats, not puppy dogs. I'm sorry you were hurt, but I'll hurt you again if you stay. It's inevitable. I'm just trying to spare you further suffering."

"I've been alone most of my life," said Toby. "You don't know a damn thing about suffering. Don't you care about my feelings at all?"

"No," said Gayle. "I told you; I hate it when they get all clingy."

She looked back at Carys, whose scowl had deepened. "You are cruel," said the Waking Beauty.

"Cruel to be kind," said Gayle. "Be grateful you only got a glimpse of the lines, Toby. You have seen what links the material and the immaterial worlds, what holds existence together. It is said that if you could see the source and origin of those lines, see from where and what they draw their power, the sight alone would blast the reason from your mind." She hesitated, and then offered Toby a neatly folded handkerchief. "Here. Wipe your face. It's wet."

"I know." Toby mopped clumsily at his sweat-covered face with an unsteady hand, and then gave back the hanky. "So, have you ever seen the source of the ley lines?"

"No, she hasn't," said Carys. "Neither have I. I don't know anyone of the material planes who has, and survived it. Some mysteries are hidden even from the greatest of us, and it's best we don't ask why, for our own protection and peace of mind."

"We don't know everything," said Gayle. "Which is just as well, really. Think how boring life would be, if there were no more surprises."

"Some surprises I can do without," Toby said darkly. "From now on, keep your hands to yourself. Though I never thought I'd hear myself saying that. My eyes feel like they've been scoured with wire wool."

"Very well," said Gayle. "Let's get back to business. You've been very free with your advice just lately, Carys Galloway. Why don't you tell Toby all about yourself. Who and what you are, and why your words are worth listening to. And maybe along the way I'll remember some reason why I shouldn't make you rue your distant birth, for interfering in my affairs. Pay attention, Toby. It's a cautionary tale."

"I'm older than I look," Carys said to Toby, ignoring Gayle with admirable thoroughness. "I'm older than the town, older than the races that have lived in it; so old the very language I spoke as a child no longer exists. Britons, Romans, Celts, Saxons, and Normans have come and gone, and I was here before and after all of them. But I have paid a terrible price for my longevity. I cannot sleep. Cannot, dare not, sleep or dream or really rest. I don't sleep because something is waiting for me in my sleep. It waits for me, on the other side of consciousness, and if ever I weaken and allow myself to sleep or doze even for a moment, it will be there, and it will take me at last."

"What is it that's waiting for you?" said Toby. "Death?"

Carys laughed briefly. "If it were just death, I wouldn't be half as scared. No, it's something worse than death. Something from my ancient past, old and awful and unrelenting. My longevity must be paid for and promises must be kept. I'm always tired, Toby. Always.

Weary, even to my bones. I can't remember what it was like to be able to sit down and relax, to close my eyes and rest. I must always be alert, ready, prepared."

"Then die," said Gayle. "I can help you, if you like. One time pays for all. And material contracts have no power in the immaterial realms."

"I can't die yet," Carys said immediately. "Not when there's still so much left to see." She smiled at Toby, suddenly seeming a lot younger. "When you've been around as long as I have, you can't help hearing things, interesting things. Bradford-on-Avon is an open book to me, and has been for centuries. I know all its history, the light and the dark, the official records and the secret deals, the sacred and the profane. I've seen a lot of it firsthand. Because of who and what I am, I can exist in both worlds, the real and the magical. Everyone in Veritie just accepts my presence, and never even thinks to question it; though generations of families have known my company down the years. I'm here because I've always been here, and no one ever thinks beyond that point. It's part of my nature. Luckily I don't show up on recording devices. I think I'm too weird for them.

"There have always been people here, and I have seen them come and go. Go back two and a half thousand years, and there were people living here. Before there was a town, there was an Iron Age settlement five centuries before the Christ was born, to save or damn the world. A dark and ugly kind they were, savage and brutal and tenacious, maintaining a community in defiance of all that the elements could throw at them. I was there. I remember them. I saw them dance and sacrifice to things best forgotten, in the name of survival.

"The Romans wiped out such unhealthy worship when they finally arrived, though they had their secrets, too. No one in the city of Bath now remembers why the old spa baths were originally built, but I do. It's still down there somewhere, sleeping. I remember when the Saxon armies drove the last Celtic forces out of this area, and named this town *bradanford,* or 'broad ford.' They kept the old Celtic word for river, though: *afon.*

"I have seen men butcher each other on the hills surrounding this town, seen the river run red with blood, for good reasons and bad. But I have seen wonders and miracles, too, as the town has grown down the centuries, acquiring grace and hope and civilization. I have seen it all . . . but never been part of it. For all my longevity, I have never been a force or a power. Never been able to fight the shadows or embrace the light, protect the innocent or punish the wicked. I watch and I remember, and I forget nothing—it is my blessing and my curse. For every joy and every pain I ever knew is as fresh to me now as the first time I experienced it. I am the town, its history, and its legend. So when I tell you *Something Bad* is coming, you listen, Gayle."

"Something bad is always coming," said Gayle. "But the world goes on turning. Are you the oldest human being, Carys?"

The Waking Beauty frowned. "I don't know . . . there's always Tommy Squarefoot."

"Yes, but he's a Neanderthal."

"Don't try to distract me!" snapped Carys. "You came here to talk to me, so listen! I don't normally pay much attention to the future or the past. I try to concentrate on the present. Otherwise I'd lose my focus and be twice as crazy as I already am. And for all my fascination with gossip, I usually keep important information to myself. People have tried to kill me before now, for what I know or what they think I know and might tell." Carys smiled. "I'm still here and mostly they're not. You don't live as long as I have without learning a few survival tricks, some of them quite spectacularly nasty."

"Get to the point, Carys," said Gayle. "You love to talk so much it's a wonder you haven't had your tongue hinged in the middle so you could flap both ends at once. What does any of this have to do with Toby and me?"

"One of my survival tricks," said Carys to Toby, "is to pay attention. Sometimes, when vital or terrible or momentous things occur, they make such an impression on time they send reverberations back down its spine. And people like me, rooted so firmly in the timestream, can detect such things. Something is going to happen, and it's almost upon us. Something so important that it will affect Veritie and Mysterie and the nature of existence itself. It's going to happen here, and it's going to happen soon, and you and Gayle will be a part of it. Whether for good or bad is beyond me. Events just are. Beware The Serpent In The Sun and his earthbound son, the Hob. Whatever it is that's coming, they're a part of it, just like you, whether you like it or not."

"If this future event is so damned important, why didn't you detect it earlier?" said Gayle.

"Someone's been hiding it," said Carys. "Want to guess who?"

"Hold everything," said Toby determinedly. "Let's take some time out. Will somebody please explain to me just who or what The Serpent In The Sun is, and why you both look so worried about him?"

Carys and Gayle looked at each other, and then Gayle looked at Toby. "The Serpent . . . is the oldest of us all. Our progenitor, in many ways. No one knows exactly what he is. We call him the Serpent because we have to call him something. Real and magical, both and neither, he lives inside the Sun."

"*Inside* the sun? Our sun, the one our world orbits?" Toby looked incredulously from Gayle to Carys and back again, but both women looked entirely serious. "Oh, come on! Nothing could live inside the sun; the whole thing's one bloody great nuclear reaction!"

"And the Serpent lives there," said Carys. "Think about that. Think how powerful he would have to be, how large and potent, compared to us small things . . . In the Bible, the Serpent was the physical incarnation of evil in the Garden of Eden, the Enemy of all that is, now and forever, eternally, implacably evil. There are many who call The Serpent In The Sun the old Enemy. And this being, this old adversary, has turned his gaze upon you, Toby Dexter. Because even the greatest of the Powers and the Dominations can be shaken or changed or brought down by the implacable forces surrounding a focal point."

"I am dead," said Toby. "I am so dead you might as well nail down the coffin lid right now and start choosing the hymns."

"Not necessarily," said Carys. She was glaring at Gayle again. "She could protect you, if she wanted. She could put a stop to what's coming. All she has to do is stop slumming, stop pretending to be human, and assume her rightful mantle, and then even the Serpent would stop and think twice. But she doesn't want to do that. The comfortable illusion of the life she's built for herself, the lie she hides behind to avoid her responsibilities, is more important to her than you or me or any other mayfly human life."

"That's not true," said Gayle. Her voice was still calm, but she did seem just a little perturbed by the raw anger in Carys's voice. "My only real responsibility is not to interfere directly in people's lives. I have to stand back, remain uninvolved. People have to learn to stand on their own two feet, to take responsibility for their own destiny. Otherwise free will would be nothing more than an illusion, and the whole point of being human would be lost. People have to be free to make their own mistakes, or they'll never learn anything."

"Even if they destroy the whole planet in the process?"

"Even then," Gayle said firmly.

"And how many innocents suffer every day as a result?"

"As many as necessary." Gayle looked at Toby almost apologetically. "I have to take the long view. And Waking Beauty here only thinks she knows what that is. I was already far older than she when she drew her first breath." She turned back to Carys. "Why did you send Toby to me? There have been focal points before. Why send this one?"

"Because you're linked," said Carys, with smug satisfaction. "The skeins of fate are wrapped around you both, so strongly I'm surprised you can't see them yourself. You think ley lines are impressive, Toby; you should see fate's workings. It's like looking behind the world, to see the stagehands at work. In my experience, life isn't nearly as arbitrary as it seems. Patterns and statistics have a way of working out, whether we like it or not."

"Crazy," said Gayle. "Crazy, and mean-spirited with it. There is no fate, no destiny—only possibilities."

"Believe what you like, if it makes you happy," said Carys. "Fate doesn't care. But you two have been linked ever since you let him follow you through the door you conjured up at the railway station."

"I didn't let him follow me! I didn't even see him!"

"And how likely is that? He was right there, in plain view . . . You couldn't have missed him, unless you were meant to. It's no use kicking and screaming, Gayle. This has been decided where all the things that matter are decided—in the Courts of the Holy. Someone's pulling strings again—"

"Excuse me," said Toby, raising his hand like a child in class. "But I could have sworn I heard someone mention *free will* just a moment ago. How does that fit in with all this talk of *Something* interfering with people's destinies?"

"Oh, hell," said Gayle. "As if things weren't complicated enough. Look; individually, you have free will. Everyone does. But sometimes the worlds that be get a nudge, from Upstairs. And then it's up to us how we cope with it. For example, you are a focal point, but you could still choose to forget everything, and walk away from it."

"And then . . . someone else would be the focal point?" said Toby.

"Damned if I know," said Carys. "Focal points are tricky things. I don't think the town would actually get hit by earthquakes, volcanoes, and swarms of killer bees, all at once, but I wouldn't rule it out either. Once you start mucking about with fate, you have to be prepared for a backlash, and there's no telling where the psychic bricks would fall. It's like pulling one can of beans from the bottom of the pyramid; it might collapse or it might not."

"If you believe in fate," said Gayle.

"I'd say it's more to the point whether fate believes in you," said Carys. "It doesn't matter anyway. Toby won't walk out on you. His feelings for you won't let him."

Toby could feel his face growing warm. "My feelings are my own business, thank you very much."

"Not anymore they're not," said Carys. She smiled knowingly at Gayle. "I don't know why you're making such a fuss. You've had mortal paramours before."

"And every single one of them came to a bad end," said Gayle. "They might start out loving me, but they all end up worshiping me, and I hate that. I haven't taken a mortal lover in more years than I care to remember. I got tired of them dying on me. I hope you're paying attention to this, Toby."

"Hell," said Toby. "I'm taking notes."

Gayle shook her head. "We are going to change the subject, right now. Let us talk instead of Nicholas Hob."

"If we must," said Carys. "Nasty little toad. The Serpent's Son is back in Bradford-on-Avon, and has taken up residence at Blackacre. Only fitting, I suppose. It's the only place in town that's as corrupt as he is. No one knows what's brought him back after all these years, but he's taken the woman Angel as his companion." She paused, and looked at Toby. "Nicholas Hob is the Serpent's only living offspring, a product of rape and horror in the early days of the world. Hob's almost as bad as his father, but luckily he's trapped in human form, which limits the damage he can do. Angel used to be an angel. The whole wings-and-halo bit. Demoted to the material worlds for a crime the likes of which you and I can only guess at. So we're now faced with two beings, both powerful enough to tear this town apart at the seams on a whim, even before they joined forces. And you're still not convinced fate is stirring things?"

"I don't think I feel very well," said Toby. "Every time I turn around the odds get worse. I could shoot an albatross and not get luck like this."

"Aren't I worth it?" said Gayle.

Toby sniffed. "I'm thinking about it. Trust me, I'm thinking about it."

"There's more," said Carys.

"Surprise, surprise." said Gayle. "Hit me with it."

"You've seen the news. There are stirrings in the sun, solar flares leaping out to caress the world. The Serpent is flexing his muscles. He's planning something. Hob and Angel are his chosen instruments. And all we have to stop them is a focal point who doesn't understand his own purpose . . . and you. If I had anywhere else to go,

I'd be packing. I have a horrible suspicion this town has been designated ground zero for something truly appalling, something that
will crack open all the worlds and let the blood run out. You have to
intervene, Gayle, and soon, before it's too late for all of us."

"Do you know that for a fact?" said Gayle.

The Waking Beauty sighed and sank back in her chair. She
looked suddenly tired and older. "No," she said reluctantly. "I can
see the pieces but not the pattern."

"Sometimes you need to be reminded of that." Gayle considered
the matter in silence for a while. "All right; something's going on.
And Toby isn't just another focal point, or he wouldn't be linked so
closely to me. Could he be the next in line to be Humanity's Champion?"

Carys looked startled for the first time, studying Toby with new
eyes. "I don't know. He could be, I suppose. It's been so long since
Humanity needed a Champion . . . You know, it does make a kind
of sense."

"Yes," said Gayle. "Unfortunately, it does." Both the women
looked at Toby in a curious but unsettlingly speculative way.

"If I am Humanity's Champion," Toby said firmly, "then we are
all in really deep trouble."

"You should be honored," said Gayle, and Toby couldn't quite
tell whether she was mocking him or not. "True Champions are few
and far between. They are heroes, warriors, legends, defenders of
Humanity against the forces of darkness. Of course, most of them
end up dying horribly, but . . . Toby! Toby, sit down! You're not
going anywhere and you know it."

"Every time I think it can't get any worse, it does," said Toby,
slumping back into his seat. "I'd just got my head round being a
focal point, and now you want me to be a hero and a warrior? Trust
me: you have got the wrong guy."

"Not even for me?"

"Not even for Kate Bush dipped in honey."

"If you won't do something," Carys said suddenly to Gayle, "I
will."

"If you do," said Gayle, "I can't protect you. You're long-lived and you know a lot of things, but at the end of the day you're still only human, Carys, while Hob and Angel are so much more. You sit tight and leave this with me. Let me think on it."

"Time is running out. . . ."

"It always is." Gayle smiled suddenly. "You know; I think I'll go and see the Mice. They're bound to have noticed something."

"Mice?" said Toby ominously. "You want to talk with a bunch of mice?"

"Oh, you'll like them, Toby. They're very charming. A bit rough and ready, but then, that's Mice for you."

"They're newcomers to the town," said Carys, frowning. "What could they possibly know that I don't?"

"Outsiders are often better suited to seeing the big picture," said Gayle. "And besides, they have the advantage of not being human. Which should, if nothing else, at least guarantee a fresh perspective. As Mice, they're closely attuned to the natural world. Whereas I have allowed myself to become rather distant, over the years."

Toby gave Gayle a hard look. "If they start singing about Cinderella and dragging in a pumpkin, I'm going to lay traps and put down poison."

"They're not that kind of Mice, dear," said Gayle. "You'll like them, provided you're not too judgmental. Good-bye, Carys. Do the sensible thing for once and stay out of this. If even half of what you and I suspect is true, the whole town is currently trapped between a rock and a very hard place. Not a good time to be drawing attention to yourself."

"Are you going to do anything?" said Carys.

"Perhaps. There's always the chance this will all sort itself out without me. But just in case . . . Come along, Toby."

Toby scrambled to his feet as Gayle rose gracefully to hers, and just had time to nod a quick good-bye to Carys before Gayle was sweeping out of the Dandy Lion. Toby sighed and hurried after her. It had started out as a weird day, and the general strangeness factor showed no signs of decreasing. Surely it was only yesterday when his life still seemed to make sense? Of course, it had been a pretty bloody boring life, and he hadn't actually met up with Gayle then . . . so it all really came down to whether Gayle was worth the candle or not. Toby grinned. On the whole, yes, she was.

He got outside to find that Gayle was already striding off down the street, and he had to run to catch up with her. On the one hand, Toby was beginning to feel just a little pissed off at being dragged around by Gayle like a dog on a leash, but on the other hand, she had quite definitely called him "dear" just now. Probably a slip of the tongue on her part, but an encouraging one. Toby liked to think he was making progress. He needed to do something, something big and memorable that would impress her, help her to see him as an equal partner in . . . in whatever the hell it was they were currently caught up in. *A hero, a warrior, a legend* . . . Toby scowled and bit his lower lip. He'd never seen himself as a man of action. In pub fights, he was always the one bravely fading into the woodwork. But whatever Humanity's Champion was supposed to be, he was pretty damn sure it involved more than being Gayle's lapdog.

As Toby accompanied Gayle through the middle of the town, he couldn't help noticing that an awful lot of people were openly staring at him. Not just because he was a new face in Mysterie, but because he was with Gayle. Most were curious, some were intrigued, a few actually looked impressed. But there were some who looked scared, as though he were a new, unpredictable factor in the equation, someone who might either change or ruin everything. Presumably these were the ones who knew a focal point when they saw one. Toby began to feel increasingly nervous. It was bad enough having to come to terms with the fact that great things were expected of you, without being forced to admit that you didn't have a damned clue as to what those things might be. What if he was supposed to kill a dragon, or something? No, forget the something, what if it actually *was* a bloody dragon? Toby had always visualized a dragon as being something very like *Tyrannosaurus rex,* only bigger and faster and with more teeth, probably breathing fire, too. Maybe he'd be allowed to start on something smaller first.

Like a dog with a bad attitude.

They were crossing the old bridge across the River Avon when the Howling Thing scared the crap out of Toby. He'd been walking along, lost in his own thoughts, vaguely aware of a sound like an angry siren growing steadily louder, and then just as he passed the old stone Chapel, something inside it threw itself against the confining walls. The whole structure shuddered and the Howling Thing's voice rose like a damned soul in torment. Toby all but jumped out of his skin, and grabbed Gayle by the arm.

*"What the hell was that?"*

"It's all right, Toby," Gayle said reassuringly, prising his fingers from her arm. "It can't get out."

Toby began to get his breathing back under control, though his heart was still thudding painfully in his chest. "What's it doing in there anyway?"

"It's doing penance," said Gayle. "Every town has its monsters, and its bad seeds. This one is doing time. Every damned bit of it."

That was when something even worse emerged slowly from the dark waters under the bridge, reeds and river water falling away from its pallid gargantuan bulk. It was huge, easily thirty feet tall, all bone and thick slabs of muscle, with an elongated skull like a horse. Its pockmarked skin was the dead white of things that live far underwater, rarely leaving the unending dark to venture to the surface's light. Its eyes were black, bulging painfully from wide sockets. The mouth was long and narrow, with great square teeth that looked as if they did a lot of chewing. Its shape was more human than not, and it just seemed to get bigger and bigger as it leaned over the bridge.

One huge weed-wrapped hand rested on the wall beside the old Chapel and the Howling Thing was suddenly quiet. The long head came sweeping down for a better look at Toby and Gayle, and it was all Toby could do to keep from falling back. Hell, anywhere else and he'd have run like fun for the horizon; but he couldn't abandon Gayle. She was standing very still, staring at the huge creature as though mesmerized. Toby put a hand on her arm to pull her away, but she wouldn't move. Toby glanced around, but everyone else had disappeared. He didn't blame them. *Every town has its monsters . . .* The huge bony hand tightened on the bridge's wall, and the ancient stonework cracked and shattered under the pressure of that awful grip.

*Oh hell,* thought Toby. *I should have settled for a dragon. Maybe if I run, I can decoy it away from Gayle . . .*

"Don't move," Gayle murmured, as though guessing his thoughts. "It's faster than you can imagine."

"What the hell is it?"

"That is a troll. All really old bridges have trolls underneath them in Mysterie. Their presence holds the bridge together, against the ravages of time. In return for which, they demand a toll. . . . Now would you please let go of my arm? You're cutting off the circulation."

Toby reluctantly tore his gaze away from the lowering troll and saw that his knuckles were white where he had Gayle by the arm. He made himself let go, and then took a deep breath and moved to put himself between Gayle and the troll. Even that was enough to bring cold beads of sweat popping out on his forehead. The troll was a killer. You just had to look at it to see that. But he couldn't let Gayle be hurt. Stood to reason it was after her. Someone as important and as long-lived as Gayle was bound to have made enemies. And by accompanying Toby back into Mysterie, she had made herself vulnerable to them. That thought put a little steel into Toby's bones, though his legs still felt decidedly shaky. He couldn't let her be hurt because of him.

He tried frantically to think of something he could do, but given the sheer size of the troll . . . He wished he had a gun. Hell, he wished he had a bazooka. It came to him then that there was only one useful thing he could do and that was to try to keep the troll occupied, buy some time, so that Gayle could get away. The creature would almost certainly kill him, but Gayle would escape. The thought chilled him, but didn't deter him. *Am I really ready to die for her? For someone who doesn't even like me much?* He seemed to have all the time in the world to consider that, but the answer was never in doubt. *Love, you're a cold cruel bitch,* he thought calmly. *I wanted a great romance in my life; I just never thought it'd be this short. Guess now we'll never get to find out whether I was Humanity's Champion. Ah well; it was worth it in the end. To be in love, really in love, for the first time in my life.*

He was just getting ready to tell Gayle to make a run for it when the troll suddenly leaned forward, fixed Toby with its dark goggling eyes, and spoke in a voice like stones crashing together in a stream, like all the cold horrid things that live in the depths.

"I have come for you, little human," said the troll, its great voice shaking in Toby's bones. "Little Toby Dexter. Thinks he's so brave. Thinks he's going to be Humanity's Champion. Wrong. It all ends here, in blood and tears and splintered bones. This is my bridge, given to me under the old compact, and no one crosses it without my permission. Do you know the rules, little human, little Champion? The old game of riddle, of question and answer? If you do, and if you're clever enough and fast enough and brave enough, you might just live to fight another day. But you're a modern man, a child of your times, so it's much more likely that I'll feed on your tender flesh and make toothpicks out of your bones."

*A gun, a bazooka, a bloody slingshot . . . It doesn't want her, it wants me . . . Well, when in doubt, bluff.*

Toby drew himself up to his full height, fixed the troll with his best menacing glare and lowered his voice as far as it would go.

"Who the hell do you think you're talking to? You back off right now, or I'll have your balls for this! I am Toby Dexter, focal point and Humanity's Champion. This is Gayle. I don't suppose I have to tell you who and what she is, do I? I thought not. Do you really think you can get either one of us to do one damned thing we don't want to? Now back off, or I'll show you what happens when I get really upset."

"Oh, hell," said the troll, slumping just a little. "You're a focal point? Really? Shit. No one said anything to me about your being a focal point. *Shit!* I never get to have any fun anymore. Is that you, Gayle? I didn't know you were out and about again. How's things?"

"Don't you *how's things* me," said Gayle in a decidedly frosty tone. "*Bad* troll!"

"Oh, go on, rub it in," said the troll. Toby was amazed to see that the huge creature was actually pouting now. "Make fun of me. Everyone does. No one respects you once you've reached a certain age, and your eyesight isn't what it was. I'm just doing my job, you know. No one cares about riddles anymore, anyway. It's all computer games and bloody Pokémon now. I can remember when monsters were respected, when teeth and claws meant something. Go on; walk across the bloody bridge, then. Run back and forth, see if I care. You do your best, spend ages working out a good set of threats, individually tailored, too, and they laugh in your face. I'm going back into the river for a good long sulk."

And as quickly as that, the troll disappeared beneath the dark and murky waters, and was gone. Toby looked at the damaged stone wall where its great hand had rested, and then turned to Gayle.

*"Bad troll?"*

"He's no real threat," said Gayle easily. "Hasn't been for centuries. He was bluffing. Mostly. Unless you'd run. Then it might have got a bit nasty. But you didn't run. You put yourself between me and harm. Quite unnecessary, of course, but still . . . I'm glad to have had a glimpse of what you're really made of."

"What I'm really made of very nearly ended up filling my trousers," said Toby hotly. "Are you telling me you were never in any danger at all?"

"Of course not. But you were still very brave, Toby. I'm impressed."

"I am so mad I could spit soot. I do not want to have to feel like that again, *ever*. If I'm going to be Humanity's Champion, unlikely as that still seems, I want a weapon of some sort. Something to give me at least a fighting chance."

"What do you expect me to do?" said Gayle. "Find you a big stone with a sword stuck through it? Whistle you up a magic lamp,

or a ring with three wishes? Forget about weapons, Toby. It isn't
going to be that kind of battle. Hob could break Excalibur across his
knee, and Angel would probably eat it. And from now on, I will
look out for myself, thank you very much."

"Fine," said Toby. "The next big monster to come along is all
yours. You can handle it, while I make for the horizon like a dog
with its arse on fire."

Gayle looked at him consideringly, and her expression softened
just a little. "You won't run, Toby. You're not the running kind.
When push came to shove, you stood your ground and kept your
wits about you. Which is good to know. The kind of beings, forces,
we'll be facing will be more impressed by brains than bravery."

"Pity," said Toby. "I could have faked bravery. I still don't feel like
any kind of hero."

Gayle patted him gently on the cheek. "That's the best kind.
Now come along. We've got a lot of ground to cover, and the day is
young."

"I will never wash that cheek again," said Toby, and Gayle had to
laugh.

They made their way through the town, and everywhere people
fell back to give them plenty of room. A few even turned and ran.
Lots of people were still giving Toby the fish eye, but he found that
smiling straight back at them, like he knew something they didn't,
was usually enough to make them turn quickly away and pretend to
be interested in something else. Even when there was nothing else.
There did seem to be an awful lot of people about, even for a Saturday morning, often gathered in little groups buzzing with animated conversation. Toby was surprised to find he recognized quite
a few faces. Apparently more people than he ever suspected were a
part of Mysterie, and always had been. It made him wonder about
the connections between the two worlds, and how much he might
have noticed before, if he'd only ever suspected the truth.

And most surprising of all, he felt comfortable in his new, magical world, for all its monsters and weirdness. He felt vaguely that he

ought to be more . . . *upset* by some of the things he'd seen and been told. The truth alone would have been enough to set a lot of people gibbering and frothing at the mouth, and the Howling Thing . . . In Mysterie all the rules were suspended, and everything was up for grabs. Toby could think of a lot of people who wouldn't have been able to cope with such madness and anarchy for even a moment, and just a few days before he would have said he was one of them, but . . . He liked it here, in Mysterie, for all its uncomfortable truths and hidden dangers. He felt alive, for the first time in years.

It probably helped that his old life had been so utterly bloody boring, that he was glad to be rid of it.

Gayle indicated a row of old houses they were passing, mostly seventeenth- and eighteenth-century. Well preserved, but blunt and functional rather than charming. "That place there, a little back from the road, used to be the old Hobshouse Bank. A failed venture by the Serpent's Son, a few centuries back. For a time, that one bank controlled all the town's finances. Owned a lot of property, and gave out even more promissory notes. Everyone who mattered came to Hob with their hat in their hands, looking for a piece of the action. They knew his reputation, even then, if not exactly who and what he really was, but they were prepared to overlook any number of, er, character faults, in the pursuit of obscene amounts of money. And there was a lot of gold to be found in Bradford-on-Avon in those days, when the cloth trade flourished.

"There's more than one way to power, Toby, and Hob's tried most of them. He ran this town for years. When his overextended bank finally collapsed, its vaults full of nothing but unrecoverable debts and piles of worthless paper, and Hob disappeared into the night with what little cold cash there was, a lot of people's fortunes were destroyed, from the highest to the lowest. Financial disasters have a way of trickling all the way down. It took the town generations to get over it. The town's forefathers should have remembered the old adage; if you must sup with the Devil, use a long spoon. Even if it's only the Devil's Son. And certainly don't use your own money."

"Money," Toby said thoughtfully. "That's something other people have, isn't it?"

Gayle looked at him. "I thought you said you were in publishing?"

"*In* is perhaps too strong a word," said Toby. "*Connected with* is probably more accurate. Suffice it to say that money and I seem to have only the most fleeting of relationships these days. I don't understand where it all goes. It's not like I have any expensive vices. I never had the chance to acquire any. How much further, before we get to these Mice of yours?"

"They're right out on the edge of town. They like their privacy, in Mysterie as well as Veritie. Place called Manor Farm."

"The hippies?" said Toby. "Oh, wonderful. We're going to end up sitting around on bean bags, drinking strange herbal teas and trying not to choke on the fumes from dodgy joss sticks, I just know it."

"You know, you're very judgmental, for a shop assistant."

"You did know!"

"I'm afraid so. Carys knows everything, remember? Not to worry. I'm sure you were a very good shop assistant. Probably got a degree in stacking. You'll like the Mice; charming creatures."

"Yeah, well," growled Toby. "They'd better have some cheese. I'm starting to feel distinctly peckish."

A pleasant enough stroll took them through the rest of the town and out into the countryside beyond. It was a leisurely walk in the bright sunshine because Toby had slowed Gayle down by the simple principle of refusing to keep up. Gayle soon got tired of conversing over her shoulder with someone who might or might not be there, and reluctantly slowed her long stride to a more reasonable pace, much to Toby's relief. He hadn't done this much walking in years. The old Manor farmhouse was all that now remained of what had once been a thriving farm. But the land had gradually been sold off in small parcels over the years, and the livestock and outer buildings with it, till all that was left was the old Tudor farmhouse itself.

Someone had recently given the exterior a quick lick of paint and a good clean, and the half-timbered structure looked to be in reasonably good condition, for its age. Toby and Gayle trod noisily up the long gravel path that led to the great front door, but there was no response from inside the house. Most interesting to Toby, the windows weren't boarded over, as they were in Veritie.

All in all, walking up the gravel path was like walking into the picture on the lid of a jigsaw box. It was the kind of perfect bucolic image that had become quite rare in the modern, mechanized, and impoverished countryside. Everything looked just right. Of course, this was Mysterie. Toby hadn't been out this way in so long he couldn't tell if the farmhouse usually looked this perfect, but he rather thought not. Upkeep on historical buildings like this could be ruinously expensive, in Veritie. The whole setting seemed utterly tranquil, calm and peaceful, with wide open green fields stretching out around the farmhouse, bordered on the horizon by traditional low stone walls. There didn't seem to be anyone about.

Gayle walked right up to the impressive front door, a great solid slab of oak, and banged firmly with the black iron knocker. The sound carried loudly, but there wasn't even a twitching of the lace curtains at the downstairs windows. Still, Toby had a strong feeling of being observed by unseen eyes. He hoped they were friendly, though just how dangerous a bunch of Mice could be . . . He looked up sharply as the huge door before him swung slowly inward, silent as a breath. There was still no sign of anyone, and only darkness within. Gayle strode straight in, without waiting for an invitation. Toby shook his head, squared his shoulders, and followed her in.

Just inside the door there was a sudden flash of light, revealing the farmhouse's interior, and Toby stumbled to a halt. The door closed silently of its own accord behind him as he stared about him, openmouthed. Just when he thought he'd grown accustomed to all the curves Mysterie could throw at him, it came up with a whole new approach. All the interior structure of the old Manor farmhouse had been removed; all the walls and the first-floor ceiling, and all the rooms were knocked through into one, so that the whole place was now one big barn. Or one very big mouse cage. The vast open floor was covered in straw, much of it days old and well trampled down. There were piles of food all over (mostly raw vegetables), left dotted here and there with no discernible pattern or purpose. An old stone horse trough had been dragged in and filled with water. Brightly colored objects of all shapes and sizes were scattered here and there, as though picked up and enjoyed, and then just dropped carelessly wherever they happened to land.

And everywhere, scampering across the floor, running up the walls and even across the high raftered ceiling, laughing and snuggling and fighting and eating and drinking: the Mice. Six-foot-tall, vaguely human, Mice.

There were lots of them, covered in fur of varying shades, with muzzles and twitching whiskers, clawed feet and long tails, but still just human enough to make it clear that they were no natural creatures. They spoke, or rather chattered, in human voices, though their movements were swift and entirely animal-like. Mice so large should have been disturbing, even scary, especially to Toby, who had a morbid horror of rats, but somehow they just weren't. If anything, they were sweet, even charming, just as Gayle had said.

They were like fairy-tale mice, magical in form and character. The Mice ran up the walls and along the ceiling with equal ease, as though gravity was just a matter of convenience for them. Most were too busy playing together to pay any attention to their new visitors, but eventually four Mice came pattering over to meet them. Two were brown, one gray, and one was pure white with rather fetching pale pink eyes. Even up close, the oversize Mice weren't in the least bit disconcerting. They were just bumbling, cartoonlike creatures, with kind eyes and wide, happy smiles. The four Mice squatted down on their haunches before Gayle, lifting their twitching muzzles to her in open adoration. They managed a few quick head bobs in Toby's direction, so he wouldn't feel left out, but it was clearly Gayle who fascinated them. Toby could understand that.

"All hail, most noble—," began the gray one, only to be immediately interrupted by the darker brown one.

"That's not the right form of address, Tidy! Not right at all!"

"You're always arguing about things like that, Bossy," said the lighter brown Mouse, patting his front paws together. "And you're always wrong. You carry on, Tidy. You're doing very well."

"I think we're supposed just to call her Lady," said the white Mouse diffidently. "But of course I'm just Sweetie, so I'm probably wrong."

"Exactly," said Tidy crushingly. "Now I—"

"You look very lovely today, Lady," said the lighter brown Mouse. "I dreamed you were coming here—"

"Ooh, you did not, Dreamy!" said Bossy at once. "You're always claiming you dream things, but somehow you never remember to mention them in advance. Ignore her, Lady. She's been at the Red Leicester again."

"I did dream her, I did!" said Dreamy, stamping all her paws in quick succession.

"All hail, most noble Lady," said Tidy doggedly, and then Sweetie turned suddenly to look at Toby. He just had time to smile at her before she launched herself at him, and knocked him to the floor. The straw soaked up most of the impact, but Toby still found himself lying on his back with a Mouse's face staring into his.

"You're *cute*," said Sweetie.

"That's nice," said Toby. "Now do you think you could get off my chest, please? I have a feeling I'm going to need to breathe again in the near future."

Sweetie backed off and allowed Toby to sit up before immediately cuddling up against him and holding him in her white furry arms. "I like him," she said to the others. "Can we keep him?"

"Actually, he's with me," said Gayle. "Try not to damage him, Sweetie."

The white Mouse shrugged, but continued to hold Toby close to her. Toby decided that if he could handle a thirty-foot troll, he could handle being groped by an oversize Mouse. Even though it did absolutely nothing for his dignity. Tidy sighed resignedly and fixed his attention on Gayle, but he'd hardly got two words out before Bossy

interrupted him again, and there then followed a long, rather confused argument as to whose turn it was to be the official
spokesMouse. It didn't help that they weren't actually sure what day
it was, anyway. They almost came to blows over that, until finally
Tidy and Dreamy slammed Bossy to the floor and sat on him till he
shut up. Bossy subsided reluctantly, clinging to as much dignity as
he could with his face peeking out from under Dreamy's furry rump.
He made apologetic eyes to Gayle, who nodded to show she quite
understood. Tidy bowed yet again to Gayle, a little breathlessly,
frowned as he tried to remember where he'd got to and then
shrugged and started again.

"Welcome to Manor Farm, Lady Gayle. Yes. If I'd known you
were coming, I'd have cleaned the place up a bit. The others are just
animals, you know. No sense of order, they just drop things everywhere. I keep telling them, we may be Mice now, but we can still
have standards. This lot would piss in the sinks. If we had sinks. *Be
still,* Bossy, or I'll groom your fur the wrong way again."

"Bully," said Bossy indistinctly.

"Things have been happening in Mysterie," said Dreamy in a
soft hesitant voice. "I see them in my dreams. Things call to me,
from the natural world. The banished Son has returned, and we are
all endangered. Sweetie, *leave the human alone.* And stop licking his
hair, I think it's supposed to look like that. Who is the human, Lady
Gayle? He smells very interesting. I think I may have dreamed of
him."

"That is Toby," said Gayle. "He's a newcomer to Mysterie. And
a focal point."

Sweetie let go of Toby so fast he almost fell over. Tidy and
Dreamy got up off Bossy, and all four Mice huddled together to give
Toby a good looking-over.

"Bit small for a focal point, isn't he?" said Tidy. "I'd always
thought they'd be more impressive."

"Size isn't everything," said Toby.

"How true," said Sweetie.

"I suppose you brought him here to hear our story?" said Bossy, pawing at his rumpled fur. "Fair enough. I shall tell it. It is an interesting, cautionary, and instructional tale, and I do so love to tell it."

"Never knew a tale you didn't like to tell," said Tidy. "Sometimes I swear you'd rather talk than eat. Though you have been known to do both simultaneously, and I do wish you wouldn't. All right, get on with it, but don't drag it out. There's still lots to do today."

"You mean there's lots you want to do," said Dreamy. "I don't know why you make such a fuss. The whole point of becoming Mice was so we wouldn't have to bother with *doing things* anymore."

"I like to keep busy," said Tidy defensively.

"Then you should have become a bee," said Sweetie.

It took a while, but eventually Gayle got them all settled down, sitting in a semicircle facing herself and Toby. He was a little hesitant about sitting on the bare straw, but couldn't figure out how politely to avoid it. In the end he gritted his teeth and sat down beside Gayle, making a mental note to fumigate and if necessary burn his trousers later. Luckily the story turned out to be so fascinating he quickly forgot about everything else.

Once upon a time, back in the sixties, in what passed then for the real world, the Mice had all been human, young men and women embracing the spirit of the times. Hippies one and all and proud of it, living the marvelous new dream of peace and love and freedom. They turned their backs on the old ways, of insane wars and corrupt politics, and looked for a more spiritual path. They also believed in sex, drugs, and rock 'n' roll, preferably simultaneously. They dropped out, turned on, tuned in, and thought they could change the world by their example. It was, in many ways, a more innocent time then.

The world did change, if slowly, for the better; but mostly as a result of direct action. The old order might be going down, but it was going down fighting. Still, it was a grand time to be alive. When to be young was everything, and you could watch your dreams come true. Unfortunately, it didn't last.

The sixties became the seventies became the bloody eighties, and one by one the dreams died. The hope and joy of the hippies became the savage nihilism of punk, which became the self-interest of Generation X. *We shall overcome* became *No future* and *Greed is good.* Drugs that were meant to free the mind instead enslaved the body. And one group of aging hippies decided they'd had enough. They gave up on the failed world of Veritie and moved en masse into Mysterie, where dreams still came true. They *changed,* willingly giving up their troubled Humanity to become Mice, warm, loving, furry animals who lived only for the day, and for each other.

Toby couldn't decide whether it was a sad story or not. Looking round at the other Mice, he didn't think they knew either. Most were still running around the cavernous interior of the old farmhouse, immersed in the moment, not even interested in listening to their own story. Here and there they cuddled together and fell asleep in great furry clumps, as the mood took them. No work, no duties, no responsibilities, driven only by animal needs and thoughts and emotions, but with just enough of a human overlay to enable them still to appreciate it. Toby was irresistibly reminded of the old novelty song about a whole bunch of mice who lived in a windmill in old Amsterdam.

Except, what did the Mice have to live *for,* anymore? Everyone needs a reason to get up in the morning, don't they? Toby suddenly realized that Bossy had finally stopped talking, the story over, and he quickly tried to think of something intelligent to say, to prove he'd been paying attention.

"So . . . what do you all *do,* now that you're Mice?"

"Doing isn't important to us anymore," Dreamy said patiently. "It's enough just to be, and be happy."

"We think," said Tidy. "We dream, we philosophize, and watch the world go by. We have a good scratch. We ponder the mysteries of Mysterie."

"And we make love like you wouldn't believe," said Sweetie, grinning. "Sometimes we go out at night and frolic in the moonlight. Sometimes we sell tickets."

"That's just in Mysterie, of course," said Bossy. "In Veritie we keep to ourselves. We can still be human there, when we have to. We remember our old bodies, and pull them on like coats for the few occasions when we still have to deal with the real world."

"They can change more than their shapes," Gayle said to Toby. "They can change their size as well: very useful side effect of the spell they bought. They can become ordinary-size mice at will, which can be very useful if someone needs a little surreptitious spying done. They do things for me sometimes. No one notices a few more mice coming and going."

"We know everything," said Sweetie, clapping her pink paws together.

"Funnily enough, practically everyone I've met in Mysterie claims to know everything," said Toby dryly.

"Well," said Sweetie, shrugging. "We know everything we care to know. People care about such silly things."

"I knew you were coming," said Dreamy. "I knew you were a focal point, too."

"Ignore her," said Tidy. "She's just desperate for attention." He turned to Gayle. "Are you sure about this, Lady? Focal points are usually preceded by signs and portents, and we've seen nothing."

"The Waking Beauty vouches for him," said Gayle. "And that's good enough for me, though I'd never tell her so."

The Mice muttered respectfully at the mention of the Waking Beauty's name and looked thoughtfully at Toby—even Sweetie.

"We know Carys Galloway," said Bossy. "She's one of the reasons we came to settle here in Bradford-on-Avon. That and the ley lines. And the fact that this little town is practically Spook Central for the whole country. There's more weird shit goes down here than in any number of cities."

"Got that right," said Bossy. "We lived in London for a while, in happier times. Had a nice place down in the old docklands, an abandoned warehouse right by the river. We were still human as often as Mice in those days, so we got out and about in the big city, following our noses and crashing every party that was going. Now you'd think that London would be one of the main supernatural centers in England, and mostly you'd be right. London is an old city, older than you'd think. It was already a seat of power when the Romans occupied it and called it Londinium. There are many special people and places in and around and under London, most of them pretty damned dangerous."

"Oh, yes," said Dreamy. "There's lots to be found under the streets of London, apart from the Underground."

"The Soul-trading Center of Cheapside," said Sweetie. "The Temple of Lamentations, the Running Tigers of Old Bond Street."

"But it all went bad, over the years," said Bossy. "The real movers and shakers moved out long ago, looking for fresh pastures and less corrupt sources of power. Too much bad magic polluting the path of the Thames, and filling the aether with black static."

"This town is older than any city, but somehow it's still largely uncorrupted, for all the Hob's attempts to dominate it," said Tidy. "Powers and Dominations have always been drawn here, from all the many worlds. And not just because of the ley lines. This is a place where things happen. Important, interesting things."

"So we came here because we wanted to see them," said Sweetie.

Toby frowned. There was a question he felt he had to ask. "You said you can become people again, when you have to deal with the real world. Don't you find you miss being human?"

The Mice all laughed quietly, and Tidy looked at him almost pityingly. "Do you miss being a child? We have moved on, not back."

"The only thing we miss is the sixties," said Dreamy. "Even the real world seemed magical then. The sixties was the last time people dreamed they were awake."

Toby looked at Gayle. "Am I supposed to understand that?"

"Not yet," said Gayle. "You've got a lot of waking up to do yourself yet." She turned back to the Mice. "Talk to me, honored friends, of Hob's return and of his connection with Angel. I have been asleep myself, for a long time, and I have missed much."

"Hob," said Dreamy, in a faraway voice. "Was it he who brought the plague to Bradford-on-Avon, in 1752?"

"The Serpent's Son has sunk himself in Blackacre," said Tidy.

"Bad place," said Bossy, his tail lashing restlessly. "Dead a long time, but now enlivened by the Hob's presence."

"He must be very lonely," said Sweetie. "He is the only one of his kind. Even one such as Angel could never really hope to understand him."

"He is evil," Bossy said flatly. "He is death and destruction and the passing of all good things."

"But what choice has he ever had?" said Sweetie. "He is what he was made to be. His father's weapon and instrument in the worlds of men. Abandoned by his violated mother, forever dominated by his absent father. It's easy to love the lovable. To love one's enemy is harder."

"Hob wouldn't know love if you injected him with it," said Tidy. "He is a predator, and everyone else is prey."

"But now he has Angel," Sweetie said stubbornly. "Another outcast, thrust into a world that can never understand her. Perhaps they will be good for each other."

"You always were a helpless romantic, even when we were all still human," said Bossy crushingly. "All those two have in common is that they're both monsters." He looked at Toby. "As Mice, we're linked more closely than most to the natural world. We *feel* changes, in Veritie and in Mysterie. With Hob and Angel in residence, Blackacre has become a stain upon nature. An open sore, oozing corruption . . ."

"The point," Tidy said heavily, "is that ever since Hob thrust Blackacre out of Veritie and into Mysterie, nothing natural can get anywhere near it, in either world. Birds and beasts and insects all avoid the area. To cross into that dark territory now is to imperil your soul. Hob has put his stamp on the burned land."

"There are dead men in the dead woods," said Dreamy. "Raised up by the Hob's power. Death surrounds him, drawn to him. People died at his hand, at the railway station last night. I saw them die in my dreams, heard them cry for help that never came. So sad."

Gayle frowned. "The Reality Express. I heard it running last night."

"The thunder godling was there, too," said Dreamy. "You should talk with him. It is his business to find the answers to questions."

"Excuse me," said Toby, just a little desperately. "But am I ever going to understand any of this?"

"If you keep your mouth shut and your ears open, possibly," said Gayle. "They're talking about Jimmy Thunder. He's the town's only private eye."

"He saw the people murdered," said Dreamy. "And afterwards, he fought with Angel."

"And survived?" said Gayle, raising an eyebrow. "I'm impressed."

"Does this have something to do with the destroyed railway station this morning?" said Toby, suddenly making a connection.

"You see?" said Gayle. "You can keep up, if you try." She looked round at the Mice. "You understand the way the world turns. Better than I do, at the moment. What can you tell me about the changing weather patterns?"

All the Mice stirred unhappily, glancing at each other. "But you're . . . ," said Tidy finally.

"I've been real for a long time," said Gayle. "By my own choice. Now I'm out of touch with my . . . full potential. Tell me what you know."

"The Serpent is stirring. The Sun is waking up," Dreamy said flatly. "Veritie and Mysterie are closer than they have been for many centuries. This can't be a coincidence."

"You should lose the human," Bossy said brusquely. "Focal point or not. There are others who can lead and advise him. If you care for him at all, distance yourself from him. If you are to become your true self again, Lady Gayle, you cannot afford to be distracted by merely human concerns. Let him find his own path. You do him no kindness by taking him where you must go. The human mind is limited, and fragile. Mortal must not love immortal, but even more important—"

"No!" Dreamy said suddenly. Her voice rose, fey and powerful, her eyes blazing. "I have dreamed them together, in a time not far from now. In that time of great need, he will stand between all that lives and great danger. I saw him stand alone, wrapped in light, with the weight of worlds upon his shoulders."

There was a long pause, as Dreamy slowly subsided, her gaze turned inward. Tidy looked apologetically at Toby.

"I wouldn't take that too seriously, if I were you. Dreamy does see a lot of things in dreams, but her accuracy rate isn't all that impressive."

*"Beast!"* Dreamy threw herself on Tidy and the two of them rolled back and forth on the straw, wrestling each other furiously. The other two Mice sighed wearily and moved in to separate them. Gayle gestured to Toby that it was time for them to leave.

They went to see Jimmy Thunder, the godling.

Once again Gayle led the way through Bradford-on-Avon, pointing out things of historical interest to an increasingly fascinated Toby. He was a Bradfordian born and bred, had lived most of his life in the small country town, and still Gayle knew all kinds of things that he'd never even suspected. And always there was something in the casual way she said things, in the little details she let drop, that made him more and more sure that these weren't things she'd learned in books, in libraries. She was telling him things she knew because she'd seen them.

She knew, for example, that St. Margaret's Street was named after an old leper hospice from medieval times, the hospice of the Blessed Saint Margaret. Gayle remembered the place vividly, and they were not happy memories.

"It was just a place where they put people to die. No doctors, no nurses, no help. The doors were kept locked, and the windows were nailed shut. Food and water were pushed in through a slot, when anyone remembered. Leprosy was considered God's punishment. So there were no comforts, no treatment, no hope of recovery or escape. Just a prison for the dying, hidden away so people wouldn't have to see them suffer. Sometimes a healthy wife or husband or child would volunteer to go into the hospice with a loved one, to look after them. Once in, they were never allowed to leave. Leprosy was thought to be God's will, so compassion was in short supply. Some things never change."

Toby looked around at the ordinary houses lining an ordinary street, and tried to see it as Gayle saw it, but wasn't at all surprised when he couldn't. His viewpoint, his understanding, was too small, too limited. Too human.

*Mortal must not love immortal. . . .*

They came at last to Jimmy Thunder's house. Toby was a little surprised when they stopped in front of what appeared to be just another in a long line of characterless semi-detacheds; traditional commuter houses thrown up in lots to meet the needs of newcomers, as Bradford-on-Avon slowly became a dormitory town for the surrounding county. Gayle watched, smiling, as Toby studied the supposed godling's house with growing perplexity. The front lawn had been replaced by gravel, though here and there tufts of grass and weeds were sprouting defiantly through. A single plaster gnome with peeling paint was fishing despondently in a small, murky-looking pond. Toby looked challengingly at Gayle.

"You're telling me a god lives here?"

"A very minor god, but yes. Descended from the Old Norse pantheon, though divorced from the original power by more generations than the human mind can comfortably cope with. He's a good sort, in his own way. Don't try to talk religion with him. He can become very short-tempered on the subject, and then you have to start ducking lightning bolts."

"Am I allowed to mention that his place looks like a dump?" said Toby. "I mean, I'm a man living alone, I understand that a certain amount of appalling mess is expected of us, but this . . . Mess like this doesn't just happen. It has to be cultivated."

"You should mention it to him," said Gayle. "But I think I'll stand well back while you do it. Come on. Let's see if he's at home."

She crunched across the gravel in a straight line, ignoring the path, and Toby followed reluctantly after her. He wasn't sure he was ready to meet a godling. He certainly wasn't going to kneel to anyone. Or put money in a collection plate. Gayle stopped before a per-

fectly ordinary-looking front door, and it took a moment for Toby
to realize that the small businesslike brass plaque said GOD FOR HIRE.
REALLY. There was, however, no bell or knocker. Gayle sniffed and
glared at the closed door.

"All right; let's have no nonsense. You know very well who I am.
Open up right now, or I'll have your poltergeist's licence revoked."

*Don't want to!* snapped a voice in Toby's mind and he jumped despite himself. The voice was sharp and more than a little sulky, but
in no way human. It was also utterly silent, outside his head, and
presumably Gayle's. *His Divinity was out all last night, and I don't
want him disturbed,* the voice continued. *He needs his rest. Galli-
vanting about at all hours, and never making the time for a decent
meal. He'll never make two hundred at this rate. I've just got him off to
sleep, and I won't have you bothering him. Come back later. Or not at
all; see if I care.*

"I really don't have the patience for this," said Gayle. "Open up
right now, or I'll do something really distressing to your hinges."

*Shan't! Bully!*

"You do know who I am, don't you?" said Gayle dangerously.

*Don't care. Someone's got to look out for Jimmy's interests. People are
always bothering him. And rarely for any good reason. Be as important
and snotty as you want. I can keep you waiting here forever, if I choose
to.*

"Gayle, might I suggest you try the magic word?" Toby said quietly.

Gayle turned an icy glare on him. "What do you know about
magic, or Words of Power?"

"Watch and learn," said Toby. He took a step closer to the door
and smiled winningly. "Please let us in. It really is very important, to
Mr. Thunder as well as to us. He could be in danger."

*Well, why didn't you just say so?* The door swung open before
them. *So nice to hear a little common courtesy. Everyone thinks they can
push me around, just because I'm a door.*

"You see?" Toby said to Gayle, careful not to sound even a little
smug. "All you need is the magic word."

"Don't look so self-satisfied, Toby. It doesn't suit you. But you're right, of course. This is why I prefer to stay real. It's too easy here to forget the things which really matter when everyone else insists on worshiping you. Thank you, door."

*You're welcome! I'll tell him you're here. But don't blame me if he's in a really crabby mood.*

Gayle and Toby stepped through the doorway and once again Toby was lost for words. The hall stretched away in front of him for what seemed like miles. Floor, walls, and ceiling were all fashioned from varying kinds of wood, from the polished dark red of the floor to the great golden-brown walls covered in carved runes and sigils, to the high, raftered ceiling overhead. Toby felt as if he were standing in one of the old Viking long ships. He jumped as the door slammed shut behind him and looked at Gayle, who, as always, was taking it all in her stride.

"You want to explain this?" Toby said hopefully.

"This is a god's place," said Gayle, smiling. "A very minor god, as such things go, but still . . . This is his territory, and here time and space obey his will. Or to put it another way, space expands to fit his ego. It's one of the perks of the job. Semi-sentient simulacra for servants is another."

"What do you mean, *semi*-sentient?" said a long mirror on the wall beside them. "I'll match my IQ against the population average any day of the week, and spot you ten points if they work in television. And ten shekels to an obol I can outthink any of those damned computers Veritie is so proud of. I've been serving thunder gods for over twelve centuries now, and I've never once cracked or forgotten a message. Now, who are you, what do you want, and, most important, do you have an appointment?"

The fact that the mirror talked didn't upset Toby as much as the fact that it was using his reflection to do it. The effect was frankly unnerving.

"You know very well who we are and what we want," said Gayle. "Don't tell me you and the door have any secrets. But just for you,

Toby; no, we don't have an appointment, but *please* may we see Jimmy anyway? It is a matter of some urgency."

"Not a chance in Niffleheim," said the mirror flatly. "You might be able to bluff the poor door, but you won't get past me that easily. If I let through everyone who thought their case was important, Jimmy would never get a moment's peace. You'll have to make an appointment to see him, just like everyone else. I have an afternoon free, about three months from now. How would that suit you?"

Gayle looked at Toby. "Know any other magic words? Preferably ones with an element of threat and imminent mayhem to them?"

Toby thought for a moment, and then grinned and produced a thoroughly filthy crumpled gray handkerchief from his trouser pocket. He held it up so the mirror could get a good look at it. His reflection studied the appalling handkerchief with fascinated eyes as things fell out of it.

"That is the ugliest thing I've ever seen that wasn't actually under a curse. Why are you showing it to me?"

"I want you to study it."

"I can hardly take my eyes off it. The last time I saw anything that filthy Hercules had been using it to clean out stables. Tell me it's a clue, or a piece of evidence. I'd hate to think you kept it about your person by choice."

"This gray handkerchief was a white handkerchief when I first put it in my pocket," said Toby, not without a certain amount of pride. "It has been in my pocket for so long that whole colonies of bacteria have grown on it, evolved into sentience, created space travel and left my pocket to go in search of other trouser worlds. This hanky is now so filthy it could make the ebola virus vomit. And unless you agree to call Mr. Thunder *right now,* I am going to use this hanky to clean your surface. Give it a good rub. *All over.*"

*"You wouldn't dare!"*

Toby brought the hanky close to the mirror, which actually shuddered in its silver frame. "Call him," said Toby, in a deadly serious voice.

"Never! *Never never never!* I am his security, sworn to protect him . . ."

Toby rubbed his hanky all over the mirror's surface, putting plenty of elbow grease into it. Streaky marks appeared.

"All right, all right!" sobbed his reflection in the mirror. "*Animal!* I'll call him, I'll call him!" Toby stepped back, his handkerchief still ostentatiously at the ready. The mirror made loud hacking and spitting noises, and then Toby's reflection glared venomously at him as it raised its voice in a desperate bellow. "Mr. Thunder! Mr. Thunder! *They're bullying me again!*"

Gayle studied Toby approvingly. "That is a really vicious streak you have there. You'll go far in Mysterie with an attitude like that. Good to see you're learning. Nice use of lateral thinking. You're . . . you're not actually going to put that back in your pocket, are you?"

"Why?" said Toby innocently. "Do you want to borrow it?"

Gayle snorted, and actually backed away.

Footsteps sounded, from far away. Steady, purposeful footsteps, growing gradually nearer. Toby's reflection looked at him spitefully. "See! He'll be here soon, and then he'll make you pay for persecuting me. I wouldn't want to be in your shoes, waking him up so soon after he's gone to bed. I just hope he hasn't caught a chill. Out all hours of the night, not enough sleep, and never time for a proper breakfast; it's no wonder he's a martyr to the sniffles. And I hate nursing him when he's ill. All he does is wrap himself in a blanket in a chair by the fire, and yell endlessly for fresh cups of beef tea and more chocolate Hobnobs."

"Talk a lot for a mirror, don't you?" said Toby.

"You needn't look so smug, Mr. *I've-got-a-hanky-and-I'm-not-afraid-to-use-it*! I can play dirty, too, you know. Here, take a good look at what you're going to look like in fifty years' time!"

Toby's reflection in the mirror leaned suddenly forward, grinning maliciously. The smile stretched unnaturally as wrinkles spread across his face in quick spurts, like ice cracking on the surface of a pond. His cheekbones rose sharply as his face sank back onto his skull like an ill-fitting mask and his eyes peered darkly from the sunken caverns of their sockets. His hair receded rapidly, till nothing was left but bare mottled skin and a few white strands. His whole posture changed, becoming stooped and tired and thin. But for all the changes, it still looked like him.

The reflection still wore Toby's present clothes, making the change even more disturbing. Toby wouldn't let himself look away. He tried hard to accept the aged image dispassionately, but it felt as though someone had hit him in the heart. Intellectually, he'd always known that how he looked would change as he grew old, but to be faced with such grim evidence of his own mortality and frailty, so bluntly and suddenly, took his breath away. The old, shrunken, broken-looking man before him was a blow to his spirit as well as his pride. No one likes to admit that in the end we all die by inches, gradually losing all the defining visual characteristics that make us *us*. Toby fought to keep his face calm, and tried hard to come up with something positive, if only to spite the mirror.

"Ah, well," he said finally. "At least I'll have lived to reach eighty-three. The way everyone else has been talking, I was beginning to wonder if I'd make it through the afternoon."

"No guarantees!" snapped the reflection in the mirror, reverting instantly to its normal appearance. "That was just a maybe. Jimmy! Jimmy! They're ganging up on me!" The heavy footsteps drew still nearer, but clearly had some way to go. The mirror sighed, and pouted with Toby's face. "Look, this could take some time. The Thunder residence is a lot bigger than it needs to be, but then that's gods for you. The master bedroom's practically in another time zone. I think you'd better both go through into the parlor and wait there until he reaches you. It's the second door on the left. And don't touch anything! Half the stuff in there's booby-trapped, and the rest bites. Who'd be a secretary? The hours are murder and the pay sucks. I should have been an oracle, like Mother wanted . . ."

The mirror was still muttering darkly to itself about unionizing when Gayle and Toby located the second door on the left and let themselves into the parlor with a certain amount of relief: only to discover another long mirror on the wall, talking to itself in the same annoyed voice, but this time using Gayle's reflection. In the interests of self-defense, Toby decided to take a careful look at the contents of the room. The parlor was really quite impressive, as thunder gods' parlors went. The room was easily the size of a banqueting hall, with bare wooden floorboards polished to within an inch of their life, under pelts and furs from a variety of large animals, and solid stone walls covered with great metal shields and many displays of crossed weapons. The swords were all over six feet long, and the great axes looked far too heavy for mortal man to lift without the help of a very supportive truss. The ceiling was so high Toby had to crane his head all the way back to look up at it. Bats of a disturbing size hung upside down from the arching wooden rafters, their eyes shining redly.

Toby looked across at Gayle, but she was still taking it all in her stride. In fact, she had her arms tightly crossed and was tapping her foot impatiently with an expression that suggested, thunder god or not, Jimmy Thunder had better have a pretty damned good reason for keeping her waiting. Toby decided he'd had enough of being impressed for one day and wandered over to study a row of glass display cases in the hope of finding something tacky he could sneer at. The cases held a series of unusual exhibits, each complete with a neatly printed card that provided a name, but no other useful information. Toby moved slowly past THE MIRROR OF THE SEA, THOR'S GAUNTLETS and SURTUR'S TOOTH, and was no wiser for the experience.

The first item was a remarkably ordinary-looking, and blessedly silent, hand mirror in a battered steel frame. It could have been any age, from any period, and there was nothing obviously of the sea about it, until Toby leaned closer for a better look and thought he heard, faintly and far away, the sound of whales singing in the deep. The sounds were gone almost as soon as he identified them, and didn't return, no matter how closely he pressed his ear against the glass case. He glanced round to see if Gayle had heard anything, but she was still busy being impatient. Toby straightened up and moved on.

Thor's Gauntlets were just a pair of ratty old leather gloves, studded with sigils and runes of black iron, all but falling apart despite much patching and mending. And Surtur's Tooth . . . was just a bloody big tooth, about ten inches long, culminating in a jagged broken end, as though it had been ripped right out of the jaw of something sufficiently big that Toby decided he didn't want to think about it.

"Curios and artifacts from some of my old cases," said a deep, commanding voice, and Toby looked round sharply to see Jimmy Thunder standing in the doorway of the parlor. Or, to be more accurate, filling it. The huge red-headed warrior figure was immediately impressive, even though he was wearing a flannel dressing gown and pale pink bunny slippers. Just standing there, entirely at ease, the thunder godling was thoroughly intimidating. His sheer bulk made Toby feel puny by comparison. He just knew he could work out with weights all his life and still never end up with a build like that. He'd never seen so many muscles in one place, on one person.

Jimmy smiled easily and strode forward to clasp Toby's hand in a grip that was nicely calculated to be firm without threatening, though the godling's huge hand all but swallowed Toby's. Toby tried for a polite, unimpressed smile, but it didn't feel particularly successful. Certainly Jimmy wasted no time in moving quickly on to clasp Gayle in a huge hug, lifting her right off the floor and swinging her round, feet clearing the ground. She laughed happily and tugged playfully at his long red beard. He grinned, set her down again, and made to hold her buttocks in his hands before she pushed him firmly away.

"Big old bear," she said fondly. "Good to see you again."

"Always good to see you," said Jimmy, his voice so deep now it was practically rumbling in his chest. "You spend far too much time being real, you know. It can't be good for you. You need to get out more, like me, and savor the best of both worlds. You weren't always so . . . retiring." He looked across at Toby, grinning. "You know the two of us used to be an item?"

"She hadn't actually got around to telling me that," said Toby. "But yes, I'd sort of guessed. So . . . you're a godling?"

"Damn right," said Jimmy Thunder cheerfully. He sat on a handy wooden bench and pulled Gayle down beside him. She hit him playfully on the shoulder, but he didn't even feel it. Toby sat down on another bench facing them. Jimmy slipped an arm round Gayle's waist and Toby tried not to seethe too obviously.

"Long, long ago, back in the mists of time, when Veritie and Mysterie weren't quite as separate as they are now, my ancestor was the god Thor," Jimmy said easily. "Hard to tell exactly how long ago, but still—Thor. Norse god of storms and lightning, Odin's son, big hammer, the whole bit. And somewhere along the line he paid a visit to Veritie, had his way with a willing Norse lass, as gods were prone to do in those days, and got her with child. Many, many generations later, I came along, my divine inheritance greatly diluted by so much mortal blood. Essentially, I'm powerful, long-lived, but not actually all that special. Especially in a town like this. All I really inherited from my distant progenitor was a hammer that can't find its way home, more red hair than I know what to do with, and the ability to know when it's going to rain. There was a horse with eight legs, but it ran away. Never liked me anyway. Ugly great thing." He sighed heavily, suddenly morose. "Not much of a god really, as gods go. No powers, no miracles, can't even change water into mead. Family history's a bloody dirge, all gloomy Eddas and prophecies of getting our arse kicked at Ragnarok. Why couldn't I have been descended from one of the Greek gods? Those guys knew how to have fun."

"Don't you put yourself down like that!" said the mirror sharply. "There are always plenty of people only too willing to do that for you. You have a famous and vitally ethnic heritage, and more muscles than a whelk farm. That's the trouble with you Norse gods; always prone to mood swings. Now introduce me properly to your guests or I'll start singing opera again. In German. With all the vibratos."

"The loud and obnoxious thing hanging on my wall," said

Jimmy, smiling in spite of himself, "is Scilla. Apparently once a Rhine Maiden (though the second part was often loudly disputed), whose spirit ended up inhabiting a mirror as a result of cheating at cards with a rather bad-tempered dwarf. In her own annoying way, she's probably more immortal than I am. My dad wished her on me in his will, and I still haven't forgiven him. She currently works as my secretary, in charge of making appointments, overseeing the paperwork, billing clients and keeping track of ongoing cases." Jimmy paused for breath. "She also nags me about my weight, the length of my hair, and my unmarried state. She seems to think she's my mother, and that I couldn't manage my life without her."

"Well, you couldn't," said the mirror. "Some days I'm lucky if he's wearing the same color socks. And if I didn't constantly remind him about his weight, he'd pork out so fast it would make your head swim. You should see his waistline during the winter months. Some years I wouldn't be surprised if he started hibernating. And someone's got to think about the next generation of thunder godlings! I don't see why you can't meet a nice Norse goddess and settle down . . ."

Jimmy looked apologetically at Gayle and Toby. "Sorry about this, but she'll go on forever if I don't get us out of here." He snapped his fingers sharply, and the world dropped out from under Toby. The parlor disappeared, swallowed up in a darkness that rushed in from every direction at once, and Toby grabbed frantically for something to hold on to as he plummeted through nothing at all. And then the light returned, the sensation of falling was abruptly gone, and Toby was sitting in a cheap plastic deck chair, clutching at his chest with both hands to try to stop his heart from palpitating. Jimmy and Gayle were sitting opposite him, also in deck chairs. Jimmy looked rather smug, for the second or two before Gayle slapped him hard about the head.

"Dammit, Jimmy! Give us some warning before you do that. You know teleporting screws up my inner ear."

"Sorry," said Jimmy, not all that convincingly. "But some days that mirror gets on my tits something fierce. I'd get rid of her, if only she wasn't so damned efficient. She pretty much runs the business these days, and don't think she doesn't know it. I've never been very good at organizational skills. Gods aren't, mostly."

Toby took in his new surroundings. The three of them were now sitting in a completely different room. Small, filthy, and cluttered, it looked very much like a garage. Lit by old-fashioned hanging oil lanterns, there were work areas, spare parts, tool benches, and any amount of tools scattered around (on the walls, the floor, the benches, everywhere), and the center space was dominated by a huge, partially dismantled motorbike of some vintage. The whole place smelled of oil and petrol and less pleasant odors. Toby gave Jimmy a hard look.

"Excuse me? How the hell did we get here?"

The thunder godling shrugged easily. "This may not be Valhalla exactly, but it is my place; so space here does what I tell it to. If I say we're in a different room, then we are. I often come here, when I need to be alone, to do some important thinking. I find working on mechanical problems very soothing. Whatever the problem is, there's always a straightforward answer, if only you can find it. Probably God felt the same way when he was creating the universe."

Toby had to raise an eyebrow at that. "You believe in God?"

"Of course," said Jimmy. "I may be a godling, but I know my place in the scheme of things. Do you like the bike?"

Toby looked it over. Even partially dismantled it was still a huge beast of a machine, all gleaming black and silver. The exposed engine was a lot bigger than some car engines Toby had seen. He didn't even want to think about how much the damned thing must weigh; certainly he couldn't have shifted it on his own. Even standing still, the bike reeked of power and speed. Toby didn't know much about motorbikes, except that they had a wheel at each end and lived for the chance to kill you in horrible and messily disfiguring accidents, but even he was impressed by this monster of a machine. He looked it over in what he hoped was an intelligent way and tried to think of something relevant to say.

"Get a lot of miles to the gallon, do you?"

Jimmy kindly ignored that and ran one hand lovingly over the shiny black frame. "This is a 1936 Brough Superior, the luxury edition. Goes like the wind . . . inhabited by the spirit of a Valkyrie. You should see the speeds she can touch at two hundred feet . . . I once buzzed Concorde out over the Atlantic, but they were too embarrassed to report it. Unfortunately, it's getting hard to conjure up the parts these days." He grinned suddenly at Gayle. "I suppose I should apologize about the mess, but hell, I'm a man who lives alone. It's expected of me."

"I knew there was a good reason why I always insisted on your place rather than mine," said Gayle.

Jimmy looked at Toby. "Is this your latest, Gayle? He's a bit smaller than you usually like them."

"Hey!" said Toby, not at all sure how to take that. He considered saying *size isn't everything,* but thought he'd better not.

"He's a focal point," said Gayle, not actually answering the question.

"Oh, bloody hell," said Jimmy, slumping back in his deck chair and looking disgustedly at Toby. "We've only just got over the last one. Focal points are more trouble than an earthquake and a volcano put together, and twice as destructive. My life's complicated enough as it is. . . . Couldn't we just kill him quietly and hide the body?"

"Don't think I haven't considered it," said Gayle. "Unfortunately, the Waking Beauty says we need him. He just might be Humanity's Champion."

"I wonder if it's too late to go into hiding now and not come out till it's all over?" Jimmy said plaintively. "I may be a godling, but there are limits to what I should have to put up with. I mean, Hob and Angel I could cope with, probably, but focal points are so . . . arbitrary. I think the Norns invented them just to mess with our heads."

"I am getting really tired of this reaction," said Toby, trying hard for dignity. "I didn't choose to be a focal point. . . ."

"Yes, you did," said Gayle. "You chose to follow me through the doorway. So this is all your fault." She looked back at Jimmy. "You seeing anyone these days? I did hear you had some lovesick mortal trailing after you again. . . ."

Jimmy shrugged easily. "You know how it is with mortals; they're so easily impressed. And they get so upset, just because you don't call them for a few years. I'm currently in between, at the moment. Women have always tended to drift into my life; usually when it's most inconvenient. Mortals are like candy: sweet, but of the moment."

"What happened to the last one?" said Toby.

"Something ate her. It's all right, though, I avenged her."

"I'm sure that made all the difference," said Toby.

"You want some mead?" Jimmy said suddenly, all smiles again. "The new batch is almost ready. I make it myself. Real kick-arse stuff. Cleans out your tubes like you wouldn't believe."

*"No,"* said Gayle firmly. "Don't you touch it, Toby. That stuff he makes isn't alcohol, it's sudden death in liquid form. Jimmy's system only handles it because he's immortal and he can outlive the side effects."

Jimmy sniffed, pouted, and looked disparagingly at Toby again. "Are you sure he's important? He doesn't look like he's got much in him. Whatever Hob and Angel are up to, I can handle it."

"Like you handled the Reality Express situation last night?" Gayle said sweetly.

"Ah," said Jimmy. "You heard about that."

"Hob and Angel got away, a whole trainload of refugees got barbecued, and the railway station was trashed? Of course I heard! I should think the whole town's heard by now! Now make nice with Toby. I have a feeling we're all going to have to work together on this case."

Jimmy shook his head unhappily. "A focal point . . . The town's still recovering from the last one, and that was a century ago. Please let me kill him, Gayle. I'll be ever so humane about it."

"Hey!" said Toby.

"Toby is under my protection," Gayle said firmly.

"All right, all right!" Jimmy sighed heavily. "You and your damn strays . . ."

"How come everyone keeps talking about me like I'm not here?" said Toby loudly.

"Wishful thinking," said Jimmy. He'd gone back to pouting again.

"Play nice, boys," said Gayle. "And try to concentrate on the matter at hand. If Carys is right, and I hate to admit it, but she usually is, the whole town's in danger. Let's start with you, Jimmy. Tell us exactly what happened with the Reality Express last night."

Jimmy brightened up at that, and launched into his tale with some enthusiasm. It was reasonably accurate, once you discounted the rather obvious boasting and exaggerations. Jimmy wasn't exactly lying or stretching the truth; he just naturally saw himself in larger-than-life terms, part of the territory when you're a godling. Toby studied him thoughtfully as he talked, emphasizing things with wide sweeping gestures. It was hard to dislike Jimmy; he was so open about who and what he was, almost childlike, for all his years. In many ways the thunder god was the kind of action hero Toby had always secretly wanted to be: all muscle and bravado and straight-forward decisiveness. If only he had a few brains to go with it . . . As the story unfolded, Toby began to frown. Even allowing for Jimmy's self-centered rendition, Toby couldn't help feeling that there was something missing from the story, that they were all missing something important. When Jimmy finally wound down, somewhat glossing over the unfortunate events at the end, Toby leaned forward in his chair.

"Why did the Waking Beauty want you to investigate the Reality Express yesterday evening? She must have known it was running before this, and if she's as good as everyone seems to think she is, she should have known about Hob and Angel's involvement long ago."

"Maybe she just wanted confirmation," said Gayle.

"Maybe." Toby thought some more, frowning hard. "Now that Hob has murdered his passengers, the odds are the Reality Express won't be running again for some time to come. Did Carys somehow know this would be your last chance to see it in action? Did she know that involving you would inevitably put an end to it?"

Gayle nodded slowly. "That sounds like Carys. She'd use anyone to further her schemes."

"Even you and me?" said Toby.

"Good point," said Gayle.

"All right, how about this?" said Toby. "Follow the logic through. Given that Hob is no longer able to gain power, or whatever else he needs, from Reality Express refugees, where is he going to get it from now? What or who will he turn to? Who's most at risk?" Toby shook his head. "Sorry, Gayle, but I need you to explain the magic situation here more thoroughly if I'm going to make sense of this."

"Very well," said Gayle. "One more time, in words of one syllable or possibly less, especially for the hard of thinking. In Mysterie, everyone is defined by *what* they are. Their role dictates the shape their lives must follow. People can have great power and abilities, but severe restrictions are placed on how they can use them. Only in the real world, in Veritie, are people free to grow, evolve, and even transcend themselves. Veritie is thus the quieter, subtler world, with the greatest prospects for each individual. Refugees flee Mysterie for Veritie on the underground railway because only in the real world can they choose who and what they will be.

"Take Jimmy here, for example. He's a thunder god because all his ancestors were. He's managed to adapt his lifestyle a little, by becoming a God For Hire, but that's only because there's so much mortal, real, blood in his past. He still has to follow the role laid out for him at birth, to be a warrior."

"To be fair," said Jimmy. "I am rather good at it. Usually."

"The Mice said a lot of people had been coming to Veritie on the Reality Express," said Gayle, frowning now herself. "Why now? What did they know, or think they knew, that made it so important and so urgent for them to leave Mysterie?"

"Maybe something bad is coming to Mysterie," said Toby. "Some new threat . . ."

"Maybe," said Gayle. "Jimmy, you're the god of stormy weather. Have you noticed the strange weather patterns recently?"

"Of course. Are you saying you don't know what's behind them?"

"I've been . . . out of touch for a while," Gayle said defensively. "I've buried myself in reality for so long, even my instincts have gone to sleep. But I'm waking up fast."

"You need to talk with Luna," Jimmy said firmly. "She can always be relied on to have an overview of the situation. Of course, there's no guarantee it'll be a useful overview. . . ."

"Who's Luna?" said Toby.

"My sister," said Gayle, grimacing. "We don't get on. Not least because she's as crazy as a loon. Sweet, but crazy. But Jimmy's right. Luna sees things other people don't. Often strange and disturbing things. The trick is figuring out which if any of them mean anything."

She got to her feet suddenly, and Toby scrambled to his as fast as he could. It's not easy getting up out of a deck chair when you're caught by surprise. Jimmy took his time getting up, just to remind them that this was his place, after all, and then fixed Gayle with a stern gaze.

"You're getting very involved with this, Gayle. Does this mean you're coming back? All the way back?"

"I haven't decided," said Gayle. "You of all people should understand how desperately I need to stay real; to be free of the demands that Mysterie would seek to put on me."

"Sure." Jimmy hesitated for a moment. "Luna sees things that other people miss. Do you think you could ask her if she knows of any Norse goddesses? Anywhere?"

"I'll ask her," Gayle said kindly. "But as far as I know, you're the last of your kind."

"Ah. I was afraid of that. Every godly line comes to an end, eventually. Only the mortals go on forever." He looked at Toby. "Hey, you want to know what drives her absolutely wild in bed?"

"Well . . ."

"You keep your mouth shut, Jimmy Thunder," said Gayle. "And don't take on any new cases. I may have need of your services yet."

"Wonderful," said Jimmy. "Another damned freebie."

Gayle and Toby walked through the Shambles, in the middle of town, a narrow lane between two rows of buildings whose construction went back to the seventeenth century and earlier, though the Shambles itself was a hell of a lot older. There were a lot of people about, doing their weekend shopping or just standing around chatting, enjoying the summer day. All of them stopped to bow their heads to Gayle as she passed. Some even knelt. Gayle smiled graciously, but kept going, making it clear she didn't want to talk to anyone. No one bowed to Toby, though a few of the older inhabitants crossed themselves or made warding signs against evil.

"Do you know why this place is called the Shambles?" Gayle said conversationally.

"No. But I have a strong feeling you're about to tell me."

"Someone's at home to Mr. Grumpy."

"Well . . . is there anything you don't know?"

"Oh, you'd be surprised. The Shambles takes its name from the old Anglo-Saxon word *scamul,* a small bench from which goods were sold at market. People have been coming to this place to shop for over a thousand years. And I remember them. I was here then, and before that. I saw you glaring at Jimmy, being jealous. Don't. For all his centuries, he's still little more than a child, compared to me. And though I may have taken some comfort from his company, in times past, he can no more have a claim on my heart than you. You are all passing things, and I am not. Be told, Toby: there can never be anything between us. Concentrate your mind on more important matters. Look up, at the roof to your right."

Toby looked up and there was Angel, perched on a gabled roof like a brooding gargoyle contemplating the world and spitting on it. Toby knew immediately who she was, who she had to be. Gayle had described her very specifically. A sudden chill went through him, as though a shadow had fallen over him. All he had to do was look at Angel to know she wasn't human, and was never going to be. There was something of the bird of prey about her, crouching on her gable, her pointed chin resting on one pale fist, viewing the world below through unblinking crimson eyes, as though everyone she saw had but one function, or purpose, or reason for being: to be prey for her. Down in the street, in the Shambles, everyone else was carefully avoiding looking up, as though afraid of drawing Angel's attention to them.

"She must find it all very confusing," murmured Gayle.

"Find all what?" said Toby, wrenching his eyes away from the disturbing figure on the roof. His heart was beating fast, as though he'd just narrowly avoided some deadly peril.

"Life. Existence. She is from the immaterial, after all. As far beyond us as we are from chalk drawings on the ground."

"Then . . . how did Hob persuade her to work with him?" said Toby. "What could he possibly offer her, or promise her, in return?"

"He's keeping her mind occupied, like a child with a new toy. So she doesn't have to think about how far she's fallen. About how small and limited she's become. Essentially, Hob and all his plans are just a distraction to her, which is perhaps a good thing. She's dangerous enough now. If she were to lose her focus, give in to rage and loss and the horror of what's been done to her . . .

"Keeping her under control must be a constant delicate balancing act for Hob. For all his power, and he is very powerful, he's still part of the material worlds. She's one of the few beings he can't threaten or coerce, and I'm sure I don't know what he could have promised her, or bribed her with. Perhaps it's enough that he keeps her busy . . . and amuses her."

"The words *divide and conquer* come to mind," said Toby. "Separate them, play up their differences, and their partnership might just fall apart. Or if there really is something she wants, maybe we could offer to get it for her instead."

"Probably," said Gayle. "I like the way you think, Toby. Though I hate to think what kind of things a descended angel might develop

a taste for. Look at her. What's she doing up there? What's she looking at? What is she seeing, feeling?"

Toby shuddered, despite himself. "Could anyone stop her, if she
got out of control? Could you?"

"Good question. She's material now. Mortal. Theoretically, she
can be hurt, even killed. But in practice . . . she burns with life, like
a furnace. We have no way of knowing what materials went into her
making, or how much of her old nature persists in this new form.
Whatever she is now . . . she'll take a hell of a lot of stopping."

They walked on, through the Shambles and out the other side,
and neither of them looked back at Angel again. Toby mulled over
what he'd heard. No matter how many questions he asked, the answers just seemed to lead to more questions.

"So . . . ," he said finally. "Angel came from the immaterial
realms. What are they, exactly? I mean, if she really was an angel,
originally . . . where do God and the Devil, or whatever, fit into Veritie and Mysterie?"

"There are many worlds," Gayle said patiently, "some so far away
we can't even see them from where we are. Think of a pyramid, with
the material worlds at the base, growing more strange and magical
as they rise, until they become so *unreal,* so far above and beyond reality, that they leave the restrictions of matter behind and become
immaterial. Spiritual realms, with gods and devils and everything in
between. And right at the top of the pyramid, beyond such narrow
concepts as life and death, real and unreal: The Creator. Far above
and beyond the worlds we know, are worlds we cannot know. The
shimmering realms, the glory plains, the Courts of the Holy. Can
you imagine what it must have been like for Angel to descend from
such heights, to mire herself in the material worlds? From pure
thought and spirit to flesh and blood and bone? From marvel to
meat? Still, the most important question concerning Angel is, did
she fall, or was she pushed?"

Toby looked sharply at Gayle. "You mean her presence here
could be a punishment? She's been imprisoned in the limited worlds
for a crime of some kind?"

"Perhaps," said Gayle. "Then again, there's always the danger of becoming too limited in our thinking. Things aren't always a matter of good and evil, right and wrong. It could be she was sent here as a learning experience because there was something she needed to understand. Something she could learn only on the material planes . . . The immaterial are subtle beings, in every sense of the word. We underestimate them at our peril."

Up Market Street they went, puffing up the long steep hill, until just before the sharp fork off to the left, into Wine Street and New Town, Gayle stopped suddenly to stare across the busy road at the great stone wall on the other side. Toby stopped with her, glad of a chance to catch his breath. It was a hard climb up the steep hill, and Gayle was still setting an uncomfortably fast pace. Toby couldn't help noticing that while he was struggling for breath, Gayle wasn't even breathing hard. He joined her in staring at the great wall, though there wasn't anything immediately interesting about it, for someone who saw it every day. Over thirty feet tall, it towered above them, built from old local stone, blackened now by long years of passing traffic. It was all that remained of what had once been The Priory, a fifteenth-century building long since demolished. Thick mats of ivy clung to the upper half, and there were still faint traces to be seen of old filled-in archways. But essentially it was just a wall.

Gayle plunged suddenly into the busy road, heading for the wall with a brisk indifference to the passing traffic. Toby stuck doggedly at her heel with his heart in his mouth, trying not to hear the blaring of outraged horns as cars missed them by inches. Somehow they made the far side of the road without causing a major incident, and Gayle knocked on the dark stone. A door opened in the wall, retreating slowly inward. Toby blinked a few times. He should have been getting used to it by now, but it still rather threw him when a door opened where a door had no business being. Particularly when, in the world he remembered, he was pretty sure there was nothing on the other side of the wall except lots and lots of open space. Yet the door was undeniably there, and Gayle was already striding confidently into the gloom beyond, and so once again Toby took a deep breath and followed her into the unknown.

For once, the room he ended up in seemed relatively normal. A little old-fashioned, with bulky, heavy furniture, but charming in a Victorian retro kind of way. Latticed windows let in streams of sunlight, and everything was bright and cheerful and airy. There were great bunches of flowers in pretty china vases on every surface, filling the air with a thick and heady perfume. One wall was covered with shelves of tightly packed hardback books, while another held shelves of decorative plates. It took Toby a moment to realize what he *wasn't* seeing. There were no modern conveniences of any kind, not even an electric light. He might have stepped back a hundred years, into a quieter, less cluttered age. But he had no time to consider that, because Luna was smiling at him.

Short and blond and palely glamorous, she sat in a huge rattan chair that made her seem even tinier by comparison. She wore an enveloping dress of butterfly pastels, from which her delicate long-fingered hands emerged to hold a half-spread fan. A straw boater was perched on top of her long curls, and her heart-shaped face boasted an old-fashioned bee-stung rosebud mouth under a long thin nose and pale china-blue eyes. She looked like a fragile and very expensive doll, and while her smile was warm enough, there was an odd vagueness to her gaze.

She rose jerkily from her chair, laughing breathlessly, and fluttered around Gayle and Toby, hugging them both briefly and kissing the air near Gayle's cheeks before settling them both in comfortable chairs. She pressed cups of hot sweet tea on them and little sugary cakes she'd baked herself just that morning. "I had a feeling someone was coming. . . ." She moved with graceful little darting movements, never still for a moment. Toby felt almost dizzy trying to keep up with her. Gayle didn't even bother trying, addressing her remarks to the room in general. Luna finally sank back into her rattan chair again and fanned herself briskly, peering almost coquettishly over the edge of the fan.

"So nice to have visitors," she said breathlessly. "So nice! People come and go, but they hardly ever stay. . . . Isn't it a lovely day? Lovely. Though of course I don't get out much anymore. You're new, aren't you, Toby? Yes, I thought so. You have that deer-caught-in-the-headlights look. I'm usually very good with faces, but names often escape me. . . . My memory isn't what it was. If it ever was. And Gayle doesn't come to see me nearly as often as she should. . . . Sisters should be close. Should be. In an ever-changing universe, family is all we have that lasts. . . ."

And then Toby almost jumped out of his chair as Luna's entire appearance suddenly changed. In the blink of an eye, the pretty dress and straw boater disappeared, and Luna was wearing a top hat and set of tails, a starched white shirt and fishnet stockings rising out of leaf-green ankle boots. Her hair was still blond, but it was now cropped right back to the skull, little more than yellow fuzz. Her face seemed subtly sharper, enhanced by bright, almost gaudy makeup, with dark pandalike eyes and unnaturally pink lips. She was still chattering away, apparently unaware of or uninterested in the dramatic change of look. Toby jumped again as Gayle's hand closed firmly on his arm, and when he looked at her, she shook her head slightly. Her tightly closed mouth was all the hint he needed. Don't talk about it. Right?

Luna crossed her fishnet legs with disturbingly erotic grace and folded her arms tightly across her chest. She fixed Toby with a bright, unwavering gaze, and her eyes were a cold, cold blue.

"You're here because you need to know things. That's the only reason Gayle comes to see me these days. I disturb her, you know, Toby. I remind her of possibilities she'd rather forget. Of who and what she could be, should be . . ." She stuck out her tongue at Gayle, who didn't react. Luna laughed charmingly, like a child who's just gotten away with something. "I'm not all I used to be, I know that. I'm not stupid. A bad thing happened . . . and in order to forget it I had to forget a lot of what holds me together. So now I'm just a ghost, haunting myself. Tra-la-la . . . But I am still large. I contain multitudes. Especially on Saturdays."

With an almost perceptible lurch, the room changed. The

slightly old-fashioned setting was gone, and was replaced by a medieval scene, all rough wooden furnishings and hanging tapestries and glowering family portraits on the wood-paneled walls. Even the chair Toby was sitting on squirmed under him as it changed in shape and character. He looked quickly at Gayle and was relieved to see that she still looked the same, though if anything her mouth was even tighter. Once again she indicated silently for him to go along with it. Toby swallowed hard. He had a strong feeling he was sitting in a room from the old Priory; a room that hadn't existed for centuries. He wondered what he would see if he got up and looked out of the window, whether he would see people and places that had disappeared long before he was born. He decided he really didn't want to know, and sat tight. The teacup in his hand had become a metal goblet half full of wine.

The conversation continued in jumps and starts, as Luna's butterfly mind roamed all around the subject despite Gayle's promptings, sometimes touching on it and sometimes not. Luna's thoughts were almost willfully vague, never staying in one place for long. Both she and the room continued to change without warning, jumping back and forth in time and fashions, to no obvious pattern or effect. Toby never quite got used to it, but made himself concentrate on what Luna was saying.

"So," Luna said brightly to Gayle. "Who are you these days? Still playing at being real?"

"I'm Gayle. And yes, I still prefer to be real, as much as possible."

Luna sighed. "Must be nice, to be so sure of who you are. . . . Why do you never come to see me anymore?"

"I do," Gayle said gently. "You just forget."

"I forget so many things," Luna said sadly. "But then, it's a matter of self-defense, really." She smiled radiantly at Toby. "And I so rarely go out, these days. The town is always changing, changing . . . real and magical. Sometimes I think I'm the only one that endures, in spirit at least. . . . Are you enjoying your tea, Toby?"

The tea had become wine, coffee, Cherry Coke, and was now something that smelled suspiciously like urine. Toby would have liked to put the cup down, but he didn't know what he'd do with his hands if he did.

"Very nice," he said, smiling politely. "What do you do here, Luna? To keep yourself busy?"

The question clearly confused her, and she leaned back in what was now a rocking chair, patting her white-silk-gloved hands together in a distracted way. "What do I do? I have enough trouble being myself, without trying to achieve things as well. Objectives require timescales, and time . . . time is a trouble to me. Yesterday is tomorrow is yesterday, with hardly any time to be today. Did you come here before, or am I just dreaming of what will happen after you come? Sorry, sorry. I drift, you see. My anchors cannot hold, my self . . . is variable. It's all the fault of The Serpent In The Sun. He broke my connections. I used to know what he was . . . but he did something bad to me, so bad, long and long ago. I had to forget it, so I forgot him . . . and so many other things. He hurt me. And now you're here because . . . because . . ."

"There are things we need to know," said Gayle.

"Yes! Yes! I'm not stupid, not senile! Not yet!" Luna leaned forward in her chair to snap at Gayle, her eyes sharp and piercing and entirely otherworldly. "My mind may not be what it was, but I'm still Luna, your little sister. I am a Power and a Domination, just like you, and I know secrets that are hidden from everyone. The night is still my domain. Even you must bow to me, *Gayle,* on occasion."

She changed again. The room was now blinding white walls, with steel and glass and high-tech consoles, and Luna wore a sharply cut chauffeur's outfit in black leather, complete with a peaked cap over a pure white quiff. She wore tight black gloves and thigh-high black boots, dark as the night, and her jacket hung open at the front, baring high, firm breasts. Her nipples were as black as ink, standing out starkly against her pale, almost milky skin. Her face was sharply defined now, almost foxy. She had long, heavy eyelashes, and lips of darkest red. She reeked of sex, an almost painfully erotic presence. Toby was having trouble breathing. He couldn't have looked away from her now if his life depended on it, and she knew it. She smiled coldly at Toby, and it was all he could do to keep from groaning.

"I know that Nicholas is back," said Luna, in a slow, sultry voice. "The Hob. The Serpent's Son. I know about the changes in the world's weather, and the way the sun is acting. I know that Angel has joined Nicholas at Blackacre, and that he is tearing the dead from the town's cemeteries. Do you want me, Toby?"

"Leave him alone," said Gayle, but her voice was a small, distant thing.

Luna smiled, a wicked, abandoned, awful smile. "How could I not know Nicholas was back? The wolf always returns to the fold, and the murderer to the scene of his crime. Or the dog to his vomit. Perhaps he's just come back to foul the streets, because it's been so long since he marked his territory."

"This town was never his," said Gayle. "And never will be. You and I have always seen to that. Can you see what his purpose is?"

"He's been talking with his father," said Luna, stretching slowly in an unbearably sensual way that brought beads of sweat to Toby's forehead. "They think I don't know, but I know . . . Nicholas was always ambitious, but in the end he is still his father's son, and will follow the Serpent's will. The old Enemy is planning something, something new, and he has summoned Hob back to be a part of it. Something bad is coming . . . something terrible . . ."

"Yes," said Gayle. "But *what?*"

Luna fixed her blue, blue eyes on Toby, and leaned forward so that her breasts seemed to surge toward him. "Do you want me, Toby? Do you long to trail the tips of your fingers along my pale flesh? To sink yourself in me? Men have always wanted me, even as I drew and maddened them. It's been so long since I was allowed anything for myself, just for me . . . Toby, dear; I could just eat you up."

"You can't have him," said Gayle, in a calm, steady voice. "He's a focal point."

Then Luna was back in her pastel dress in her rattan chair, and her eyes were just eyes and her smile was just a smile. Toby felt the tension run out of him like a fading pain; he sat slumped in his chair, breathing heavily. Luna looked at him sadly.

"Must be nice, to be a focal point. To be so . . . focused. To have such a straightforward role to play."

"But I don't know what I'm supposed to do," said Toby. His voice was weak but steady, like someone recovering from a harsh illness. "I'm also supposed to be Humanity's Champion, but no one will tell me what that involves, either."

"I know just what you mean," said Luna. She looked at Gayle, her eyes suddenly clear, her mouth firm. "The solar flares are signs that the Serpent is stirring. Sometimes I hear him when he talks to Nicholas. Even after all these years, after everything I've done to myself to be free of him, we're still connected. By what he did . . . and what I did later. The Serpent plans to change everything. Veritie, Mysterie—everything and everyone. You've got to do something, dear sister. *Do something.* I would, but . . . I'm just me, poor broken Luna. Even holding myself together long enough to talk like this takes everything I have."

"What do you think I should do?" said Gayle. Her voice was quiet, unusually subdued.

"Kill him. Nicholas. The Hob. Kill him, if you can. You know I can't."

"Yes, I know." Gayle frowned, and Toby realized with a slow chill that she was seriously considering the idea. Killing a man in cold blood, because it was necessary. "But what if that's what the Serpent wants me to try? Because I'd have to change to do it, become my true self, my whole self. And I was happy being human, damn it!"

She got up and turned away from them both, her arms crossed tightly across her chest, scowling at something only she could see. Luna looked kindly at Toby and he almost flinched. For a moment, back then, he would have done anything, anything at all, just for the touch of her, the taste of her. Even though he knew, on some deep, primal level, that she would have chewed him up and spat him out, ripped the heart out of his chest—and made him love every moment of it.

"Gayle remembers when this town was new," Toby said slowly, searching for safe ground. "What do you remember, Luna?"

She laughed breathily, a happy, guileless sound. "I remember when it was all new. We had such plans then . . . such hopes. Oh, yes. The things we were going to do . . . But the Serpent, the old Enemy, wouldn't let us. He was so much older than us, you see. We depended on him. It took us so long to break free of his will, to make our own lives, our own destinies. It was mostly her, even then. I was never strong, like her. This world could have been a paradise. It *should* have been a paradise. But the Serpent has always had his own plans, so afraid of anything that might challenge his power . . . And then, of course, there was the Hob. Nicholas. Dear, damned Nicholas."

She sat brooding for a while, and then glanced at Gayle, still lost in her own thoughts. "You love her, don't you, Toby?"

"Yes," said Toby. "Even though everyone tells me it's a bad idea."

"Oh, it is," said Luna. "Really. You can't conceive how bad. You're afraid of me, but you should be much more afraid of her. Still . . . she's not a bad sort, not really. She's just been hurt so often. Be kind to her, Toby Dexter. Not many are. I can almost see the skeins of fate connecting you two. The chains of destiny and purpose. Don't turn away, Toby. You're capable of much more than you think. Eventually you're going to have to face Nicholas and Angel. And if Gayle can't or won't give you the support you need, try Jimmy Thunder. He's always been a generous man to those in need. And you may find it easier to trust a man like Jimmy rather than Gayle, who is so much more than a woman."

And then her eyes went vague again, and her speech began hopelessly confused and rambling. She could tell she wasn't making sense anymore, tried to pull herself back together and broke into loud, wet tears when she couldn't. Gayle immediately snapped out of her mood and tried to calm her sister, but what little coherence and clarity Luna had been able to summon had slipped away. She didn't even know who Gayle and Toby were anymore. So they said their good-byes and left, leaving Luna mumbling querulously to herself as she and her room changed, again and again and again. Out in the street, Toby looked furiously at Gayle.

"What the hell did the Serpent do to her, to make her like that?"

"He raped her," said Gayle.

# Six ~

# The Comforts of Strangers

IN THE DEAD WOODS, in the dead house, in the dead room, Nicholas Hob and Angel were drinking winter wine. Old wine, cold wine, wine so cold it frosted the outside of their glasses, and snowflakes swirled endlessly in the ice-clear liquid. Not a drink for mortals, poor delicate mayfly creatures born to die too soon. Winter wine had the delicacy of snow crystals and the strength of glaciers, and a taste like all the cold drinks on all the hot days that ever were. Hob and Angel drank their wine in slow appreciative sips, and their breath steamed thickly on the hot air in the rotten room.

Blackacre farmhouse was in an appalling state, held together by spite and inertia, and the parlor was particularly foul, with its seeping walls and filthy floor; but Hob found the presence of so much corruption consoling, and Angel was above or beyond noticing such things. The room attracted flies, which buzzed aimlessly back and forth on the still air, confused by so much decay without a source. Every now and again they'd stray too close to Hob and spontaneously ignite, burning fiercely for a moment before dropping silently to the floor like so much soot. None of the flies went anywhere near Angel. The light from the hanging oil lamps had a sickly yellow glow, and the sweaty heat in the room came from the continuous process of corruption.

Hob and Angel sat at ease in their comfortable chairs, on either side of a hideously valuable coffee table Hob had picked up for a song some centuries earlier, and tried to find things to talk about. Fate, and the implacable will of The Serpent In The Sun, had made them partners and companions, but for all their more than human characters, they had little in common. And, for all his improbable age and ancestry, Hob was still basically human, while Angel's grasp on her new human state was precarious at best.

"This is good wine," said Angel. "I like this. The pleasure of its taste is fleeting, but still it has in it hints of immortality."

"The world turns, but winter always returns," Hob said smoothly. "Winter wine would be one of the wonders of the world, if the world only knew it existed. It's rarer than gold or frankincense or myrrh, but you can find pretty much anything in Mysterie, if you know where to look. This fine vintage came to us courtesy of Ultima Thule Distilleries, the old firm, purveyors of the coolest booze in this world or any other. The price for such a treasure of the grapes is normally a lien on your soul, or someone else's, but Ultima was kind enough to send me a whole crate of the stuff, in the hope of . . . future considerations. They can feel changes beginning in the patterns of fate, in the warp and weft of destiny, and like others, they are hurrying to hedge their bets by establishing credit with as many sides as possible. Not that it will save them from my father's plan, of course."

"Of course," said Angel, draining her glass and pouring herself a fresh libation. Hob winced, just a little.

"Do try to savor this one, Angel. I swear, the subtler pleasures are wasted on you."

"Pleasure," said Angel, licking frost from her dark lips with a surprisingly pale and pointed tongue. "An interesting concept. Much like pain. So much is new to me, filtered through this body's senses. You tell me some things are good and some are bad, but I have no background against which to judge your conclusions. I have to try them for myself, to see what they are, what they mean . . . and my senses are such limited things, now." She scowled suddenly and glared at Hob. "Why do we have to stay here? I've seen so little of this world since I was exiled here. I want to go out and play with things. Hear them laugh and scream and praise my name. I want to do other things . . . and I don't even know what they are yet. I don't want to be here, in this place. It smells of failure."

"We're here because we're following the Serpent's plan," said Hob carefully. "Everything's going as it should. You have to be patient."

"I don't have to do anything I don't want to! You keep talking about your father's plan. Why can't I know what it is?"

"It's dangerous to say some things out loud," said Hob, holding her unsettling gaze with his. "You never can tell who or what might be listening. Even in this dead place, behind all my shields and protections, there are still presences who could hear our faintest whisper, and perhaps even some of our louder thoughts. You're just going to have to trust me, Angel. I tell you as much as I can, as much as I dare. There'll be work for you shortly. Bloody work. The kind you like best."

Angel stirred in her chair, glaring sulkily into her wine. She was restless. This was a new sensation, and therefore intriguing, but she was pretty sure she didn't like it. Hob sighed quietly to himself. Sometimes Angel was like a small child, who has to be kept endlessly fascinated and placated with new things, for fear she'll throw a tantrum. Or go wandering through the town again, freaking the locals.

"How would you like to go after Jimmy Thunder again, my dear? You can learn a new thrill. It's called revenge. You'll like it."

"But not yet, right?" said Angel pointedly.

"No," said Hob. "Not just yet."

He closed his eyes, just for a moment. He was deathly tired, after a hard day's work raising the dead and summoning them to Blackacre, and he had hoped for a little peace and quiet this evening, a little rest, but he should have known better. Baby-sitting Angel was getting harder all the time. More of his father's instructions, of course. No one realized just how much hard work there was in necromancy, how much concentration and willpower was required to pull the dead from their graves, walk them unseen through the town's streets and then set them to guard the dead and empty woods of Blackacre. He had a fearful headache. The wine was helping to soothe it, but Angel very definitely wasn't.

It was also hard work baby-sitting someone who could destroy the farmhouse and the woods and possibly the whole damned town, if she ever got angry enough to put her mind to it. He'd survive, of course, because he always did, but his father would be displeased with him, if he let Angel off the leash too soon. And just the thought of that was enough to make Hob shudder.

"Talk to me," Angel said implacably. "Tell me what you're feeling. It helps me understand what I'm feeling. You were thinking about your father just then, weren't you? I can tell. When you speak of him, I hear only hatred in your voice. Love and hatred are different, yes? One is good, one is bad. I have trouble making such distinctions. I have so few references to set them against. You don't want to do what you're doing now, but you do it anyway. Why?"

"No, this isn't what I'd rather be doing," Hob said tiredly. "But I don't have any choice in the matter. Like so many only sons, I inherited the family business. Mine just happened to be Evil. Luckily, I'm rather good at it, but still . . . I had to follow in my father's footsteps. Carry out his plans and ambitions. It was expected of me."

"What did you want to be?" said Angel, studying him with her unblinking crimson eyes.

"I never got the chance to find out," said Hob. "All my life I've danced to my father's tune, one way or another. Rarely had any time to myself. I've always been alone. No close family, or friends, or . . . lovers. Love isn't for the likes of me. Anyway, being the Hob is a full-time job. Women have been drawn to me, down the years, for various reasons. Ambition, usually. Villains and adventurers and the occasional romantic who saw herself as consort to my Prince of Evil. It's always the bad boy that makes a girl's heart beat that little bit faster. I've known companionship, but never love. Sex, but never tenderness. Alliances, but never friends . . . There were even a few women brave enough to try to use me for their own ends. I think I liked them the best. But no matter why they came to me, it always ended badly, for them and for me. I try to have fond memories of some of them, for the few bright moments they brought into my life. I have known some remarkable women. Sweet Susie Slaughter, also known as The Suffering. What times we had, in Revolutionary France, dancing in the blood around the guillotines. Then there was Crow Jane, the Eidolon. I had to kill her. Twice. It was for her own good. And not to forget dear Annie Abattoir of London's East End, the scheming little minx. I hammered a stake right through her cheating heart."

"Ah," said Angel. "She was a vampire."

"No." Hob stared moodily into his empty glass. "They always end up leaving me, one way or another. Sometimes I just outlive them. Humans are such transitory things. Another of the damned tricks fate played on me, making me what I am. Just human enough to tease me with thoughts and dreams of things I can never have, and not quite monster enough not to care. Doomed to live among mortals, while ensuring I can never share the sweet, passing joys they all take for granted. And so I hurt the world, as it hurts me, every day." He smiled humorlessly at Angel. "You don't understand a damned thing I've said to you, do you? And that's probably why I can talk to you like this. Because you can never use it against me."

"I understand what it is, to be alone," Angel said slowly. "Ever since I first fell to earth, I've found nothing and no one who can match what I am, let alone what I was. Except perhaps you. You are my anchor. A rock I can cling to, in a storm of things that make no sense to me. Your singular nature is comforting. Emotions confuse me, especially those connected with love. Sexuality. Sensuality. I know the words, but . . . I feel things I don't understand. Don't know what to do with." She leaned forward suddenly, and slowly stroked the side of Hob's face with the back of her hand. He sat very still as she ran a single soft fingertip down his face, from brow to cheek to chin, and then back to his lips, frowning as she concentrated on the sensation of skin touching skin. Hob was careful not to react in any way. This close, Angel was like some dangerous animal from the wild, some unknown creature that might do anything, anything at all. The hand that touched him so lightly was the same hand that had punched holes through the solid stone walls of the railway station. He didn't think she could really damage him, but still . . . Angel took her fingertip away from his lips and held it up before her, studying it closely, and Hob allowed himself to breathe a little more easily. He controlled Angel only because she let him, and more and more just lately he was beginning to think she knew that. Angel sniffed her fingertip and then licked it, but there was no more to it than some great cat licking its paw. Angel shrugged suddenly and let her hand fall.

"The Serpent," she said calmly, as though nothing of any note had happened. "Your father. The Serpent In The Sun, the Old Enemy. Have you ever seen him? Do you know what he really is?"

"No," said Hob, and was pleased at how calm and steady his voice was. "As far as I know, the only person ever to see my father in the flesh, so to speak, was my dear mother, and the experience drove her quite mad. Sometimes I hear my father's voice, in my mind. When he wants to give me orders. And that is always . . . unpleasant. His voice is awful, unbearable. Overwhelming. There's nothing human about the Serpent. He's so much bigger than that. No one knows much about The Serpent In The Sun, not really. Most of the world's religions have taken a guess or two, down the centuries. I've read up on most of them, and I'm no wiser. All anyone knows for sure, from records that predate Humanity, is that my father was the Firstborn, the very first living consciousness in the solar system. Everything else came after him; all the Powers and Dominations, all the lesser presences, all the way down to poor benighted Humanity. Sometimes I wonder—"

Hob convulsed in his chair, his wineglass flying from his spasming hand. He cried out in pain, a terrible, animal sound, and then his mouth snapped shut, forced into a grinning rictus by the straining muscles of his face. His whole body was shaking and twisting now, seized by an outside force that racked him unmercifully. He screamed behind his locked teeth, and tears flew from his wide-stretched eyes. The convulsions grew worse, throwing him from his chair, and he crashed helplessly to the floor, unable even to put out his arms to break his fall. He hit the floor hard, twitching and shuddering all over as his limbs flailed wildly.

His body stretched unnaturally, muscles tearing and bones cracking, as his shape and form altered violently, struggling to contain something from outside, something too big and too strange for the human form to accommodate. Hob was crying out all the time now, awful animal sounds of unbearable pain and horror, forced out of a twisting mouth. His body grew and shrank in sudden spurts, convulsing muscles tearing themselves free from bones that couldn't transform fast enough. He still looked basically human, but moment by moment he was leaving that state behind, his whole being racked by invasive, inhuman energies. Tears ran down his face in sudden jerks and streamings. Hob reached out one hand, with its crooked, foot-long fingers, in helpless supplication to . . . *someone.*

Above it all, a great Voice filled the rotten room, loud beyond bearing, terrible beyond belief and utterly inhuman. It spoke in a tongue beyond all human languages, or perhaps the root of them all, unknowable, unfathomable, to anyone in the mortal world except the Serpent's Son. Angel flinched back in her chair just at the sound of it, not understanding a word and yet somehow drawn to it, as though it reminded her of some other tongue, from her time before this world. The Voice was as loud as thunder, an earthquake or a volcano, and just as implacable, a force that could not be denied.

And then, at last, the message came to an end. The Voice was gone, and the only sounds in the dead room were the quiet creakings of muscle and bone as Hob's body slowly returned to normal, and his exhausted, pitiful sobbing. Even after his human shape was restored, he lay curled up on the filthy floor, crying and whimpering and hugging himself tightly, as though to stop himself from falling apart. The great and mighty Nicholas Hob, sobbing like a hurt child.

Angel looked down at him from her chair. In all her short time in the material world, she had never seen anything so clearly evil, so remorselessly cruel and malevolent, done by one living creature to another. She rose slowly from her chair and knelt beside the shaking, helpless Hob. And without quite knowing why, she took him in her arms and held him to her. She held his face gently to her breast, and his tears soaked her black rags. She'd never seen him so weak, so helpless. She felt helpless, too—not something she was used to feeling. She tried to comfort Hob, in her own awkward, ignorant way, and in her helpless anger at what had been done to him she found a new, different link between herself and Hob; that in the end, for all their power, they were both at the mercy of forces greater than themselves.

Finally Hob stopped shaking, and after a while he stopped crying, too, or perhaps he just ran out of tears. He lay limply in Angel's arms, his head still resting on her bosom. His breathing gradually slowed to something like normal, and tears and sweat no longer dripped off his chin.

"He always hurts me," he said quietly. "My father. When he talks to me. I may be his son, but I'm still mostly only human. Sometimes I think he hurts me deliberately, unnecessarily, just to remind me who's in charge. There's never been any love between my father and me, in either direction. I'm just here to carry out his orders. I'd love to hurt him, the way he hurts me, love to punish him. Kill him. But I never will. I can't even defy him. I've tried to outthink him, out-maneuver him, but in the end, as old as I am, with all my hard-earned experience and knowledge, he is immeasurably older and far more powerful. The Serpent. The Old Enemy." Hob sounded horribly tired to Angel, hurt and defeated, even broken. She held him a little tighter, and tried to understand why. Hob sounded like a small child, beaten for reasons he could never hope to understand. Angel lowered her head next to his, to catch his last quiet words. "I'll never be my own man, never be free. Never be anything more than my father's bloody puppet!"

He started to cry again, helpless with rage and frustration, and suddenly he pounded one fist against the floor, till the skin on his knuckles broke and blood flew on the air. Angel reached out and

restrained his bloody hand with her own. Hob raised his face to look
at her, and for a long moment they stared into each other's eyes.
Something passed between them, something new to both of them.
And then Hob began trying to sit up, and Angel immediately let
him go. She knew better than to help him, as he forced himself back
onto his feet and then collapsed into his chair. She resumed her seat
on the other side of the coffee table. Neither of them said anything.

Hob remembered how it all began.

The Serpent saw Angel fall. Saw her plunge through the shimmering realms, down and down and finally out into the material,
and Mysterie. He watched as she burned across the sky like a me-
teor, at last plummeting to earth like a falling star, landing with a
crash that shook the world in more ways than one. The Serpent then
spoke to his son, Hob, and told him to go to a certain place and retrieve what he found there. Which was how, just under a year ago,
Nicholas Hob came to be standing beside his elegant and powerful
car, deep in the heart of southwest England, looking dubiously at
the ancient burial mound known as Silbury Hill.

There was a cold wind blowing, though up until now it had been
a hot and muggy day. He hunched his shoulders inside his long
leather coat and flexed his fingers inside his heavy driving gloves. He
didn't like being back at Silbury Hill. It had been seven hundred
years since he'd last been here, and the place still disturbed the crap
out of him. To the casual eye it was just another burial mound, big
enough to be named a hill but otherwise unremarkable. Even the
legends surrounding it were pretty generic. That the mound held the
body of some ancient chieftain, along with his treasures. Or perhaps
it was the secret tomb of some great and potent hero, sleeping in
majesty, waiting to be called forth again in the time of England's
greatest need. There'd been several fairly major invasive digs here in
this century alone, but no traces of a tomb or a body or treasure had
ever been found. The legends persisted. Of King Sil, or the King in
Gold, or The Rider On The White Horse.

Hob knew the truth. That the mound was thousands of years

older than that. He knew what was really buried there, deep and deep in the cold wet earth, held down by the weight of the mound, wrapped in iron chains blessed with terrible prayers and curses, doomed and damned to lie deep in the ground till Judgment Day, and perhaps beyond.

Grendel Rex, the Unforgiven God.

Hob shivered, and not just from the cold wind that always blew around Silbury Hill. There were giants in the earth, and some of them slept badly. Still, if you were looking for a fallen angel, a morally ambivalent spot like this was certainly the right place to start. A hill older than history, where good and evil, reality and un-reality, and even Time itself became uncertain when the wind blew in the wrong direction. Hob took a deep breath and started up the hill. The steep, grass-covered mound was strangely unsteady under his feet, as though it wasn't always there. Hob stared straight ahead as he climbed, careful never to look down. It took him a lot longer to reach the top of the hill than it should have, but then, there was more to Silbury Hill than just three dimensions.

When he finally reached the summit, and had stood there for a while bent over and gasping for breath, he saw that Angel was lying curled up at the bottom of a deep crater, like a sleeping child. The grass all around had been burned away by the shock of her impact, leaving only dark scorched earth and a pit twenty feet deep. Angel lay in its center, pale and naked and unharmed, like a worm in a bit-ter fruit. Her bare skin was so bright a white it almost glowed, and Hob could feel the power in her, like a presence on the air. She sat up suddenly, alerted to his arrival by some unknown sense, and her bloodred eyes locked on to his. Hob froze in place, staring back at her, unable to look away, knowing he was finally face-to-face with something as powerful and primal as himself. Angel was breathing unsteadily, as though breathing was a new thing to her, and when she finally smiled at him it was a tentative, uncertain thing.

"Hello, Angel," said Hob. "Welcome to the material world."

"I hate it here," said Angel, her voice thick and slurred. "I feel . . . small, limited. Vulnerable. They have given me body and mind and language, but they've taken away my memories, of who and what I used to be. I fell so far, diminishing all the time, and it hurt all the way down. Thrown down. Thrown out. I don't want to be here!"

She shrieked that last to the gray skies, but no one answered. Hob made his way carefully down the steep side of the earth pit, took off his long coat, and wrapped Angel in it. His heart was beating uncomfortably fast, but when he spoke he was pleased to find that his voice was calm and steady, despite his dry mouth. "The material worlds aren't so bad, Angel. There are lots of entertaining things to do to pass the time. Come with me. I'll look after you, teach you the ways of the world. It'll be fun."

"Yes," said Angel. "I want to go out into the world . . . and do things to it. But I don't know what, yet. So I'll stay with you. You know things. And you feel . . . something like me. Who are you?"

"I am Nicholas Hob, and I am just what you need. No one else can teach you the things I've learned. Thank your lucky stars I got to you first. Not everyone could understand you like I do."

But Angel had already lost interest in his words and was staring intently at the leather coat around her, concentrating on the feel of it against her skin. Touch was a new thing to her. Hob had to smile—Angel was a blank slate, on which he could write anything he wanted. The thought excited him, and the fact that she was so very dangerous, and could turn on him in a moment, and just might be able to destroy him, only made it that much more exciting.

Hob poured Angel another glass of winter wine with a hand that was perfectly steady. He noted that they were getting near the bottom of the bottle, and mentally ordered one of his dead servants to bring another. Hob drank, like he did everything else, to excess. One of the joys of such a powerful and long-lived body was that it could take practically any amount of punishment and abuse. And after one of his father's little chats, Hob felt he was entitled to a pick-me-up. Angel was studying him thoughtfully over the rim of her glass, but Hob pretended not to notice. Awakening Angel's emotions had never been part of the deal. She was there to be his partner, and that was all. Anything else frankly scared the crap out of him. For many reasons, not least of which was that if Angel ever decided she was a woman scorned, well . . . In years to come they'd probably be able to point at a ten-mile-wide crater and say, *That's where Bradford-on-Avon used to be.*

The dead servant strode soundlessly into the parlor, carrying a fresh bottle of winter wine. The thick layer of frost coating the bottle had already crept up to cover his gray hand and arm, but the dead man hadn't noticed. Hob signaled for him to put the bottle on the table and open it. In many ways, Hob preferred his servants to be dead. You never had to worry about their loyalty, or paying them, and you never had to put up with any backchat. Of course, they weren't nearly so much fun to maltreat, but then, you couldn't have everything. Or at least, not yet.

"I'm going to have to piss soon," said Angel, with that matter-of-fact directness that Hob never failed to find disconcerting. "Such a curious thing, this body, with its needs and appetites and functions. But then, so little of the material makes sense to me. I know I should stay out of Veritie; just being there diminishes me even further, but . . . there's something about the real world that draws me to it. Things seem to matter more, there. Things can be decided in Veritie, and brought to conclusions."

"Change is dangerous for such as us," Hob said carefully. "It threatens what we are. We're weaker there, less significant. That's why the thunder godling was able to knock the snot out of you at the railway station."

Angel scowled immediately. "Next time we meet, I'll rip out his heart with my bare hands and he can watch me eat it as he dies. I want to meet him again. It was fun, fighting someone who could fight back. Most things break too easily when I play with them."

The dead man happened to be leaning over the table beside her, opening the new bottle. Angel gripped him casually by the arm and tore the limb right out of its shoulder socket with no obvious effort. The dead man lurched, but didn't fall, and when he straightened up his face was still expressionless. Hob sat very still. A few beads of sweat had popped out on his brow. It did him good to be reminded that the same arms that had held him so comfortingly could just as easily tear him apart at a moment's notice.

Angel looked at the dead arm thoughtfully, turning it over and over in her hands, as though looking for some significant detail that had escaped her. Finally she sniffed dismissively and dropped the arm to the floor. She drank her wine and looked at Hob again, as though nothing of any import had occurred. To her, it hadn't.

"Angel, dear," said Hob. "Please don't damage the merchandise. They're needed, all of them, for the next stage of my father's plan."

"More of this plan that I can't know about," said Angel moodily, her dark mouth pouting like a child's. "Was that what your father wanted to talk to you about?"

"Among other things, yes. The opposition is gathering together. We can't have that. So I've been ordered to do something about it."

He gestured for the dead man to pick up his discarded arm and leave. Angel ignored him, staring into her glass again, her crimson eyes far away.

"It's not easy, being mortal," she said suddenly. "This body they gave me is as near-perfect as anything can be in the material worlds, but it will run down, eventually. Everything does, here. Nothing lasts."

"As opposed to where you came from?" said Hob. "Are you perhaps remembering something of who and what you were, before you were . . . demoted?"

Angel looked at him sharply. "You have to keep asking, don't you? You're desperate to know whether I was cast out from Heaven or Hell. Well I don't know. I've forgotten so much because I had to, to stay sane. I couldn't function here, on this messy, limited plane, if I still remembered the glories of the shimmering realms. I try to remember things about my past existence, even small things, but they're all gone. And I have to wonder, were my memories taken from me, or did I choose to forget? Did I *agree* to my descent, for some forgotten reason? There's a hole inside me, Hob, a great aching wound that I can sense but not comprehend the shape of. I have been robbed of all the better parts of myself, and been left just aware enough to know it. *Bastards!*"

The wineglass shattered in her hand as it closed convulsively. Shards of glass fell to the floor, apart from one great sliver that protruded from her palm. Angel looked at it for a moment, entirely unmoved, and then pulled it out. She didn't wince, and only a spot of bright red blood showed where the sliver had been. She studied the piece of glass for a moment, and then let it fall, too.

"Pain. Pleasure. So bright, like sparks in the flesh. Hard to tell apart, sometimes. They're all part of this body's weaknesses, its vulnerabilities. I hate the arbitrary nature of this place, where damage and death can come out of nowhere, at any time, for no real reason or purpose. Once, everything I did, everything I was, had purpose. I know that. And if I ever find out who has taken that from me, I will punish them for all eternity."

"Even if it turns out to be you?" said Hob.

"Perhaps especially then," said Angel.

Hob handed Angel his glass of wine, hoping to distract her. Angel's brooding made him nervous. Curious as he was over her origins, it better suited his purposes, or rather his father's, if Angel remained lost and uncertain. It made her easier to manipulate. Angel accepted the glass, but didn't drink from it.

"I will return to the immaterial," she said softly, implacably. "I will go back to where I belong, reclaim my due, even if I have to destroy all the material worlds there are to be free of their grip on me. I will tear whole civilizations apart and dance laughing in their ruins. I will see the end of all the breathing, bleeding, lesser things, if that's what it takes. And not all the Powers and Dominations there are shall stand against me."

Hob felt very cold. She could do it.

"Unless . . . that's what I'm supposed to do." Angel was frowning hard now. "Perhaps that's why I was sent here, to be made angry enough to become the destroyer of peoples, and of worlds. In which case . . ."

"When you can't depend on logic," Hob said reluctantly, not liking at all the ways Angel's thoughts seemed to be going, "rely on your feelings, your intuition. Do you feel Good or Evil?"

Angel shrugged. "I'm not sure I understand the concepts properly yet. Morality is so confusing. I'm not sure either term applies to me. Feelings and instincts are both useless to me, with so little frame of reference to place them in. I feel . . . confused. Tired. Trapped."

"All right," said Hob. "Then follow the argument through. If you need so badly to be free of your material existence, why not kill yourself? If you die, your spirit should return to the immaterial. I say *should*; I have no direct evidence that that's what occurs. Even after all my very long life, some things still remain mysteries to me. If you can't do it yourself, I'm sure I could help. After we've carried out my father's plans, of course. He wouldn't allow either of us to die while he still had a use for us."

"If I were to die, they'd just send me back again," said Angel. "Thrust me back into the meat, into blood and bone and hair. I just know that's what they'd do, the bastards! I have to stay here, until . . . until I do whatever it is I was sent here to do."

She shrugged suddenly, and drank her wine. Some of the tension had gone out of her, perhaps because she'd realized she'd followed the argument as far as she could, for now. Hob allowed himself to relax a little, too. Angel was never so dangerous as when she was thinking.

"Tell you what," he said casually. "It could be that you were sent here to help me. Once the Serpent's plans go through, the nature of the material worlds will have changed so much, that perhaps that will be enough to free you. Certainly by the time we've finished with them, Mysterie and Veritie won't be anything like they were."

"Perhaps," said Angel, apparently no longer interested. "I want to go back into town, find the thunder godling. Descendants of lesser gods should know their place. Perhaps he was behind the man we caught watching us, the man who followed the dead man back here." She frowned suddenly and looked sharply at Hob. "Why so many dead? You don't need them to protect you. You have me."

Hob grinned wolfishly. "The dead are my army, my weapon.

Our target has a blind spot, you see. Being so closely linked to the living world, *she* can't see, detect, or defend herself against the dead."

"Why are you always so careful never to refer to her by name?"

"Because to name her is to evoke her, to raise her from humanity. Neither my father nor I want that. We daren't attract her attention before all the parts of the plan are safely in place."

Angel considered him thoughtfully. "You're afraid of her, aren't you?"

"Of course," said Hob. "I'm just the Serpent's Son, while she is . . . so much more."

"But . . ."

"Change the subject," Hob said steadily.

"All right," said Angel. "Answer me this: How did something as great and powerful as the Serpent produce a merely mortal son like you?"

"By design," said Hob. "In those days, my mother lived in Mysterie and Veritie, occasionally playing at being human with her sister. They were closer, then. The Serpent raped her in Mysterie, the only place where they could meet, knowing she would choose to give birth to the child in Veritie, to limit its power. And so it would be as little like its father as possible. The Serpent wanted a human agent in the real world, and didn't give a damn how many lives he ruined in the process. Any more questions, dear Angel?"

"Yes. How is it that you're able to raise the dead?"

Hob smiled sourly. "Technically speaking, I don't. Only one man was ever able to give life to the dead, and I'm very definitely not Him. I just raise dead bodies and move them with my will. You don't live as long as I have, and move in the circles I've known, without picking up a few useful tricks along the way." He leaned back in his chair, eyes hooded, suddenly reflective. "I've done a lot of things, down the many years, wonderful, terrible things. I tried so hard to build something that mattered, so I'd have something to call my own. But nothing ever lasted. And besides, destroying things was always so much more fun. Nothing really lasts, anyway, except reputation. Everyone knows who Nicholas Hob is."

Angel raised a perfect eyebrow. "Everyone?"

Hob smiled easily. "Everyone who matters."

"And a lot of them live in Bradford-on-Avon," said Angel. "Aren't you afraid someone in authority here will try to stop you?"

"Not really," said Hob. "In the magical world there is no authority, as such. The powers that be pursue law and chaos, light and dark, good and evil as their natures and functions suggest and compel. The more powerful people are in Mysterie, the more they tend to cancel each other out."

"What about the Waking Beauty, and the thunder godling?"

"For every meddling would-be hero, there are any number of villains ready to stand in their way, in return for vague promises of vast rewards, once my plan is complete. Villains are always suckers for inside information. And they all know better than to argue with the Serpent's Son."

"How does that feel?" said Angel, leaning forward. "To know people are frightened of you?"

"It feels . . . safe, secure. Anyway; I have spoken with the Painted Ghoul, the Bedlam Boys, the Murder Waltz, even Nasty Jack Starlight. From a distance. Between them they'll cause more than enough trouble to distract any interfering busybodies who might develop an interest in what I'm up to. In the end, most people will quite sensibly choose just to keep their heads down, and hope not to be noticed till it's all over. With the Serpent at one end and *her* at the other, no one wants to get caught up in an Apocalypse." He grinned suddenly again. "By the time everyone realizes that's exactly what it is, it'll be too late. And afterwards . . . I have been promised complete dominion over Mysterie. Pity about what's going to happen to Veritie, but I never liked the place anyway. Far too many people in the world today. Get rid of most of them, and maybe I'll be able to hear myself think at last."

Angel looked at him thoughtfully. "And what will you do with the world, once it is yours?"

"Punish it, for not loving me."

Angel smiled. It was an unpleasant sight. "I like the way you think, Serpent's Son. Maybe I won't kill you, after all."

Hob's mouth was dry again. He made himself smile easily. "We must stick together, Angel. Who else would have us?"

# $Seven \sim$

# The Death-walkers

TOBY DEXTER AND GAYLE strode down an almost empty Church Street, side by side, neither of them talking to each other. Toby vaguely noted that they were back in the middle of town *again,* but just at that moment he couldn't bring himself to give a damn. He had a lot on his mind, very little of it positive, most of it to do with Luna—enigmatic and powerful, undeniably beautiful, disturbingly sexy and quite clearly as crazy as a loon. All along he'd been following Gayle because he assumed she knew what she was doing, but having seen the state of her sister, for all her power, Toby had to wonder whether he should be trusting Gayle so completely. He really knew very little about the real her: who she was, what made her tick, and what her motives might be. He still loved her, but . . . she'd said more than once that she didn't love him. And she'd done nothing at all to indicate that she had his best interests at heart. (He remembered the ley lines and shuddered briefly despite himself.) He wanted to believe that she knew what she was doing, but he had to consider the possibility that she was just as lost in all this craziness as he was.

In which case, he was in even more trouble than he'd thought.

He realized that they were almost at the end of Church Street, presumably heading back to the new bridge. Most of the light seemed to have gone out of the day, and there were hardly any people around. Toby looked up at the sky and was shocked to find it was now early evening. How long had they spent at Luna's endlessly changing residence? Did Time move differently there, too? As he looked around, his gaze fell upon the cash machine on the other side of the street, and he quickly looked away. He didn't think he could stand being serenaded again. At least the machine's showering him with money made a little more sense now. Presumably it knew a focal point when it saw one, and wanted to be remembered kindly. Unless it really had liked his face . . . Toby walked a little faster, and had actually got a few yards ahead of Gayle before he realized he didn't know where they were going. He slowed and fell back beside Gayle and cleared his throat politely.

"Sacred Heart," Gayle said briskly. "Twelfth-century, Norman architecture, built over an old Saxon place of worship."

"Ah," said Toby. He wasn't much of a churchgoer usually. "Feel in need of a little spiritual guidance, do we?"

"Churches are for mortals," said Gayle. "We are more interested in the cemetery."

"We are, are we?" said Toby. "Any particular reason, or are we just looking for interesting rubbings and tombstones with funny inscriptions?"

"You can be very irritating sometimes, Toby."

"Good. I like to think I'm contributing something to this little mystery tour. Why the hell do we have to visit a cemetery?"

Gayle sighed, not particularly patiently. "It's not so much the cemetery, as what lies beneath it. I want you to meet the death-walkers."

She pushed the pace again, to make it clear that she'd said all she was going to, for the moment. Toby gave her a deep sigh of his own, just to show he could do moody, too, and then scowled thoughtfully as he strode along beside her. The Sacred Heart cemetery was one of the largest and oldest graveyards in an old town, and the source of a great many spooky stories, including one very down-to-earth one from his childhood. Following the narrow path through the cemetery and out the other side was a well-known shortcut, but when Toby was very young his mother warned him sternly that there were old, sunken graves on either side of the path, often overgrown and impossible to see, so if he ever did take the shortcut, he had to promise to *stay on the path,* because otherwise you never knew what you might be treading on.

All the kids got that warning, and it was much discussed at school, with exaggerated tales of brave or careless children who walked on the grass and crashed right through rotting coffin lids. And there were other, darker stories, of moldering arms that burst up out of the ground to grab children who'd strayed too far from the path, and drag them down to keep the corpses company in their ancient, lightless caskets. And, of course, *they were never seen again.* Kids loved to tell these stories over and over again, in the safety of brightly lit playgrounds, adding and inventing all kinds of grisly new details until it became a generally acknowledged dare to walk all the way through the graveyard after the sun had gone down, and see how close to the edge of the path you could get . . . or even how far onto the grass . . . Toby had never worked up the courage to leave the path, or even go all the way through the cemetery. He'd never been particularly brave, as a child.

And now here he was, stopping with Gayle before the open metal gates, with the last of the sun already sliding down the sky. It was very quiet. There was no one else around, not even a bird singing. This was the point in horror movies when the audience started shouting, *Don't go in there, you idiots!* Beyond the open gates the neatly cropped grass looked very green, as though well nourished by underground sources, and the hundreds of well-tended graves made it seem a very peaceful place. Not many fresh flowers, though. And yet the sounds of the town seemed far away, and an old fear curled around Toby's heart. He could feel the hackles on the back of his neck rising, just at the thought of entering those open gates.

"You're thinking about the old cautionary tales," said Gayle, and Toby jumped despite himself. She smiled briefly. "Don't. They're just a cover story that got out of hand, to protect the secret of what goes on beneath the cemetery."

"All right," said Toby, a little sharply. "What does go on, down among the dead men? But bear in mind that if your explanation involves the words *ghosts* or *ghouls* or *zombies,* you are going in there on your own, and I am heading for the nearest horizon, at speed."

"Nothing so commonplace," said Gayle. "This is much more scientific in nature. The death-walkers are great believers in technology, these days. And recent advances in computer science have given them a whole new lease of life, if that's the right phrase. They've been here a long time, in one form or another."

"How long?"

"Oh, centuries. The town has always attracted and encouraged freethinkers, and those of an . . . experimental disposition. Sacred Heart has long been a center for spiritual power in the town. There used to be an old town ceremony, very old, called the Clipping of the Church. Once a year the townspeople would come and form a circle around the church and cemetery, and hand in hand, sing holy songs. It was a ritual, to harness the sacred power of the church, to drive the Devil and his influence out of the town. And this is Veritie we're talking about, not Mysterie. No one knows how far back the ceremony started, but it only came to a halt in 1905, after it was mistakenly reported that Nicholas Hob was finally dead. Word was the Walking Man got him; but Hob's always been hard to kill."

"What are death-walkers?" said Toby, firmly refusing to be distracted. "And why do I just know I'm not going to like the answer?"

"Death-walkers are explorers, travelers in the lands of the dead," said Gayle. "As astronauts investigate the planets, death-walkers travel to the afterworlds, the territories beyond life. Crazy bastards, one and all, but occasionally very useful. They have access to sources of information that even I don't. They know things no one else knows, or would want to know."

"Oh, wonderful," said Toby, annoyed but unable to keep a certain amount of relief from surfacing in his voice. "It's sit-around-a-Ouija-board time, is it? Knee to knee with broody spinsters and tweedy pensioners, translating messages from dyslexic ghosts? Or are we going to be holding hands at a séance, hoping you won't fart just when the medium asks, *'Is there anybody there?'* in their best spooky voice? One knock for yes, two for no, three for *'Sorry the line is busy right now.'* I can't believe you're a believer in this voices-from-beyond shit, Gayle. It's all self-delusion and confidence tricks, preying on the gullible and the bereaved. I'm warning you; it's only a short step from this to crystals, aromatherapy, and using the tarot to choose your lottery numbers. Surely there must be something more profitable we could be doing with our time."

"Are you in for a surprise, o skeptical one," said Gayle. "This is Mysterie. Things are different here."

She led the way through the metal gates, striding off down the narrow path, apparently entirely unconcerned. Toby hurried after her, still troubled by old childhood memories, but the cemetery turned out to be much less impressive than he remembered, and nowhere near as threatening. And then Gayle suddenly left the path, walking quickly across the uneven ground. Toby hesitated for a long moment before following her. His heart was beating faster, and his mouth was dry. In the end he finally stepped off the path and onto the grass like a swimmer off the edge of a pool, not at all sure how deep or how cold the water was going to be. He took one step, and then another, the ground entirely normal and supportive beneath him, and he let out his breath in a long sigh of relief. He hurried after Gayle, who was some distance away now, moving confidently among the standing headstones. She finally stopped by one, and waited for Toby to catch up with her. The old gray stone was pocked with moss and lichen, and was leaning slightly to one side, as the earth beneath had slowly subsided over the years. Toby moved in beside Gayle and studied the carved lettering, its details softened by the ravages of time and weather.

DEATH IS NOT THE END.

Toby sniffed loudly. "He's not fooling anyone but himself. What's so special about this grave, Gayle?"

She put one hand on the stone and pushed hard. The headstone tilted smoothly backwards, there was a loud click, and the whole grave suddenly slid sideways, disappearing under the grass, revealing itself to be a shallow fake. Where the grave had been there was now a set of wooden steps, leading steeply down into darkness. A light came on somewhere below, quite a long way below. Toby swallowed hard.

"All right, I'm impressed. But I don't like this, Gayle, I really don't like this."

"You'll like what's to come even less," said Gayle. "Even I feel uncomfortable around the death-walkers. But they're the only ones who might be able to point us where to go next. They know things, usually disturbing, unsettling things. Stick close to me, Toby."

"Give me one good reason why I should go down there, into God knows what?" Toby said hotly. "Hell, give me one bad reason."

Gayle looked at him directly for the first time. "You said you'd follow me anywhere."

"This is very definitely not what I had in mind." Toby frowned unhappily under Gayle's unwavering gaze, and then shrugged angrily. "All right! You lead, and I'll follow. But this had better be worth the strain this is putting on my nerves."

"Trust me," said Gayle, starting down the wooden steps. "If nothing else, I guarantee you won't be bored."

"Isn't that what General Custer said to the Seventh Cavalry?"

Gayle's dry chuckle floated back up from the gloom she was fast disappearing into, and Toby reluctantly went after her. He had to believe she knew what she was doing. She was all he had.

There were no railings, nothing to hold on to, just the bare wooden steps falling away before him. Gayle was just a dark figure some distance below. The stairway had been cut directly into the earth, with nothing shoring it up, and Toby couldn't help wondering how safe it was. And whether, if he put out one hand to steady himself against the wall, he'd feel worms wriggling in the damp soil. He kept his arms firmly at his sides and his eyes straight ahead, and eventually he reached the end of the steps and the beginning of a tunnel.

There was a bare lightbulb hanging from the low ceiling, giving the scene an eerie blue cast Toby could very definitely have done without. It was utterly quiet, and very cold. Gayle fumbled at the earth wall and found a hidden switch. There were faint grinding sounds from up the stairs, and Toby realized it was the false grave sliding back into place. They were sealed in down here now, with whatever they'd come to find. Toby glared about him, ready to jump right out of his skin at the first hint of an excuse. The narrow tunnel leading off before him was barely seven feet high, and not much wider, and it didn't go far before it branched off into several new tunnels. There were signs on the various walls, but they were all in Latin. Toby decided he wouldn't ask Gayle if she could translate them, just in case one of them said ABANDON HOPE, ALL YE WHO ENTER HERE. Gayle set off confidently down a side tunnel, and Toby hurried after her, not wanting to be left on his own.

The tunnel branched again and again, until Toby was quickly lost and totally disoriented. He visualized a subterranean maze of tunnels, crisscrossing endlessly under the unsuspecting visitors to the cemetery. He tried hard not to think about the coffins and bodies that were presumably interred somewhere above the tunnel's earth roof, making himself concentrate on what was before him. Everywhere he looked there were long trails of wiring, stapled into place along the earth walls in a bewildering rainbow of color codings, enough to run all kinds of technology. Presumably there was a generator down here somewhere, but Toby couldn't hear it running. In fact, the whole place was eerily quiet. Adding to the deserted feel of the tunnels were the piles of rubbish strewn across the tunnel floor. It was pretty recent stuff, too; pizza boxes, fast-food wrappings, and all kinds of crumpled paper. There were also a large number of primed, oversize mousetraps, which Toby preferred not to think about. Gayle sniffed loudly as she kicked something out of her way.

"This whole place could use a woman's touch. I suppose when you're preoccupied with solving the mysteries of existence and eternity, you can't be bothered with cleaning up after yourself."

The tunnel suddenly opened out into a wide cavern that was again cut directly from the earth, easily thirty feet across but with the same uncomfortably low ceiling. All around the walls stood banks of very much state-of-the-art computer systems, with monitors and terminals piled up and pushed together on rows of wooden tables. There were three different coffee percolators going, and any number of abandoned plastic cups on every available surface. There was a pervading smell of ozone and cheap air freshener. The whole room had an improvised feel to it, as though the many and varied items of equipment had been compiled piece by piece over the years, as required, to no particular plan or order. Gayle stopped, so suddenly Toby almost crashed into her from behind. He looked quickly past her and found that a man was standing directly before them, even though Toby hadn't seen or heard anyone enter the chamber.

Given the setting, and Toby's growing fears of what the death-walkers might turn out to be, the newcomer was something of a disappointment. He was of average height, average-looking, and wore the scientist's traditional white lab coat, complete with pens and pocket protector, over slacks and a shirt that had clearly gone too long between washes. His face was wide and open, his manner calm and pleasant. He was just the kind of person Toby always imagined working on nuclear bombs and germ warfare.

"Hi," said the newcomer easily. "I'm Glen Jensen. I run things here, as much as anyone does. We're more of a cooperative really, these days, working together on whatever interests us. We had word from the afterworlds that you'd be coming. Been a long time since you last honored us with a visit, Lady. I'm sure you'll be impressed by the improvements we've made."

"Don't put money on it," said Gayle. "This is all still just a step up from rooting around inside a sheep's guts and making guesses according to which way the liver's pointing."

Toby was rather surprised at her tone. There was a genuine edge of anger in her voice that he hadn't heard before. If Jensen was at all intimidated, he hid it well. He just nodded to Gayle, then beamed happily as he stepped forward to shake Toby firmly by the hand.

"Not often we get visitors down here. Usually it's all need-to-know, and all that security nonsense. Still, any friend of the Lady . . . And we're always glad of a chance to show off our latest toys."

"Really?" said Toby, his voice a little uncertain; he'd just noticed that Jensen was carrying a gun in a shoulder-holster under his lab coat. "Gayle's told me so little about you. What exactly do you people do down here?"

"We are death-walkers," Jensen said proudly. "Explorers of the unknown, scientists dedicated to uncovering the secrets of the last great frontier. Going where no living man has dared to go before, and doing our very best to come back to talk about it afterwards. It's a dangerous business, venturing out into the afterworlds. There are all kinds of hazards. Some of us don't come back. Quite a lot, actually. Membership drives are a real problem, and you wouldn't believe the difficulties we have collecting dues. But the rewards can be . . . exhilarating."

"Yes," said Toby. "But what do you *do,* precisely?"

"We die," said Jensen. "We let our spirits leave our bodies, allow them to explore, for a designated time, and then our resident necromancer draws the spirit back into the body, before it can move on, and he then revives the body. A whole new Near-Death Experience, scientifically evaluated. It's such fun, and terribly exciting. We're learning all kinds of things, all the time."

Toby felt seriously out of his depth. He looked plaintively at Gayle, who shrugged.

"Don't get too impressed. These people are just the philosophical equivalent of bungee jumpers and skydivers. A Really Dangerous Sports Club for complete headbangers. They say they're doing it for Science and Knowledge, but mostly it's just for the kicks."

"Facing our fears is what makes us strong," Jensen said easily. "And fear of death is the greatest fear of all. We have moved far beyond that, here."

"You've moved far beyond sanity," said Gayle.

"And yet still here you are, coming to us for what you can't find anywhere else." Jensen turned pointedly to Toby. "Come with me, and let me show you how we overcome that old devil, Death, every day. Just for the hell of it. We are taking Science into areas where even Einstein and Hawking never dared to go."

He led Toby around the chamber, ignoring Gayle, naming and explaining the various pieces of high-tech equipment, while Toby smiled and nodded and did his best to look as though he understood more than one word in ten. He could work a word processor and find his way around the Internet, but after that he was pretty much lost. One thing was increasingly clear, though: this was all major-league equipment. Nothing off-the-shelf here. It had the look of cutting-edge technology, where you couldn't even explain what it was for without speaking fluent maths. Still, Toby felt he ought to say something, since Gayle was manifestly so uninterested and unimpressed by any of it.

"Who pays for all this stuff, Glen? You didn't get any of this equipment through mail order."

"Various corporations," Jensen said smoothly. "You'd be surprised how many top-rank firms are ready to ship us anything we might want, under the counter, in return for access to whatever information the equipment might produce. None of them wants to be left behind, in case we come up with anything interesting, or useful. Corporations are technically immortal entities, these days, so they're more prepared to take the long view. But, even with all this help, the nature of our business still remains . . . highly experimental."

"Translation," said Gayle, "they don't know what they're doing."

"We learn by doing," said Jensen. "Our limitations arise out of the limits of the human mind. Our explorers into the infinite can only retain and bring back the merest scraps and fragments of information. What we see when we die is apparently so big, so overwhelming, so conceptually *alien,* that it's hard for the human mind to comprehend it, once it has returned to the material word. What we get mostly are impressions, guesses, and dreamlike memories. Through extensive correlation and cross-checking, we have been able to obtain a few nuggets of hard information . . . Unfortunately, they often tend to contradict one another.

"It's possible that the nature of the afterworlds is, at least at first, determined by the thoughts and beliefs of the observer; the human mind translating unfamiliar information into acceptable metaphors. It's all very quantum, really. As below, so above. And of course so much of what we get is meaningless without a context or useful frame of reference. But we persevere! Every scrap of information our volunteers drag back with them is fed into our computers, there to be sorted like with like, in order to build up a clearer, larger picture.

"The death-walkers have been compiling information for centuries, but recent advances in computer technology have made our lives a lot easier. We're currently comparing and contrasting our compiled data with all existing religious texts, searching for useful correlations and insights. The living human mind may be too small and limited to encompass the afterlife experience, but computer models are theoretically infinite in application. We fully expect to have detailed maps of all the afterworlds, within our lifetime."

"How long have you people been down here, doing this?" said Toby.

"We have written records going all the way back to the Roman Conquest. Of course, methods then were much cruder. We really peaked during the reign of Elizabeth I, after we'd finally broken away from the Catholic Church and its inflexible doctrines. Of course, we did tend to lose a lot more people in those days. They relied mostly on the terminally ill as subjects, in return for a promise to look after their families. Nowadays, we use volunteers."

"And what exactly have you learned for sure, after all these centuries," asked Gayle, "even with your precious computers? What can you tell us for a fact, about where people go when they die?"

"Not a lot that makes sense," Jensen admitted reluctantly. "Some of our people have reported quite lengthy encounters with the recently deceased and departed, but either the newly dead lie a lot, or they've got a really weird sense of humor."

"The more I hear, the less I like this," Toby said frankly. "You're trying to know things we're not meant to know. Aren't you afraid someone's going to turn up and shut you down?"

"No one's turned up yet," said Jensen. "Actually, we'd rather like it if *Someone* did. There are all sorts of questions we'd just love to put to Him. Or Her. Or Them. We try to be open-minded around here. Though of course we have to be careful. Keep your mind too open, and you never know what might walk in."

"Show me a door," said Toby. "Right now."

"We were all terribly excited to hear of Angel's arrival in town," said Jensen. "An actual one-time occupant of Heaven or Hell! The things she could tell us . . . Unfortunately, she didn't take too kindly to the emissary we sent, asking for her cooperation."

"What happened?" said Gayle.

"She sent back his lungs," said Jensen unhappily. "Gift-wrapped. We think she ate the rest. We did try to make contact with the poor man's soul, but we couldn't find a trace of it anywhere. Presumably he was too traumatized to hang around, or just possibly she ate that, too. There's a lot we don't understand about the nature of the soul. Still, that's why we're here! Learning something new every day."

"I'm here for information," said Gayle. "Much as it pains me to admit it. I need to talk to the recently deceased. Do you think we could make a start, please?"

"Of course, dear Lady," said Jensen magnanimously. "I quite understand your embarrassment, having to come to us for what you can't do yourself, for all your power. But try not to be too uncomfortable. We're happy to help anyone who comes to us in need, even those who have insulted and belittled our efforts in times past. Come with me, and we'll get things moving. I'm sure we can help you out with whatever little problem is currently troubling you."

He headed for an open doorway on the other side of the room without looking back, and Gayle and Toby trailed after him. Gayle was scowling dangerously. Toby leaned close to her.

"If he lays it on any thicker, we'll end up drowning in it. Can we trust these people?"

"They really can do a lot of what he says they can," Gayle said quietly. "Whether we get anything useful out of it is open to question. I need you to be brave, Toby."

Toby was about to ask why, when they passed through the doorway and into the adjoining chamber and he was immediately struck dumb. This new cavern was even bigger, some fifty or sixty feet wide, much of the floor taken up with basic cots, placed side by side in long rows. And on those cots lay still bodies, corpses; men and women with staring eyes and their death wounds still bloody on them. Toby's gorge rose in his throat as he moved slowly forward, looking quickly from one corpse to another. *We die,* Jensen had said, but that hadn't prepared Toby for the awful reality. These people had died in a variety of ways, none of them easy or natural. There were bullet holes and stab wounds, blood still pooling and drying around some of the cots. Some had cut wrists or throats. Several had cords pulled tight around their necks. One had a plastic bag over his head. Toby's head swam sickly, and he felt suddenly faint. Gayle was at his side in a moment, holding him up with firm hands.

"Be brave, Toby. I need you to be strong for me."

Toby made himself breathe deeply, and his head slowly cleared. He glared furiously at Jensen. "This is sick! What the hell is going on here?"

"I told you," Jensen said calmly. "People die here and go forth to explore the worlds to come. Only we can't just stand around waiting for people to die, so we kill them. No faked, technical near-death here; our volunteers go much further than that. They have to, to get the results we need. It can get a bit messy sometimes, I admit, but our resident necromancer is quite capable of repairing all tissue damage. And you have to understand, Toby; nothing happens here that our volunteers don't agree to in advance. You see, when you die, over and over, when you get used to dying, you get bored with doing it the same old way. The thrill goes out of it. So our people are constantly experimenting with new and more unusual, more violent ways of dying. Some of them have become quite inventive."

"I told you," said Gayle. "Bungee jumpers, all looking for the next big kick."

"You're crazy," said Toby, looking with loathing at Jensen. "You're all bloody crazy."

"Couldn't agree more," said a thick, slurred voice from the far side of the chamber. "Stupid bloody sensation-seekers. I'd have the lot of them committed, put on industrial-strength Prozac and locked up in rubber rooms; but no one ever listens to me."

They all got something of a shock as a figure that had been lying on a cot at the back sat up slowly, took a long drink from the bottle in its hand, and then lurched to its feet. Toby distinctly heard Jensen sigh heavily as the new figure shuffled across the chamber to join them. As he drew nearer, he turned out to be fat, middle-aged, and shifty-looking, with a great bushy beard and a shiny bald head. He wore an old sweater with fresh food stains on it, over battered khaki shorts that had seen better days. There was a cigar sticking out of one corner of the beard that waggled when he talked or when he took a swig from the dark bottle of rum that never left his hand. He staggered to a halt far too close to the others, sneered at Jensen, leered at Gayle, and sniffed suspiciously at Toby.

"I hate visitors. Who the hell are you, boy?"

"I'm Toby Dexter. Who the hell are you?"

"I'm Trash. Child prodigy, eccentric dancer, and necromancer-in-waiting to the Court of St. James, the bastards. I do all the real work around here. I count them all out, and I count them all back. I hold their hands, mop their fevered brows and help them into nice new jackets that tie up at the back. It's my magic that makes this appalling proposition possible. Not that you'd know it from the way I get treated around here. It's a disgrace. I should have been a girl, like Mother wanted."

Toby looked at Jensen. "You have a sorcerer named *Trash*?"

"Hey!" Trash said indignantly. "I am a necromancer! If you're going to insult me, at least have the common decency to be accurate. And I like the name. Chose it myself. It's got style, charisma, it's . . . me. And for some reason, people never seem to have any trouble remembering it." He took a good swig from his bottle, blew nasty-smelling cigar smoke into Jensen's face, and farted loudly. Trash giggled. "Quick, get a match! We'll catch the next one!"

"You're drunk!" said Toby.

"Too bloody right I am," snarled Trash, lurching even closer so that he could glare at Toby more efficiently. "You don't think I could deal with all this shit sober, do you? Place is full of dead people! And crazy dead people, at that. Depressing situation for a man of my refined sensibilities. And it stinks like an abattoir."

Toby had been trying very hard not to notice the smell. "Do I take it you've never done this yourself?"

"Do I look crazy? Anyone tries to kill me, I'll send him home crying with his balls in his hands. I am strictly managerial. I'm only here because someone has to look out for these poor bloody psychos."

"And because we pay you an entirely extortionate amount as a weekly retainer," said Jensen calmly.

"That does help," Trash admitted. "Never be a necromancer, Toby Dexter. The hours stink, the conditions are appalling, and you have to deal with complete loony tunes. I was much happier as an undertaker. Till I got found out." He took another drink and looked expectantly at Gayle. "What are you doing down here, Lady? Come to shut them down at last?"

Gayle had been looking sadly at the dead men and women on their cots. Some of them were quite young. But when she answered Trash, her voice was calm and businesslike. "Everyone has the right to go to Hell in their own way. I don't interfere. No matter how much I may . . . disagree." She looked at Jensen. "Do your lives mean so little to you, that you'd risk them so lightly? Are your lives so empty that only death can fascinate you? This is the antithesis of everything I believe in and stand for."

"Life is not enough," said Jensen, almost condescendingly. "We don't accept any limitations to our search for knowledge. Life is only the beginning; death is forever. We want to know where we're going, if only so we can prepare properly to get the most out of it. Science has always been about pushing back the boundaries. Here, we are taking the first faltering steps into a much larger world. Our volunteers may be doing it mostly for the thrills, but the driving force in the death-walkers has always been a love of knowledge, first and foremost."

"I don't like being here," said Gayle, cutting Jensen off abruptly. "And I don't like having to ask for favors, but it seems I have no choice."

"Ask us anything, dear Lady," Jensen said amiably. "Only too happy to help, to prove our worth."

"What the hell are we doing here, Gayle?" said Toby. "This place is seriously freaking me out."

"We're here to find out what you want to know," Gayle said sharply. "Namely, what precisely it is that makes you so important. Now be quiet and let me handle things. And don't question me. I know what I'm doing." She took a deep breath and turned back to Jensen, who was still smiling his condescending smile. He could tell Gayle was uncomfortable and was being especially friendly and helpful just to rub it in. She wasn't fooled. "I need to talk to the recently dead, Jensen. To be specific, I have questions for those members of the underground railway who were murdered at the station last night, Nicholas Hob's victims. I need information from them."

Jensen shrugged. "Shouldn't be too difficult. Their spirits won't have gone far yet."

He looked at Trash, who belched loudly. "No problem. I've got a girl ready to go out. She's talked to the dead before. Doesn't freak her. Though I'd be hard-pressed to think of anything that would. She's a hard case, even for this place. You can piggyback her, she won't mind. She's died lots of times. Can't keep her away. Knows her way round the afterworlds, and never has any trouble finding her way home. We'll send you off together, and she'll hold the spirits in place so you can ask your questions."

"You know I can't go," Gayle said flatly. "My nature makes it impossible. It has to be Toby."

"*What?*" Toby spun round to glare at Gayle, who looked steadily back at him. Toby was so angry he could hardly get the words out. "*Me* go? Are you out of your mind? Let one of these crazy bastards kill me, in the hope they'll be able to bring me back? There is no way in hell I am doing this! Shit! You had this in mind all along, didn't you?"

"I told you," said Gayle. "I need you to be brave, Toby."

"It's not that dangerous," said Jensen. "Not these days. All right, we lose a few, now and then, well, more than a few, actually. I think they just don't want to come back, which is understandable really."

"Keep that psycho away from me!" Toby glared around him, his hands balled into fists. "I am leaving, right now. Just point me down the right tunnel, and I am out of here."

"Toby," said Gayle, and something in her voice chilled him. "Toby, you can't leave."

"Want to bet? Just watch how fast I can move when I'm properly motivated."

"I need you to do this for me. For both of us. You said you'd do anything for me."

"This isn't what I had in mind, and you know it! You're taking advantage of my feelings for you."

"You said you'd do anything. You said you'd die for me. I need this, Toby. You're the one who said he loved me."

"I can't believe you're asking me to do this," said Toby. "This is emotional blackmail."

"I can't force you to do anything, Toby. It's up to you, and how much I mean to you."

"Come and see our volunteer," suggested Jensen. "When you see how easy she is about it, I'm sure you'll feel a lot better."

"Don't put money on it," muttered Toby, but he allowed Jensen to lead them all to the back of the great chamber, where a tall, busty young woman was lying on her back on a cot, listlessly smoking a cigarette. She sat up as they approached and smiled sardonically at them. Her skin was so pale it was almost luminous, especially when set against the basic black she was wearing. She also had long black hair and wore heavy black eye makeup. The only touch of color was in her blue lips. She had a dozen piercings on her face and ears. She was every Goth girl Toby had ever seen, cranked up to the max. She didn't look healthy. Her bone structure was far too prominent in her face; there were deep hollows under her eyes that the makeup couldn't conceal, and there was a disturbing languor to her movements. As far as Toby was concerned, she looked half dead already. She offered him a limp, cold hand, and he shook it gingerly in case it might come off in his grasp.

"This is Betty Bones," said Jensen, smiling approvingly at her. "One of our most enthusiastic death-walkers. She holds the current record for the most deaths and successful returns."

"Yeah," muttered Toby. "She looks it."

"Oh, we're all very proud of dear Betty. Game for anything, aren't you, dear?"

"Damn right," said Betty, in a breathy whisper. "Nothing is too extreme, that's my motto. I did heroin chic for a while, but this is much sexier. Dying's better than any orgasm."

"Sometimes," said Trash, to no one in particular, "I think I'm the only normal person down here. Which, given my background, is a truly disturbing thought. Lie down, Betty, and I'll send you on your way in a minute. If you meet Elvis again, ask him where he's really buried. Toby, you can have the cot next to hers. One size fits all."

Betty lay back on her cot immediately, smiling as though waiting for a lover. Toby sat reluctantly on the empty cot next to hers and glared at Gayle as she stared impassively down at him.

"I can't believe you're asking me to do this."

"You only think you know me, Toby. I've done harsher things than this, in my time, when I've had to. And this means a lot to me. You will do it for me, won't you?"

Toby's anger ran slowly out of him and was replaced by a tired, bitter acceptance. "Of course I'll do it. You knew I would before I came here. Women like you have always been able to get what they want from men like me."

"You attached yourself to me," Gayle said steadily. "I told you not to. There are good reasons why mortal must not love immortal. But . . . I will be here, all the time you're gone, and I'll be waiting for you when you come back."

"Well, that's a comfort, I suppose." Toby took a deep breath, that didn't calm him nearly as much as he'd hoped it would, and lay back on his cot. The stretched canvas barely gave under his weight, and there was no pillow. He was careful not to look at the cot immediately to his left, already occupied by an especially bloody corpse. Toby's heart was all but leaping out of his chest and despite his hurried breathing, he couldn't seem to get enough air. He wanted just to get up and run, but he didn't, couldn't. Even if Gayle didn't love him, to be needed was something. She sat on the edge of the cot beside him and held his right hand in both of hers.

"I'm scared, Gayle."

"Of course you are. I'm here, Toby. I won't let go. I'd do this myself, if I could . . . but there are some things even I'm not permitted."

"Don't I get a local anesthetic?" Toby tried to smile, but his lips were already trembling too much to cooperate. The presence of death was thick in the room, like another person. "Even the dentist will give you a local."

"Are you scared of the dentist?"

"Terrified. What if this goes wrong?"

"It won't."

"But what if it does?"

"Then I will kill Jensen and Trash slowly and horribly, and send them after you to explain."

"Oh ye of little faith," said Jensen breezily as he joined them. "We do this every day and things rarely go wrong anymore." He stood at the base of the cot and smiled cheerfully down at Toby. "So, how do you want it? We usually recommend poison for first-timers, but that can take time, and our Lady here is looking impatient. Or you could cut your wrists; that's very popular right now among the Goth community."

"Razors are cool," said Betty dreamily from her cot. "You can feel your life just slipping away from you along with the blood."

"Sorry," said Toby. "I'm not the suicidal type."

"Fair enough," said Jensen. "Murder it is."

He drew the gun from the shoulder-holster under his lab coat and shot Betty Bones in the chest. The bullet took her right between the breasts and she spasmed on the cot, her legs jerking. Her head lolled to one side, and Toby saw the light go out of her staring eyes.

He started to say something, but even as he turned back to yell at Jensen, the scientist was already aiming the gun at him. There was a sound louder than thunder, and something punched him hard in the chest. The impact drove him back into the cot, the canvas absorbing the pressure. The bullet knocked the air right out of him, and when Toby tried to breathe more in, he couldn't. There was blood all over his chest, he couldn't breathe and his head was still full of the sound like thunder.

But he didn't die. His body fought stubbornly to cling onto life. His lungs sucked and fluttered in his chest, already filling with blood. He tried to lift his arms and couldn't. There was no pain yet, only a terrible, terrifying numbness. He tried to scream and blood came up his throat and filled his mouth. He jerked on the cot like a fish caught on a hook, going nowhere. He tried to speak to Gayle and thick blood spilled down his chin. She held his hand in both of hers, pressing so hard her knuckles went white, but he couldn't feel it. There was only the new, growing pain in his chest, worse than he could ever have anticipated, and the slow awful fragmenting of his thoughts as the thunder filled his head.

Everything seemed very far away. Darkness was creeping in from all sides. He wanted to tell Gayle he'd changed his mind, that he didn't want to die, that it had all been a terrible mistake, but there was just the blood bubbling in his mouth and Gayle holding his hand, looking down at him with a calm, horribly implacable face. And that was the last thing he saw as the darkness finally, mercifully, swallowed him up.

And then he died.

There was no great tunnel rushing past him. No wondrous light, calling him home. No choir of angels and St. Peter at the gate. No downward-bound train to a lake of fire. No old familiar faces to welcome him in, not even his whole life flashing past one last time.

It was dark and then it was light, and then Toby was sitting in a waiting room so typical it was practically generic. The bare walls were painted in institutional pale green, and there was a vaguely uncomfortable chair and a coffee table almost buried under old issues of the kind of magazines no one really reads anyway. At least there wasn't any Muzak. Toby looked slowly, unhurriedly about him. There was no one else waiting with him. The room felt calm and very peaceful, and it seemed to Toby that he knew this place, that he'd been here before.

Perhaps while he was waiting to be born.

A door opened on the opposite side of the room and a young woman in a stylized nurse's outfit entered and smiled prettily at him.

"Mr. Toby Dexter? Death will see you now."

Toby nodded to her, rose to his feet, and walked over to the door she was holding open for him. It never occurred to him not to. The door closed behind him with a solid-sounding thud, and he found himself in a bare white room, just big enough to hold a standard office desk with a chair on both sides. Sitting behind the desk, which held two wire trays overflowing with official-looking papers, was a beautiful woman. Her smile was warm and welcoming. Toby trusted her immediately. He knew he'd never seen her before, but her face was immediately familiar, as though he'd always known her. He sat down in the empty chair, while Death studied the thick file in her hands.

"Toby Dexter. You really shouldn't be here, you know. It isn't your time yet."

"I couldn't agree more," said Toby. "I'm supposed to be piggy-backing one of the death-walkers."

"Oh, *them,*" said Death, pulling a face. "Bloody nuisances. They've been shooting back and forth so often just lately I've been seriously considering installing a revolving door. It won't do them any good. Their spirits can't travel far enough to learn anything really interesting without leaving their bodies permanently behind. You'd have thought they'd have figured that out after all these years. Still, hope springs eternal in the minds of the seriously deluded."

"You don't mind?" said Toby dubiously.

Death shrugged easily. "Let them play. Everyone has to come to terms with dying, and this is their way."

"Do they all get to meet you?"

"No. They've never seen me. You only got this short interview because you're special."

Toby groaned loudly. "You have no idea how tired I'm getting of hearing that. All right, I'm a focal point. But can you at least tell me why?"

Death smiled. "It was decided where all the things that matter are decided. You have been given the power to decide the fates of peoples and of worlds."

"But I don't want that kind of responsibility!"

"Then you're the very best kind to have it."

"Why *me*?" said Toby, almost plaintively.

"Don't ask me. I don't move in those kinds of circles. For what it's worth, I think the Creator occasionally likes to test his creations, to see what they'll do. To see how far they've come."

"But . . . what am I supposed to *do*? No one will tell me!"

"You'll know, when the time comes. Every martyr has to choose their own cross. Be strong, be brave . . . and be yourself. Follow your heart, Toby. And if it does all go wrong, I promise I'll be here, waiting for you."

"Where is this place?" said Toby.

"Don't ask me. It's your mind we're talking in. See you again, Toby. See you again."

Toby sat up suddenly on his cot, his lungs sucking in air. There was blood in his mouth, and he spat it out, but there wasn't much. He clutched at his chest, but the wound was already healed. Gayle was still holding his hand in both of hers. Toby looked wildly about him. Everything looked very sharp, very bright. At the next cot, the necromancer Trash was leaning over Betty Bones, who was lying very still. Toby breathed harshly; his body felt like a small and fragile thing, and very precious. He also felt cold, terribly cold. He was shuddering violently now, full of the chill of death. He started to cry, and Gayle took him in her arms, holding him close, warming his body with the heat of her own. Toby would have liked to push her away, but he didn't have the strength. And besides, right then he needed to be held. Gayle rocked him slowly back and forth, containing his shivers in the resilience of her own body, until gradually they died away.

"Hush," she said. "Hush, hush, it's all right now. It's all over."

"You don't know what you did to me," said Toby, forcing the words past his tears. "You don't know what you made me do."

"I'm sorry I hurt you, Toby. I always hurt the ones who get closest to me. I'm not allowed to have favorites. Goes with the job."

After a while he stopped crying and stopped shaking, but Gayle still held him, and Toby let her hold him. He needed to believe, if only for a while, that she cared for him on some level. But eventually pride made him push her away, and she let go of him immediately. They sat there on the cot for a long moment, just looking into each other's faces.

"I'm back," Toby said finally. "Surprised?"

"Not at all," said Gayle. "I always knew you were too stubborn to be beaten this easily. I never doubted your strength of will to return for a moment. Welcome back, my hero."

"More like your fool," said Toby.

"Where did you go?" said Gayle. "What did you see?"

Toby frowned. "It's like a dream, the details already fading. But . . . I wasn't with Betty. Where—?"

He looked past Gayle to see Trash working fiercely on Betty's unresponsive form. He leaned over to breathe air into her slack mouth, and then hit her hard on the chest, again and again, all the time chanting angrily in a language Toby didn't recognize. Jensen hovered nearby, capturing it all on video. And then, finally, Betty Bones convulsed on her cot and sat bolt upright, almost hitting Trash in the face. She made a sound like being born, opened her eyes, snatched his cigar from his mouth and stuck it in hers. Trash stopped chanting, patted her fondly on the head, and took a long drink from his bottle. Betty ran her hand slowly through her hair and blinked a few times.

"That was intense," she said dreamily. "I went a lot farther than

I've ever been before. But I lost the new guy. Something just . . . ripped him away from me."

Jensen quickly turned his camera on Toby. "So where did you go, Toby Dexter? What did you see?"

"She was very beautiful," Toby said slowly. "But I can't remember . . . what she said."

Jensen lowered his camera, looking disappointed but not surprised. "Don't worry, Toby. Few people bring back much from their first trip."

"So it was all for nothing," said Toby, looking at Gayle. "Everything you put me through; everything I did for you. All for nothing."

"I learned something," said Gayle. "I learned what you're made of, Toby. And how much you love me."

She reached out to touch his face, and he flinched back. Gayle looked at him sadly. Jensen coughed politely.

"Yes, well, let's see how our little Betty did. She's a much more experienced traveler."

He turned the camcorder on Betty, who smiled into the lens with practiced ease. "I found Hob's victims, or some of them, anyway. They never knew what Hob was really up to, only that his plans, or rather his father's plans, were a threat to the whole of Mysterie—a threat to its very nature. That's why they thought they'd be safer in Veritie."

"But the nature of Mysterie never changes," said Gayle, frowning. "That's the point. What could the Serpent possibly be planning that could threaten the very essence of Mysterie?"

And that was when all the dead people on the cots came back to life simultaneously. One moment they were just so many bloodied corpses, and the next they were all sitting up at once, thrust back into life. A lot of them were screaming. Trash and Jensen and even Betty Bones ran back and froth, holding and comforting the returnees and asking what had happened. It quickly emerged that the death-walkers had been thrown out of the afterworlds, though they couldn't or wouldn't say by what or by whom. All they knew for sure was that *Something Bad* was coming, heading right for Mysterie and Veritie, and that they were banned from the realms beyond life until it was all over, one way or another. A lot of them mentioned Toby Dexter's name. And on learning that he was right there with them, these men and women who were so unafraid of death that they did it every day, just for kicks, looked at him with spooked and wondering eyes.

"I think it's time we were leaving," said Gayle.

"You took the words right out of my mouth," said Toby.

They waited till they were well out of the death-walkers' lair, and were walking back through the Sacred Heart cemetery, before they had their argument. Toby's anger had plenty of time to build, and by the time he finally spoke to Gayle, who seemed as cool and calm as ever, it was all he could do to keep from shouting at her.

"You used me."

"Yes. We didn't get nearly as much out of it as I'd hoped, but then, I always knew it was a long shot."

"You used me! You knew I couldn't say no to you. And all for what? What do we have now, that was worth what I went through?"

"I did what I had to," said Gayle. "You don't know what it cost me, to ask favors from them."

"Since it didn't involve getting shot through the chest, I don't think I care! So what if it hurt your pride? I can still taste blood in my mouth!"

"Keep your voice down," said Gayle. "You never know who might be listening. Especially here."

"I thought you knew what you were doing. But you're just as lost and confused as the rest of us, only you won't admit it. I don't know who or what you really are, or used to be, but it's clear you've been human too long. You're out of touch. I don't know why I've followed you this far."

"Because you love me."

"Do I? Do you care for me at all, Gayle? Does my pain mean anything to you?"

"I care about it. But I can't let it matter to me. I have to see the bigger picture."

"You can't see anything anymore! You're as divorced from what's really going on as your crazy sister. She said I ought to ask Jimmy Thunder for help, and I'm beginning to think she might be right. He has good contacts, in Veritie and in Mysterie, and I don't think he'd lower himself to betray me the way you did."

Gayle stiffened at the bitterness in his voice. "I did what I had to! You can't see things as I have to. And you can't trust anything Luna says. She's crazy."

"Then why did we go to see her?"

"Don't you question me, Toby Dexter. You don't have the right!"

"I don't have the right? I died for you, Gayle!"

"I never said I loved you," said Gayle. "I tried to warn you away, told you you'd only get hurt if you insisted on hanging around me. I do care for you, Toby, but I'll sacrifice you in a moment, if I have to. I have greater responsibilities, greater duties, than you can imagine, and I can't put them aside for one lovesick young fool who followed me through the wrong door."

"I died for you because I trusted you."

"I've seen a lot of people die."

"Damn you."

Gayle looked at him tiredly. "What do you want from me, Toby? I can't feel for you the way you want me to feel. I never asked you to love me, never wanted it. I care for lots of people, and often I can't save them either. If you weren't a focal point, I'd have cut you loose long ago. As it is, we might as well talk to Jimmy again. I've run out of ideas."

Toby sniffed. "I feel safer already."

# Eight ~
# At Home with Leo Morn

SAFE AND SECURE in the real world, Leo Morn lived in a charming little seventeenth-century cottage on the banks of the Kennet and Avon Canal. It was a pleasant, isolated domicile, with thick, solid walls of the local creamy-gray stone, heavy oaken doors, and latticed windows, topped with the traditional thatched roof. The only sign of modernity was the television aerial holding up the rather rickety-looking chimney stack. There was a burglar alarm, but Leo hardly ever bothered setting it, on the unanswerable grounds that he owned nothing worth stealing. The cottage was a comfortable distance away from the hustle and bustle of the town center, while still within easy walking distance of the nearest pub. From the outside, Leo's cottage was a picturesque, even enchanting sight, a relic of times past and qualities not forgotten. Inside, it was a dump, and visitors had to be very careful where they put their feet. Some men just aren't suited to living alone. In fact, some men are absolute pigs when they don't have a woman running around cleaning up after them.

Leo Morn didn't give a damn. Mostly.

Today he scowled fiercely as he kicked his way through the accumulated junk and rubbish cluttering up the floor of his living room. Normally he wouldn't even have seen it, but right then he needed something to take out his bad temper on. So old pizza boxes, stacks of old newspapers and magazines, and mounds of general refuse best not investigated too closely went flying this way and that under the urging of his boot, making the living room even more of a disaster area than it had been before. Leo ran out of energy before he ran out of bile, and reluctantly slumped into his favorite chair. He looked moodily at the antique Moroccan table beside him, still layered with the debris of several meals. Leo only ever cleaned up after meals when there wasn't any room left for the latest addition. In fact, he didn't think he'd ever taken the cloth off the table since the day he first put it on. This in turn reminded him of the tottering piles of dirty crockery currently filling the kitchen sink, but he pushed the thought firmly aside. He was depressed enough as it was.

Leo chewed cheerlessly at the week-old slice of pizza he'd found stuck to the top of his bedside table. The cold crust was overly crunchy, but the pepperoni still had a pleasant tang. Leo was a great comfort eater, when he couldn't get sex. The cottage had always been his shelter, his safe haven, his refuge from all the demands the world insisted on making on him, and the growing certainty that he was going to have to leave it depressed him mightily. Not that he had any choice in the matter. Hob had seen him, back at Blackacre farmhouse, and it was only a matter of time before he, or more likely one of his nastier agents, came looking for the poor deluded fool who had dared to spy on the great and powerful Nicholas Hob. Leo had decided not to be around when that happened. In fact, very soon now he was going to choose a horizon and then disappear over it at speed. He finished the last of the pizza, licked his fingers, and scowled about him. He was really going to miss this cottage. Particularly after all he'd gone through to acquire it.

The cottage was a listed building, an architectural treasure of historical interest protected by the National Trust, and therefore not surprisingly worth at least a hundred and fifty thousand pounds on the open market. Leo couldn't have raised that kind of money if his life had depended on it, but he'd set his heart on living there, so he acquired it the way he usually got things he wanted but couldn't afford: by being sneaky, underhanded, and utterly conscienceless. In this case that involved tracking down the pleasant fortyish widow who owned the property, and sleeping with her. He went on sleeping with her until she agreed to sell him the cottage, for a staggeringly low sum, waited till all the contracts had been signed and exchanged, and then stopped sleeping with her. Leo wasn't much of a one for looking back. He never answered her phone calls, didn't even bother opening her letters, and in the end she left him alone to enjoy his cottage. Leo had heard about guilt, conscience, and integrity, and wanted nothing to do with any of them. They just complicated things and got in the way of a comfortable life.

The cold pizza left him even hungrier. He surged up out of his chair and stomped off into the adjoining kitchen. He headed straight for the fridge, not even glancing at the packed sink, and tugged open its filthy, fingerprinted door. Next to the piled-up six-packs was a fat leg of lamb, fresh from the butcher's that morning—still raw and bloody, the way he liked it. He took it out and ripped off the shrink-wrapping, forcing the fridge door shut again with his shoulder. His nostrils twitched at the delicious smell, and he chewed hungrily at the raw meat and gnawed on the bone as he made his way back into the living room. The simplest pleasures were the best. And he always got hungry when he was planning something.

Right now he was planning on running away, and the only thing left to be decided was how far he'd have to go before he could be sure he was safe.

The voice of his Brother Under The Hill intruded on his thoughts, the usual nagging reminder of things left undone. *I thought we were going to talk to someone about what we discovered at Blackacre Farm? About Hob raising the dead from their graves?*

"*I have thought about it, and the only thing I feel like saying is good-bye,*" Leo said firmly. "*I am not stupid enough to go up against the likes of Nicholas Hob and Angel. They could chew me up and spit me out, and not even notice unless part of me got stuck in their teeth.*"

*Even after they dragged your friend Reed up out of his grave and sent him walking through the town?*

*"All the more reason not to stick around so he could do the same thing to me. Reed would understand. He knew he couldn't depend on me, even when he was alive."*

If Nicholas Hob is up to something big, where can you go and still be safe?

*"I'll lose myself in London. I've done it before. There's always enough magical shit going on in the Smoke that even the Hob won't be able to find me. I still have my old contacts in the clubs, from the last time I toured there. They loved me at Strangefellows. Whatever Hob's up to, it isn't my responsibility to do anything about it."*

No. It never is, is it?

*"Look, whatever's going to happen, I do not want to be here at ground zero when it goes off."*

Are you planning on telling anyone before you leave?

*"No."*

Are you planning on taking anyone with you?

*"No."*

I would say I'm disappointed, but I've known you too long. Your father—

*"My father got himself and my mother killed, trying to play the hero! Trying to live up to what you wanted him to be! I've got more sense."*

The Brother sighed heavily. *I've raised Morns for generations. Been guardian to a line of heroes and warriors. Where did I go wrong with you, Leo?*

*"You let my parents die."*

Leo realized he'd eaten all the meat off the bone. He cracked the bone in two to get at the marrow, got out as much as he could be bothered with, and then threw the pieces of bone away. They disappeared into the sea of rubbish on the floor. Leo dropped back into his comfortable chair, all his energy suddenly gone. He knew he had to leave, and soon. He knew that every moment he delayed was a risk, but leaving his home and his town didn't come easily to him. He'd put a lot of effort into establishing a comfortable, undemanding, *safe* life, and he fiercely resented having to give it up. All Leo had ever wanted was to be left alone, to drift through his life as he saw fit, with no encumbrances and no commitments. And mostly, he'd achieved that. No great accomplishments, no triumphs to boast of, but no duties and no dependents either. No responsibilities to anyone, or for anyone. And now, because of his curiosity, and a vague feeling that he ought to avenge a dead friend, he was going to have to give it all up, leave behind the few things he genuinely valued, to run off and hide in the grubbier bolt-holes of the Smoke. It wasn't fair.

*Will you be taking anything with you?* said his Brother, echoing his thoughts.

"*Would you?*" said Leo. "*It's all junk. Stuff that fell off my life when I wasn't looking. There's nothing here I can't replace in London. Travel light, travel fast. I'll still be able to hear your nagging voice. What else is there that matters?*"

*Are you really going to leave your whole life behind?*

"*A life?*" said Leo, with sudden bitter honesty. "*That's something other people have, isn't it? My life ended the day my parents were taken from me. I was ten years old, remember? Hell of a birthday present. Since then, there's just been me. Doing what I have to to get by. Lots of acquaintances, but few real friends. Too wild an animal for most people, civilized people. I never fit in, never really wanted to. Damned by my father's legacy to be a lone wolf. All I've had, all I've ever really had, is you. And that's only because the exorcism didn't work.*"

*What about your many girlfriends? Shouldn't you at least call them, tell them you're leaving? Some of them might actually worry about you.*

"*I seriously doubt it. If you'd been paying attention, you'd know that none of them are currently speaking to me. I keep telling them I don't do the commitment thing, but they never listen. They just smile and nod and think,* This time it'll be different, *until finally I have to rub their noses in it. And then they get all upset. Sometimes I think I should prepare a form letter to hand out in advance, just so they've got it in writing.*"

*It certainly might have helped the one who cut her wrists.*

"*I drove her to the hospital, didn't I?*"

*Why are you always breaking up with them, Leo? Some of them really do care for you, though God alone knows why they should.*

Leo sighed tiredly. *"If you leave them first, they don't get a chance to hurt you by leaving."*

*Like your parents left you?*

*"Shut up. Just shut the hell up. Let me think."*

Leo lurched to his feet and kicked the hell out of everything around him, including the fittings and furniture. He broke a satisfying number of things, and generally redistributed a lot of the junk on the floor, but in the end nothing had changed. His life was still the same. He stood in the middle of the room, breathing heavily, head hanging down, and couldn't say he felt any better. Things had come to a pretty pass when even casual violence and destructiveness couldn't comfort him. As always, when pushed into a corner, Leo lashed out.

*"Stop trying to make me feel guilty about leaving! There's nothing I can do here, and you know it! Not against Nicholas Hob and Angel!"*

*I know many things,* said his Brother Under The Hill calmly. *I see the past as well as the present, and sometimes hints of things to come. I see the ever-changing web of fate, and the way its strands reach subtly out to entangle people, struggle as they may. Whatever Hob is planning, it must be something big, something unprecedentedly significant, even for him. It's hard for me to see him at the best of times, given who and what he is, but right now the skeins of fate are boiling all around Black-acre, changing and reforming with every moment, with every thought and decision Nicholas Hob has. I've never seen such terrible potential in one place before. Whatever he's planning threatens the whole of Mysterie.*

"Good," said Leo. *"Let it all burn. Nothing good ever came out of Mysterie, only threats and dangers and madness. And cursed, damned lives like mine."*

*And me? Am I a curse?*

*"Look, even if I was prepared to stay, which I'm not, what the hell could I do? I'm not a power in this town; let one of the real movers and shakers deal with Hob. Someone who's happy to play the hero. I am out of here."*

There was a sudden, and very unexpected, knock at the front door. Leo froze where he was, hardly breathing. No one should be able to approach his cottage without his Brother noticing. No one *normal.* Leo looked quickly about him. There were no lights on in the cottage, no sounds, nothing to show that anyone was at home. He stood perfectly still, listening. Beads of sweat popped out on his forehead. He could hear someone moving restlessly outside the front door.

*"Can you see who it is?"* he said mentally to his Brother.

*No. Which is unusual, in Veritie. Only one of the really major players would be able to shield themselves that thoroughly, in the real world. But I think we can safely assume it isn't Nicholas Hob or Angel, on the grounds that they wouldn't have bothered to knock.*

*"But why would a major player come looking for me? No one else even knows I was at Blackacre."*

Whoever it was knocked at the door again, a little more firmly. They clearly weren't going to go away. Leo scowled, and very reluctantly crossed the room to the front door. With his current luck it was probably someone from the Inland Revenue. He opened the door just enough to look out, and then wider as he took in his visitor. She was pretty in an unfinished kind of way, only just out of her teens, all blond hair and wide eyes and an innocent smile, and Leo was damned if he recognized her at all. He was pretty sure she wasn't an old girlfriend. He usually liked them a little older and a lot more experienced. She was wearing a light summery frock and a cute little black beret over long blond hair that fell straight to her shoulders. Her hands were clasped tightly in front of her, the knuckles white with tension, but her smile was sweet and open. It took Leo a moment to realize that for all her youth, she had icy-blue eyes as old as the world.

*Hell and damnation!* said his Brother, something very like shock in his mental voice. *I don't believe it! That's Luna!*

*"Jesus!"* said Leo.

*No, I'm pretty sure it's Luna.*

*"What the hell is she doing out in the real world?"*

*Ask her in and find out. I'm absolutely dying to know.*

Leo quickly remembered what passed for his manners, and

stepped back from the door, inviting Luna in with a mute wave of his hand. She glided forward into his living room, moving with more than natural poise and grace. Then she stopped and looked about her, frowning prettily, politely appalled by all the mess but too well bred to say so. Leo stared at her for a while, honestly enchanted, then pushed the front door shut and hurried forward to clear the best chair for her to sit in. She regarded the chair dubiously for a moment and then smiled and settled into it as if it were a throne. Leo pulled up his other chair and sat down facing her. Something about her took his breath away, even apart from knowing who and what she was. Luna turned the full force of her beaming smile on him, and Leo did his best to smile back. It felt rather like having a lion in his living room. Luna was a Power and a Domination, not to mention as crazy as a loon, and could crush him like a bug if the notion took her.

"So," said Luna, in a light, breathy, and not at all threatening voice, "I have tracked you to your lair, Leo Morn, last of the line of Morn. Not quite what I expected, but then I so rarely know what to expect anymore. The world is a complete surprise to me. Yes. You know, you really are going to have to do something with this place. Preferably involving fumigation."

Leo laughed politely. "How did you find me?" he said, careful to keep his voice entirely respectful. "I didn't think people like you knew people like me even existed."

"I see all, from my high vantage," Luna said airily. "Nothing is hidden, nothing is ever lost, nothing is ever forgotten. That's always been part of my problem."

Leo studied her openly and for the moment she seemed content to let him. Luna hadn't walked in Veritie, the brutal and unforgiving real world, for as long as anyone in the town could remember. Her home only existed in Mysterie, a magical refuge surrounded by ancient and powerful spells of protection. *As much,* some whispered, *to protect the town from her, as vice versa.* And there she lived her quiet, insane life, troubling no one, asking only to be disregarded and left alone. And anyone with any sense did just that. One does not wake the dragon without good reason. Now here she was, out and about in the real world, without even a warning. She looked small, vulnerable, and really quite ordinary. Pretty enough, but nothing spectacular. And she had a sad, battered, beaten-down look that was immediately familiar to Leo; a harsh reminder of every woman he'd ever used and hurt and abandoned. Despite himself, he felt obscurely guilty.

He knew the story of Luna's rape. Everyone did.

"I came to you," Luna said suddenly, "because I know your Brother Under The Hill. I've known him for a long time. And I have been out of touch for so long that he is the only one in this town that I can still remember. Apart from my sister, of course. Poor Gayle, still trying so very hard to be human. Your Brother is very special. I remember him from before he was Under The Hill."

Leo's ears pricked up immediately. "Really? I don't suppose you know who put him there? He won't talk about it to me."

"He's never told you? Then perhaps it's not my place to say either. I know so many things, and it's hard to remember which of them are supposed to be secrets. But if you need to know . . ."

*I put myself Under The Hill,* said the Brother heavily. *I killed the first of your line, Leo. The first Morn, long, long ago. He was a good man, and a great hero, though I didn't realize that until it was too late. This is my penance, to be interred forever and a day because I was wrong. Because I was blind, and would not see.*

"And now you see everything," said Leo, "and you're still killing Morns."

*I have raised and guarded heroes, preserved the line from its many enemies. But for all my years, I am not infallible. Yes, I failed your parents, Leo. Is that what you want me to say? I mourn their loss just as much as you do. I am your Brother.*

"What was he?" Leo said to Luna. "Originally, I mean. Do you remember?"

"Of course I remember. That was back when giants walked the earth, and he was one of them. He was Nephilim, child of angels. So beautiful, and so cursed. Hello, Brother. Hello."

*Hello, Luna. How are you?*

"Better than I was."

Leo looked sharply at Luna. "You can hear him? I thought I was the only one."

"I hear everything, from my high station," Luna said sadly. "That's always been part of my problem."

It was clear to Leo that if he followed up all the questions he wanted to ask, he and Luna would still be sitting here this time tomorrow, so he made himself concentrate on the matter at hand. "What brings you here, Luna? To me, in reality?"

"My sister, Gayle, came to see me," Luna said slowly. "Her presence awoke me from my long stupor, from my dreams. She came to me for advice and help, which shows how desperate she must be. There was a young man with her, a focal point. His presence helped to focus me, to collect my scattered selves, if only for a while. I feel stronger now, more . . . coherent. Together. Yes. Gayle's words stay with me. What she said, and what she didn't say. For once, I didn't forget.

"So I went out into the town, to look around. It seems much the same in spirit, though the details have changed. Not for the better, I suspect, but then, I'm no judge. And as I walked in Veritie, my reason no longer clouded by my own protective spells, I could see the Hob was planning again. He's had plans before, his own and those of his accursed father, but this . . . this is something new. I can tell. The Serpent's never been this ambitious before. He knows something, or thinks he does. I think this time he's planning to play for all the marbles. . . ."

Leo didn't know what to say to that. Anyone else of her rank and station he would have believed immediately; but this was Luna, whose very name was a byword for madness. And yet . . . he'd seen Hob and Angel, sitting together in that rotting farmhouse, seen the dead men standing guard in the dead woods.

"How are you enjoying reality?" he said finally, just to be saying something, and then winced as he realized how that sounded.

"It's very cramped," said Luna, quite seriously. "Much too small and confining, compared to what I'm used to. But I couldn't go traveling in Mysterie without Hob noticing, so I was forced to translate myself into the real world. It was quite a shock. I haven't been real in such a long time . . . but I am more centered here, more focused. Less crazy. I've been able to think here."

"Why haven't you gone to see your sister?" said Leo. "She's still a Power. She can do much more for you than I can."

"Gayle has been human too long," Luna said flatly. "All those years of being real have limited her thinking. She's reluctant to embrace her responsibilities and take on her aspect again. She could leave it too late, and find herself unable to stop Hob. And she's emotionally linked to the young man, the focal point. Dangerous things, focal points. This link, whatever it turns out to be, makes her unpredictable. Bottom line: We can't trust her to do the right thing."

"But why come to *me?*" Leo said plaintively.

"Because I need a hero. I need a Morn. Thanks to the Brother Under The Hill, those of your line have been champions of the good and the just for centuries."

"But I'm not like them!"

"You'd better be," said Luna. "Or we're all dead."

Leo felt like whining. He had a very sick feeling in the pit of his stomach. "Define *all.*"

"Everyone, in all of Veritie and Mysterie, perhaps. Or maybe worse than dead. You can't outrun what's coming, Leo Morn. No one can. Not even me."

"What is coming?"

"I don't know. But it feels like the End. Of everything."

There was a long pause, and all Leo could think, over and over, was *oh, shit.* He searched frantically for some hole in Luna's argument.

"How could even Nicholas Hob hope to hurt your sister?" he said eventually. "Given who and what she is? Hob may be the Serpent's Son, but she's a lot bigger than that. Even with Angel at his side, surely there's a limit to the damage he can do?"

Luna cocked her head on one side. "You know about Angel? Ah, yes; you went sneaking out to Blackacre, and saw them in conference together. I know there was a particular reason why I came to you. You found a way in, past all Hob's defenses. Quite remarkable. I want you to do it again. Take me back there, into the dark heart of Blackacre."

Leo could feel cold fingers wrapping tightly around his heart. This just kept getting worse and worse. If there was one place in the world he definitely didn't want to see again . . . There had been a definite air of madness and awful intent about the dead house in the dead wood, a sense of danger to body and soul. But he couldn't just say *No, thank you,* or, *Not a chance in hell,* not to as powerful and potentially crazy a personage as Luna. Even here in reality, sitting in his chair, all sweetness and innocence, Luna was scarier than Hob and Angel put together. She could turn him inside out with a thought, and still keep him alive and suffering for as long as it amused her. She'd done worse, in her time.

*"What about you, Brother?"* he said finally, desperately. *"Can you see anything of Hob's plans? Or anything to suggest that the worlds are in danger?"*

*No,* said the Brother thoughtfully. *But given the nature and strength of a creature like Hob, I wouldn't expect to. In fact, if he put his mind to it, he could be standing outside your front door right now, and I wouldn't know it until he'd burned the cottage down.*

"Now there's a comforting thought." Leo looked unhappily at Luna. "What exactly are you planning to do, if I can get you to the farmhouse?"

"I will talk to Hob," said Luna. "He is my son."

"I see. And when did you last talk to him?"

Luna considered for a while. "Do you know, I don't think I ever have. So it's probably well past time we sat down and had a good mother-and-son chat. I've been neglecting my duties."

"Look," said Leo, "I really don't think this is such a good idea. . . ."

Luna stood up abruptly and took just a little of her aspect upon her. The cottage was suddenly full of a shimmering silver light,

almost too bright to be borne. It suffused Leo's body and mind like
a howl of ancient days, of running free in the wild woods, and his
heart leaped in response. He wanted to fall to his knees and worship
her, to hunt down some fleeing thing and lay it bloody and smoking at her feet. She was the mistress of his soul, of his wild and un-
tamed lone-wolf soul, and he would have done anything for her
right then, anything at all, sacrificed or been the sacrifice, all for her,
for she was the goddess of the hunt.

The light snapped off and was gone, and Leo was unsurprised to
find himself on his knees before Luna. But even as he tried to find
a voice to say something, Luna frowned and the whole cottage
*shifted* as she translated it out of Veritie and into Mysterie, by sheer
act of will. For a moment the living room was full of the ghosts of
its previous owners, drifting and flickering through the room, until
Luna dismissed them with a wave of her hand. Leo bowed his head,
sweating and shuddering, in the presence of something so much
greater than himself.

Luna smiled terribly upon him, and then shut down her aspect
and became just a woman again. She sat down in her chair, arranged
herself comfortably, and smiled sweetly on Leo as he scrambled to
his feet and all but collapsed back into his chair.

"I have need of you, Leo Morn," Luna said, calmly, implacably.
"The Morns have always been heroes."

"But I abdicated!" said Leo, whining.

*And of course, you have so many other important things to do. . . .*

*"Whose side are you on?"* said Leo, feeling outnumbered and distinctly hard-done-by.

*Wait a minute. Someone's here . . . I didn't see them coming. Why
didn't I see them coming? Hell's teeth, it's Angel! She's found us, now
we're in Mysterie! She's right outside the front door!*

Leo surged up out of his chair and sprinted across the room to
lock and bolt the front door.

*That won't stop her. Steel plating won't stop Angel, if she wants in.*

*"Then think of something that will!"*

"I don't suppose you have any weapons in this place?" said Luna, rising unhurriedly from her chair. "Arthames, Elder Signs, shaped curses?"

"Never felt the need for any before now." Leo looked quickly about him. "Come with me. There's a back door. . . ."

And then they all fell silent as they heard Angel run up the outside wall of the cottage. It was a light, eerie sound, like an insect the size of a man scuttling over the uneven stone. She strode unhurriedly across the roof, her great heavy footsteps crushing the thatching, to let them know where she was. The room shook under the impact of each awful tread and Leo was afraid she might come crashing through the roof at any moment. Luna craned her neck back to look up, seeming more interested than anything. It occurred to Leo that this was his worst nightmare come true: to be trapped between two powerful women who might destroy him in their fight over him. He tried to smile at the thought but there was no humor in him, and anyway his mouth was too dry. Angel had come to kill him, and there was nowhere left to hide.

The heavy footsteps stopped. Leo and Luna looked around them. It was very quiet. And then there was a thud outside the front door as something heavy hit the ground, and even as Leo spun round, Angel smashed through the locked and bolted door in one sudden movement. The solid oak tore like paper, and the hinges flew across the room like shrapnel, torn from the doorjamb. Angel stood framed by the wreckage of the doorway, a menacing figure as pale as a ghost, wrapped in black tatters, grinning fiercely and with glowing, bloodred eyes. Leo made a sound in his throat. Angel took a step forward and laughed happily as he took a step back.

"Little animal, I have sniffed you out," said Angel, smiling her inhuman smile. "You shouldn't have come spying to Blackacre. Shouldn't have made yourself known to us. Nicholas Hob wants to talk to you. I'd just as soon kill you now, but he's curious. Maybe after he's finished with you, he'll let me play with what's left of you."

"I don't play well with other people," said Leo. He tried to sound calm and composed, even threatening, but Angel didn't look at all impressed.

"Pretty Angel," said Luna. Her face had gone all vague, and her eyes were unfocused. Her summery frock had changed to a gypsyish outfit of brightly colored blouse and skirt, and her blond hair now had thick curls in it. The black beret had been replaced by a knotted kerchief. Leo's heart sank. Luna was drifting again. Being in Veritie had kept her focused, but the move back to Mysterie must have weakened her grip on herself. Angel looked at Luna and frowned.

"I feel I should know you. But it doesn't matter. Stay out of my way or I'll kill you."

Luna giggled and brought one hand up to her rosebud mouth so she could suck on her thumb. Her eyes were very far away now. Angel turned back to Leo.

"Come with me. Come with me now, or I'll hurt you. I think you'd break very easily."

"Ah, hell," said Leo resignedly. "Some days fate just won't leave you alone."

He reached deep inside himself, called on his father's heritage and *changed*. Thick fur burst out all over his body. His legs lengthened. Claws erupted from his feet and hands. His back arched and a tail burst out of his hindquarters. His face shot forward, forming a long muzzle crammed with sharp fangs. His clothes disappeared as he fell forward onto all fours, seven foot long, three hundred pounds, all wolf and angry with it. Like his ancestors before him, Leo Morn was a shape-shifter. A lycanthrope. A *werewolf.*

"Cute little puppy," said Angel. "You are full of surprises, aren't you? Still, time to go walkies, Leo Morn."

Leo went for her throat.

His powerful back legs propelled him forward faster than the human eye could follow, his vicious jaws gaping and slavering as he launched himself, but Angel didn't even fall back a step. She caught him by the throat with one hand and held him fast, absorbing his speed and the impact of his weight as though it were nothing. Leo kicked and scrabbled helplessly as her fingers closed around his windpipe like steel bands. Angel laughed in his changed face and threw him from her. He flew across the width of the living room and smashed into the far wall, hard enough to crack the plaster. He hit the floor already back on his feet again, and went to meet Angel snarling as she advanced on him, her pale fingers crooked like claws. Luna wasn't even watching.

Leo ducked under Angel's reaching hands and tore a wide rip across her belly. The blood that flowed was thick and dark, intoxicating in the wolf's flaring nostrils. He howled, an ancient, primal sound full of rage and defiance and blood lust. He and Angel circled each other for a moment, respectful of each other's strength, and then Angel lashed out and her more-than-human fist crushed the side of his skull, driving the bone sharply inward. A killing blow, under normal circumstances. Leo grinned widely as the bone popped back out again, and the wound healed in seconds. He was *were,* and only silver could hurt him now.

*For God's sake, Leo!* The Brother Under The Hill was yelling in his mind almost constantly now, forcing his words through the wolf's killing frenzy. *Grab Luna and get the hell out of there! I'll think of something to slow Angel down. You can't beat her! She really is a descended angel!*

"*What makes you so sure?*" said Leo, allowing some of his human mind to resurface for a moment.

*Because I recognize her.*

Which was a very interesting statement, and one Leo would have liked to follow up, but Angel came at him again, and the blood lust drove all other thoughts from his mind. They slammed together, pounding and clawing at each other, ignoring the damage they took in their determination to bring the other down. To Leo's enhanced wolfish senses, Angel seemed more than real, burning bright like a flame at night, elemental and almost pure in her fury. Part of Leo wanted just to curl up at her feet and be petted, but that only made him fight all the more fiercely. His emotions were larger now, more extreme. He could still taste her blood in his mouth, and he wanted more.

He surged forward, ignoring the pale hand that clawed his left eye clean out of its socket, and fastened his jaws around her throat.

The flesh actually resisted his fangs, but he bore down, forcing his mouth shut with great wolfish jaw muscles, and blood spurted into his mouth as his teeth sank in. They fell to the floor, tearing at each other like lovers in the heat of a furious passion, and Angel grabbed Leo's elongated head with both hands and forced his jaws away from her throat. She was bleeding heavily and laughing breathlessly. She brought her knees up sharply, and Leo's ribs splintered and broke under the impact. He coughed harshly, his own blood flying from his muzzle to spray Angel's face.

She kicked him away and rose quickly to her feet as he lay scrabbling on the floor, struggling desperately for breath. And then she stepped forward and stamped on his head. The skull fractured, and Angel stamped again and again and again, not allowing the splintering bone to repair itself. Sharp bone fragments were driven deep into Leo's brain and all he could do was howl like a soul newly damned to Hell.

And then Luna woke up. She stood tall and proud in a long gown of shimmering samite, and light blazed from her face as she took her aspect upon her. The silver light hit Angel like a hammer, forcing her away from Leo. The harsh, implacable light drove Angel back, for all her struggles, and something in that light seemed to diminish her, making her smaller and more human. In the end Angel screamed with rage and turned and fled, rather than face a light and a presence that was so much greater than she was.

Leo lay on his side on the floor, panting hard, listening to the sharp popping sounds in his head as his skull repaired itself. Angel's blood was still sharp in his mouth, and he surged to his feet, turning his head back and forth as he tracked the sound of Angel's departing footsteps.

*Don't you dare,* his Brother said firmly. *You were lucky, Leo. For all your heritage, you are not in Angel's class. Now change back. We need your human mind, your common sense, because we sure as hell aren't going to get it from Luna.*

Leo became a man again, in a series of twists and jerks, his bones cracking loudly as his shape changed. His fur sank back into his skin and his clothes reappeared—a very useful rider spell to the original curse. Luna applauded, her clapping hands a surprisingly soft sound. Leo looked at her carefully. She was back in the summer frock and beret again, but she was at least a foot taller. Leo decided he wouldn't mention it.

"Well fought, Leo Morn. And now you will take me to Blackacre."

All Leo could say was, "Yes, ma'am."

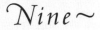

## Dead Indoors

GAYLE AND TOBY DEXTER exchanged hardly a dozen words as they headed back, through an increasingly empty town, to Jimmy Thunder's godly semidetached, which was probably just as well, as Toby had a lot of hard thinking to do. So far he'd been more or less content to follow where Gayle led, partly because she knew this magical world so much better than he did, and partly because he was so utterly captivated by her; however, he didn't feel he could do that anymore. He no longer trusted her, not after the death-walkers. Not after what she'd made him do there. But if he couldn't rely on Gayle, that meant he'd have to take charge himself, and Toby liked that idea even less. He'd never been comfortable about making decisions, for himself or others. He was much happier to stand back and let someone else do all the hard work and shoulder the responsibility.

And if Gayle couldn't, or wouldn't, help him discover what the hell he was supposed to do as a focal point (and just possibly as Humanity's Champion, though he still had strong reservations about that), he was going to have to work it out for himself, unfortunately. Toby had drifted through most of his life, taking it as it came, and the longer he spent in the magical and disturbing world of Mysterie, the more likely it seemed such an attitude was going to get him killed, in any number of appalling ways. Everywhere he went the shadows had teeth, and quite often an agenda. More and more Toby felt he was under threat from all sides, and being backed into a corner, from where he would *have* to do something. And time, as treacherous as always, was running out on him.

There was a part of Toby, the calm and reasonable part, that wanted simply to walk away from Gayle, and go to talk with Nicholas Hob, lay the whole situation out before him and listen to his side of the story. Toby didn't believe in villains, not in people who were simply evil and nothing else. Surely if he could just sit down and talk with Hob, man to man, they could work something out together. Arrive at a basic compromise, where everyone got something they wanted in return for giving up something else. That's how the world worked. And then he, Humanity's bloody Champion, might not have to do anything after all.

But he'd seen Angel, crouching on a rooftop overlooking the Shambles, like some malevolent living gargoyle, and just the sight of her had made his skin crawl. She was a predator in a world of prey, a dark and dangerous force with none of the human weaknesses such as conscience or restraint or sanity. Toby knew, on some level as deep and primal as instinct, that there was no point in being reasonable with Angel. And she was Hob's creature, his trusted right hand, his supernatural attack dog. Which meant . . . Toby sighed unhappily. This was Mysterie, not Veritie. They did things differently here. Maybe there were villains, here.

Which was a pity because he sure as hell didn't see himself as any kind of hero. He was just Toby Dexter, shop assistant and wage slave, the man who had turned underachieving into an art form. And for all his journeys through this strangely transformed town, he was no nearer understanding what he could, or should, do. His frown deepened into a scowl as he strode along beside Gayle, thinking hard and long about the problem of Nicholas Hob, and Angel, and Blackacre.

\*　　\*　　\*

The door to Jimmy Thunder's place swung open even as they approached it, and there was the godling himself, large as life and twice as broad, this time dressed in black biker's leathers, complete with gleaming steel studs and dangling chains. Toby couldn't help feeling that Jimmy looked less like a Norse deity and more like the god of Harley-Davidson worshipers, the kind of people who probably recited braking distances under a full moon, and sacrificed a Kawasaki when they needed to beg a favor. The thunder godling looked more relieved than happy to see them again, and beckoned them in with an urgent wave. Gayle stalked right past him, not even looking round, and Toby was hard-pressed to manage more than a polite smile. Luckily, Jimmy was so excited and full of his news that he didn't notice. He ushered them into his great hall, and the front door slammed shut by itself as he turned to address them.

"Damn, it's good to see you two again! I was about to go out looking for you; I've been hearing stuff you wouldn't believe! The whole town's talking about you!" He finally took in Gayle's forlorn, beaten-down expression, and the excitement leaked out of him like a burst tire. "Gayle? What's happened? You look exhausted."

"It's been a long, hard day, Jimmy," said Gayle, smiling wanly as she reached up to kiss him on his bearded cheek. "And I think I may have really screwed up, this time."

"You? Impossible," Jimmy said loyally. He offered her a huge, leather-clad arm to lean on, and she accepted it gratefully. All the certainty and arrogance had gone out of her and she looked somehow smaller, more vulnerable. Jimmy led her to the nearest door leading off the long corridor, and it swung smoothly open before him as he led her through, murmuring soothing words like an adult with a hurt child. Toby went after them, quietly annoyed that Jimmy hadn't thought to offer him an arm. Not that he would have accepted it, of course, but it would have been nice to be acknowledged, at least. He was just as tired as Gayle, and with more reason.

They were back in Jimmy Thunder's huge medieval hall, that looked more like the inside of an old Viking long ship than ever.

Toby couldn't help visualizing it with two great ranks of oars, surging proudly up the River Avon to ransack the towns beyond, set fire to government buildings, and pillage the big corporations. He wondered if he was getting light-headed from fatigue.

Jimmy insisted Gayle sit down on the nearest wooden bench and conjured up from somewhere an oversize mug of his own home-brewed mead. It was a mark of how dispirited Gayle was that she accepted it without comment. Jimmy waved for Toby to sit on the bench facing Gayle and provided him with a mug of mead, too. Toby studied the thick golden liquid dubiously as he sat down. It had things floating in it. But he was tired, and it felt so good to be sitting down, and he was thirsty, so . . .

It was actually quite pleasant, in a thick, glutinous and oversweet sort of way. It warmed him nicely, and it wasn't until the third gulp went down that the alcohol content hit him like a flying brick to the head. His eyes misted for a moment, and he was glad he was sitting down. He could practically feel the stuff putting a polish on his fillings. But once the shock had passed, he did feel decidedly perked up. He looked across at Gayle, and of course she was drinking the stuff with no visible reaction whatsoever. Jimmy Thunder sat down beside her with his own mug and put a comforting arm around her. She sighed, and leaned heavily against him, her eyes closing, and Toby tried not to bridle too obviously. Jimmy looked from Gayle to Toby and back again.

"So, is there any particular reason why you two aren't talking to each other?"

"Ask her," said Toby, not quite growling the words.

Jimmy nodded understandingly. "It's a hard thing to be human and mortal, in a world of Powers and Dominations. Harder still to be a mortal in love with an immortal. It always ends, and it usually ends badly. You have to understand, Toby, Gayle's concerns are always going to be so much larger than yours. She has responsibilities far beyond your comprehension. She can't live for the moment, like you. In her life, you're just the blink of an eye."

"Responsibilities?" said Toby, too tired to disguise the anger and betrayal in his voice. "What about her responsibilities to me? To someone who loved her, trusted her?"

Jimmy shrugged. "I'm the wrong person to ask, Toby. Mortal women have never been more than passing fancies for me."

"Yes, but that's because you're a bastard," said Gayle. "I've been human, I'm supposed to know better. Tell me your news, Jimmy. I could use a good distraction right now. What's happened that's got you so excited? Is Hollywood planning a remake of *Girl on a Motorcycle?*"

"Even stranger!" said Jimmy, getting quite animated again. "Luna has left her home! She dismantled all her protections, left her sanctuary, and went walkabout! In Veritie!"

"That's impossible!" Gayle said sharply. She sat upright, pushed herself away from Jimmy, and glared at him. "Luna hasn't translated herself out of Mysterie in centuries! I'm not sure she even knows what the modern world looks like. Why in God's name would she want to go traveling in reality, where she's even more diminished?"

"Hey, don't shoot the messenger," said Jimmy. "I've been asking questions all over town, but no one knows where she's gone, or why—not even the Waking Beauty. Once Luna became only human, she dropped off everyone's radar. She could be anywhere by now. Could this be something to do with Hob and his plans? Could he have lured her out? Or developed some kind of influence over her?"

"Unlikely," said Gayle, frowning deeply as she considered the matter. "I helped her set up her protections, long, long ago, and most of them were designed specifically to keep her safe from Hob, or anything he might send against her. I'd have known immediately if they'd been broken, even in my human condition. No, it's much more likely this is all my fault. I took Toby to see her earlier today. She seemed agitated, though admittedly with her that's hard to tell. It's entirely possible that my visiting her after such a long absence stirred her up in some way. God knows, she's capable of practically anything once she gets a bee in her bonnet."

"Then why did you go to her?" said Jimmy, honestly baffled. "You must have known—"

"All right, it was a mistake, I admit it! I should have known better. But I was desperate. And so out of touch." Gayle shook her head. "I've been human so long, and out of the loop for ages by my own choice, and I didn't know who to talk to anymore. I don't even know who the real movers and shakers are these days. It's been centuries since I last took on my aspect, becoming my full self. I wanted, needed, to steep myself in being just human, and as a result I've become isolated, dangerously isolated. I didn't even know Hob was back in town, and I should have known."

"The answer seems obvious," said Jimmy. "Take on your aspect again. Become who you really are. I don't understand why you're so reluctant to embrace your full domain."

"Because . . . what if that's what Hob wants? What if that is what this is all about, the object of his plans? I can't believe all the changes, all the threats, all the provocation I've been put through are just coincidence. I think Hob wants me to take on my aspect and jeopardize all my hard-won humanity. I haven't *become* in so long, that I'm no longer sure just *what* I might become. It took me so long to learn the simple, everyday human concepts of compassion and mercy . . . and love. I won't give them up."

"I've been searching for answers everywhere," said Jimmy, tactfully changing the subject. "After your last visit, it seemed to me that I'd been missing a lot of things I should have noticed before now. I contacted all my usual sources, only to find that most of them had gone into hiding. So I barged into a lot of places where I'm not usually welcome, and threw my weight around a bit, but still nobody wanted to talk, except about Luna. Everyone's talking about Luna. In the end, I came back here and put Scilla on the job. As a magic mirror, she has the most amazing and unsuspected links with all kinds of simulacra and sentient paraphernalia all over the town. Including quite a few objects whose owners don't even suspect are sentient. Don't praise her too much; she's been insufferably smug all afternoon."

"Thank you, Scilla," said Gayle, nodding graciously to the mirror on the wall.

"It was me! All me!" said the mirror triumphantly, using Jimmy's voice and image, just to rub the point in. "He couldn't find out anything, but I did! I am wise and wonderful. I know so many things now, I'm thinking of applying to be upgraded to oracle. The whole town's in an uproar, behind the scenes! You wouldn't believe what's going on out there!"

"*Thank you,* Scilla," said Jimmy heavily. "I'll tell them." He glowered at Toby. "Nothing worse than a self-satisfied talking mirror."

"I heard that! There's nothing worse than an ungrateful thunder godling! And by the way, Toby, you look awful, like death warmed up. Have you been taking your vitamins?"

"Ignore her," said Jimmy. "I do, as much as possible, but then, I've had practice. Anyway, the point is, all across the town the seers and soothsayers are crapping themselves. All of a sudden, no one can see the future anymore. And the skeins of fate have become so convoluted that none of the patterns make sense. It's like both fate and the future have been put on hold . . . until something significant has happened."

He looked meaningfully at Gayle, and then at Toby, who pulled a face. "Yeah, I know," he said heavily. "Focal point, Humanity's Champion, all that bullshit. Haven't any of your contacts been able to tell you something useful?"

"Maybe," said Jimmy. "Something is happening in the sun, and I don't just mean the solar flares. Apparently the sun has actually grown in size, just a little."

"That can't be possible," said Toby.

"The Serpent is stirring," said Gayle, hugging herself tightly, "The Serpent In The Sun, the Old Enemy. We were wrong all along; it was never Hob's plans we were dealing with, but his ancient father's. The Serpent, operating through his son, pursuing his old ambition, the utter subjugation of all living things to his will."

Jimmy and Gayle looked at each other for a long time, their faces unreadable. Toby stirred uncomfortably on his bench and cleared his throat tentatively. "Just how dangerous could Nicholas Hob be, if he put his mind to it? Is he some kind of sorcerer? Does he have . . . powers?"

"He's bigger than that," said Jimmy. "He was born human, but he's still the Serpent's Son, and older than you can imagine."

"Hob has always preferred to act through agents," said Gayle. "Never puts himself at risk. But he has been responsible for a great many evils and atrocities, down the years. He's supposed to have started the Great Fire of London, after one of his plagues got out of hand. The fires of the sun have always been his to command, for short periods."

"You don't have to tell me," said Jimmy. "I saw him incinerate a whole crowd of refugees in one moment. There was nothing left of them but ashes floating on the wind. Scary."

"The Hob's always taken an interest in disease," said Gayle. "Suffering and human mutability fascinate him. He's known to have been responsible for at least two outbreaks of plague right here in Bradford-on-Avon, back in the seventeenth century. One in three died then, for his pleasure."

"Why does he keep coming back here?" said Toby. "Someone as powerful as he is should be working in the centers of power, deciding the fates of nations. What's the appeal for him of one small English country town?"

"I thought you'd have worked it out by now, Toby," said Gayle. "Bradford-on-Avon is the secret heart of the world. What is decided here, decides how the world will go. If Hob, or rather, the Serpent working through Hob, can control and dominate the powers that operate here, the world is his for the taking. That's why Hob has returned, following his father's orders."

"All right," said Toby. "How are we going to stop him?"

Jimmy looked at him and raised an eyebrow. *"We?"*

"Damn right, *we,"* said Toby, giving Jimmy a hard look in return. "This is my town, my home. I'm involved. I would be even if I wasn't a bloody focal point. Hob has to be stopped, so what are we going to do?"

"Maybe there's nothing we can do," said Gayle. "If the Serpent is stirring . . . If the sun is growing . . ."

She sounded lost. She looked exhausted, as though she'd been running on reserves for too long and had finally given out. Her face was slack and empty, her eyes were dull, her shoulders slumped. Toby had never seen her look so . . . small. Jimmy put his arm around her again, and hugged her to his broad chest. She nestled against him like a weary child. Toby tried not to be jealous.

"Big old bear," Gayle murmured drowsily into Jimmy's warmth, as though wanting only to escape into sleep and leave all her worries behind her.

"This is all your fault," Jimmy said to Toby, scowling. "You've run her off her feet, dragging her all over town today."

"*My* fault?" snapped Toby. "I got bloody shot! I have been through a Total Death Experience, up close and personal! I died and came back for that bloody woman, and I still can't get a straight answer out of her about anything!"

Toby and Jimmy were both on their feet now, glaring at each other. The thunder godling was easily twice Toby's size, but Toby was so mad he didn't give a damn. After everything he'd been through, he was in no mood to take any shit from anyone, least of all one of Gayle's old boyfriends. It still came as something of a surprise when Jimmy placed a hand flat on Toby's chest, gave him a bit of a push and threw him ten feet backwards. Toby sailed over the bench he'd been sitting on and crashed to the floor some distance beyond it. He came down hard, the breath knocked out of him. He was still groaning and trying to get up on one elbow when Jimmy stepped over the bench and advanced on him grimly. Toby scrabbled backwards, common sense pushing aside his hurt feelings to make a sudden comeback. Toby had never been much for fighting, and especially not with bikers built like brick shithouses who carried a bloody big hammer on their hip. Toby kept retreating and Jimmy kept coming. He was smiling now, and it was a really unpleasant smile.

"What part of *immortal godling* didn't you understand, little human?" said Jimmy, cracking his huge knuckles loudly. "You don't talk like that in my presence. I think you need a lesson in manners, tiny mortal."

*I think I need a Magnum .45 and a good running start,* Toby thought, just a little desperately. *Maybe if I hit him hard enough with my face I'll damage his hand. What the hell was I thinking of, challenging Godzilla in biker leathers? So; apologize loudly, kiss his leather-clad arse, and maybe later I can sneak up behind him with something large and heavy and preferably pointed . . . oh, shit, this is going to hurt.*

Jimmy loomed over Toby, grabbed a handful of his shirt, and lifted him easily off the ground. Toby's heels kicked a good two feet above the floor, as the thunder godling glared right into his face. Toby opened his mouth to apologize, and then thought, *Hell with that,* and spat into Jimmy's right eye. The godling roared deafeningly with rage and drew back an enormous fist, and then Gayle was suddenly there, hauling on Jimmy's arm with both hands and yelling at him to put Toby down.

"Do it right now, Jimmy Thunder! Do you hear me? Put him down or I'll never speak to you again!"

Jimmy growled deep in his chest, glared at Gayle, and then opened his hand and let Toby drop to the floor. He fell hard again, but was so relieved he was still in one piece he didn't care. Gayle crouched down beside him and helped him sit up. Jimmy glared at both of them.

"Mortals should know their place."

"Don't you judge him, Jimmy Thunder, don't you *dare*. He's been through things for me, suffered things for me that even you would balk at. He's one of the bravest souls I've ever met. Even if he does have a tendency to speak before engaging his brain. Are you hurt, Toby?"

"Don't worry, I'm getting used to it." Toby rose slowly to his feet, leaning on Gayle a little more than was strictly necessary. "Good thing you intervened. I was just getting ready to kick his arse."

"Of course you were, Toby. Now come and sit down before you fall down."

Toby winced. "I think I'd rather stand for a while."

"Ah," said Gayle. "Did you hurt your—?"

"Yes, I did, and I don't want to talk about it, thank you."

Gayle smiled suddenly. "I could always kiss it better."

Toby managed a small smile, too. "Maybe later. I don't think I'd appreciate it right now."

"I think I'm about to be sick," said Jimmy.

Gayle gave him a hard look. "I don't want any more trouble between you and Toby, do you hear me, Jimmy? We're going to need Toby's brains, and his outsider's viewpoint, to get us through this. I think that's why he was chosen to be the focal point. And I can't pretend I'm in charge anymore. I've been away too long."

Jimmy shrugged and sat down on his bench again. His anger had subsided as quickly as it had been aroused, and he was all business again. "Whatever you say, Gayle. He's your pet."

Gayle turned her back on him and persuaded Toby to come and sit, gingerly, on his bench again. This time she sat down beside him. He tried not to read too much into that. He couldn't help reflecting on how easy she'd seemed in Jimmy's company, as opposed to his. Not really too surprising, considering Thunder was an immortal, too. How long had they been an item, and how long ago? How could a mere man hope to compete with a godling? He realized Jimmy and Gayle were talking again, about how best to take on Nicholas Hob, and he made himself pay attention.

"I could always smash my way into Blackacre and go berserk on him," said Jimmy. "One of the more useful parts of my godly heritage. There's not a lot can stop me or stand against me when I'm berserking."

"Not much except Hob," said Gayle. "And let's not forget Angel. Even if you could get through all the defenses Hob's bound to have strung up all around Blackacre, Angel would probably stop you right in your tracks, rip off your arm and beat your head in with the soggy end. Berserking's overrated. Your ancestor Thor was always going berserk with any problem that required too much thinking; it was one of the reasons he and I never got along. Though his mother was always matchmaking . . ." She noticed the look on Toby's face and smiled. "Don't let it throw you, Toby. I've been around a long time and met a lot of famous people, but very few of them were worthy of their legend. I've noticed you becoming increasingly less impressed or intimidated by the various supernatural personages we've encountered, and that's a good thing. Where a lot of humans would have frozen, or run away screaming, you've stood your ground and outthought or outmaneuvered most of them. And when you couldn't, you endured trials for my sake that would have broken most, lesser people. I'm impressed, Toby. Really.

"Of course, one of the reasons why you were able to outthink a lot of those personages was because most magical beings aren't too tightly wrapped. That's what comes of having to believe ten impossible things before breakfast, just so you can get on with your neighbors. In Mysterie they're all bound by their roles and natures, which seriously limit their thinking. Being human and mortal, you aren't. You're free to be greater than you think you are. That's what makes you so important. Your unclouded mind is a weapon we can use against Hob and The Serpent In The Sun, and bring them down."

Toby got angry all over again. "You were doing really well there, Gayle, and then you had to blow it. I really was starting to think that you cared about me, about what you'd put me through, but in the end it came back to making use of me. That's all I am to you, a weapon. An expendable weapon, that you can throw against your enemies. Well I have had it up to here with being useful to you, being your weapon, your pet. I don't care anymore. Not about Hob, or this town, or you. I am out of here."

He started to lurch back onto his feet, but Gayle grabbed him by the arm and made him sit down again. Either she was stronger than she looked, or he was even weaker than he felt. Either way, he wouldn't struggle against her. He wouldn't give her the satisfaction. He stared straight ahead, not looking at Jimmy, or at Gayle as she talked.

"You're right, Toby. You have every reason to be angry with me.

I have used and misused you. And I am sorry you have suffered so very much, for me. But you must stay."

"Why?" said Toby, still refusing to look at her.

"Because you're a focal point," said Gayle, "and the town needs you. And because I need you."

Toby turned his head to look at her. "Keep talking. I'll listen. But if you say the wrong thing again, I will leave, and you'll never see me again."

Gayle sighed. There was just a hint of tears in her eyes, though her gaze was steady and her mouth and her voice were both firm. "You only know the human side of me, Toby Dexter, and that's really such a very small part of who and what I really am. All the centuries I've invested in being human are only a moment in the long span of my existence. If I am forced to take on my aspect, there is a very real chance that the whole of me would sacrifice you, without hesitating, for the greater good, to save the town and the worlds. That's why I can't afford to care for you, to let you matter to me. I mustn't love you, Toby. Because it would hurt me so much to lose you."

"Too late," said Toby softly. "Too late . . ."

Their faces were very close now, feeling each other's breath on their lips and in their mouths as they stared into each other's eyes, saying more in that lengthening moment, in that silent communication, than they could ever bring themselves to put into words. Off to one side, entirely forgotten, Jimmy Thunder was shaking his head resignedly. The mirror on the wall was quietly singing the theme from *Love Story*.

"What am I going to do with you?" said Toby, after a while.

"We'll think of something," Gayle murmured, "later."

"If there is a later," said Toby, pulling back a bit. He looked away and his breathing began to return to normal. "Something has occurred to me."

"Really?" said Gayle. She was smiling when Toby looked back at her.

"About our current problem," said Toby, frowning to show he

was being serious again. "Given that Hob and Angel, and possibly the Serpent, are such a clear and present danger, why don't we put out a general alarm and raise the whole town against them? Get together all the most powerful people, form our own army and take Blackacre by force? Surely if we all worked together . . ."

He trailed off. Gayle and Jimmy were both shaking their heads. "Never happen," Jimmy said bluntly. "First, because most of the people here wouldn't want to get involved. Too afraid of backing the wrong side. And second, those whose natures might impel them to get involved are already too busy. Someone, whose name probably begins with an H, has persuaded all the main villains in the town to run wild simultaneously, so that all the heroes who might have helped us have their hands full trying to contain the villains. Right now there's blood in the town's streets and a fair amount of structural damage, and the fighting's still going on."

"In other words, Hob has removed all the major players, good and bad, from the equation," said Gayle. "I should have known. He wants this to be his story, and his alone. We're on our own."

"There's always the Mice," said Toby.

Jimmy sniffed dismissively. Gayle raised an eyebrow. "I think we're a bit past the need for spies."

"I have something else in mind for the Mice," said Toby, smiling mischievously. "I've been thinking about how best to take the fight to Hob, and certain strategies have come to mind. Certain . . . off the wall, unprecedented strategies."

"You've got a plan, haven't you?" said Gayle.

"Maybe." Toby looked directly at Jimmy Thunder. "Luna said I should ask you for help, that you were a good man at heart. Are you game? Can I count on you?"

"Luna sent you to me?" Jimmy looked honestly surprised. "I didn't think she even knew I existed. I never met her, even when Gayle and I were an item. Never wanted to, to be honest. No offense, Gayle, but just her reputation scared the crap out of me."

"Very wise of you," said Gayle. "She worries me, and I'm her sister."

"To get back to the subject," Toby said firmly. "There are a few things I still need to get straight, if I'm going to make this work. Starting very definitely with what it actually *means* to be a focal point. Do I have any powers? Any magic of my own?"

Jimmy and Gayle looked at each other, their expressions unreadable to Toby. "Well, yes and no," Gayle said carefully. "You're not powerful in and of yourself, but you have been made significant. At the most important point, whatever that turns out to be, you will be placed in a position where you will have to make a decision, and whatever you decide at that moment will shape and determine the outcome of this present struggle. I can't say what that might involve. No one can, until the time comes."

"But . . . why? What's the point of a focal point?"

"People have been asking that question, in increasingly aggrieved tones, for a hell of a long time," said Jimmy. "It's one of the great mysteries of Mysterie. There are a lot of answers, depending on who you talk to, and how drunk they are, few of them particularly helpful or satisfying. The best bet seems to be that God, or somebody fairly high up in the celestial chain of command, has got a really twisted sense of humor. I know which way I'd bet."

"All right," said Toby, pressing on determinedly, "I'm not sure I'm any wiser than I was before, but then, that's Mysterie for you. Next big question. I need to know exactly who and what you are, Gayle. All I've got from you so far is a whole bunch of hints and allusions. Why does it have to be such a big secret? Why can't you just come out and say it, whatever it is? What could be so shocking that you don't think I could handle it, after all I've seen and been through today? Everyone else seems to know."

"Everyone else does know, in Mysterie," Gayle said slowly. "There's a reason why I haven't told you, Toby, or let anyone else tell you, and it's not a very nice reason. I don't want you to know, because once you do, you . . . you might not love me anymore. And I might need to rely on that love for you to save me, to save us all, when you have to make your fateful decision."

And that was when the dead starting appearing out of nowhere, dropping out of the empty air and into the long Norse hall. There were dozens of them, and more appeared every moment, dead men and women raided from the cemeteries of Bradford-on-Avon, sent forth to tear down the living, driven by Hob's overpowering will. They were in varying stages of preservation and decay, and grave mold spotted their funeral clothes and sunken faces. They smelled of earth and formaldehyde and corruption. They had unkempt hair and long fingernails, grown long in their graves. They moved stiffly, old bones creaking loudly as an awful magic forced motion from shrunken muscles. And all their gray faces had the same malevolent expression, from the single mind that moved them all and saw through those who still had eyes.

Hob had come to the thunder godling's home, in dozens of dead bodies, the unliving forced into an act of horror against the living by one man's hateful intent. They lurched down the hall toward their victims, grinning horribly, their hands like claws.

Jimmy and Toby jumped to their feet and looked wildly about them, but Gayle just sat where she was and looked at them, baffled. "What?" she said. "What's the matter?"

"What's the matter?" Toby said incredulously. "It's *Night of the Living Dead* time! The whole place is crawling with zombies!"

"She can't see the dead," Jimmy said quickly. "It's a blind spot, part of her special nature. Toby, listen to me. We can't let these bastards get anywhere near Gayle. She mustn't be hurt or damaged. It's vital, for everyone's sake."

Toby looked immediately for the nearest exit, but there were already a whole crowd of the dead between him and the door. There was no way for him to get Gayle out. He moved to stand back to back with Jimmy. To his surprise, he wasn't as scared as he thought he should be. The dead looked distinctly upsetting, but he'd seen much nastier things in horror movies. Mostly he felt angry, even outraged, that Hob should seek to hurt the woman he loved.

"*Hate* liches," said Jimmy, his voice thick with loathing. "Never a fair fight, and never any honor in it. Not a real enemy, just . . . things, that can't be killed because they're already dead."

"I know how to deal with zombies," said Toby, trying hard to sound confident. "I've seen all the movies. Just shoot them in the head. Take out the brain."

"You're thinking of the wrong movies," said Jimmy. "This is more *Evil Dead* territory. Tear them apart, rip them into pieces, or they'll just keep coming at you. Every part of them is a part of Hob's will. I'm going to have nightmares for weeks after this, I just know it. *Hate* liches. Feel free to grab any weapon from the wall you like the look of. And whatever you do, *keep them away from Gayle.*"

He gestured at the weapon plaques on the walls bearing fine displays of swords and axes. Most had clearly been designed to be wielded by someone of Jimmy Thunder's size and strength, but Toby quickly spotted a sword he thought he could handle. He darted over to the wall, pulled the sword from the plaque, and hefted it in his hand. He'd never handled a sword in his life, but the solid weight felt comforting, even reassuring, and he'd seen enough swordfights in films that he thought he could fake it. He glared about him, sweeping the shining blade back and forth before him, doing his best to look dangerous. The dead were closing in from all sides now, and none of them looked impressed in the least.

Gayle had stood up by now, but was still looking blankly around her, unable to see or appreciate the danger they were in. Toby grabbed her by the arm, hauled her over to the nearest wall and then dragged wooden benches into position around her, forming a basic barricade. He managed to pile it three benches high before the first dead got too close, and he had to leave her. He was breathing hard now, not all of it from the exertion. He really didn't like the odds. He would have run—if there'd been anywhere he and Gayle could have run to. He tried to smile reassuringly at her, but his mouth was very dry, and he wasn't sure how it came out. She smiled and nodded back at him, trusting him, expecting him to save her. Toby looked around him, at the zombies shuffling forward, dragging their dead feet, and he grinned suddenly.

*Ah, hell; how often in real life do you get the chance to play the hero?*

*To be the good guy, protecting his lady fair from the forces of darkness? So stop thinking and worrying, suck it in, and go for it!*

He moved to stand back to back with Jimmy Thunder again. The godling had his hammer in his hand and was hefting it thoughtfully.

"Don't try confusing them, or setting them against each other," he said tersely. "There's only one mind guiding them, and that's Hob's."

"How can he control so many bodies at once?" said Toby.

"Same way he got past all my defensive shields," Jimmy growled, "because he's the Hob. Fight well, Toby Dexter. Or if you can't manage that, at least try to die well."

He drew back his great arm and launched his hammer Mjolnir like a guided missile. The ancient weapon smashed into the nearest zombie, punching a ragged hole through its chest and out of its back. The hammer sped on, hardly slowed at all by the impact, and slammed through half a dozen more bodies. The zombies were thrown to the floor, but the terrible damage hardly affected them, and they were already rising awkwardly to their feet. A whole group of the dead lurched deliberately in front of the flying hammer, slowing it down until dead hands could snatch it out of the air and then pull it down, holding it to the floor by the sheer weight of their bodies. Jimmy snarled angrily.

"Some days, things wouldn't go right if you paid them. All right, we do it the hard way. Watch your back, Toby."

The dead surged forward, and the thunder godling went to meet them. He lashed out with his great fists, smashing skulls and tearing heads from bodies. Some of the dead he tore limb from limb and others he smashed to the ground and trampled underfoot. The dead fell, unable to match his inhuman strength, but there were always more to replace them. They clustered about him, clutching at his arms and back and trying to drag him down. He flexed his great arms and bodies flew from him. But still they came.

Toby watched Jimmy fight and envied him his godly abilities. All he had was an all-too-human body, already tired out from a really hard day, and courage that was more stubbornness than anything else. But still he stood his ground before Gayle's improvised barricade, and didn't even think about retreating. He tried to hold his sword like he knew what he was doing, and was surprised at how steady his hands were.

The first of the dead reached him: an old man in his best black suit, a shock of white hair hanging down around his gaunt face. The eyes and mouth were open, the edges ragged from where they'd torn through the mortician's stitches that had held them shut. He stank of the grave, and his reaching hands were crooked like claws. His yellowed eyes were deeply sunk, but full of awareness and hate. Toby stepped forward, and swung his sword with both hands like a golf club. The long blade flashed round in a great sideways arc, and sheared clean through the dead man's neck and out the other side. The blow staggered the zombie, and the grimacing head toppled from the shoulders. Still the body staggered forward. Toby scowled. He moved to one side, and tripped the body so it went crashing to the floor. Toby then gave the severed head a good kick, so it went rolling away, well out of reach of the body's grasping hands. Toby grinned. Not bad for a first attempt. He looked down at his sword, that had suddenly seemed so light and effective in his hands. Trust Jimmy Thunder not to have an ordinary sword on his wall.

More dead came lurching forward and Toby went to meet them with a confident smile on his lips and a dangerous gleam in his eyes. His sword was a blur as he moved quickly among the slow-moving dead, cutting them up and easily evading their grasping hands. He was soon breathing hard from the exertion, and his arms and back ached fiercely, but his success put new vigor in him, and he felt as if he could have done this all day. To his great surprise, he found he was actually enjoying himself. After a day of being the butt of everything that happened to him, it felt good to be involved in something simple and straightforward, with a whole bunch of tangible bad guys for him to take out the day's frustrations on.

But still, for every dead body he dismembered and sent crashing to the floor, there were still more coming forward, and appearing out of nowhere to join the crush. Good as he felt, Toby knew he couldn't keep this up forever, and just maybe they could: the dead didn't get tired. It occurred to Toby to wonder just how many dead Hob had at his command. There were a lot of cemeteries in Bradford-on-Avon: very old, very large cemeteries. As he thought that, the crowd of risen dead around him seemed even thicker, and the smell became almost unbearable. Toby set his back against Gayle's barricade, and fought on.

There was a sudden cry from across the hall, and Toby looked round sharply just in time to see Jimmy Thunder fall beneath an unstoppable wave of the dead, that was dragging him down by sheer weight of numbers. The thunder godling was still fighting, throwing broken bodies away from him, but the dead held him down, clawing at him with their cold hands and fastening on him with their yellowed teeth. Toby got a brief glimpse of Jimmy's face, already streaked with blood, as he looked right past Toby to Gayle.

"Dammit, Gayle, take on your aspect!" he yelled, his voice touched with hysteria. "Your presence might be enough to block Hob's sending!"

"I daren't," Gayle said miserably. "That has to be what the Serpent wants. He must have set up some way to turn it to his advantage. It's the only trump card I've got. I daren't play it too soon."

"Gayle, damn you . . ." And then the thunder godling was lost to sight and sound under a mass of the dead that writhed like a pile of maggots.

Toby heard the mirror on the wall scream, right behind him. He looked round to see three of the dead hammering at the mirror, trying to smash and shatter it with their cold fists. Toby cut all three of them down before they even knew he was there, and was back defending Gayle in a moment. He rather thought he was getting the hang of this. Even if his arms hurt like hell, and it was growing harder to get his breath with every minute. His image in the mirror babbled thanks, and then raised its voice urgently.

"Use the artifacts in the display cases!" the mirror shrieked almost hysterically. "They're all weapons!"

Toby looked over at the rows of glass display cases. His sword was getting harder to wield. The dead were taking longer to go down. He didn't have a godling's strength, but if he had a godling's weapons . . . Most of the cases were already out of reach, overrun by the dead, but the first few . . . He used the last of his strength to clear some space with his sword and then sprinted forward to smash the glass of the first case with his swordhilt. The sign said Mirror of the Sea.

His prize, when he got it out, turned out to be a small hand mirror, in a battered steel frame. Toby lifted it uncertainly in his free hand, not at all sure what he was supposed to do with the bloody thing, and then the carved runes on the back of the mirror seemed to come alive, twisting and squirming before him, and words came from his mouth before he was even aware he knew them. He didn't understand what they meant, but the mirror did. He could feel power roaring in the ancient artifact, like a head of steam that had been building for centuries, and was only now breaking loose. The mirror shook and shuddered in his hand and then a jet of dark water shot out of the mirror's face.

The water came flying out like a fire hose, an endless stream under enormous pressure, bowling the dead clean off their feet and casting them away. None of them could stand against the crushing impact, even for a moment. Toby grinned fiercely as he turned the mirror back and forth and the pounding stream of water mowed down the dead around him. The mirror was a gateway to the ocean, to the deep dark bottom of the sea, where water under unimaginable pressure never knew the light of day. He knew this, just as he'd known the right words to activate the mirror. And more: where the waters hit the dead and soaked their clothes, they were slowly dissolving. Their mouths screamed silently as dead flesh melted away. It was the salt in the ocean water, Toby realized. Salt had always been a defense against zombies. He laughed aloud and advanced on the dead and they fell back before him.

Until a dark, rubbery tentacle studded with twitching suckers suddenly burst out of the mirror's face, blocking the flow of the water. Something in the depths of some faraway ocean had discovered the hole, and become curious. Toby shook the mirror hard, but the face remained blocked. The tentacle snapped back and forth, curling and uncurling, until it encountered a zombie that had ventured too close. It snapped around the dead body, crushing the midriff to pulp in a moment, and then tried to pull its prize back through the mirror. Toby swore disgustedly and threw the mirror to the floor. The tentacle had made it useless to him.

The dead were already regathering and advancing once again. Toby turned to the next display case.

Thor's Gauntlets turned out to be a pair of ancient, ratty leather gloves, falling apart and much mended with assorted patches. Like the mirror, they were covered in sigils and runes, this time spelled out in black iron, but Toby didn't need to be able to read them to know what you did with a pair of gloves. He put his sword to one side and snatched the gloves out of the shattered display case, pulling them on carefully. They were so delicate the leather felt like lace, but they fitted him perfectly. Toby felt a new strength flooding through him and smiled confidently as the first zombie came within reach. He drew back and hit the dead man square in the face. The zombie's head shattered and flew apart, and the glove all but disintegrated under the impact, falling away from Toby's hand in scraps of crumbling leather. Some artifacts just weren't built to last.

Toby swore loudly, pushed aside the headless body that was still reaching for him and hurried over to the third display case. Some of the dead were getting too close to Gayle's barricade. From the way she was glaring desperately about her, it was clear she could sense the danger, even if she couldn't see it. Over to one side, Jimmy Thunder was still fighting desperately under the mound of dead bodies holding him down, crying out angrily as they clawed at his flesh and snapped at his face. And that was when Toby realized he'd left his sword behind. He snarled, and smashed the glass case with his elbow, yelping at the pain. This had to be the one. There was no way he'd be able to reach another case.

He was hoping for the mystical equivalent of a tactical nuke.

What he got was Surtur's Tooth. Just a bloody big tooth, yellowing into brown, easily ten inches long, that culminated in a jagged broken end from where it had been ripped out of something's jaw. There were no runes, this time, just the tooth. Toby cursed dispassionately and reached for the tooth anyway, only to jerk his hand back at the last moment as the mirror on the wall screamed at him.

*"Don't touch it with your bare hand! It burns!"*

Toby tried again, with the hand still wearing one of Thor's Gauntlets, and gingerly picked up the tooth. It was surprisingly heavy, but it didn't burn him. A dead man came out of nowhere to go for his throat, and Toby reacted instinctively, jamming the tooth deep into the zombie's chest. The dead body burst into fierce yellow flames. It fell to the floor, kicking and arching its back, and then was still as the leaping flames consumed it. Toby allowed himself a sigh of relief, and then went to meet the dead as they came crowding in around him. Whenever the tooth touched dead flesh, the bodies burned, and soon the floor of the great Norse hall was littered with charred and blackened forms with no movement left in them.

Hob's unwilling army was at rest again, all his unnatural life burned right out of it.

Toby was soon able to rescue Jimmy, and with the somewhat battered and bloodied thunder godling at his side, quickly finished off the rest of the dead. No more new dead came popping out of nowhere to attack them. Hob had clearly seen the futility of losing any more of his dead servants to Surtur's Tooth. When it was finally over, Toby and Jimmy stood together, both grinning fiercely. Toby felt good, pleased, at having finally achieved something. And, for the first time, he didn't feel intimidated by the big thunder godling's presence.

Jimmy clapped him on the shoulder, staggering him for a moment. "Not bad, Toby Dexter. Not bad at all, for a mortal."

They shared a smile, and then Toby looked down at the great tooth in his gloved hand. "What is this thing, anyway?"

"My ancestor Thor had a run-in with Surtur, back in the old

country. Surtur was a major fire demon. Still is, as far as I know. Certainly if he ever turns up here wanting his tooth back, I plan on giving it to him with all the politeness at my command. Nasty things, fire elementals."

They went back to dismantle the barricade around Gayle and she emerged to hug Toby tightly. She was shaking, but it took Toby a moment to realize that it was from laughter, not fear. She pushed herself away from him and grinned at him.

"My brave hero. I'm sure it was all very perilous, Toby, but you have to understand that all I could see was you and Jimmy charging back and forth, attacking empty air. I couldn't see the dead until you burned Hob out of them, and they were just everyday bodies again. Poor souls."

"Wonderful," said Toby. "My big moment, and I'm the only one who saw it."

Gayle looked around her, at the dozens of smoldering corpses scattered across the hall floor. "None of this was their fault. They didn't ask for their rest to be disturbed. But that's Hob's way, to let the innocent suffer, rather than put himself at risk."

Toby looked around him, and for the first time saw his recent enemies simply as men and women, their final peace desecrated in the name of Nicholas Hob's ambition. He felt ashamed. He'd enjoyed fighting them, cursing them, destroying them.

"What am I going to do with all these bodies?" said Jimmy, just a bit plaintively. "I can't keep them. I don't have the cupboard space. Besides . . . they're really creeping me out. *Hate* liches."

"They're all going to have to be properly identified and returned to their proper resting places," Toby said firmly. "We have to do the right thing by them. None of them wanted to be here. They're just more of Hob's victims. The death-walkers can probably help."

"Yeah, well, those people give me the creeps, too," said Jimmy. "But I suppose you're right."

"First," said Gayle, "we have to stop Hob."

"Damn right," said Toby. "I won't stand for this. He has to pay. I think it's time we took the fight to him. No more reacting to whatever he does. We have to go to him, catch him wrong-footed. We have to go to Blackacre."

"Now you're talking!" said Jimmy Thunder. "No more messing about. Just barge right in and bust everything up. It's what I do best. I'll take care of Angel. Once we're both in Mysterie, I'll really kick her arse."

Gayle looked at Toby. "Like I said, limited."

"I think we need a plan first," said Toby, diplomatically. "I've been thinking. First we need to talk to the Mice. . . ."

# Ten~

# Unexpected Encounters

O N THE EDGE OF TOWN, isolated and abandoned, stood Black-acre. The trees rose still and tall, though life had left them long ago, and no animal or bird or insect disturbed the suffocating silence. But in this place where nothing lived, something moved. A thick fog, blue green and shimmering with its own unearthly light, came stealing through the trees, billowing slowly out from the ancient farmhouse that was the foul and rotten heart of Blackacre. The fog pulsed and heaved like a living thing as it progressed, swallowing up everything in its path, until it reached the boundary of the dead wood on every side, and then it stopped abruptly and was still, waiting for some poor damned fool to come and disturb its domain.

Night had fallen by the time Toby Dexter, Gayle, and Jimmy Thunder came to Blackacre. A focal point, a God For Hire, and a woman who was so much more than just a woman. It was a clear night, but no stars were out, leaving only a ghostly silver light from the full moon to show their way. If anything, the evening seemed even hotter than the day had been, and the night air was close and sweltering. Toby pulled his sweaty shirt away from his chest as he played the beam of his flashlight ahead of him. He felt increasingly uncomfortable, and not just from the unrelenting heat. He'd never been to Blackacre before, even though it lay only just outside the town where he'd spent most of his life. No one went to Blackacre, not even in calm and reasonable Veritie. Everyone knew the stories. Now here he was in Mysterie, where such stories had power, approaching the last redoubt of the Serpent's Son to face the dragon in his lair; and suddenly all Toby's plans and preparations seemed as nothing, compared to such ancient, established evil. If Bradford-on-Avon really was the secret heart of the world, then Blackacre was the hidden canker in that heart.

Toby still wasn't at all sure what he and his companions were going to do, once they finally came face-to-face with Nicholas Hob and Angel. He only knew, on some deep, instinctive, primal level, that direct confrontation was the only strategy left to them that had any chance of success.

They had come to Blackacre because they were meant to be there.

Gayle had insisted they wait for darkness before setting out. And so they watched the enemy sun sink slowly down the sky, as the sky turned as red as blood, and then disappear into the dark purple of evening. Darkness would hide them from the Serpent's sight, and the watchful, sorcerous gaze of his Son. Toby still had a hard time accepting that the familiar sun that shone every day, the giver of life and light, was actually the home of Humanity's most ancient and awful Enemy; but he had to admit, a night attack made sense. The element of surprise was practically the only thing they had going for them.

He led the way up the long, gradual hill that culminated in the old forbidden wood, glaring into the dark and shining his torch ahead of him like a weapon. The moonlight helped, but the blue-white glow made everything seem unreal, like walking through a dream. Toby had the only flashlight. Apparently thunder godlings didn't need such things, and Gayle stuck close to Toby. She'd grown ever more silent as they left the town behind them, and she seemed to stumble more in the dark than Toby and Jimmy put together. She was holding on to Toby's arm, and it seemed to him that the growing pressure of her fingers was more for comfort than support.

Jimmy Thunder was quiet, too, only cursing under his breath from time to time as earth turned unexpectedly under his great weight. And so, in silence and with uncertain courage, they came at last to the dead place, the scorched land, and stood at the boundary of the dead wood, looking in.

The thick fog enveloping the trees came as a surprise to them. It hung about the trees like a shroud, thick and impenetrable. Toby shone his light into the fog, and the glowing mists swallowed it right up. He looked back at the town, laid out below in a patchwork map of glowing amber lights, and there was not a trace of fog anywhere in the slow, hot summer night. He turned back to the eerie glow of the blue-green mists, and swallowed hard. He didn't need to be told that there was nothing natural about this fog that shone with its own unclean light and stopped impossibly abruptly at the edge of the dead wood. Just looking at it made his skin crawl. Whatever Hob was up to in there, he really didn't want it seen. Suddenly Toby realized that Gayle was clinging tightly to his arm, breathing heavily, and actually shuddering as she looked at the fog before them. Toby didn't blame her. He had an unpleasant feeling that if he stood and looked into the fog long enough, something would come out of it to look back at him. Something he wouldn't want to meet at all.

"Are we going to stand here all night?" said Jimmy Thunder, and Toby all but jumped out of his skin.

"I don't know," he said sharply. "Maybe. Are you telling me this fog doesn't disturb the hell out of you, too?"

The thunder godling shrugged. "I've seen stranger shit than this in my time. The fog's actually a good sign, if you think about it. It means that Hob's fallen back on the defensive. He can feel things are coming to a head, and he's worried someone might come to stop him. This fog might look impressive, but it's really only a protective shield. According to the Waking Beauty, the real defense here is the small army of walking dead Hob has staked out around his farmhouse, ready and waiting to slice up any uninvited visitors. And since none of my artifacts is of any use this close to Hob's seat of power, we'd better hope your plan to get us in is going to work."

"It'll work," Toby said immediately, trying at least to sound confident. "I'll get us to Hob. Hopefully by then you and Gayle will have worked out what the hell you're going to do to him. Because if you haven't, I am going to start running and I won't stop until I'm in a different time zone. Mice! Where are you?"

They came tumbling up the hill toward him, a whole crowd of large furry animals, leaping and pirouetting and jostling each other, laughing breathily from high spirits. Toby felt better immediately, just from looking at them. Life blazed so brightly, so freely, in the Mice. They piled up before Toby, pushing and shoving each other and grinning broadly. Toby grinned back as he took in four familiar Mouse faces.

"Is this all of you?"

"Oh, yes," said Bossy importantly. "I made sure no one was left out. Always up for a bit of organizing, me. We're here, all twenty-three of us."

Toby raised an eyebrow. "I thought there were only—"

"There are always more of us than you think," said Sweetie, leaning languorously against Toby's hip and batting her big eyelashes at him. "For you, we've called out all the reserves. We are the Mice. Fear our playfulness."

"It looks like you're going to need all of us," said Tidy, studying the fog just a little doubtfully. Other Mice joined him, their noses twitching unhappily. Tidy snorted loudly and turned back to Toby. "Nasty stuff. Stinks of bad magics. Going to be hell getting the smell out of our fur later. Still, anything for the Lady. And you, Toby. Don't worry; we can handle this. Dreamy, you're about to say you dreamed of this, I can tell. Don't you dare."

"I dreamed something," said Dreamy doubtfully, her eyes very wide. "But I can't remember what. I'm sure it was very important. . . ."

"Yes, well, we can talk about that later," said Toby diplomatically. "Now, in you go, all of you. Spread yourselves wide and cause as much trouble and distraction as you can, but *don't* risk getting caught."

Bossy sniffed dismissively. "There isn't anything in there that can catch us. Mice! Forward! Tally-ho!"

The Mice charged forward, laughing and hallooing, and streamed into the thick, enveloping fog, bounding along and eager for fun. Toby tried hard to remember that they were perfectly capable of taking care of themselves. Jimmy Thunder watched the last of them disappear into the mists and nodded approvingly.

"Hob can have as many dead guards in there as he likes; those Mice will run them ragged all night long."

"One of your better ideas, Toby," said Gayle. She sounded tired, washed-out. She realized Toby was looking at her worriedly, and managed a reassuring smile for him. "This place . . . upsets me. There's nothing natural here, nothing of life and the natural order. It's a setting dedicated to death, carved out of the living world. I don't know how long I can operate, or even survive, in such a place."

Toby frowned. Gayle looked fragile, vulnerable. Weak. He wasn't used to seeing her like that. He didn't like it. "Maybe you should stay here, while Jimmy and I—"

"No," Gayle said flatly. "You're going to need me when you finally get to Hob—my dear little nephew. Come on. Let's get moving before I change my mind."

She let go of Toby's arm, took a deep breath, and strode forward into the thick, pulsing fog. Toby and Jimmy quickly followed her in.

Gayle barely managed a dozen steps into the dead wood before she staggered to a halt, unsteady on her feet and gasping as though she couldn't get her breath. Toby moved in quickly beside her, and she grabbed his arm with both hands, leaning heavily on him for support. She was trembling all over now, and her face was pale and beaded with sweat. Jimmy drew his hammer Mjolnir and looked fiercely about him for some sign of a threat, but there was nothing. Toby murmured soothingly to Gayle and tried to get her to take deep breaths. She laughed shakily.

"God, I feel bad. Sick. I don't belong here. I remember . . . this place, before it died." She stopped to swallow hard, and shook her head as though to clear it. "It was a long time ago. Just a pleasant little wood, then. A warm and shadowed copse for young lovers to walk in. Until Hob came, and did the terrible thing that cursed the land and made this place forever Blackacre. A cold scar on the body of the world, never to heal, never to regenerate, never to know life again."

"Why did he do it? Why would Hob want to do something like that?" Toby was more interested in distracting Gayle from her obvious distress than anything else, but even as he spoke he realized he needed to know the answer, if he was ever to understand why Hob was the way he was.

"He did it to show that he could," said Gayle. "To stamp his mark on the world, his brand. So that no matter what we or anyone else did, there would always be one place that was forever his, always apart, always hurting. Just like him."

Toby glared about him into the thick fog. Blackacre was horribly silent. The dark, dead trees loomed around him, shadows in the shimmering blue-green curtains of mist. He hardly needed his flashlight anymore. The fog's own glow was like burning marsh gas, or spoiled moonlight. Gayle signaled that they should move on, and Jimmy quickly took the point. He knew where the farmhouse was, though he'd never been there before. Apparently he made it his business to know things like that. Gayle and Toby followed after the thunder godling, sticking close so as not to lose him in the treacherous fog. The ground beneath their feet was soft and unpleasantly yielding. Toby looked down and saw that they were treading through a thick layer of ash. He looked back over his shoulder, but they'd already come far enough that he could no longer see the boundary, lost as it was in the fog. There were only the dead trees and the ashes at his feet, and the fog, thick enough to blur the surrounding world and muffle the few sounds he and his companions made. It felt to Toby now as though he was walking at the bottom of the sea. He kept a careful lookout for sharks.

Strangely, it was even hotter inside the fog than out. The heat seemed to come from everywhere at once, as though they'd stepped into an oven. The air was thick, full of the corrupt stench of the wood, and the sweltering heat was almost overpowering. Toby's shirt was soaked with sweat, and more ran down his face to drip off his chin. Gayle was leaning ever more heavily on him now, her face shiny with sweat and her eyes half closed, but she didn't complain. Jimmy did, but had enough sense to keep it mostly to himself, grumbling constantly in a growl of Old Norse. Norse gods were built to endure cold, not heat. Toby switched off his flashlight and put it away, so he could have both hands free to support Gayle.

"I shouldn't be able to see this," she said suddenly. "Any of it. I have a blind spot where death is concerned. But Blackacre is as vivid to me now as any nightmare I ever had. This is Hob's doing—his place, his rules. He wants me to see his work, be impressed by his power and his evil. He's very insecure, in some ways. Comes from his being an only son, dominated by his father, abandoned by his mother . . . We should have done more for him. In a way, all of this could be laid at my door."

"Stop that," said Jimmy immediately, not looking round. "Hob made himself what he is, and took great delight in it. He is the Serpent's Son, and you could no more have changed his nature than you could make the world turn backwards."

"Well . . ."

"And if you're about to say what I think you're about to say, I don't want to hear it. Just let me get him within range of my hammer, and I'll change his nature for him. I'll give the top of his head such a bash he'll end up having to hear out of his arse."

"Is it just me," said Toby, "or does this fog have a distinctly *oily* feel? I can feel it, crawling on my skin. It's like walking through wet curtains."

"The fog is alive," Gayle said tiredly. "It's an extension of Hob's will. Just by passing through the mists and disturbing them, we're telling Hob someone is coming. Though he shouldn't be able to tell who, as yet. My nature shields us from him. But there will be other defenses, as we draw nearer to the old farmhouse, even apart from the dead guards."

Toby looked quickly about him, but the thick fog threw back his gaze. He hadn't spotted any of the dead standing guard yet, but still he had a strong feeling that he was being watched. It also worried him that he hadn't seen any of the Mice yet, or heard them. He couldn't stand the thought that he might have brought them here to their capture, or injury . . . or death. They were, essentially, innocent creatures. Toby felt isolated, and horribly helpless. There could be any number of threats or enemies out there in the wood, in the fog; and he wouldn't know anything about them until they were right on top of him.

"Angel's the one I want," said Jimmy, not at all for the first time. He'd been going on about her all the way up the long slope to Black-acre, and for some time before. Apparently he'd taken his defeat at the railway station the previous night very hard. His pride had been hurt, and he wasn't used to that. "You just leave Angel to me. I'll take her down this time, you'll see. We're both in Mysterie now, where my powers are at their peak. I will show her the true rage and power of a Norse god in his glory, and she will kneel to me."

Toby had heard all this before, and a great deal more like it, and was getting bloody tired of the whole subject. He glared at Jimmy's broad back.

"You know, I have a major slap with your name on it, in my pocket. Now keep the noise down, so we can at least hear if something nasty is coming our way."

Jimmy didn't even deign to look back, but he did shut up, for a while. Toby was grateful for small mercies. He was becoming increasingly worried about Gayle. She was trembling violently all the time now, and leaning on him so that he was almost carrying her. Toby was secretly pleased and flattered that she should have chosen to depend on him rather than on her old flame, the great hero Jimmy Thunder. He knew this was small of him, but . . .

And then the dead came lumbering forward out of the fog, chasing after scattering Mice. Jimmy, Toby and Gayle stood very still, and the dead guards ignored them, fixated on the taunting Mice that kept just ahead of them, and generally ran rings around them. The Mice shot back and forth between the dead trees, throwing up clouds of ashes with their pounding paws, the disturbed fog billowing around them. The dead guards didn't have a chance, or a clue. They stumbled after whichever Mouse came nearest, reaching out with slow dead hands after furry bodies that were already long gone.

More and more of the dead appeared, drawn from their stations, bumping into each other, or into trees, or being tripped up or bowled over by the darting Mice. Soon there wouldn't be a single dead man left to stand between Toby, Gayle and Jimmy and the Hob's lair. The Mice were having a grand old time. As longtime hippies, firmly committed to peace and nonviolence, they couldn't and wouldn't fight directly, or lend their paws to open destruction, but this . . . this was just playing. Another triumph for the mousy pranksters.

"One of your more inspired ideas, Toby," said Jimmy, smiling despite himself. "With so many Mice dashing around like mad things, any signals Hob might get from the fog will be hopelessly confused. He won't know what's happening until we're right on top of him."

One of the Mice stopped suddenly before Toby, eyes wide and breathing hard. It was Dreamy.

"I remembered!" she said, trembling distractedly. "I dreamed about this, I did. About all of us here, in this place, at this time. Great things will happen here, and bad things. Someone dies, screaming in the night."

And then she was off again, running through the dead trees, chasing and being chased, tormenting and distracting the dead guards. Toby looked at Gayle and Jimmy.

"Her dreams aren't reliable," said Gayle. "The other Mice said so."

"Stands to reason someone's going to die here," Jimmy said gruffly. "Either Hob and Angel, or one of us. No way we can all hope to walk away from this alive. I knew that going in."

"No one's ever been able to kill the Hob," said Gayle, her eyes fixed on Toby's. "Even the Walking Man couldn't finish Hob off. And Angel is an unknown factor. She was created in Heaven's forges, and even in her new, lesser form, she is mighty indeed. The best we can hope for is to make both of them back down, dismantle whatever operation the Serpent had them set in motion. And no, Toby, I don't know how we're going to do that yet. But we have to be here. We have to face them, in the center of their power. I can feel it, even without taking my aspect upon me. You, Toby, of all of us, have to be here. You will be the focal point, upon which everything else turns."

"Don't rely on me to save the day," said Toby, looking away from Gayle. "I'm not the kind of person you can rely on. I haven't got a clue what I'll do when I finally come face-to-face with Hob, except probably wet myself. Look, I've already died once today. I should be exempt from further unpleasantness in that area."

"What do you want," said Jimmy, "a note from your mother?"

Luna and Leo, two very different shape-shifters, approached the Blackacre boundary, not knowing that from another side, another group was doing the same thing at the same time. Luna was still disturbed though, sensing the presence of other powers, and kept looking distractedly about her. Leo didn't really notice; as usual he was entirely taken up with his own concerns. In fact, he was still thinking wistfully about the chances of doing a runner and legging it for the nearest horizon. But . . . he knew there was nowhere he could run where Luna couldn't see, and find him, and punish him in all kinds of inventive and unpleasant ways. His nature and hers meant that they were forever linked. So he sighed and growled and shook his shaggy head, sniffing unhappily at the eerie blue-green fog smothering the dead trees before him. It smelled unhealthy.

"This is new," he said finally. "Wasn't here the last time I came through. Hob must have set it up, after I evaded all his other security measures. We walk into that stuff, we might as well send Hob a singing telegram saying we're coming."

"I want him to know we're coming," said Luna. "I want him to know I'm coming, and to worry. I have a great deal to say to my errant son."

Leo looked at her uneasily. All his instincts were yelling at him to get the hell away from the unnatural fog and what it contained; but right then, Luna was scarier than anything he might encounter in Blackacre. Her voice was horribly cold and angry, and her eyes were blue chips of ice—goddess's eyes. Having a direction and a purpose had served to focus her again, even in Mysterie, and of course she was much stronger in the moonlight. She was dressed all in white furs now, the pure silver pelts still spotted with the dark blood of the furs' previous occupants. Her face was thinner, almost gaunt, her close-cropped hair shining silver like her furs, her mouth a thin scarlet line. Her appearance had changed several times on the long trek through the town and out, but her mind was fixed and relatively sane. Leo just hoped fervently that she would know what to do when she finally came face-to-face with her discarded son, the Hob. There was more to Luna, now—a presence and a power, even though she had yet to take her aspect upon her. She was waking up, after centuries of sleep, and beginning to remember who and what she was, and could be. Leo did his best not to bring himself to her attention except when necessary.

"He's in there," Luna said abruptly, staring into the thick fog as though she could see right through it—and perhaps she could, at that. "He knows company's coming, but he doesn't know who. He's curious, but he isn't scared. Yet. And . . . there are other presences abroad in the night, heading into Blackacre with retribution on their minds. Events are approaching a climax. There will be blood and suffering—oh, yes, and death and reckonings long postponed. You must listen when I tell you these things, Leo. The life you save might be your own."

"Wonderful," said Leo. "I'm so lucky to have you here to point these things out to me. How do you want to do this?"

"We will walk into the wood, and keep walking until we reach Hob's redoubt. And if anything gets in our way, I will walk right over it."

"I have a strong suspicion it's not going to be quite that easy," said Leo, carefully. "Apart from this fog, there are all kinds of other defenses in the wood, set up specifically to keep out people like us."

"There are no people like us."

"Yes, well, be that as it undoubtedly is, the fact remains that there is a small army of the risen dead standing guard in there, with orders to make offal out of unannounced visitors, quite apart from a whole bunch of free-floating defensive spells, all ready to trigger if anyone gets too close to them. Shaped curses, malignant hexes, demolition charms; all the usual black-magic crap designed to really mess up your day. I only avoided them on my last little incursion because of my dual heritage, and you can bet Hob will have reprogrammed them by now to take that into account."

Luna sniffed, fixed the unmoving fog with a hard look, and then thrust one very pale hand into the blue-green mists. The fog churned violently about her hand, as though in pain, and bright lights flared suddenly, deep in the mists, and were followed by the sound of distant explosions. Leo could feel his jaw dropping as he listened to the Hob's defensive spells detonating under the pressure of Luna's will. So much power, linked to a mind of fluctuating sanity . . . Leo didn't even want to think about what might happen if Luna ever turned such a gaze upon him, but he couldn't seem to help himself. He felt very much like whimpering, and did actually jump just a bit when Luna nodded once, sharply, withdrew her hand and spoke to him.

"Come along, Leo."

All he could do was nod, and say, "Yes, ma'am."

She walked into the fog with her head held imperiously high, and Leo slunk in after her. He felt a sharp sinking sensation in his stomach as the thick, oily blue-green mists swallowed him up, like the maw of some hungry beast. His skin crawled at their touch, and all his hair stood on end. He glared about him, tensed and ready for any form of attack, but there were only the dead trees, like dark smudges in the fog. Leo considered turning wolf, and then thought better of it. This place was upsetting enough to his merely human senses. He glanced at Luna and wasn't surprised to find she'd changed again. She was dressed in chased silver armor now, from shimmering helm to dainty boot, the shining metal traced with frost despite the heat, and scored all over with marks in a language Leo didn't even recognize.

*I know it,* said his Brother Under The Hill, sounding distinctly unhappy. *No one uses it anymore. It's Enochian, a language for speaking with angels.*

"Be quiet," said Luna. "Your chattering distracts me."

*Listen to me,* the Brother said stubbornly. *There are others in there with you, powerful presences. Not Hob or Angel.*

"Oh, shit," said Leo. "It's going wrong already, isn't it? Maybe we should come back later?"

*Too late.*

Suddenly a whole gang of mice came charging out of the fog, racing around and past Luna and Leo, laughing and whooping. Dead men came stumbling determinedly after them and the Mice chased and pestered them mercilessly, taking turns to see who could get the closest to the grasping dead hands and still escape untouched. The dead stubbornly pursued the Mice, who led them off into the wood again until all of them were gone, swallowed by the fog. The last Mouse to go was Sweetie, who paused just long enough to drop Leo a saucy wink.

"Friend of yours?" said Luna.

*Oh, tell me you didn't . . . ,* said his Brother.

"Today just keeps getting worse and worse," said Leo.

That was when the dead hands burst up and out of the ash-covered ground all around them, grasping blindly for Luna and Leo's ankles: dead men and women, buried in the dead ground, hidden from view as another line of defense. Cold fingers dug deep into Leo's ankles and feet, tearing the skin and crushing flesh and bone with horrid, implacable strength. Leo yelled, from shock as much as pain, and tried to change, but the pain distracted his thinking, preventing him from concentrating. He fought to keep his balance, knowing that if he fell, the rotting hands protruding from the ashes, opening and closing like bear-traps, would tear him apart in moments.

But where the hands touched Luna's cold armor they recoiled in a moment, seared and twisted, as though blasted by some unseen force. They could not bear the touch of her. Luna glared about her, and wherever she looked the hands sank quickly back into the broken ground, driven away by the awful power of her will. Some of the more slowly retreating hands actually withered under the pressure of her gaze and fell apart. The ground itself rippled and roiled as the hidden dead tried to dig themselves deeper into the earth, to get away from her. It took Leo a moment to realize that his ankles were free, too, now that she'd looked in his direction, and he quickly knelt down to press his tattered ankles together with his hands, to speed up the healing. And so he wouldn't have to look at Luna, and perhaps meet her terrible gaze.

"That was Hob," Luna said calmly. "My son, working through the dead. Now he knows I'm here. Good. I want him to know. And to worry."

In another part of the dead wood, Toby and Gayle and Jimmy stood together, watching a bright golden gleaming will-o'-the-wisp, as it danced in the mists ahead of them. It was drawing steadily closer, a golden glow bobbing on the air like an unblinking flame. Then suddenly there were two of them, moving paired together, racing forward through the fog. Jimmy hefted his great hammer Mjolnir and braced himself. The golden glowing things became the two golden eyes of a huge dark cat, stalking out of the mists toward them, overpoweringly huge and menacing. It stood easily five feet tall at the shoulder, and was perhaps ten feet long. Thick cords of muscle bulged under the night-dark hide, but for all its size, it wasn't a panther or a puma or a leopard, or any known species. Instead, it was somehow all cats and none, every kind of cat rolled into one and grown to an impossible size. The abstract, perfect, primal Cat. The ground shook under its tread, as though afraid. It came to a halt disturbingly close to Gayle and Toby and Jimmy and looked at them with calculated insolence.

"Well, hello," said the Cat, in a slow, self-satisfied drawl that Toby immediately knew was how all cats would sound if they could talk. "You really shouldn't be here, you know. This is a dangerous place, for the uninvited."

"Do you know who I am?" said Gayle, her voice perfectly calm and steady.

"You, Lady? Always. I would bow my head to you, in other places. But this place belongs to another, and so I do not bow to you. Soon, everywhere that is will be taken from you, and then I will bow to you no more, Lady."

"Can we cut to the chase, please?" said Jimmy, in his best commanding, godlike voice. "I haven't got the time or the patience for the usual veiled threats and insinuations. Who the hell are you?"

"So swift, so uncourteous," said the Cat. "You would take all the fun out of it, little god. Your ancestors understood the need for civilized banter, a crossing of wits before the slaughter. It is expected of us, as symbols and avatars. But style is going out of the world, along with so many other things. I am the King of the Cats. And the Hob has bound me to him with promises of free reign in the world that is to come, the world that he will bring about. No more pets, no more zoos or sanctuaries. All mankind will be my prey, or all of Humanity that survives the transition. My prey, to run naked and squealing before me, to hunt and kill at my pleasure. Such fun. And all I have to do to earn that joy is to kill fools like you, who intrude where they're not wanted."

"You know who I am, and dare to challenge me?" said Jimmy, as calm and collected as the Cat.

"Oh, yes," said the King of the Cats. "Such a pleasure, to have such notable victims to rend and tear, such godly blood to lick from my claws. I'm going to enjoy running you down, and hear you plead for your little lives. The diluted god, the diminished Lady and the tiny mortal. You will run for me, won't you? Who knows; I might not chase all of you."

"Shove it," said Jimmy Thunder, hefting his hammer in his hand.

The Cat looked at Mjolnir thoughtfully, his great muscles rippling under his fur. He didn't look especially impressed. If anything, he seemed to be smiling. And then Toby stepped forward, putting himself between Gayle and the Cat.

"So," he said brightly. "How did you get to be King of the Cats?"

"What?" said the Cat, not looking away from Jimmy Thunder. His tail was lashing slowly behind him. He might have been starting to crouch.

"How did you get to be the King?" said Toby. "Start at the bottom and work your way up? Perform marvelous feats of bravery and derring-do? Or is it a purely constitutional title these days, with no real power and responsibility?"

"*What?*" said the Cat, turning his glowing golden eyes on Toby. "What kind of questions are these? I just . . . knew. When the old King died, I became the King, ruler of all the cats, in all the worlds."

"And that's it?" said Toby. "No examinations, no discussions, not even a ceremony? You just think you're the King? Hardly seems likely, does it? I don't know about this. You could be wrong, you know. Have you checked? How do you know there aren't other contenders for the Kingship? Some of them might actually be better qualified than you. And isn't the idea of an absolute monarchy dangerously outdated, in this day and age? Perhaps you'd be better off with a committee, or some form of proportional representation. What are your qualifications to be King?"

"*What?*" said the Cat, actually backing away as Toby advanced on him. "The . . . the Voice told me the old King was dead, so I was King. That's how it works!"

"Ah," said Toby, nodding interestedly. "Now we're getting somewhere. How long have you been hearing voices?"

The Cat screamed, turned abruptly, and ran off into the fog.

"How about that?" said Jimmy, lowering his hammer. "He ran away, rather than have to listen to you anymore. Mind you, I often feel the same way."

The King of the Cats didn't get far before he ran into Luna and Leo. Still screaming, the Cat took one look at Luna standing tall and imposing in her silver armor and skidded to a halt, his fur standing on end. Leo turned wolf in a flash, and threw himself on the Cat.

He'd been looking for someone to take out his grievances on all day. They hit the ground in a cloud of ashes, a hissing, growling mess of teeth and claws and bad temper, tearing savagely at each other. But the Cat was outweighed, outclassed, not to mention already severely demoralized, and besides, Leo could heal all his wounds in a second. Soon the Cat was fighting only to break away and run. Leo pounced, snapping his great wolf jaws shut on the nape of the Cat's neck. He took a firm grip, braced himself, and shook the huge Cat violently back and forth, ignoring his pitiful howls. Leo then dropped the Cat, bit him fiercely on the arse, and chased him up the nearest tree. Leo sat at the base of the tree, his long red tongue lolling out of the side of his grinning mouth as he peered up, while the Cat clung precariously to the highest branch that would still bear his weight.

Luna came over to stand beside Leo, and stared haughtily up at the treed Cat. "Bad kitty. No more sour cream for you."

"Oh, God, she's going to start talking to me now," said the Cat. "I think I'm going to have one of my turns."

"A cat may look at a Queen, but even the King of the Cats should know better than to annoy me," said Luna. "Now come down here and apologize, before I think of something amusing to do to you."

"I am not coming down while that hairy thing with the thyroid problem is still down there!" said the Cat, trying to hang on to the last vestiges of his dignity. "Your Majesty," he added, as an afterthought.

"I could go up there and fetch him for you," growled Leo. "In fact, I could chew him up and spit him out again, and make you a nice pair of slippers out of his hide. If you like."

"I don't really think we've got time," said Gayle, behind them. "Besides, they'd clash terribly with that armor."

Luna and Leo looked round sharply as Toby and Jimmy and Gayle came out of the fog to join them, drawn by the noise of the conflict. Up in the dead tree, the King of the Cats cringed pitifully.

"Please don't let him start talking again! I can't stand it! My head hurts. . . ."

Everyone ignored the Cat as the two sisters stared at each other thoughtfully and Toby and Jimmy looked interestedly at the werewolf.

"Thunder god," said Jimmy. "Jimmy Thunder, God For Hire."

"Focal point," said Toby. "Toby Dexter, very confused."

"Werewolf," said Leo. "But I think you already guessed that. Hang on while I change into someone less comfortable." He rose up on his hind legs and quickly became human again. He was actually glad of the excuse. The dead wood was too overpowering and upsetting for his enhanced wolf senses. Toby blinked a few times as he tried to work out where Leo's clothes had suddenly appeared from, but was otherwise suitably impressed. Leo gave Toby and Jimmy his best friendly smile. "Leo Morn, acting hero, unpaid, under protest. Is that really Gayle?"

"Yes," said Jimmy. "Do I take it you're on your way to see Hob, too?"

"Much against my better judgment, but yes. Luna said I was going with her, and you can't argue with facts like that. I'm here to look after her, watch her back, remember who she is for her, that sort of thing. Of course, now you're here, I'm sure you could take care of all that better than I ever could, so I'm not really needed here anymore, am I? In fact, I'd probably just get in your way. So I'll just say Good Luck, and Godspeed, and be sure to let me know how it all turns out. . . ."

"Stand still, that wolf," said Luna, still looking at Gayle. "You're not going anywhere, Leo Morn."

"Oh, bugger," said Leo miserably.

The two sisters were still staring into each other's eyes. Neither of them seemed all that pleased to see the other.

"You shouldn't be here," said Luna. "Not here, of all places."

"I could say exactly the same to you," said Gayle. "I can't protect you here."

"I have the better right," said Luna. "He is my son, after all."

"He's the Serpent's Son. When have you ever cared about him,

Luna? You didn't even want to see him after he was born. I had to take him away."

"Yes," said Luna. "And we all know how that turned out."

"All right, I screwed up. Fostering him with the Green Man probably wasn't the wisest decision I ever made. But I couldn't just kill him. He won't listen to you, Luna. Why should he? You've never spoken to him before."

"You shouldn't be here," Luna maintained stubbornly. "This is a dead place. You have no power here. It's outside your nature."

Gayle smiled slightly. "Looks like we're both just following our natures. We're here because we feel we have to be. Duty can be a real bastard sometimes. How are you feeling, Luna?"

"Surprisingly coherent, for a change. I find anger concentrates the mind wonderfully. So, we're off to see the Hob. Do you have a plan?"

"Do you?"

"I thought not." Luna looked at Toby interestedly. "You always did have lousy taste in lovers. A focal point! Well, that should complicate things marvelously."

"Excuse me," said the King of the Cats diffidently, still up his tree. "Would anyone object if I were to come down now, and perhaps run away? I'd really like to run away, if that's all right with everyone. There are far too many powers and avatars in one place for my liking. It can only mean that something dreadfully important and significant is about to happen, and I would personally prefer to be incredibly far away when the shit starts hitting the fan."

"Be quiet," said Gayle. "Or I'll let Toby talk to you some more."

"Shutting up right now," said the Cat.

And that was when a whole crowd of Mice suddenly came running out of the fog, streaming past the startled group at the foot of the tree without stopping. All twenty-three Mice stampeded past Toby in full flight, not even pausing as he called out to them, their purpose forgotten and abandoned as they headed for the Blackacre boundary with all the speed they could muster. The fog swirled thickly about them, disturbed by their passing. There was no sign of any of the dead, left behind as they ran.

For behind them came Angel.

She came striding out of the fog, walking on the air, as silent as a ghost, as remorseless as revenge. She advanced unhurriedly on the group by the tree, who closed their ranks instinctively, ready for trouble. Angel came to a halt before them, hovering some ten feet above the ground: flesh white as winter, wrapped in black tatters, with bloodred lips and eyes. Even standing still in midair, the fog around her was disturbed, as though by the slow flapping of unseen wings. She smiled down on them, and that smile was a terrible thing to see. Leo was whining softly. Toby felt like doing the same. Gayle and Luna stood shoulder to shoulder, glaring at Angel with cold, implacable faces. But Angel's attention was all for Jimmy Thunder.

"I knew if I waited long enough, you would come to me," she said happily. "You, at least, know how to show a girl a good time. Not that I expect this to last long. We're both far from our beginnings, but here in Mysterie I am more than you'll ever be. So how about it? Want to dance, little godling? Want to bleed and suffer and die? I almost envy you the sensations you're about to endure."

Jimmy Thunder threw Mjolnir at her. The ancient hammer flashed through the fog, too fast for mortal eye to follow, and struck Angel squarely in the gut, folding her over and knocking her out of the air. She dropped to the ashy ground like a wounded bird, making horrid noises as her crushed lungs strained for air, but though Mjolnir struggled to return to Jimmy, she clung grimly to the hammer, refusing to let it go. Jimmy ran forward to take it from her, and she rose up like a demon from the pit to face him.

Luna looked at Leo. "Help the thunder god. Destroy the angel."

Leo looked back at her. "Are you kidding?"

*Don't you listen to her,* said his Brother. *You wouldn't stand a chance, Leo.*

"I had worked that out for myself, actually," replied Leo. "Sorry, Luna. Scary as you undoubtedly are, Angel is a whole different class of homicidal maniac."

"But you're a Morn!"

"And I'd very much like to stay one, rather than become a small pile of meaty chunks after they've passed through Angel's digestive system. I know my limitations."

"You get in there and help the thunder god or I will personally spread your limitations over a very large area," said Luna sternly.

Leo pouted. "This isn't at all fair, you know."

"Now you know how I feel," said the King of the Cats.

"Shut up," said Leo. He shook his head and growled. "I should have joined the union when they asked me."

He stretched and twisted into his wolf form, and raced forward to help the thunder godling, who was currently on the wrong end of an appalling beating.

Jimmy had lost his hammer and was going head to head with Angel, both of them giving and receiving dreadful blows that shook the foggy air like thunderclaps. Any of those terrible blows would have killed a lesser being immediately, but Jimmy Thunder and Angel crashed back and forth through the wood, knocking down or destroying the dead trees when they got in their way, leaving a wide trail of devastation and churned-up ash and earth. Great trees that had stood for centuries, even after they were dead, were now uprooted and set leaning at impossible angles as Jimmy and Angel fought on.

The thunder godling was losing, and he knew it. He was strong and fast and could soak up staggering amounts of punishment, but in the end Angel was just so much more than he was. Blood ran thickly down his pulped face as he gasped for air through a crushed mouth and broken nose, and it was all he could do to see his opponent through his swollen and closing eyes. His back was still straight and his blows were still strong, but he could feel the strength going out of his legs. He'd never fought so hard, for so long, to so little effect. It was like smashing his fists against a mountainside. Angel drove him back, steadily, remorselessly, laughing as she hit and hurt him.

Leo circled the fight, looking for an opening. He wasn't sure what he could do. All right, he was a werewolf, but truth be told he wasn't even in Jimmy Thunder's class, never mind Angel's. And then Jimmy Thunder roared with rage and hurt and frustration, and went berserk. Veins popped up all over his body as his muscles distended and all his wounds stopped bleeding. His eyes were wild and fey, everything he was now focused only on attack. He surged forward, shrugging off Angel's blows, and clasped her in a vicious bear hug, pinning her arms to her sides and crushing the air from her. All her greater strength couldn't stand against his berserker rage. For a moment Angel was actually helpless, and Leo saw his chance. He launched himself at Angel and, with one vicious snap of his great wolf jaws, tore out her throat.

He hit the ground hard, and spun round impossibly quickly, just in time to see Angel break Jimmy's hold with one great flex of her arms. She hit him once, throwing him to the ground with such force that all his berserk power was knocked right out of him. Blood ran in a flood from the terrible wound in Angel's throat and air bubbled in it, but she didn't fall. The pale flesh closed over, knitting together, and the wound was gone. She laughed at Jimmy lying on the ground before her and stamped on him. Ribs cracked and broke loudly. Angel did it again, and Jimmy cried out in spite of himself. Leo threw himself once more at Angel, and she snatched him out of midair with one hand and threw him thirty feet, to smash against a tree and break it in two. Leo fell limply to the ground.

Jimmy Thunder, last of the Norse gods, last of the line of Thor, drew on the remains of his strength and his heritage and called down a lightning bolt.

The stark and brilliant leven bolt slammed down through the fog, throwing back the night, and grounded itself through Angel. She shrieked like a damned soul, shuddering and shaking, but held in place like a beetle on a pin. All her hair stood out, and her skin blackened and charred. She shook violently, still screaming. The lightning bolt finally snapped off, and Angel's scream stopped. She fell forward onto her face and lay still, smoke rising from her black and twisted body.

Toby hurried over to the broken, bloody thunder god, and got him back on his feet. His wounds were slowly healing, but his eyes were vague and confused. Leo Morn came limping over to join them, human once again.

"We'd better get moving," Luna said calmly. "Angel's down, but not out. Nice try though, Jimmy. Leo, look after him. Toby, you help Gayle. She's only going to get weaker as we approach the farm-house. I'll lead the way, while I can."

They set off slowly through the fog. Up in his tree, the King of the Cats watched them go. When he was sure it was safe, he climbed carefully down, went over to sniff at Angel's still smoking body, and then headed resolutely for the Blackacre boundary. Cats know when to cut their losses.

Gayle was leaning more and more heavily on Toby now, and sometimes she didn't seem to know where she was, or why. According to Luna, they were almost at the farmhouse clearing, but Toby didn't know how much faith to put in her. She seemed sane and collected enough, but the details of her armor kept changing when he wasn't looking, and sometimes she addressed him by his own name and sometimes by others, confusing him with lovers from Gayle's extensive history. Jimmy Thunder looked worn out, and Leo Morn looked frankly dispirited. All in all, they were not much of an army to take on the Serpent's Son.

Part of Toby wanted just to take Gayle and get the hell out of the dead wood. Blackacre was killing her. He could see it in her growing weakness, in the troubling vagueness of her face and eyes. Somehow the dead wood was sucking all the life out of her. But even if he could drag her out, against her will, he knew she'd only insist on going back in again. She was supposed to be here. So was he. He could feel it, on a level too deep to deny. The focal point was being drawn inexorably to the point and purpose of his existence, whether he liked it or not. The same unknown force that had brought him and Gayle together was now demanding its price, and possibly its pound of flesh. Toby wasn't as scared of death as he'd once been, not now he'd met her, but still he didn't want to die. He had so much to live for, with Gayle.

Typical of his luck, really. Finally to gain what he'd always wanted, only so it could be taken away again.

He was so lost in thoughts of fate and destiny, he didn't notice at first when the dead wood came alive around him. The ancient trees stirred slowly, their long branches bending and twisting and stretching out towards the group as they passed, while dark roots burst up through the broken ground to writhe like dreaming snakes. One by one the group became aware of what was happening, and looked quickly about them as the dead trees rocked and swayed, and tore themselves up out of the ashy ground. They walked on their roots, terrible dead giants with blind, implacable purpose.

"Hob," said Luna, making the name a curse. "His plan, his will. It's in everything."

Gayle raised her head slowly, and recited an old rhyme Toby hadn't heard since his childhood.

*"Ash do grieve, Oak do hate, Willow do follow if ye walk out late."*

The dead trees were tearing themselves free from the earth on all sides now, and the group fell back before them. No one had the strength left to fight them. Jimmy's hand went to his hammer, back in its holster on his hip, but he didn't draw it. It was all Leo could do to keep Jimmy on his feet, and both of them knew it. The trees pressed forward, blocking off all routes but one, herding the group toward the clearing, and the farmhouse.

Hob was getting impatient.

They were only a few minutes from the clearing. They stumbled out into the open space, and the fog was suddenly gone. It clung to the edges of the clearing, but would not enter, as though even it was afraid of Nicholas Hob. Toby took his first look at the farmhouse up close and felt sick. There was something foul and unhealthy about the old structure, in its shapes and angles, as though the very stone and timbers had been infected by the evil that lived within it. Gayle's head came up slowly and she gently pushed herself away from Toby. She didn't want to appear weak before Hob. She walked steadily forward, across the open clearing, and no one ever knew what that cost her. The others went with her. One by one the farmhouse windows came alight with a harsh bright glare, like eyes opening. Gayle and the others came to the front door, and it opened before them, and there was Nicholas Hob, smiling.

"Do come in. I've been expecting you."

His voice sent shivers up Toby's spine, and he looked instinctively behind him for some way out, but there, on the edge of the clearing, stood Angel, complete and unharmed and smiling a smile very like Hob's. One by one the risen dead emerged from the fog to stand with her, a dead army compelled by Hob's unrelenting will.

"Come in," said Hob. "And we'll talk, for a while. You might as well. There's nowhere else you can go."

He stood back and gestured for them to enter, and one by one the last hopes of all the worlds entered the house of their enemy.

# Eleven~

# Family Ties

Toby's first thought on seeing the interior of the farmhouse parlor was that something had died there, just possibly the room itself. The pockmarked walls were seeping with what looked awfully like pus, and there were larger craters, too, weeping like discharging wounds. The floor was thick and sticky with accumulated filth, and the sourceless light that filled the room was too sharp, too bright; overwhelming to the human eye, it gave everything the exaggerated, distorted look of a fever dream. There was a sense of sickness to the room: physical, emotional, and intellectual. It was not a place where normal, sane people could bear to live. It stank, too, a rank, horrid stench that was almost overpowering. Toby had to fight not to gag too obviously. Houses come to resemble their owners. It occurred to Toby that he was getting his first real look at Nicholas Hob's mind, or his soul.

Gayle was even weaker here, increasingly unsteady on her feet, and Toby was having to support most of her weight. There were only two chairs, on either side of an elegant coffee table, all looking incongruously normal in such a setting. Toby didn't wait for permission before settling her onto one of the chairs. Hob might have said no, if asked. Gayle's face was slack, and wet with sweat, and her eyes were dangerously vague. She didn't respond when Toby said her name. He looked round at Hob, who was sinking gracefully into the opposite chair.

"What have you done to her, Hob?"

"Just brought her down to everyone else's level," Hob said cheerfully. "I thought it was time we all had a little chat, and I don't want any . . . interruptions." He looked across at Leo Morn, who was still supporting the weakened Jimmy Thunder. "Do feel free to dump him anywhere, Leo. It's not as if either of you are going anywhere, just yet." Then, finally, he looked at Luna.

"Welcome to my home, Mother. It's not much, but it's mine, all mine."

"Oh, this place is really you, Nicholas," said Luna, still looking round the room rather than at him. "You must have put a lot of effort into getting it to look like this."

Hob smiled briefly. "You have no idea, Mother. Do make yourself at home. We have so much to talk about." He turned a charming smile on Toby. "You and I especially have much to discuss. Hi, I'm Nicholas Hob. I'm sure they've told you terrible things about me, but you should know by now not to believe everything people say. In Mysterie, there are always more than two sides to any story. And mine is more complex than most. Ask me anything, Toby Dexter, and I promise I will tell you whatever you want to know. Whether you'll like the answers . . . Where would you like to start?"

"How can you live in a place like *this*?" said Toby.

"This is where I have been forced to live," said Hob, leaning forward in his chair to fix Toby with an earnest gaze. He ignored the others with almost insolent charm, focusing all his attention on Toby. "A lot of people want me dead, Toby Dexter. People like your companions. People such as they have hounded me across the world and back, for longer than you can imagine, never allowing me to settle anywhere for long. There are only a few places left now, where I can feel safe and secure. *They* took all the good places for themselves. It's time you knew the truth about me, Toby, and the truth about them."

"Don't listen to him," said Jimmy Thunder. He was sitting on the floor now, with his back propped against the wall, breathing harshly, his voice just a shadow of its former confident self. "You can't trust the Hob. Can't trust anything he says. He knows you're a focal point, knows you're here for a purpose. He wants to turn you, make you his. He'd say anything, promise you anything, to distract you from your purpose here. You can't ever trust the Serpent's Son."

"You see?" said Hob, leaning back in his chair and crossing his long legs with elegant ease. "They don't want you to listen to what I have to say. They can't allow you to know the whole truth. Because there are some things they can't afford for you to know. Terrible secrets, that they've been hiding from you."

"The Hob is the Prince of Lies," said Jimmy. "Everyone knows that."

"Why should I lie, when the truth can be so much more damaging?" said Hob. "Take Gayle, for example. Tell me, Toby—have any of them told you who and what your lady love really is? Would you like to know?"

Toby considered, but only for a moment. "Yes, I want to know. I need to know."

He looked at Gayle, sitting slumped in the chair beside him, but she said nothing. Toby folded his arms across his chest and looked defiantly at Hob, who smiled back at him almost sadly. Jimmy tried to say something, but Hob overrode him easily.

"Gayle is the human form of Gaia. Mother Earth, the planetary consciousness, the living world that supports us all. When she takes on her aspect, she becomes the Earth, womb and parent to all humankind, and unimaginably powerful. Her sister, Luna, my dear mother, is the Moon, of course. Take deep breaths, Toby. These are big concepts, but you can handle them."

"So the Serpent In The Sun," Toby said slowly, "is . . ."

"The Sun. Yes. The Gayle and Luna you've been associating with aren't really human, the way you and even I are. They're just masks, roles they play, suits they put on when they feel like going slumming. Tiny extensions of themselves they made so that they could walk unnoticed among us. The Gayle who so entranced you is really nothing more than a glove puppet. Gaia can no more love you than you could love one of the amoebae that live in your digestive tract. That's why she would never tell you the truth, or allow anyone else to tell you. She kept you close to her, in ignorance, because you're a focal point, and as such, useful to her."

Toby's head was spinning. He felt sick. He wished there was another chair. Hob's voice was calm and reasonable, but the things he was saying were hard to swallow, even after everything Toby had seen so far, even though they explained so very much. He was careful not to look at Gayle, or Luna. He looked challengingly at Hob.

"So . . . all the planets are alive?"

"Everything's alive, on some level," said Hob. "Everything's conscious. And the further up the scale you go, the bigger you get, the more powerful that consciousness becomes. Gaia and Luna and the Serpent are the real Powers and Dominations, because they have power and control over everything we do and are. We only exist on their sufferance because we're useful, sometimes. I've spent all my long life fighting them, struggling to be free. For all of us to be free."

"But . . . you're saying Gaia, and Luna, are physically the Earth and the Moon?" said Toby, needing to be sure he'd got that right.

"It's more of a metaphysical thing," said Hob. "The women you've been allowed to see are only the smallest tips of very large icebergs. Time for a history lesson, I think—the true and terrible origins of life in the solar system, and not at all what they teach you in school. In the beginning was the Firstborn, what we now know as The Serpent In The Sun—the first living consciousness. The Sun, alive and aware and terribly alone. Then, later, the planets awoke and took on sentience, and developed needs and aims of their own. In the beginning they were all one happy family, or so I've been told, but it didn't last. When new life, new sentience, began to appear on the worlds, things changed.

"The Serpent was the Sun, and always would be. An individual consciousness, perfect and unique, but never to know the joys of raising and nurturing life of its own. Gaia, on the other hand, gave birth to teeming hordes of life, great and small, over the millennia.

And all kinds of beings grew strong and sentient in her loving care. As long as they didn't forget their place. Remember the dinosaurs? Cocky bastards, by all accounts. Anyway, Humanity came along very late in the day, the very last species on earth to achieve sentience. They were the weakest creatures, but the most subtle; and as a result, the race with the greatest possibilities for growth and even transcendence. Which is why Gaia continues to tolerate our poisonous presence, despite all the damage we do her. But don't misunderstand me, Toby. Gaia may approve of our species as a whole, but she's never given a damn for individual members of that species."

"You flowered in the real world of Veritie," said Luna, unexpectedly. "You made it your own. The greater powers and presences always preferred Mysterie."

"Because they're afraid of Humanity," Hob said quickly. "Afraid of our potential, of what we might become."

"That's not true," Gayle said heavily. "He lies, Toby. He always does. It's his nature. Tell the truth for once, Hob, and shame yourself. You planned all this, didn't you?"

"Oh, yes," said Hob. "I planned it all, every detail."

"Why?" said Gayle. "Why did you want us here?"

"Direct and to the point, as always," said Hob. "I've always admired that in you, Gaia. Dear Auntie. Never any messing about with you. Your answers to problems have always been very straightforward—an earthquake, a volcano, a plague. You've wiped out whole civilizations, in your time. Compared to you, I'm an amateur." Hob leaned forward suddenly to glare at Gayle. "And you call me evil . . . my body count is nothing compared to yours." He settled back in his chair and looked apologetically at Toby. "Sorry about that. I just find hypocrisy so *irritating*. Now, where was I? Oh, yes. Everything I've done since my return here was planned with a single aim in mind: to bring you and Gayle here. Spreading rumors, planting information here and there, even my attack with the risen dead on the thunder godling's home were all a ruse, to distract you from my true intentions and lure you here, into my parlor, my world. Blackacre, the one place where I have power, and Gaia does not."

"Tell him why," said Gayle. "Tell him about the terrible thing you did here, little monster."

"I've always been very proud of what I achieved here, but then I'm biased, I suppose," Hob said easily. "But no one else has ever torn a part of Gaia away from her and made it their own. It's a unique achievement. Until now . . . But I'm getting ahead of myself. Long ago, Toby, I called to my father the Serpent, and he sent out a great and powerful solar flare. I called it down to this place, to this very spot, channelled it through me, and that supernaturally charged blast of heat scorched all life from this wood. All that was left were dead trees in a dead land. It became the one place on Earth where Gaia no longer had any hold, or influence, or power, or access. Blackacre became my place, my world, where I could be safe at last. The view's not up to much, but you can't have everything."

"He killed it all," said Gayle. "Every living thing here, from the highest to the lowest. And now I am here, in this unnatural place; I'm isolated from the living world. I cannot become Gaia, or call on any of my power. Here, I'm only my human self. Small, limited, and very vulnerable—the perfect trap. And I walked right into it."

"Exactly!" said Hob, clapping his hands together. "I knew your mighty pride, your ancient arrogance, wouldn't let you see me or this place as a serious threat to such as you. You've been human too long, Gayle, forgotten too much."

"No," said Gayle. "That isn't why I came here."

Hob looked at her for a moment, and then shrugged. "No matter. I needed you here, and here you are. And you, Toby. You're just as important to me. In fact, you're much more important than they ever told you."

"What about the others?" said Toby.

Hob shrugged. "Angel wanted Jimmy Thunder here. She's a bit peeved with him. She wants to rip out his heart and eat it, and who am I to deny Angel her little pleasures? Luna's presence was unexpected. Who knew she'd actually leave her wretched little bolt-hole after all these years? I haven't had the pleasure of her august presence in the same room as myself since she abandoned me as a baby. And, it must be said, I had no wish ever to see her again, except at her funeral, perhaps. Still, what only son doesn't want his mother to see the great things he's achieved? To be awed, when he becomes so much more than she ever was? It's fitting she should be here, in the moment of my greatest triumph. You will try to pay attention, won't you, Mother dearest? I'd hate you to miss any of it. Ah, well—it's not as if I need worry about your interfering." Hob looked at Toby almost apologetically. "She's still a Power, but much weakened by centuries of feeble-mindedness. Frankly I'm amazed she remembers who I am, or who she is."

"I remember many things," said Luna. "That's always been my problem." She looked at Hob sadly with her ice-blue eyes. "The Serpent raped me. Took me against my will, hurt me till I could no longer resist him, and then made me carry his seed. A metaphysical rape, but the horror was very real. Such was his power that I could not abort you, drive your unnatural presence from my body. And so I reduced myself to the human, gave birth to you in blood and suffering and inflicted you on Humanity. That was the Serpent's curse, and my crime. Everything else since then has been your responsibility."

"Aren't relatives embarrassing?" Hob said to Toby. He smiled at Luna. "You know, humility suits you, Mother. You should try it more often." Hob's charming smile disappeared. "It didn't have to be like that. You could have kept me, raised me, cared for me, protected me from my father. But you chose not to. You helped make me what I am."

"I hated your father," Luna said tiredly. "Hated what he did to me, hated the result—you. I let Gayle take you away because . . . I wanted to forget what happened, forget you. And we all know how well that worked out. I'm here now, Nicholas. We can talk."

Hob showed his teeth in an unforgiving smile. "Too late, Mother dearest—far too little, and far too late."

"Excuse me," said Leo Morn diffidently. "What about me?"

"What about you?" said Hob, and Leo nodded quickly, shut his mouth, and hoped not to be noticed again.

"Why Blackacre?" said Toby. "If you wanted a place of your own, why make it such an awful place?"

"Because I could," said Hob. "It felt so good, to hurt the world as she hurt me. And because the Serpent demanded it. He would allow me a place of my own, but only on his terms. Typical father, I suppose. Still, I have power here. You'd be surprised at what I can do, here."

"Then why did you leave?" said Jimmy Thunder.

"The Serpent again," said Hob. "I have always been my Father's servant, his weapon in the world of men. He had a use for me, and so he drove me out of here, with whips and scorpions, to do his bidding. He does so love to meddle. And it's really so very typical of him, and of all my family. I've never been allowed to have a life of my own."

"So what's the plan?" said Gayle. She was sitting up a little straighter now, though she still looked very weak. "Why do you need me here, Hob?"

"You're the key to everything," said Nicholas Hob reasonably. "Through you, my father and I will change everything that is. Or, to be more exact, through your death. Soon the Serpent will send out a massive solar flare, the one he's been building up to all this time. And I will call it down, target and channel it through me, and send it out to sear all the life from this town, the secret heart of the world. Not one living thing shall survive here, in Veritie or Mysterie. The Serpent's natural and supernatural heat will scour the town clean from boundary to boundary, and Bradford-on-Avon will become just part of a much bigger Blackacre.

"And of course, as goes the town, so goes the world. Because here in my place, dear Gayle, you are only human. You have no power, no defenses; you will die with all the others. The earth will live on, but you, the soul and heart and intelligence of Gaia, will be dead and gone. The Serpent will take control of the new, mindless Earth, and remake it according to his wishes. Without you to stop him, he will send out more solar flares, to scorch all the life from the world. And then he will combine Veritie and Mysterie by force of will into one world, which he will restock with creatures of his own choosing and design—new life, answerable only to him. And I will rule them, in my father's name."

"You are crazy," said Toby, too taken aback to be anything but honest.

"You wish," said Hob. "Let the old worlds die. They were never very kind to either of us, were they? It's time for a change."

Toby looked at Gayle. "Is it possible? Could he actually do that? He and his father?"

"Yes," said Gayle. "The Firstborn was always the most powerful of us. With Gaia gone, and perhaps Luna, too . . ."

"The end of the old and the beginning of the new," Hob said cheerfully. "We should be celebrating! The new, joined world will be far superior to what we have now. None of the deadly dull grayness of Veritie, none of the capricious madness of Mysterie. No more Powers and Dominations, screwing up people's lives . . ."

"None of the logic and sanity of Veritie," said Gayle. "None of the wonders and joys of Mysterie. Just the Serpent, to screw up everybody's lives . . ."

"With you and your kind gone, the Serpent will have no reason to interfere," said Hob. "No more gods and monsters, just . . . ordinary people. Something very like Humanity, I'm sure. To be frank, the Serpent isn't very imaginative. I'm sure he'll end up leaving a lot of the details to me. He usually does. The Serpent will be an absentee landlord. And I will be whatever I want to be. At last . . . Let the old worlds go. I never liked them anyway."

"You don't have to do this," said Luna. "It's not too late, even now, to turn and walk away. You can still stop this."

"Can you protect me from my father?" said Hob.

"No."

"Then I do have to do this. And I would anyway, because I want to. Payback can be so very sweet, Mother dearest."

"I could die here, too, with Gaia."

"I know! Isn't it wonderful! An unexpected but most appreciated bonus." Hob sneered at her from his chair. "I owe you so much, for what you did to me. By choosing to give birth to me in your human form, in Veritie, you ensured I would be human, too. So much less of a threat to you and your kind. You crippled me, Mother. Condemned me to a mere human vessel, when I could have been so much more. Denied me my true heritage, my real power. What might I have been, had I been born in Mysterie, a true son of Luna and the Serpent? I could have been greater than all of you. Instead you damned me to be human, with a human's limitations, no match for my father's power. And so I became his slave, never to be free of him, never to be my own person."

"You could have been safe from him," said Luna. "If you'd stayed in Veritie, where I put you."

"And give up all my dreams of revenge? I needed the power I could find only in Mysterie. Not much power, compared to what I could have had, but enough to back my various little schemes. To make you and Auntie Gaia notice me and suffer, and regret your crimes against me. And let's face it; Veritie's a nice place to visit, but you wouldn't want to live there."

"Revenge?" said Jimmy Thunder. He'd finally got back onto his feet, with Leo's help, but he still had to lean against the filthy wall to support himself. "Is that what all this has been about? Because Mummy didn't love you? How very human of you, Nicholas. Get a life!"

The Hob snatched up a metal coffeepot from the table and threw it at Jimmy. It bounced off his skull, and his head rocked under the impact. Fresh blood ran down his face, but he still kept his feet.

"Speak when you're spoken to," said Hob. He turned back to Toby, suddenly all charm again. "Don't listen to them, Toby. They're just jealous. You can still be a part of this. You're supposed to be here. You have a role to play, as a focal point. You were chosen, by Powers far greater than any here present, to help make all this possible. I know it's a big thing, to give it all up and start anew in a brave new world; but was your old life really so special that you want to hang on to it? I'm offering you the chance to be a god, along with me, to rule over a wonderful new age. A new beginning, of wonders and miracles and glorious new life. What is there in your old life that you'd miss? A lousy job, rotten prospects, growing old, useless, and forgotten? To be mortal, to age and die? You could be worshiped, in the world that's coming."

"You want to kill Gayle," said Toby.

"So should you," Hob said reasonably. "She's used you and lied to you all along the way. She doesn't love you. She can't love you. *Gayle* is a lie. She has no real existence of her own, no real personality, that could feel anything for you. She's just a mask, a puppet. The shadow Gaia makes against a wall. Whatever you might think you feel for her is just an illusion, like the crush you might have on a film star on the big screen. She knew that, but she used that love to bind you to her. So that when your moment came, your short moment of power and destiny, you would do what she wanted. Toby, listen to me. I know what it is to be used by one of Them. My new world will be free of such lies, such influences. It might not be a strictly human world, but it will be much more humane. Make the big jump, Toby. Throw off your shackles and be free!"

"You can't expect me to agree to the slaughter of all Humanity! To the extermination of the human race!"

"Why not? The Serpent will produce something very similar, to take its place. Every god needs worshipers." Hob shrugged easily. "When you've lived as long as I have, Toby, and seen Humanity at its worst, the charm wears off pretty damn quickly. They're a spiteful, vindictive bunch, with few redeeming qualities. I'm sure the Serpent and I can improve on them."

"That's not why the Serpent wants to kill off Humanity," said Gayle, some of the old steel in her voice. "He's afraid of them. He sees Humanity's potential as a threat to him because they're always evolving, growing, becoming more than they are."

"Or were supposed to be," said Hob. "Who knows what they might become, in time? They have no limits on them, in Veritie, to protect the rest of us from their ambitions. They've already learned how to leave this planet. Eventually, there might come a time when they won't need the Earth, or the Sun, anymore. They already seek to control this world, gutting it and poisoning it in the process. Given time, they'll wear it out and move on, leaving this world and the Sun behind."

"Finally," said Luna. "Finally we come to the truth. To the Sun's words and motivation. He won't allow Humanity to grow, because they might grow beyond him. Might learn to do without him. Might even go away and leave him alone, as he was in the beginning. He'd destroy them all first, and replace them with something that could never grow and would never leave him."

"Well, yes," said Hob. "After the Sun's wiped the Earth clean, with my help, he'll subsume Veritie into Mysterie, and ensure that this fused world will remain weakened, forever under his and my control. Everyone in the new world will know their place and their function, and will never again grow beyond their purpose, transcend what they were supposed to be."

"No more choice," said Gayle. "No more freedom of thought."

"Why should they have what I've never known?" said Hob. He turned the full force of his charm and personality on Toby. "Join with me. Help bring about a new start, a new beginning. You can't love her. She isn't real. She isn't a person. She'll never love you."

"You're wrong," said Toby. "Gayle may be only a small part of Gaia, but she's real, she's human. She made herself real, by living as a human among humans, by not just accepting her limitations, but learning from them. You spent so long regretting what you could have been and obsessing on revenge that you never learned to appreciate the simple joys and pleasures of the human condition. What might you have been, Hob, what might you have achieved, if you'd concentrated on being real? All these centuries you've lived, all the people you've met—didn't you ever love any of them?"

"No," said Hob. "For a long time I thought . . . maybe some day . . . but love isn't in me. I don't think I'm capable of it. How can you feel, how can you know what you've never had? There's only ever been me and the Serpent's orders. All my life, others have only ever sought to use me for their own ends. From the highest to the lowest, from the Serpent down to foolish, limited humans. Open your eyes, Toby. You've been used, too. *They* made you a focal point, arranged for you to meet Gayle and fall in love with her, knowing she wasn't a real person and could never return your love. All so you'd do what They want, when the time came. Don't be a sucker all your life, Toby. Fight back. This is your chance for revenge, to make them pay for promising you a love you could never have."

"You're right," said Toby. "You don't understand love. They, whoever They are, probably did arrange our meeting yesterday. But I loved her long before that. I loved her from the first moment I saw her. I never expected anything to come of it, never expected her to love me. It's enough that I love her. She's real, she's human, and she's very special. I won't betray her, and I won't agree to the death of all Humanity, just because you're pissed off because you couldn't get a date."

"Ah, hell," said Hob. "It was worth a try. Angel! You can come in now!"

The door slammed open, and there was Angel. She strode into the room, her scarlet eyes bright and hungry. Hob indicated Jimmy Thunder.

"He's all yours, Angel. Feel free to make a mess."

Jimmy had only started to push himself away from the supporting wall when Angel was upon him. She snatched the hammer Mjolnir from his holster, raised it high, and brought it smashing down with inhuman speed. The hammer tried to turn in her grasp, but her strength was relentless. The hammer slammed violently against Jimmy's unprotected head, and there was a loud crack as it caved in the side of his skull. Jimmy fell limply to the floor like a steer in a slaughterhouse and lay there twitching. Angel hit him again with the hammer, just in case, and because she enjoyed it.

Leo Morn, who'd never thought of himself as any kind of hero, who knew he didn't stand a chance against Angel, turned wolf in an instant and threw himself on Angel's back. He'd always admired Jimmy Thunder, who was a real hero, and much to his surprise, he found he couldn't just stand by and watch while Angel killed a real hero. He landed on Angel's shoulders, and she cried out in shock and staggered away from Jimmy, as Leo's claws sank deep into her pale flesh. He bit viciously at the back of her neck.

*Leo!* shouted his Brother Under The Hill. *Get the hell away from her! You don't stand a chance! You don't have to do this!*

"Yes I do," said Leo. "I'm a Morn."

His great wolf teeth savaged Angel's flesh, and her hot blood sang against his tongue as his jaws piled on the pressure until his teeth grated against her neck bones. Angel dropped the hammer Mjolnir and spun round and round, screaming in pain and rage, while Leo clung grimly on, fighting to sever her spinal cord. But in the end he was just a wolf, and she was Angel. She forced her arms back until her hands could reach his hairy shoulders, and then her fingers sank into his flesh like knives. His bones cracked and broke as her grip tightened, and then she tore him away from her.

Leo kicked helplessly as she held him up before her with one hand, studying him with hot, angry eyes, and then she casually tore his left forelimb right out of its socket. Blood spurted clear across the room as Leo howled in agony, more like a man than a wolf. Angel pulled off his other legs, one by one, and only then tore off his head. She looked at the bloody pieces piled on the floor before her, her head cocked slightly on one side, as though puzzled by the extremity her rage had driven her to. Passions of all kinds were still new territory to her. Hob made tut-tutting noises.

"How many times do I have to tell you, Angel! Always clear up after yourself. Remember, we have to live here."

Angel shrugged and threw the pieces of what had once been Leo Morn out of the door, followed by Jimmy Thunder's still twitching body.

*Leo! NO! NO!*

They all heard the Brother Under The Hill screaming, thundering through their minds, a harrowing scream of rage and loss and bitter intent. And they all heard the earth rumble and break, as just outside the town a hill began to open. On the side of that hill was an ancient drawing of a giant human form, carved out of the white chalk beneath the grass in centuries past, so long ago now that few indeed remembered by whom and why. There are chalk carvings on hillsides all across the country. Some say they mark the worship places of forgotten gods; others, that they are fertility symbols. Only in Mysterie did a very few remember that chalk giants marked the resting places of dead or sleeping Nephilim, the giants in the earth. And under the carving on the hill outside Bradford-on-Avon a giant was stirring, his ancient blood awakened by a terrible loss. The hill shook and trembled and broke apart, the cold wet earth splitting open, and out came the Brother Under The Hill, roaring in his anger even as he wept for the last of the line of Morn.

He was twenty feet tall, a great and muscular figure of more than human grace and perfection. Entirely naked, wet mud still daubing his golden skin, the old wounds still showing on his back from where he'd torn away his wings long and long ago. He cried out, and his great voice filled the night. No longer resting in the earth, no longer bound by his ancient oath, the last of the Nephilim in the world of men headed for Blackacre with blood and vengeance on his mind.

Nephilim: human–angel hybrid. Sterile, like all hybrids, they adopted human families as their own. The Brother had adopted the Morns, watched and guarded them down the generations, had taken pride in their heroic deeds. Now they were all gone. The Brother came striding through the night with inhuman speed, to stop the Serpent's plan in Leo's name.

In a matter of moments he was upon Blackacre, and crashed through the boundary without slowing. The thick fog shrank back from him as he passed, unable to bear his overwhelming presence. The dead guards came to stop him and he swatted them aside easily, sending their broken bodies flying and tumbling through the night. The great trees lurched forward on their roots to form a barrier before him, and he crashed right through them, rending and breaking the dead wood with his huge golden hands. He was Nephilim, semidivine, touched by the Holy, driven by loss and remorse and cold, cold anger, and he would not be stopped.

He strode out of the broken trees and into the clearing, and approached the farmhouse. Hob sealed all the doors and windows with his magic, and called up all his defenses till the old building glowed in the dark. The Brother didn't care. He loomed over the farmhouse, defensive spells crackling harmlessly against his golden skin like static, and brought his huge fist down like a hammer. He beat against the farmhouse with his bare hands, and the old stone and timbers creaked and groaned under the onslaught. One by one the defensive spells went down, shattered by the Nephilim's presence and resolve. Stone cracked and crumbled, roof tiles exploded, and the whole structure shuddered, as though afraid.

Inside, dust was falling thickly from the groaning ceiling and wide cracks opened up in the walls, leaking unhealthy fluids as though they were bleeding. The whole room rocked like a boat at sea. Hob was screaming with rage. All his plans were being put at risk, by the one thing he hadn't bargained for. He glared furiously at Angel.

"I can still do this. You, buy me some time. Get out there and do something!"

"No!" said Luna, moving swiftly to put herself between Angel and the door.

Hob didn't hesitate. "Kill her, Angel. We don't need her. We've got Gayle. But do it quickly, please. She is my mother, after all."

Angel turned her crimson gaze on Luna, who didn't flinch. If anything, she looked sad. "From my high station, I see everything. I saw you fall, Angel. And I remember what you have forgotten. Look at my armor, Angel. Read what is written there, and know the truth."

Angel frowned and moved slowly forward to stand before Luna, almost as though drawn against her will. She studied the script that was graven into the shimmering metal.

"I know this," she said softly.

"Yes," said Luna. "It's Enochian, a language for talking to angels. Can you read what it says?"

"Yes," said Angel. "It's my name and my history. I remember who I am. I remember everything, now."

Her voice rose, suddenly sweet beyond bearing, powerful and potent, as she called out to the Brother in a language never spoken in the world of men. Never spoken because the human voice could not support it. She spoke to the Brother, the Nephilim, in the language of angels, and he halted his attack. There was a long pause. The night grew quiet as the house slowly settled, licking its wounds. Hob glared about him like a trapped animal. And then the front wall of the parlor split apart from top to bottom and slowly opened up like a pair of stone curtains, letting in the night. Through that great gap looked the kneeling Brother, the rage in his face replaced at least for the moment by shock and wonder.

"Uriel?" he said slowly. "Is that you?"

"Yes," said Angel. "It's me, finally. It's been a long time since I last saw you, Brother To Humans. My son."

"Is there *anyone* here who understands what's going on?" said Toby, but no one answered him. Hob and Luna and Gayle only had eyes for Angel and the kneeling Brother. In the end, Angel turned round and looked at Toby, and for the first time her face seemed calm and relaxed.

"Once upon a time, Toby Dexter—because the best stories all start that way—once upon a time, in the days before human history was set in stone, angels walked the earth. You see, there was once a Great War in Heaven, between those angels loyal to the Creator, and those loyal to the Morningstar. We all know how that turned out. But there were some angels who couldn't make up their minds as to which side they should be fighting on, and even if they should be fighting at all. So after the War was over, something had to be done with them. Not pure enough for Heaven, or evil enough for Hell; for their indecision, their lack of faith, and lack of moral conviction, the Creator sent them away. He reduced them from the immaterial to the material, and placed them on earth, there to live as mortals among mortals, and learn morality the hard way.

"Now angels have no sex of their own, no male or female. But once made mortal they became men and women, better to help them appreciate and understand the new world they moved in. And, not surprisingly, the mortal angels mated with mortal humans, and produced children. These hybrid sons and daughters were the Nephilim, giants of great power and huge emotions. Perhaps luckily for the path of human civilization, these hybrids were sterile, or their descendants would have dominated Humanity's story forever. Still, there were giants on the earth in those days, legendary kings and conquerors, statesmen and philosophers, heroes and villains— long-lived, but not immortal. Most of them are gone now, dead or sleeping, buried in the earth, at peace at last.

"The mortal angels slowly learned morality, through their own actions or those of their children, and one by one they determined their true natures, and they departed the earth as the Creator called them home, back into the immaterial. But some of us never forgot our children. I . . . had unfinished business here, that continued to haunt me. So after many restless centuries, I was allowed to return here. I descended back into the material, to meet with my only child, the last of the Nephilim still involved with the world of men.

"But it all went horribly wrong. I had to forget much of who and what I was, to be able to operate on the limited, material plane, and this left me weak and vulnerable. The Serpent In The Sun saw me fall, saw an opportunity, and interfered with my descent. He shut down all my memories and even arranged for me to materialize as a female this time, to further distance me from my past identity. Hob was the first living thing I saw, so I imprinted on him, and served him, as the Serpent intended. Sorry, Hob, but we were never truly companions. I'm just somebody else your father used."

"But why?" said the Brother. "What brought you back here, back to me, after all this time?"

"Because I never said good-bye," said Angel, or Uriel. "And because I never told you I loved you."

"You killed my Leo," said the Brother.

"Yes," said Angel. "I'm sorry, now."

"Families!" said Hob bitterly. "It always comes down to families, and the ties that bind. I've never been allowed to have anything, and now they've even taken you away from me, my fierce and bloody

Angel. In the end, you were just something else my father could use to hurt me. Well, the hell with all of you. This is my place, and I have power here. Power to punish the world and everything in it. Power to call down the sun! Father! Send me your fire!"

Angel threw herself at Hob and wrestled with him. They were both inhumanly strong, and neither could overpower the other. The Brother put his great hands on the broken parlor wall and tried to widen the gap, so he could get in and help. The house cried out as more dust fell from the ceiling. Luna watched it all with wide, wondering eyes. Gayle turned to Toby, gripped his arm, and pulled him down so that they were face-to-face. She called up the last of her strength, that she'd been saving for a moment such as this, and her gaze and her voice were strong and sure.

"This is your moment, Toby, your reason for being here. Angel can't stop Hob, not here. Not in his place, not his power. No one could. He will destroy Angel, summon his father's fire, and channel it through him, and do every awful thing he swore to do. He'll kill us all, and rape and remake the worlds of Veritie and Mysterie. He'll damn all the life that replaces us to an endless nightmare under his control, and his father's, unless you help me stop them. As a human, as Gayle, I'm helpless to intervene. But you still have a foot in both Veritie and Mysterie; you have a link to both worlds, no matter where you are. I can't access my power; but you can bring it to me."

"How?" said Toby. "Tell me how."

"The ley lines," said Gayle. "My power, the power of the living earth, travels along those lines. I put you in touch with them, earlier today. You're still linked to them. You can reach out and touch them, even here, and bring my power to me. I can use that power to become my true self, Gaia, and do what must be done to stop the Hob, and the Serpent."

"I remember the ley lines," said Toby, meeting her gaze steadily. "Just touching them for a moment hurt me beyond bearing. Holding on to them long enough to bring them to you would kill me, wouldn't it?"

Gayle nodded slowly. She wouldn't let herself look away from

Toby's relentless gaze. "Yes. You could die, Toby. Being a focal point might protect you, or it might not. I don't know. The odds aren't good. Oh, Toby . . . I have no right to ask this of you. You already died once for me today. But you're the only one who can do this. I can't make you. It has to be your choice, your decision. But we can save the worlds, Veritie and Mysterie. Or you can let them die, and be replaced by something else. Your choice."

"My choice," said Toby. "The one that changes everything."

"Yes," said Gayle.

"Hob was right about one thing," said Toby. "Looking back, it wasn't much of a life I had. But it still sounds better than anything Hob or the Serpent have planned. And I won't condemn all of Humanity to death just because I never got the breaks. I don't want to die, Gayle. I want to live on, with you. I love you, even if you are only a mask for something that could never love me. I understand now. Mortal must not love immortal, for the same reason that the moth must not fly too close to the flame. Unfortunately, love doesn't care about things like that. So I'll do what's necessary. Bring the ley lines here, and burn on their coals. Not for the worlds, or even Humanity, but for you. Because a mortal man called Toby Dexter finally found love and would rather die than live without it. Can I get a good-bye kiss, for luck?"

Gayle rose up out of the chair, put her hands on either side of his face, and kissed him. When they moved apart, she held his face close to hers, so that she could look right into his eyes.

"I don't know what will happen when I become Gaia. It's been so long . . . but whatever happens, whatever Gaia finds it necessary to do here, know this, Toby Dexter. I love you. The woman called Gayle, the human role I made for myself, loves you with all her mortal heart, and always will. You're a good man, Toby, and you deserved better than this. Now do what you have to."

Toby looked around him. Time seemed to have stopped while they were talking. Angel was still struggling with Hob, Luna was still watching, the Brother was still trying to get in. Jimmy Thunder and Leo Morn were still dead. Toby tried to take in every detail of the

scene, in case it was the last thing he ever saw. And then he reached
out, in a direction he could feel but not see or name, and there were
the ley lines, shining so bright and powerful and perfect it hurt to
look at them. He called them to him and the thundering energy of
the living world leaped forward into Blackacre and surged through
him, wild and terrible, burning him more fiercely than the Sun ever
could have. He would have screamed at the awful pain, but his voice
was lost to him. He tried to see Gayle, one last time, but she was
gone from him, lost in the overpowering incandescence of the ley
lines. They were destroying him, tearing him apart. He could have
let them go, but he didn't. He clutched them to him and grounded
them in Mysterie, in Blackacre, in the farmhouse.

Gayle saw the ley lines and called them to her, and they went immediately, like dogs to their owner's voice. Toby could feel Gayle's
arms around him now, supporting him and holding him together,
and then taking the burden of the ley lines' terrible energies from
him. She let him go and he crashed to the filthy floor, shaking and
shuddering, but still alive. He saw Angel and Hob stop fighting,
transfixed by the sight of something so much more important than
either of them. Luna was laughing. Toby couldn't move his head, but
he could just move his eyes, and so he saw at last as Gayle took her
aspect upon her and became Gaia.

She became transfigured, still human in shape and size, but of
awesome depth and quality, so much greater than Toby could ever
have imagined. She was the force that drove life through every cre-
ation, from the smallest to the largest, the source and protection of
every living thing on planet Earth. She was Mother Earth, come into
her kingdom at last. Wild and glorious, loving and sorrowful, inhumanly just and terribly impartial. She was Gaia, and she was all
those things and more.

She smiled, and Blackacre was dead no longer. Life rushed
through the dead wood like a pulse, and the trees burst into life
again. Blackacre blossomed, throwing off its long death like an old
coat, revealing what had been underneath all along. The unnatural
fog faded away and was gone, unable to bear Gaia's gaze, and the

dead guards lay down and were only corpses again, free at last. Blackacre blazed with life, and Hob screamed with rage and loss.

The one place that had been his was his no more, and much of his power had gone with it. He could not undo what Gaia had done, and with Blackacre gone and Gayle transformed, the Serpent's plan was undone. But he was still the Serpent's Son, and he would have revenge. His father's fire still burned within him. He let it all out in one great rush, a blast of supernatural heat that was more than enough to reduce the farmhouse to ashes, and everything mortal within it.

But suddenly Luna stood before him, and called up her aspect, and the Moon reflected the Sun's heat right back at Hob. He blackened and burned and finally exploded, torn apart by the great warring forces, and his ashes were scattered across the room. But all the time he burned, he laughed: a hard, bitter, defeated laughter that had no regret in it, perhaps only a little relief that his long, unhappy life was finally over. Nicholas Hob, the Serpent's Son, was dead at last, by his own hand as much as anyone else's. The Serpent In The Sun no longer had an agent in the world of men, no longer had any way to reach them, or punish them. Veritie and Mysterie were safe.

Luna gave up her aspect and became just a woman again. Her armor was gone, replaced by a simple white shift. She sank to her knees beside the scorch marks on the floor that were all that remained to show where her only son had stood. She didn't cry, but she looked very tired. She'd tried so hard not to love him, tried so hard the effort had driven her mad, and she had had to retreat from the world that held her son. And when she finally pulled herself together, and went out into the world again, it was only to watch her son die. The Courts of the Holy were cruel sometimes, in their necessity.

She'd always known he would die at her hand, eventually. Because she was the only one who could do it.

Gaia looked around upon her works, and saw them to be good. She looked down on the fallen Toby, as though from a great height, and smiled fondly. Gayle had forgotten so much, forgotten that

Gaia loved all her creatures. How could she not? She was their Mother. She put aside her aspect and became Gayle again. She knelt beside Toby and hugged him to her fiercely. The ley lines had racked him, but he still lived. He was only mortal, and she was not, but she would love him as long as he lived. Gaia knew what Gayle had forgotten: that love is worth the pain it brings with it. Toby stirred in her arms and smiled up at her. Gayle smiled back.

Angel was talking quietly with her son, the Brother from Under The Hill, when Leo Morn lurched through the door, completely intact. He stalked over to his astonished Brother, reached up, and slapped him round the head as hard as he could.

"Idiot! You of all people should have remembered that only silver can kill a werewolf. Playing jigsaw with my body parts won't do it. Putting myself back together hurt like hell, mind, and took some time. I take it we won, since we're all here and Hob isn't. So, that's what you look like, Brother. I've often wondered. I'm impressed, really. But we're going to have to find you a pair of trousers, before you give the rest of us an inferiority complex. Now would someone please fill me in on what happened while I was out of it?"

"Of course," said the Brother. He indicated Angel. "Leo, I'd like you to meet my father."

Jimmy Thunder came through the door next, wincing as he gingerly felt the side of his head. Gayle laughed.

"I should have known you couldn't kill a Norse god by hitting him on the head."

"Not with his own hammer," Jimmy agreed. "I've had worse hangovers than this. Can we go home now, please?"

"Yes," said Toby. "It's been a long day, one way and another."

# Twelve~

# The Morning After

UNUSUALLY EARLY for a Sunday morning, Gayle sat at her kitchen table in her silk wrap, working her way happily through a large plate of scrambled eggs, her enjoyment only partially soured by the knowledge that scrambled eggs are what you end up making after you start out to do something more ambitious and then decide you can't be bothered. Gayle put aside the thought very firmly. She liked scrambled eggs. Especially with toast soldiers and a large mug of steaming black coffee. Life's little pleasures . . . Gayle was also reading the main section of the *Sunday Times,* which was propped up on the table against a coffeepot, looking bulky and authoritative. It appeared that the menacing solar flares had stopped, as suddenly and mysteriously as they had begun, and that everything was getting back to normal again. Gayle snorted loudly and slurped more hot coffee. As in so many things, the real world had no idea how close to the wire it had gone. Which was just as well, really.

She looked up as Toby came into the kitchen, carrying a carton of milk and a bunch of bright red flowers. Gayle qualified her welcoming smile with a stern gaze, but Toby just grinned as he laid the flowers down before her on the table.

"I know; you don't approve of killing flowers, so I got you silk ones instead. Happy now?"

"Deliriously," said Gayle. She ran an appreciative hand over the soft petals, and then got up to give him a happy, morning-after kiss. Toby sat down at the table and wrestled with the milk carton, while Gayle retrieved his serving of scrambled eggs and toast from the oven. Toby solved the problem of the recalcitrant carton by the application of a certain amount of brute force, and a certain amount of milk sprayed all over the tablecloth. He smiled apologetically at Gayle and poured the rest of the milk into the waiting jug. Gayle put his breakfast down in front of him, shaking her head, and he got stuck in.

"Not many people about in the Shambles," he said, indistinctly, "but then, most people have more sense than to be up and about this early on a Sunday morning."

"Sorry to kick you out of bed so early," said Gayle, sitting down opposite him. "But needs must when the stomach rumbles. Sorry I had to send you down to the Shambles, too, but I'd forgotten I was so low on milk. You tend to forget things like that when you're busy saving the world. Where's my change?"

Toby dug in his pocket and came up with a handful of small change. Gayle took it from him and counted it carefully while Toby concentrated on his eggs. He wasn't normally much of a one for a cooked breakfast, but a night of good sex always left him hungry. The two of them sat together in silence for a while, happily eating, comfortable in each other's company. Sunlight poured through the open kitchen window, bringing with it the sound of birdsong, occasional traffic, and the peal of church bells from across the town, summoning the faithful to prayer.

"If only they knew how close they'd come to not waking up at all this morning, the pews would be a damn sight fuller," said Toby.

"Don't talk with your mouth full," said Gayle. "And Veritie never knows, if we've done our job right. You've got a bit of egg on your chin."

"Sorry."

"And you haven't shaved this morning, have you?"

"I did try," said Toby. "But all I could find in your bathroom was that tiny razor I assume you use on your legs. Damn near cut my-self to ribbons before I gave up. If we're going to be an item, I'd bet-ter bring some of my things over." He stopped eating and looked at Gayle. "We are an item, aren't we?"

"Well, after last night, I'd say so," said Gayle.

Toby grinned. "So, I passed the audition, then?"

Gayle laughed. "Men! Always seeking reassurance. What do you want, marks for style, endurance, and star quality?"

"God, I love it when you talk dirty. But really, that was a pretty amazing night, love. I don't think I've ever been happier."

"I'm glad, Toby. I'm happy, too. And as for the bedroom gym-nastics; you don't live as long as I have without picking up a few tricks along the way."

Toby considered for a moment, slowly chewing. "I won't ask."

"Best not to, dear. More coffee?"

"Sure. Good eggs. Like the soldiers."

"You're welcome."

Gayle finished the last of her breakfast, wiping her plate clean with the toast. Toby couldn't help noticing that for a Power and a Domination, Gayle was a really messy eater. Toby approved. He needed to feel she was as human as he was. It also made him feel bet-ter about his own lack of manners. He always felt a little self-conscious, the morning after (always—all three times . . .), when the first glow of romance has faded, and you actually have to talk to them. Discuss things like who showers first, while trying to remem-ber where you threw your socks in a moment of passion. He liked it that Gayle was so organized about things. He'd never acquired the knack, somehow, despite or perhaps because of living alone for so long. He liked the feeling of being looked after. He finished the last of the eggs and pushed his plate away with a satisfied sigh.

"So," Gayle said brightly. "When do I get to see your place?"

"Not until it's been tidied, cleared up, and possibly fumigated. With a flame-thrower," Toby said firmly. "If you were to see how I normally live, you'd dump me on the spot. I am a man who lives alone. My place is a mess. It's expected of me. I have a reputation to live down to." He stopped and looked thoughtfully at Gayle. "Why do you prefer to live as a human, Gayle? And put up with all our . . . imperfections?"

"To ground me," said Gayle. "To remind me that the small picture is just as important as the big picture. Gaia takes the overview, always thinking in the long term, for the future. If I let her, she'd forget that there are no populations, no countries, only individuals. And each and every man, woman, and child matters just as much as the fate of nations. Gaia without a conscience would be a terrible force indeed. I like to think I help keep her sane. Oh, by the way; Jimmy Thunder called while you were out."

*Oh, yes?* Toby wanted to say. *He did, did he? Your old flame, checking up on me, perhaps?*

'That was nice of him," he said neutrally. "Bit early in the morning, though. What did he want?"

"Just to bring me up to speed on what all the others are doing," Gayle said easily. "He's recuperating, and already exaggerating his exploits and his part in what just happened, to everyone who'll listen on the Internet. It's where he finds most of his worshipers these days. He spends hours logged on, listening to them talk about him, when he's not working. He has a whole bunch of tribute sites, set up by worshipers with more time and money than sense, and you can bet they'll be pumping him for every detail of his latest adventure. I'll show you, later. I guarantee you won't recognize his version of what went down at Blackacre last night."

Toby shrugged. "He probably wouldn't recognize my version. I'm a little concerned about Blackacre. What will people say when they see it's come alive overnight?"

"Beats me," said Gayle. "Some scientist will explain it, eventually. They always do. Veritie doesn't have the patience for mysteries."

"I can't believe it all happened so quickly, that all the dramas and battles and destinies fulfilled took place in a single day and night," said Toby.

"All your fault," Gayle said easily. "After all the years, the centuries, of people and places and things moving into position, all the pressures building came to a head when you decided you were in love with me. When you crossed out of Veritie and into Mysterie, to be with me, you became a focal point, and the last piece finally fell into place.

"And everything could begin, at last."

Toby considered that, thought about raising the subject of free will again, thought better of it, and finally decided to change the subject.

"What's happening with your sister?" he said carefully. "How is she doing?"

"Apparently Luna is making arrangements to go traveling. She doesn't want to stay in Bradford-on-Avon anymore, not after seeing her son die here. Now that she's feeling more herself, and less like several other people, she's looking to center herself by studying other people—real people. It's been a long time since Luna went walkabout in the real world. I can't help feeling she's in for quite a shock, and a few surprises. She missed a lot, cooped up in her cage."

"Will she be all right?"

"Of course. She's Luna."

Toby decided to change the subject. "How about Leo Morn?"

"Leo has returned to his cottage, and has let it be known that if ever we're in urgent need and trouble again, if ever we need a hero . . . would we please ask someone else. Anyone else. And, that if we ever come knocking at his door again, he's going to barricade himself in and throw things at us."

Toby had to smile. "Yeah, that sounds like Leo. Do we have any news about his Brother and Angel?"

Gayle shook her head slowly. "No one's seen anything of them since they disappeared together last night. They've dropped off the map completely, which is a pretty good trick in a town like this. Presumably they want to be left strictly alone while they do their catching up. Personally, I'm prepared to let them be lost for as long as they want. I have a feeling they could get really irritated with anyone who intruded on their reunion, the kind of irritation that ends up with the intruder being sent home in several small boxes. At least the

Brother repaired his hill before he went missing. Though the chalk giant does look a bit crooked now."

Toby looked Gayle straight in the eye. "You haven't mentioned Nicholas Hob. Is he really dead and gone, this time?"

"Yes," said Gayle. "Killed by the only people who could do it. Caught between, and destroyed by, the mother and father who gave him life."

"What's to stop the Serpent trying again?" Toby said slowly. "Could he create another child, another agent in the world of men? Could he try to . . . rape someone again?"

"We're ready for him now," said Gayle, and her voice was cold and hard. "Protections are in place."

Toby decided not to press the point any further. He didn't think he wanted to know the details. Certainly it was clear that Gayle had said all she was prepared to say on the matter. He changed the subject again.

"What happened to the Mice? Did they all get back safely?"

"Oh, yes," said Gayle. "There are few things in either world fast enough to keep up with a properly motivated Mouse."

"I still feel a bit guilty about endangering them," said Toby.

"Nonsense," Gayle said briskly. "They had the time of their lives, most fun they've had in years. The Mice live for pranks and putting one over on the bad guys." She poured herself more coffee and offered the pot to Toby, who shook his head. Gayle frowned, suddenly thoughtful. "The only real victims were the dead, torn from their graves to serve the Hob. Jimmy's arranged for the death-walkers to retrieve all the bodies from Blackacre, and from his hall. They'll use their insider knowledge to identify each body properly, and see they're put back where they belong. Minimum of fuss, for the families' sake."

"Must have been quite a long phone call, while I was out," Toby observed to his coffee cup. Gayle put a hand on his arm.

"Don't be jealous, Toby. I got over Jimmy a long time ago. I'm still fond of him, as a friend, but I have no illusions about him. He's brave and he's a hero because that's what his nature compels him to be. You were brave and a hero through your own choice. It was your decision. That's a hell of a sight more impressive. Whoever decided to make you a focal point knew what they were doing."

Toby snorted. "I hope they also know that I am very definitely retired from the focal-point business. I don't ever want to be that scared again. What if I'd chosen wrong?"

"But you didn't. You're a remarkable man, Toby Dexter. I'm very proud of you."

Toby met her gaze squarely. "But mortal must not love immortal."

"No one said this was going to be easy," Gayle said quietly. "I'm human, but Gaia is not. Long after you're dead and gone, Gaia will still be here."

"Then let's make the most of our time together," said Toby, taking her hand in both of his. "Because the small picture is just as important as the big picture."

They smiled together, lost for a long moment in each other's eyes.

"This is why I stay human," Gayle said eventually. "These transient, passing joys that are more important than sagas and destinies and the rise and fall of worlds. Because in the end, there's nothing more magical than love, my sweet."

They kissed, and for a while nothing else mattered.

"So," said Toby, eventually. "Do I take it you have no plans to assume your aspect again, any time soon? To become Gaia, the Mother of the World?"

"No," Gayle said firmly. "I decided long ago not to interfere. If Gaia were to get involved with your species's progress, how could you ever learn to grow and evolve and transcend yourselves? I might preserve your present but deny you your future. I'm your Mother, not your Nanny. Humanity's potential is too great to put at risk by meddling."

"Even if we continue to pollute the planet, and maybe some day even destroy it?"

"Even then. You have to have faith, Toby."

"So . . . what do we do next?"

"Well, first we clear the table and do the washing-up. Then . . . I have a life to get back to. My special children don't care about my problems, they have too many of their own. Humanity is something you learn by doing. How about you?"

"I am not going back to my old job, my old life," said Toby. "I couldn't, not after everything I've seen. There's so much out there that I want to know about. I'm going to go exploring in Mysterie, find all the weird places and weirder people. See everything there is to see."

"Good," said Gayle. "That should stir things up a bit."

"Of course," said Toby, scowling, "there is the problem of what I'm going to do for money. I don't suppose your teacher's pay is going to cover both of us."

Gayle laughed. "Toby, I've been around for centuries, remember? I'm rich. Compound interest will do that for you, if you just live long enough."

"I knew there was a good reason why I fell in love with you," said Toby.

What value can one ordinary man have in a magical world? What can a mortal bring to the affairs of immortals?

Insight. Honor. Morality. Perspective.

Because nothing makes love and life matter more than the knowledge that some day it must end.

After they'd finished the washing-up, Gayle produced a bottle of wine she'd been saving for a very special occasion. Old, dark wine from the borderlands where night meets day. She opened the bottle expertly and poured two long glasses. They toasted each other and drank together, a wine so dark it had stars in it.

Midnight wine.